WHEN TIDES TURN

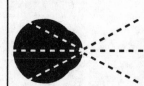

This Large Print Book carries the
Seal of Approval of N.A.V.H.

WHEN TIDES TURN

SARAH SUNDIN

THORNDIKE PRESS

A part of Gale, Cengage Learning

GALE
CENGAGE Learning·

Farmington Hills, Mich • San Francisco • New York • Waterville, Maine
Meriden, Conn • Mason, Ohio • Chicago

GALE
CENGAGE Learning

LIBRARY OF CONGRESS CATALOGING-IN-PUBLICATION DATA

Names: Sundin, Sarah, author.
Title: When tides turn / by Sarah Sundin.
Description: Large print edition. | Waterville, Maine : Thorndike Press, a part of Gale, Cengage Learning, 2017. | Series: Waves of freedom ; #3 | Series: Thorndike Press large print Christian historical fiction
Identifiers: LCCN 2017003957| ISBN 9781410499790 (hardcover) | ISBN 1410499790 (hardcover)
Subjects: LCSH: United States. Naval Reserve. Women's Reserve—Fiction. | World War, 1939-1945—Fiction. | Large type books. | GSAFD: Christian fiction. | Love stories.
Classification: LCC PS3619.U5626 W47 2017b | DDC 813/.6—dc23
LC record available at https://lccn.loc.gov/2017003957

Published in 2017 by arrangement with Revell Books, a division of Baker Publishing Group

Printed in the United States of America
1 2 3 4 5 6 7 21 20 19 18 17

Dedicated to the 86,000 women who served in the WAVES during World War II. Your patriotism, pioneering spirit, and enthusiasm inspire us today.

1

Boston, Massachusetts
Thursday, July 30, 1942

A touch of kindness and enthusiasm could transform a person's spirit, and Quintessa Beaumont delighted in participating in the process.

"This is lovely on you, Mrs. Finnegan." Quintessa lined a box with tissue paper on the counter at Filene's.

Her customer giggled and tucked a gray curl behind her ear. "Listen to me. I sound like a schoolgirl. All because of a blouse."

"Not just any blouse. The perfect blouse for you." Quintessa laid the floral fabric in neat folds in the box. At first, Mrs. Finnegan had struck her as drab and tired and dowdy. Shame on her for thinking that way — so shallow. But as Quintessa had assisted the older lady in her search, she'd sensed a sweet dreaminess. Mrs. Finnegan deserved a blouse that reflected who she was inside, something to make her happy and confident. Quintessa had found it.

She settled the lid on the box and handed it to Mrs. Finnegan. "Thank you for your purchase. It was a pleasure meeting you."

"The pleasure was mine. You certainly have a gift, Miss Beaumont." Mrs. Finnegan strolled down the aisle with a new bounce in her step.

Quintessa returned to the sales floor and straightened racks of summer blouses, which needed to be sold to make room for autumn merchandise.

Filene's fifth floor boasted fashionable women's apparel, designed to meet the War Production Board's standards to limit use of fabric. For the past ten months, Quintessa had rotated among Filene's various shops, learning the business and the wares. When her year in training was complete, she could finally put her business degree to use in the offices.

A few ladies browsed the racks. With so many women working now due to the war, business was slow on weekday mornings.

A figure in white caught her eye — a naval officer with a familiar determined gait. Quintessa's heart lurched. Dan Avery? What was her roommate's oldest brother doing here?

She smoothed her blonde curls but stopped herself. Why bother? The man was already married — to the United States Navy.

Although his stride didn't waver, he gazed from side to side like a lost child, frowning and squinting. Then he spotted Quintessa, and the frown and squint disappeared.

He was looking for her. Another lurch, with a tingle this time, but Quintessa shoved it aside. She tilted her head. "Lieutenant Daniel Avery. Whatever brings you to Filene's better blouses?"

"My mom's birthday." Dan rubbed the back of his neck and eyed the clothing racks as if they were a fleet of enemy vessels. "I tried to bribe Lillian to do my shopping for me, but she refused. Some sister. Told me you'd help me find something."

Quintessa loved her roommate's forthright nature. "Does the bribe apply to me too?"

He didn't smile. He rarely did, and she didn't think she'd ever heard him laugh, but his dark eyes twinkled. A no-nonsense man, but not humorless. "I imagine Filene's disapproves of employees taking bribes."

"I'll settle for the commission." Shifting her thoughts to her former Sunday school teacher, Quintessa contemplated the summer blouses. "Let's see. Your mother is about Lillian's size and coloring."

"Plumper and grayer."

No wonder the man was still a bachelor. "We would never say that here at Filene's. She's more mature."

"I'd hope so. Raising the seven of us, she's earned her gray."

Quintessa smiled and flipped through the blouses. Mrs. Avery handled the business end of her husband's boatyard, and she was neither frilly nor frumpy.

"How about this?" Quintessa held up a tailored cream blouse with a brown yoke and short brown sleeves. An embroidered green vine with delicate yellow flowers softened the border between cream and brown.

"I'll take it."

"Let's see what else we have."

"Why?" Dan gestured to the blouse. "Is it her size?"

"Yes."

"Do you think she'll like it?"

"Well, yes, but —"

"I'll take it."

The man certainly knew his mind. One of many things she found attractive about him. "All right then."

Quintessa took the blouse to the cash register and rang up the purchase. "How are things at the Anti-Submarine Warfare Unit?"

One dark eyebrow lifted, and he pulled out his wallet. "We're making progress, but personally, I want to get back out to sea."

"That's where the excitement is."

"And the real work. We finally have convoys along the East Coast, and we've pretty much driven the U-boats away. But they're back to their old hunting grounds in the North Atlantic, and they're wreaking havoc in the Caribbean and the Gulf of Mexico. The battle's constantly changing, and we have to stay on top of it."

Quintessa focused on making change. Concentration was always difficult when Dan Avery spoke about the war or ships or the Navy. Passion lit the strong lines of his face and animated his firm mouth. If only he'd remove his white officer's cap and run his hand through his wavy black hair. The wildness of it.

She puffed out a breath. "Here's your change. Let me wrap that for you."

"Very well." He slipped the coins in the pocket of his white trousers and glanced at his wristwatch.

Quintessa gritted her teeth as she pleated the tissue paper inside the box. What was wrong with her? She'd always been drawn to men who showered her with starry-eyed adoration. Now she was drawn to a man who looked right through her as if she had nothing of substance to stop his gaze.

Shame shriveled up her insides. How could she blame him? He had to know she'd come to Boston to throw herself at his younger brother, Jim — who turned out to be in love with her best friend, Mary Stirling. Dan had also been in Boston when Quintessa was dating Clifford White — who turned out to be married. Surely Dan saw her as a silly, selfish woman with poor judgment.

He'd be right.

She worked up a smile and presented him with the wrapped package. "Here you go. Thank you for your purchase."

"Thank you for your help. Mom will love it." He tipped his cap to her and strode away.

Just as well. She needed to set her head on straight before she started another romance. The past year had turned her topsy-turvy.

Miss Doyle arrived to relieve Quintessa for her lunch break, but Quintessa headed up to the offices on the seventh floor instead. Her former boss, Mr. Garrett, had retired last week, and she'd only briefly met his replacement, Mr. Young.

First she slipped into the restroom, powdered her nose, freshened her lipstick, and straightened her chic golden-brown suit jacket. She smiled at her reflection. Feminine, but smart and professional. Perfect for this meeting.

The business offices buzzed with a tantalizing sense of purpose. Mr. Young's office door stood open, and she lightly rapped on the doorjamb.

Her boss raised his salt-and-pepper head, grinned at her, and stood to shake her hand. "Miss Beaumont, isn't it? Yes, yes. I don't have the final sales figures for July, but you're in line to be one of the top salesgirls again. A true asset to Filene's."

An excellent start. "Thank you, Mr. Young."

He crossed his arms over his charcoal gray suit. "What can I do for you?"

"I wanted to speak with you about the next step in my training program."

"Training?" He narrowed one eye. "You're the last person who needs sales training."

A sick feeling settled in her belly. Hadn't Mr. Garrett told Mr. Young why she was here? "Mr. Garrett hired me to work here in the business offices, but —"

"You're a secretary?"

Quintessa maintained her professional smile. "No, sir. I have a bachelor's degree in business. Mr. Garrett wanted to give me a year of sales experience before starting here. He felt it was important for his assistant —"

"Assistant?" Mr. Young winced as if he had a toothache. "That might have been Mr. Garrett's plan, but I just hired a man. These offices are no place for a young lady."

"Unless she's a secretary."

"I'm glad you understand." His face brightened. "Besides, you're excellent at sales. Why would we waste your talents on boring old numbers and paperwork? And why would we hide that pretty face behind office doors?"

A pretty face. That's all she was.

"Now, off you go." Mr. Young guided her out his office door. "That's a good girl. Go make Filene's proud."

Quintessa trudged down the hallway. She'd come to Boston for nothing. She'd worked for her degree for nothing. *Lord, what's the reason for all this? What do you want me to do?*

Patriotic posters by the elevator reminded employees to put part of their paychecks into war bonds. The nation was at war, and everyone was working together. Her roommates Mary Stirling and Yvette Lafontaine worked at the Boston Navy Yard, where American warships were built and repaired. Her other roommate, Lillian Avery, worked as a pharmacist, freeing men to fight.

But Quintessa Beaumont was only good for selling blouses.

After a day like today, Quintessa needed this. She opened the door to Robillard's Bakery and inhaled the scents of bread and pastry and hospitality.

"*Bonsoir, ma petite* Quintessa." Madame Celeste Robillard raised a plump hand in greeting.

"*Bonsoir,* Madame Robillard."

"I will be with you in a minute," the bakery owner said in French, Quintessa's father's native tongue.

"*Merci.*" Her French roommate, Yvette, had introduced her to Robillard's, a gathering place for Boston's French expatriates and refugees.

With sugar on ration, Robillard's carried fewer pastries and more breads, but today a row of éclairs called from the glass display case. Why not? If she were fat, Mr. Young might *want* to hide her in the business offices.

Maybe she'd buy two éclairs. Or three.

Guilt zinged through her. No, she'd buy four, one for each roommate. How could she forget her friends? After all, she planned to indulge in their sympathy this evening. Didn't they deserve compensation in pastry form?

"Oh, *ma petite*. You are sad." Madame Robillard's brown eyes crinkled.

Quintessa waved her hand in airy dismissal. "Nothing an éclair can't fix."

"Oui." Madame Robillard opened a pink pasteboard box.

"Four, *si'l vous plait.*"

"You are so kind. Such a good friend."

That's what everyone thought.

Madame Robillard stopped and studied Quintessa. Wiry curls in brown and gray framed her face, escapees from the loose bun at the nape of her neck.

Quintessa propped up her smile.

"Come, come." Madame Robillard abandoned the éclairs, shoved open the half-door in the counter, grabbed Quintessa's arm, and guided her to the back wall. "Paris is the cure for sadness."

Quintessa had to smile at the Philippe Beaumont lithograph of the Pont Neuf, from Papa's youth in Paris, before he'd come to America in 1910 and had fallen in love with Mama. His early work sparkled

16

with color and light, influenced by the Post-impressionists.

Madame Robillard squeezed Quintessa's arm. "You are sad because of Yvette, *non*?"

"Yvette?" Quintessa blinked at the tiny woman. "Why? Is something wrong?"

"Have you not noticed? She is not herself. At our meetings, what she says is tuned down."

"Toned down?"

"*Oui.* I am glad she is not so hotheaded, but I worry. It is not like her."

Quintessa had never attended one of the meetings with Yvette's French friends, but Yvette was always one to speak her mind. "Maybe she's preoccupied with Henri."

"Henri Dubois? *Non.*" Madame Robillard fluttered her hand in front of her chest. "They are like brother and sister."

"Not anymore. Last week she told me they've fallen in love."

"*Non,* it cannot be. A woman in love is happy, not suspicious, always looking over her shoulder. Yvette is jumpy. Like a little flea."

Come to think of it, last night while cooking dinner, Yvette had jumped when the egg timer dinged. Quintessa patted Madame Robillard's hand. "I'm sure she's fine. Aren't we all blessed to have another mother watching over us?"

"You are too kind." The baker pressed her hand to her chest. "You young people are far from home with no one to look after you. And here I am, far from my Paris and my sons and my grandchildren. We must be family for each other. And now I must get to work."

Quintessa followed her back to the counter. An evening newspaper lay in an untidy mess on an empty table, so Quintessa picked it up.

The headlines made her shudder. Eight German saboteurs had landed in the US by U-boat in June and were under trial for their lives, with the verdict expected any day. And the Nazi army was advancing in the Soviet Union, unstoppable.

Awful, awful. She folded the paper to hide the madness.

"Navy making WAVES." She stood still and read the article. That morning, President Franklin Roosevelt had signed a bill establishing Women Accepted for Voluntary Emergency Service, the women's branch of the US Naval Reserve.

Back in May, the Women's Army Auxiliary Corps had been formed, and magazines showcased young ladies in olive drab uniforms. Now young ladies would parade in navy blue.

Purposeful women contributing to the war effort, selflessly serving the nation.

"*Ma petite?* Are you all right?"

"Yes." Quintessa's vision cleared. "I know what I'm going to do."

2

Anti-Submarine Warfare Unit, US Navy
  Atlantic Fleet
Boston, Massachusetts
Friday, July 31, 1942

Ensign Bill Bentley plopped a manual on Dan Avery's desk. "It's a bouncing baby boy."

"We should pass out cigars." Dan stroked the cover of the revised manual for antisubmarine warfare that would soon be distributed to the US Atlantic Fleet. The Navy's Anti-Submarine Warfare Unit had worked hard combining statistical data from the battle against the U-boats with civilian research to find the best combat tactics. If only Dan could go to sea and put these to practice himself.

Bentley leaned his hip on the desk and picked up Dan's compass. "I think this manual will make a difference."

"I know it will." Dan kept telling himself

that, his gaze fixed on the compass in Bentley's hand. Kept telling himself his work was vital to the war effort.

Stay the course.

He could hear Admiral Aloysius Howard's voice in his head. Howard had good reasons for placing his protégé in the ASWU, but Dan felt like the war was passing him by.

"Say . . ." Bentley grinned at Dan and patted the manual. "Birthing this baby was a long, hard labor, Mama. You look beat."

Dan allowed one corner of his mouth to inch up. "I've never been called a mama before."

"Yeah? Well, you still look beat. You ought to take a long, hard rest this weekend. Or go out and celebrate."

A groan rumbled up his throat. "Apparently I'm celebrating. My brother and sister insisted on a night on the town."

Bentley's pale blue eyes lit up. "Sounds swell. Where are you going?"

He shrugged. "Jim's best friend, Arch, is back in Boston. He's the one who lost his eye in battle."

"You told me. Out of the Navy, huh?"

A cold chill crept up his chest. "Yes. He has a new job in Boston, so they want to welcome him back. It's only right that I pay my respects. Besides, he'll probably marry

21

Lillian."

Bentley gave him a light punch in the shoulder. "Ah, it's good for you, Mr. Avery. All work and no play —"

"Makes Dan a dull boy." He plucked the compass from his ensign's hand. "But it might make Dan an admiral."

The sounds of Jack Edwards and his orchestra playing "Moonlight Cocktail" floated through the Terrace Room in the Hotel Statler. Dan sat squished with five other people around a table built for four, trying not to bump elbows with Quintessa Beaumont.

"Nice new stripe." Arch Vandenberg pointed to the shoulder boards on Jim's dress whites, which boasted a thick and a thin gold stripe for Jim's promotion to lieutenant, junior grade.

Jim's face scrunched up. "Say, buddy, I'm sorry —"

"I'm not." Arch wore a well-tailored gray civilian suit and a smile. Only a slight droop in one eyelid hinted at his injury and his glass eye.

Dan gave him the direct gaze the former officer deserved. "Tell us more about your new position."

"Oh, it's wonderful." Lillian entwined her

fingers with Arch's. "He's opening the Boston branch of Vandenberg Insurance, and he's hiring wounded servicemen."

"After they're discharged, of course." Arch winked at her. "I'm here for a week to scout locations for the office and to find an apartment. Then I'll train with my father for a month in Connecticut before I set up the Boston branch."

Mary Stirling, Jim's girlfriend, patted Arch's free arm. "We're glad you'll be here to stay."

"Mary?" Quintessa peered out at the dance floor. "Notice anything odd about Yvette?"

Dan frowned. Quintessa had barely spoken this evening, and now she'd changed the subject. Neither behavior was normal for her. And who was Yvette?

Mary glanced in the same direction. "Yvette? No. Why?"

"She doesn't act like a woman in love. She's looking all around the ballroom, not into Henri's eyes."

A pretty brunette danced with a dark-haired civilian. Oh yes, Yvette Lafontaine. The ladies' fourth roommate.

Lillian's lips twitched with laughter. "Why, Quintessa? Do you sense a mystery?"

"Poor baby." Mary's light blue eyes

danced. "Lillian and I both solved mysteries lately, and you haven't."

Dan's hands tensed in his lap. Both ladies nearly lost their lives in the process.

Quintessa's laughter bubbled up. "I am jealous. I admit it. Now, hush, everyone. Hi, Yvette! Hi, Henri!" She sprang to her feet, kissed her roommate's cheek, and faced the table. "You all know Yvette, of course. This is her boyfriend, Henri Dubois. He's a draftsman at the Boston Navy Yard. Henri, you know Mary and Lillian. These are Lillian's brothers, Jim and Dan, and her boyfriend, Arch Vandenberg."

Dan blinked. How could any man follow an introduction like that?

"How do you do?" Henri said in a French accent.

"I'm pleased to meet you." Dan stood and shook Henri's hand. The man had a good firm handshake, and confidence shone in his dark eyes.

"Will you join us?" Mary said. "We can make room."

"No, thank you." Yvette circled her arm around Henri's waist. "We are here for a romantic evening."

"Oh, good." Quintessa returned to her seat. "I'm glad to hear it. Are you all right?"

Yvette exchanged a glance with Henri,

and her brow puckered. "It is nothing, I am sure. I feel . . . all evening I've felt —"

"Don't, my love."

Yvette pulled away a bit. "Nonsense. They are my friends. I feel as if someone is watching us."

A leg brushed past Dan's shin. Quintessa jerked and glared at Lillian, who wore a smug "we know who was watching them" expression.

Just like Lillian to kick someone under the table. He'd felt that foot under the dining room table in Vermilion countless times.

"It was a pleasure meeting you." Henri bowed slightly and gestured back to the dance floor. "My love?"

Before Dan could blink, Jim and Arch stood and ushered their girlfriends to the dance floor too.

Leaving Dan alone with Quintessa. His stomach squirmed. Since when had Lillian danced? The traitor. Yet it was good to see her happy. And he admired how she never allowed her artificial leg to slow her down.

Dan pulled his notepad and pen out of his breast pocket so he could plan the coming week's work. It wouldn't take long before someone asked Quintessa to dance. Too bad she didn't have a boyfriend — but not a low-down heel like that Clifford. Still burned him up that a married man deceived both his wife and a nice girl like Quintessa.

Beside him, Quintessa shifted in her chair. She was a beautiful woman, and she wore a yellow dress with sparkly gold pins and things. Everything about her was as golden and sparkling as sunshine on the ocean.

Just like Joanie. Women like that needed lots of friends and social activities and attention. Good thing Admiral Howard talked sense into Dan before Joanie ruined Dan's second year at Annapolis and his naval career.

"You know, Dan. It would be polite if you asked me to dance."

He winced, but at least Quintessa's voice was teasing instead of demanding. "You wouldn't enjoy it."

She laughed. "I doubt you're that bad of a dancer. What are you working on?"

"Plans for the week." He flipped a page.

Quintessa folded her arms on the table and leaned closer. "You know what they say — all work and no play —"

"Second time today someone said that to me." He met her gaze. A mistake.

Light green eyes like phosphorescence in a tropical sea. "Maybe you should listen."

He raised one eyebrow. "Remember, we're at war. The men at sea don't get to play."

She rested her chin in her hand. "You'd like to be at sea, wouldn't you?"

"That's where I belong. My ship went to the Pacific without me. I should be there."

"The *Vincennes*."

"Yes." No one could ever accuse her of being a dumb blonde. She was extremely intelligent and remembered details most ladies couldn't be bothered with. "A good ship and a good crew. They screened the Doolittle carrier raid on Tokyo in April and participated in the Battle of Midway in June." Two of the greatest naval events in modern history.

"And you weren't there." She released a sympathetic sigh. "But how about your work here? Do you enjoy it?"

"It doesn't matter if I enjoy it or not. It's my duty, and it's important to the war effort."

"It must be terribly fascinating if you can't take five minutes to dance. What are you working on?" She edged closer.

Blonde curls brushed his shoulder, and perfume tickled his brain, feminine and mesmerizing.

"Oh, that's nice," she said.

Dan forced himself to look at his notebook. He'd been doodling without realizing it. A sailboat. Again.

Quintessa smiled at him, much too close. "Designing sailboats, just like your dad."

His stomach hardened. "I'm nothing like my father." He ripped the page from the notepad.

"Oh! Don't. It's very nice. May I have it?" She held out her hand.

Dan paused, staring at the slim fingers. Then he grunted. "Fine. I don't know why you'd want it, but —"

"Oh, thank you." Quintessa plucked the paper from his hand and studied the sketch. She giggled. "Strong lines. All black and white. Just like you."

"I'm glad I amuse you."

"You do. And I know exactly what your sketch needs."

She did?

Quintessa fetched her purse from under her chair and slipped the paper inside. "Wait and see. Now, back to work. No dillydallying. We're at war."

"Yes, ma'am." But his plans for the week had seeped out of his brain.

The last chords of "Who Wouldn't Love You?" played, and the rest of the party returned to the table.

Quintessa raised her hands in front of her, fingers wiggling. "I have an announcement. I've been dying to tell you."

Dan tucked his notepad away. One of those blonde curls would fit perfectly around his finger.

"What is it?" Mary asked.

Quintessa grinned. "On Monday I'm joining the WAVES."

Expressions of surprise exploded around the table.

Dan's jaw drifted lower. "The women's naval reserve?"

"Yes. I'm so excited. I want to do something for the war effort. I want to contribute. And the WAVES will be fun."

Fun? His jaw set. "You do realize it's the real Navy. Hard work, discipline, not much time for fun."

"I didn't mean it that way." Her cheeks darkened to the shade of a ripe peach. "I meant the work itself will be fun."

Dan clamped his lips between his teeth. She was smart, but she was too glamorous, too lovely, too sparkling for the military. "Face it, the Navy's no place for . . ." How could he say this without offending her? "Well, you even have a princess name."

"Dan!" Lillian kicked him in the kneecap.

He grimaced, but he deserved the kick. Why did he always have to be so brusque? Just as well he stayed away from women. He was always hurting their feelings.

Dan shot her an apologetic look. "I'm . . ."

She wasn't looking at him. Color high, jaw forward, eyes darting around. Then her gaze snapped to Dan, sparks replacing sparkles. "All right, then. Call me Tess."

"Nonsense." Mary reached across the table and grasped her hand. "You've never had a nickname. You *are* Quintessa. It's who you are."

Quintessa got a faraway look. "The quintessence of everything my parents wanted in their only child. A princess. Not anymore."

"Don't let my brother discourage you." Lillian knifed him with a glance.

"She's right," Dan said. "I shouldn't have said that."

"Why not? It's true. Quintessa is only good for selling blouses, but Tess — Tess can do something worthwhile." Her chin rose, showing strength and determination that only added to her beauty.

But Dan's stomach sank. Too bad the Navy would turn her down.

3

Tess Beaumont set the pot roast on the kitchen table, keeping her expression neutral, even though her insides bounced around.

Mary, Lillian, and Yvette watched her, concern etched on each face. They knew Tess's plan for the day.

"It smells wonderful." Lillian trained her big hazel eyes on Tess, not the pot roast.

"Thank you." She took her seat.

Mary fiddled with her fork. "So, how was your day, Quin—"

"Tess. Just Tess."

Mary sighed. "Lifelong habits take time to break."

"I know." Tess gave her roommates a perky smile. "I'll help you."

"And how was your day — Tess?" Mary asked.

She served up some pot roast. "Ran errands, went to the recruiting office, did a load of laundry, made dinner."

"And . . . ?"

Tess couldn't contain her excitement one more minute. "I did it! I filled out my application for the WAVES."

"Oh my goodness!"

"You did?"

"When do you start?"

Tess laughed at her friends' expressions. "If they take me, I'll start in October."

"If?" Yvette asked.

"Well, I meet the basic requirements for an officer, but there were an awful lot of girls, and I still have to take a test and a physical. They'll contact me soon."

Mary's smile fell. "But you have your heart set on leaving Filene's."

Tess motioned to the pan, encouraging her friends to help themselves. "If the Navy turns me down, I'll go to the Army. If the WAAC turns me down, I'll take a job at the Navy Yard. I'll learn to weld or rivet. I want to do something for the war effort. I don't want to be a princess. I want to be useful."

Lillian groaned and tucked a strand of dark blonde hair behind her ear. "Don't listen to that brother of mine."

"I won't." But she really wanted to prove Dan Avery wrong. He saw her as she was —

frivolous and selfish. She wanted to become a selfless person whose work provided worth.

Yvette glanced at her wristwatch and sliced her roast.

It was Monday, the evening the French expatriates and refugees met at Robillard's Bakery. "Do you have your meeting tonight?" Tess asked.

"Oui." Yvette dabbed her mouth with her napkin.

Tess's observations and Madame Robillard's questions and Yvette's suspicion that she was being watched rolled into a ball in her head. How many times had Yvette invited her to these meetings? Tess had never attended. How rude of her.

"May I join you?"

"Pardon?" The brunette arched one elegant eyebrow.

"If I'm going to join the Navy, I should learn more about the war, the situation abroad."

"Oh yes. Please come. My friends will be happy to meet the daughter of the famous Philippe Beaumont."

"Thank you. It'll be fun." Even if boring old Dan didn't think much of fun, Tess did.

Tess sat at a little round table with Yvette

and Henri, facing the back of the bakery. Solange Marchand, Yvette and Henri's good friend, sat on the far side of the room, glaring at them. Tess had never seen the blonde wear so much makeup or such a tight-fitting dress.

She leaned close to Yvette and lowered her voice. "What's wrong with Solange?"

"She thinks she is in love with Henri and that I stole him from her."

"Impossible." Henri traced one finger along Yvette's forearm. "You cannot steal what already belongs to you. I have loved you forever."

The devotion in Henri's dark eyes looked genuine, but Yvette glanced around the bakery at the two dozen people greeting each other in French.

Tess settled back and smoothed the skirt of her caramel-colored suit. She might not have a real mystery, but she could still play sleuth and use her powers of observation and intuition.

Next to Solange sat a slender man in his thirties with blond hair and an eager look. He said something to Solange, but she inched away and talked to the elderly lady on her other side.

A man in his fifties stood in the back of the room next to Papa's painting of the Pont

Neuf. *"Bonsoir."*

"Professor Louis Arnaud, our leader," Yvette whispered to Tess.

Professor Arnaud had a long face and sleepy eyes. Despite his deliberate manner of speech, Tess had a hard time understanding all his French due to his extensive vocabulary. At least she kept up with the news. The Germans had invaded France in May 1940. After the surrender, the Nazis occupied northern France but allowed a puppet government for southern France in Vichy.

The professor described how the Nazis had rounded up thousands of foreign Jews living in Paris. He described how Resistance members assassinated Nazi officials, which led the Germans to kill fifty French civilians for each murdered Nazi. And after British commandos raided Boulogne in April, the Nazis executed a hundred civilians.

The blond man at Solange's table stood. "The Resistance does right. We must confound the *Boche* at every turn."

"Jean-Auguste Fournier," Yvette whispered. "Now watch."

Tess gave her roommate a curious look, but Yvette motioned her toward the conversation.

Madame Robillard stood and clasped her

hands before her chest. "Jean-Auguste, please. We must think of our sons and daughters in France, our grandchildren —" Her voice cracked.

"My apologies, madame." Jean-Auguste bowed his head. "I get angry when I think of Germans ruling our land, but you are right. We must be careful. For every Nazi who dies, fifty good Frenchmen — and women — die. We cannot allow that."

"Nonsense!" A middle-aged man with a dark mustache sprang to his feet. "Jean-Auguste, you blow with the wind. That is what the *Boche* want — they want to scare us so we do not fight. But we must fight."

"Who's that?" Tess whispered.

"Pierre Guillory." Yvette's golden-brown eyes narrowed at the scene. "Dockworker."

"*Non,* Pierre." Madame Robillard fluttered her plump hand at the man. "My boys, they send letters through our contacts. It is not so bad in Paris. They have jobs. They have enough food. The streets are safe. We must not listen to troublemakers."

"I am not a troublemaker. I am a patriot. I took German bullets to my leg in the trenches in the Great War. I almost died from poison gas." Pierre slapped his chest. "And now? The streets are only safe because the citizens are terrorized. That is not freedom. That is tyranny."

"If you wish to fight, Monsieur Guillory . . ." Jean-Auguste swept his arm eastward. "The Atlantic is not so wide."

A smattering of chuckles circled the bakery.

Tess studied the faces. Perhaps she should follow Mary's example and take notes, but she'd rather observe. What a fascinating group of people.

"Attentisme," Madame Robillard said in a pleading voice. "That is the best policy. *Attentisme."*

Tess took the word apart. *Attentisme* . . . attentive . . . waiting in expectation . . .

Professor Arnaud cleared his throat. *"Attentisme* is not enough. We have waited, and we've seen what the Nazis do. Life for most is not as good as it is for your sons, Madame Robillard. And waiting for the Allied invasion of France is not enough either. How long will it be? Another year? Two? Three? We must resist the Nazi regime."

"We are an ocean away." Jean-Auguste sighed and returned to his seat.

"Oui," the professor said, "but we can continue to smuggle letters back and forth through Portugal, through Vichy France, and into occupied France. We can raise money to buy arms. We can arrange aid for

spies and couriers. The Arnaud château in the Loire Valley straddles the border between Vichy and occupied France. My cousin's caretaker runs messages to his brother on the Nazi-occupied side. He is very helpful."

Tess frowned. Should he share information like that in public?

Madame Robillard twisted her hands together. "We must not make the Germans angry."

"Do not be a fool." Pierre shook a meaty fist. "The Germans must not make *us* angry."

"Monsieur Guillory." Yvette's voice sliced through the tension. "Be respectful."

Pierre wheeled toward Yvette and wagged a finger at her. "Since when have you turned? You are siding with a collaborator."

Madame Robillard gasped. "*Non!* I am not a collaborator. I am only a mother who loves her sons."

"I am not siding with her thinking," Yvette said, her tone low and calm. "I am reminding you to be respectful."

Tess held her breath as the two stared each other down. At last, Pierre gave a sharp nod and sat.

How strange. That was the first time Yvette had spoken tonight, and Henri hadn't said a word. In the past, Tess had heard both spout streams of anti-Nazi rhetoric.

Just as Madame Robillard had said. Tess sneaked a glance at the bakery owner, who sent Tess a pointed look with a flick of her chin toward Yvette.

What was going on? What had changed for Yvette? And was it anything for Tess to trouble with?

4

Chesapeake Bay
Wednesday, August 12, 1942

By the rails on the main deck of the new light cruiser USS *Cleveland,* Dan scanned the skies with his binoculars. The familiar waters of Chesapeake Bay, the balmy weather, and the sounds of a crew hard at work failed to lift the heaviness on Dan's heart. Regardless, attending this exercise was an excellent opportunity. "Thank you for bringing me here, sir."

To his right, Rear Adm. Aloysius Howard peered through his own binoculars. "Yes. Well, I'm sorry about the *Vincennes.*"

A slug to the chest. On August 7, the Marines had invaded the tiny island of Guadalcanal in America's first offensive campaign of the war. Two days later in the Battle of Savo Island, the Japanese had sunk the Australian heavy cruiser *Canberra* and three US heavy cruisers — the *Astoria,* the *Quincy,* and the *Vincennes.* Four massive warships and over a thousand men. Gone.

Dan cleared his throat. "Thank you, sir." At least the admiral didn't say, "Aren't you glad you weren't there?" Of all people, Admiral Howard knew Dan's answer would be no. He should have been there when his ship was under attack and sinking, when his men were dying.

Admiral Howard lowered his binoculars, his white hair and blue eyes bright in the summer sunshine. "Today you'll see first-hand why I put you in ASWU for a year."

Dan lifted one eyebrow. Testing new fuzes for antiaircraft shells wouldn't help battle subs.

Howard flapped his hand. "This has nothing to do with antisubmarine warfare, but it has everything to do with the direction of the US Navy — toward science and technology. The admiral of tomorrow needs more than combat experience. You're on the right track to become one of America's finest admirals."

"Thank you, sir." His chest felt lighter, bigger.

Howard tugged his dress white tunic over his round belly. "Something big is coming up, and you'll be on board as an observer gathering data. You'll be proud to be involved."

Dan's heartbeat picked up a notch. He'd rather serve as a line officer, but at least he'd be at sea.

"Now hear this," a voice spoke over the loudspeaker. "The first drone failed. Stand ready for the second drone."

Dan's groan joined hundreds of others on the *Cleveland.* Radio-operated planes were supposed to simulate an attack on the cruiser so the crew could test shells equipped with the new fuzes.

The admiral shook his head. "Hope they get those drones to work. These fuzes are promising."

"Good." The waters of the Chesapeake stretched wide off Tangier Island, about a hundred miles south of Annapolis, perfect for a test. "In time, we'll overcome the submarine threat, but aircraft . . ."

The admiral rested both forearms on the bulwark. "A small, speedy, evading target. Shells with contact fuzes have to hit the aircraft to explode, and timed fuzes require precise calculations."

Dan recognized an examination question from his former Academy instructor. "But the proximity fuze sends out radio pulses. When a plane passes within seventy feet of the shell, it explodes. So does the plane."

"In theory. But in practice?"

Dan had studied the paperwork, as the admiral knew he would. "In the January test, they found a 52 percent detonation rate. And in the April test with the improved battery, it went up to 70 percent. But this is the first test against a moving aircraft."

"If they can get the drones —"

"Ahoy!" a talker yelled behind Dan. "Aircraft bearing two-seven-zero. Range seven-oh-double-oh."

Dan whipped his binoculars straight abeam to port. He brought the plane into focus, coming in low as if on a torpedo-bombing run. Like at Pearl Harbor.

Now to see how the crew would perform. The *Cleveland* was on her shakedown cruise. The gunnery department was young and inexperienced, which made this a realistic combat test.

Even though no pilot manned the plane and no danger threatened the ship, Dan's pulse raced. This sure beat sitting in his office in Boston.

The cruiser's five 5-inch dual-mount guns cranked their ten barrels into position. Inside each gun compartment, a crew would be ramming projectiles and powder cases into the breach.

"Range five-oh-double-oh."

"Now," Dan whispered.

A thunderclap shook the deck as ten guns fired as one, stirring Dan's blood. He never tired of the roar, the concussion, the smell of cordite. If only he could hear guns fired in actual battle instead of just in drills.

He refocused his binoculars on the target. The plane rocked once, twice, exploded.

His jaw flopped open as flaming bits spun down to the water. All around, sailors whooped and cheered. The radio-control operators said none of the drones had ever been shot down.

Dan turned to the admiral. "Did I just see that? Only ten shells."

Howard held up one finger, his eyes ablaze. "Yes, you saw. Now do you *see*?"

Yes, he saw. Science would win this war. Science and technology and production. Civilian and military minds working to-gether — just as they'd done on these VT proximity fuzes.

Admiral Howard clapped him on the back. "Six more months in Boston, then back to sea. Work hard, keep your nose to the grindstone."

"That's what I do, sir." He'd seen the fruit of laziness in his father's life.

"And avoid distractions, especially the feminine variety."

"Always, sir."

"I'm going up to the bridge to speak to Captain Burrough and the technological advisors. I'll be back in a few minutes. We have more drone attacks coming."

"Yes, sir." Dan squinted at the morning sky. A dive-bombing simulation seemed most likely.

Something out of the blue. Unexpected. As dizzying as a feminine distraction.

His wallet burned in his pocket, and he glanced around. No officers to see his moment of weakness. He opened his wallet and unfolded a piece of paper, the sailboat he'd sketched in the Terrace Room.

On Sunday at Park Street Church, Quintessa — Tess — had slipped the paper back to him, laughter in her eyes and her mouth.

His sketch was stark black-and-white simplicity. She'd added color — a warm oak color for the hull with a jaunty stripe of red. And she'd drawn a little man in dress blues at the helm, his chest puffed out and his chin raised to the wind. She'd labeled the little man with an arrow and the words "Admiral Danny."

Danny? No one had called him Danny since he was six years old. He'd told her that, and she'd giggled, saying she wasn't surprised. Who would dare?

Who would dare indeed? No one but Tess Beaumont.

A smile worked its way up his face. With two words she'd managed to encourage him and tease him.

Why did he like it so much? Why did he like the gesture, the teasing, the thought? Why did her addition of color bring his drawing to life?

And why on earth did he keep it in his wallet?

He was letting himself be distracted. Yet he couldn't bear to toss it into the Bay. He liked the drawing, and keeping it showed respect for Tess. He'd already hurt her feelings too much.

Dan returned the picture to hiding. Perhaps Tess wouldn't distract him much longer. Maybe she'd be accepted into the WAVES. Maybe she'd pass officer training school. Then she'd be assigned somewhere stateside — New York, Washington, DC, San Diego. The chances she'd return to Boston were as low as the chances of shooting down an aircraft with a single shell.

However, what if the Navy didn't take her? Or if she washed out? That would break her heart. And she'd stay in Boston.

Dan huffed out a breath and tucked his

wallet in his pocket.

"Ahoy!" the talker called out. "Aircraft bearing three-five-five. Elevation seven-five."

Dan swung his binoculars skyward. Yes, a dive-bombing simulation.

The gun barrels cranked to the vertical. High above, the drone aircraft weaved and dodged and started its descent.

In a few seconds, a mighty boom and roar resounded in Dan's gut.

A few seconds more, and the drone jiggled, flipped onto its back, and cartwheeled to the water.

"Wow."

Admiral Howard leaned over the wing of the bridge, beckoning to him.

"I see." Dan tapped his temple. Boy, did he see.

He jogged up to the bridge. No more complaining about his duties at ASWU. Sure, he wanted the sea breeze in his face, but this type of scientific work was vital.

Up on the bridge, Admiral Howard greeted Dan with a grin. "Two in a row."

"What do you mean, we're out of drones?" the commanding officer, Capt. Edmund Burrough, barked into the telephone. "We're supposed to conduct tests for two days straight."

"We're out?" Dan asked.

"They only have three, and the first malfunctioned." The admiral's grin spread. "We weren't expected to shoot them all down before noon. We weren't expected to shoot them down at all."

"We surprised them, eh?" Satisfaction warmed him inside. "Now let's surprise the Germans and the Japanese."

"You see. You see." Those blue eyes drilled into him. "Now, stay the course."

Dan snapped his heels together. "Aye aye, sir."

5

Boston
Tuesday, September 8, 1942

Tess studied herself in the mirror. Camel-colored suit and white blouse, chic matching hat, subtle makeup, simple gold jewelry, her curls rolled up at the nape of her neck. Smart and serious and polished. "Do I look like an officer?"

"I hope so. Then I'll have the room to myself." Yvette blew her a kiss, then returned to bustling around the bedroom.

"You won't get a new roommate?"

"No. I would like some privacy." She jammed her feet into black pumps and dashed out the door. "*Au revoir!* Good luck!"

"*Au revoir.*" She stuck one more bobby pin into her coiffure and frowned. When Tess arrived in Boston, Yvette had been the one who insisted she move into the apartment. Same when Lillian moved to town. Yvette wanted to lower her portion of the rent and also alleviate the housing shortage. Why did she suddenly want privacy?

Tess grabbed her brown handbag and the portfolio holding her documents, and she headed toward the El station at Charlestown's City Square.

Why was Yvette leaving at nine o'clock for her job at the Boston Navy Yard? Although she was always in a hurry, she'd never been late. Until recently, when she and Henri began going away to Cape Cod every weekend.

Tess's cheeks warmed as she walked down Monument Avenue under the basswood trees. Yvette went to bed earlier and overslept more often, and every Monday she made a cavalier statement about not getting much sleep on the weekends. Her morals!

But was something fishy going on?

What evidence did Tess have? Yvette said she was in love but didn't act like it. She didn't want a new roommate despite her perennial interest in saving money. She acted jumpy and thought someone was watching her. Yvette and Henri were less hotheaded than usual.

No crime. Not even a rumor of anything illegal.

Tess groaned. She needed to mind her

own business and stop sniffing around for a mystery.

If only the WAVES would take her. The Navy would keep her too busy to engage in such nonsense.

A half hour later, Tess stepped off the El at North Station. Clutching her purse to her stomach, she headed down Causeway Street under the tracks for the El. The huge modern building for North Station and Boston Garden loomed on her left, and dozens of people crowded the sidewalk — businessmen and salesgirls and servicemen.

Maybe someday soon she'd be in uniform too. *Please, Lord. Let me be useful for once.*

An office building stood at the northeast corner of Boston Garden, a dozen stories tall. In the lobby she found the directory and the location of the Office of Naval Officer Procurement.

Her stomach did the jitterbug. An officer. In the Navy. Tess Beaumont?

She drew a deep breath and took the elevator. The Navy thought well enough of her to give her an appointment. Now to pass the aptitude test, the physical, and the interview.

The office teemed with young men and women, and Tess's breath hitched. She joined the nearest line. When she reached

51

the front, she handed the sailor the letter with her appointment.

He checked her name off a list. "Down that hall, ma'am. First door on your left."

"Thank you." She followed the directions to a silent room filled with desks. A sailor handed her a pack of papers and motioned her to a desk. "One hour, ma'am."

The aptitude test. Tess glanced through — math, science, reading. She hadn't taken many science courses at Miami University, so she struggled through that section, but the reading and math were a breeze. Tess enjoyed math far more than a girl should. She'd always kept that to herself, but today it came in handy.

After she finished the exam, she was sent down another hall to a waiting room. For the next hour, she made small talk with the other ladies as they came and went.

At last, a woman in a white nurse's uniform and cap called for her.

Another hall and into a medical examination room. Tess smiled at the nurse. "Does this mean I passed the aptitude test?"

"Of course." The nurse gave her a look as if she thought they might need to regrade that test. "If you hadn't, they would have sent you home."

"Oh, thank you." One step down, two

more to go.

An hour of poking and prodding from head to toe. They counted her teeth, checked her vision and hearing, told her to dress, and sent her back to the waiting room.

Hurry and wait, lines and paperwork. The military way. She'd need to get used to it — or she hoped she'd have the opportunity to get used to it.

It was almost two o'clock, and hunger added to the jitter-bugging in her belly, but she didn't dare leave for lunch in case they called her name.

"Quintessa Beaumont."

She plastered on a smile and followed the officer into a small room. Another officer stood behind a desk. Tess shook hands with both men, Lieutenant Reynolds and Lieutenant Pierce, each in their thirties.

The men waited for Tess to sit, then seated themselves. Lieutenant Reynolds flipped through a manila folder. Were they going to send her home . . . or interview her?

He looked up with deep-set dark eyes. "Why do you want to join the WAVES, Miss Beaumont?"

An interview! She grinned, then restrained herself to a more professional expression. War posters and patriotic slogans came to mind, but Tess latched on to her own words. "I have a choice, Lieutenant. I can continue living for myself, or I can live for something bigger — for my country and freedom. I want to do everything I can to end this war as quickly as possible, and I'm not doing that in my current job."

"Why the WAVES?"

She hadn't been specific enough. Tess squeezed her purse in her lap. "I just knew, the moment I read about President Roosevelt signing the bill. And I've been reading the news, how Lt. Cdr. Mildred McAfee has been sworn in as the director and how the first class of officers began training two weeks ago. I want to be a part of it."

Their expressions hadn't changed. She needed more. "Plus, three of my friends are in the Navy, all Annapolis graduates. I've heard what they've gone through. Two of them were on the USS *Atwood* when it was sunk, and one was injured in battle — he's now been discharged. If only I could do something to help my friends — help all the men — come home safely."

The officers nodded. Did she dare try for humor? She gave a slight smile. "And with so many friends in the Navy, do you see why I'd be in danger if I joined the Army?"

They chuckled. Lieutenant Reynolds

turned a page in the folder. "You have a degree in business. Excellent. Why did you choose that field?"

Might as well be honest. "I wanted to go to college. Although my parents encouraged me, my boyfriend didn't want me to leave. He planned to expand the family store into other towns, so we made a deal. He'd let me go to college if I studied business to help him. Well, he married someone else, but I ended up loving business. Every part of it — accounting, record keeping, merchandising, sales."

"You have experience at two major department stores." Lieutenant Reynolds asked a series of questions about her time at Marshall Field's in Chicago and Filene's in Boston. He seemed particularly interested in her work in bookkeeping and inventory.

She tried to stay serious, but her enthusiasm bubbled out.

Lieutenant Reynolds crossed his arms on the desk. "What is your secret to such high sales figures?"

Modesty was essential, so she squelched her pride. "It isn't difficult. You spend time with the customer, listen to who she is and what she needs, then help her fill that need. I enjoy it."

Lieutenant Pierce slid a typed list in front

of Lieutenant Reynolds and tapped the middle of the page. Both men looked at Tess with assessing eyes and smiled.

What was on that piece of paper? It would be rude to peek, but oh, it was hard not to.

"Thank you for your time, Miss Beaumont. Please return to the waiting room."

Back in the waiting room, Tess settled into a seat and smiled at the woman beside her. "If I'd known this would take all day, I would have packed a picnic."

Older than Tess and wearing a dowdy gray suit, the woman gave a shy smile. "Indeed."

Tess offered her hand. "I'm Tess Beaumont, business major, height five-foot-five, weight don't ask." She recited the list in her best impression of the procurement officers.

"I'm Nora Thurmond, electrical engineer."

"Oh my." She'd heard of women becoming engineers but had never met one.

Brown eyes flicked to the side. "Don't be too impressed. The men I work with treat me like a laboratory assistant."

"But in the WAVES . . ." Tess squeezed Nora's forearm. "Why, they actually want women with technical training. What a great opportunity."

Nora glanced at Tess's hand, but she didn't pull away. "I hope so."

"Oh, how could they turn down someone like —"

"Will the following women please follow me?" A sailor read down a list of names, Tess's near the top.

She stood, and her stomach flipped over. Were they being accepted or rejected?

They also called Nora Thurmond's name, thank goodness. Surely, they wouldn't reject a lady engineer.

"This way please." The sailor marched down a hallway, and a dozen women followed, whispering to each other about what it meant.

"Have a seat." The sailor pointed them to a long table, and another sailor passed out packets of papers.

Contracts. Tess grasped Nora's hand. "We're in. We made it."

Nora read more carefully before she nodded. "We did."

An officer talked them through the contract, the gravity of what they were agreeing to, terms of service, reasons for discharge, prohibitions against marriage during training and against marrying a Navy man at any time.

Tess smiled. A good rule. That would put any lingering thoughts of Dan Avery out of her head.

Then the officer explained that they'd be sent home and called up later to report to officer training school on October 6.

Tess signed her contract slowly, meaningfully, gratefully. She'd make the most of this opportunity and strive to become a woman who was good for more than decoration.

After they signed, the ladies were shown into another room with the American flag at center front. "Raise your right hand and repeat after me."

Tess did so, emotion stirring inside. "I, Quintessa Beaumont, do solemnly swear that I will support and defend the Constitution of the United States against all enemies, foreign and domestic; that I will bear true faith and allegiance to the same; that I take this obligation freely, without any mental reservation or purpose of evasion; and that I will well and faithfully discharge the duties of the office on which I am about to enter. So help me God."

It was official. She belonged to the United States Navy for the duration of the war plus six months.

"What have I done?" Nora whispered.

Tess grinned at her. "You and I are about to have the adventure of our lives."

6

Boston
Sunday, September 27, 1942

Dan gazed up at the red brick façade of Park Street Church and its tall white steeple. This was his kind of architecture — simple and strong, yet beautiful.

"What should we do this afternoon?" Tess asked the group.

Dan winced. He should have escaped as soon as he stepped outside after Sunday services.

"It'd be a lovely day to take a train to the country," Mary Stirling said. "The trees are starting to turn."

"Wouldn't you rather wait until Jim comes back from sea?" Tess asked.

"You'll be gone by then. I want to savor your last week in Boston."

A trip to the country would take all day. Dan couldn't afford that. "I'll have to pass. I have a lot of work."

Lillian held Arch's hand and gave Dan a saucy smile. "It's the Sabbath, a day of rest. Even the Lord God took a day off."

"Remember, Lilliput . . ." He used the childhood nickname that put his kid sister in her place. "Jesus said, 'The sabbath was made for man, and not man for the sabbath.' And the Sabbath certainly wasn't made for times of war."

Lillian's big eyes sparked with mischief. She'd call him Dan-druff, he knew it.

"Are you sure?" Tess saved him, her brow wrinkled under her hat brim. "Everyone needs to rest now and then. And pardon me, but you seem tired and tense."

Tired and tense? He stared at her.

Her cheeks colored. "I'm sorry if I'm being presumptuous, but . . ."

But she must have seen him nodding off in the middle of an excellent sermon by Dr. Harold Ockenga. "A little tired. Nothing a nice black cup of coffee can't fix. But I'm not tense."

"Oh." Tess's light green eyes narrowed with concern. "You keep rubbing your neck."

He was doing it that very moment, and he lowered his hand. "A crick. Slept on it wrong."

"I know I'm wasting words." Arch Van-

60

denberg set his gray fedora over his blond hair. "But don't forget Tess leaves next week."

Dan hadn't forgotten. In fact, he was counting the days until the pretty little distraction left Boston. He gave her a respectful nod and turned to Mary. "I assume we'll have a going-away party next weekend."

"Oh yes," Mary said.

"I'll be there. Until then . . ." He tipped his navy-blue cover and headed down the sidewalk.

"I know the problem," Lillian called after him. "You're getting old. You're turning thirty in the spring and can't handle all that walking. Would you like to borrow my crutches?"

Dan faced the group. Arch was good for Lillian. She never used to mention her handicap, much less joke about it. "I'm too far gone for crutches. Apparently I need a nap in my rocking chair and a liniment rubdown."

While everyone was laughing, Dan's gaze dipped to Lillian's prosthetic leg.

A familiar burn smoldered in his chest.

That was the year Dan had to finish growing up because his father failed as a man. Unlike his father, Dan wasn't averse to hard work. He tipped his cover again. "Pardon me, but duty calls."

That afternoon, Dan sat in his office at the Boston Navy Yard with a sandwich and a cup of joe from the cafeteria. Although the yard bustled round-the-clock as new ships were built, the office was deserted.

All the better to get some work done.

He spread manila folders before him. So many projects. Admiral Howard had hinted Dan's special assignment would come soon, so Dan wanted to clear his desk and make it easy for Mr. Bentley to take care of things in his absence.

The first few folders were for radar projects. In October, the US Navy would start fitting out escort vessels with centimetric radar, which was more effective at detecting U-boats than the older meter-length radar. The British and Americans were also working feverishly to build centimetric radar systems small enough to fit in aircraft.

Dan sipped his coffee. Always had to stay one step ahead of the Nazis.

The next set of folders covered improved weaponry. Rocket projectiles, better depth charges, and a promising homing torpedo that could be fired by ships or aircraft.

And Dan's pet project, a series of studies

on auxiliary carriers. Aircraft were effective at keeping U-boats away from convoys, but land-based aircraft were limited by range, leaving critical regions of the ocean unprotected. If convoys could bring their own aircraft, they might put Admiral Karl Dönitz and his *Unterseeboote* out of commission forever.

A twinge of pain, and Dan massaged a knot at the base of his neck. Sure, it'd be nice to take a day off and stroll through the country with a pretty girl. Who wouldn't want that?

But his time on the USS *Cleveland* confirmed the need to avoid distractions. This technological work had merit. The VT proximity-fuzed shells had been rushed into production and were scheduled to be sent to the Pacific in November.

No days off. No leisurely strolls. And definitely no pretty girls.

He had work to do and a good reason to do it.

Dan leaned back in his chair and surveyed the office. Empty. Quiet.

And lonely.

7

Smith College
Northampton, Massachusetts
Tuesday, October 6, 1942

In an explosion of fall color, Tess lugged her suitcase across the campus of Smith College. Red maples and orange oaks and yellow elms — Tess's favorite — accented the attractive buildings in red brick and white stone.

Thank you, Lord. She prayed also to remind herself that this was what she wanted. Even if it meant leaving her friends.

Her throat felt thick. Despite humiliation and heartbreak, this past year had been wonderful, living with her best friend and making new friends with Lillian and Yvette.

She stopped and adjusted her grip on the suitcase. The bus driver had pointed her to Capen Hall, and Tess peered up the walkway through the foliage. That white building with the regal columns looked right.

Mary, Lillian. Would she make such good friends in the WAVES?

What about Yvette?

Tess let out a sigh in the chilly air. Yesterday evening when Tess had been packing, Yvette had returned from her meeting a ghostly shade of white.

Professor Arnaud had received word from his cousin in France. The Gestapo had caught his caretaker and the caretaker's brother exchanging letters and weapons. Both were arrested.

Yvette was convinced someone in the Boston group was a spy, and she was furious that one of her friends betrayed them. The professor insisted it was all a coincidence, but Yvette said he was naïve and foolish.

Of course, she'd say the same thing if she were the snitch.

Tess gave her head a brisk shake. What a horrible thought, and ridiculous. She knew Yvette better than that.

A breeze stirred through an elm tree, sending leaves fluttering. Tess plucked one from the sky. The same bright yellow as the dress she'd worn to her going-away party. Since she wouldn't have many possessions in the Navy, her friends had given her letters or cards instead of gifts.

Dan's was the shortest, so short she'd memorized it: "I pass on advice from a great man, Admiral Aloysius Howard. Stay the course, Tess. When things get tough — and they will — stay the course."

That was all, plus a drawing of a compass in black ink. She'd teased him and said someday he ought to draw her a whole coloring book.

She'd almost gotten a smile. She'd seen it wiggling in the corner of his mouth, begging to burst free. How glorious that would have been.

Tess climbed the broad stone steps to Capen Hall. Yes, it was definitely best she'd left Boston.

A desk stood inside the front door, manned by a real WAVE — a woman in her early forties in the stylish navy-blue uniform. She must have been one of the first 125 officers who trained last month, handpicked by Lt. Cdr. Mildred McAfee herself.

Should Tess salute? A bad salute would look awful, so she smiled. "Good morning."

"Last name?"

So, no pleasantries. "Beaumont."

"Beaumont . . ." She scanned a typed list. "Quintessa?"

"I go by Tess."

"Here you go by Beaumont. You'll be billeted in cabin 245 on the second deck."

"Second deck?" Tess frowned, then laughed. "Oh, the second floor. Like a ship. How cute."

Brown eyes bored through her. "This is the Navy, Beaumont. Every facility is a ship, and nothing is cute."

"Yes, sir — ma'am. Aye aye, ma'am." She sounded sillier with each word.

"Leave your civilian hat in your cabin, then report to the mess hall to be fitted for your uniform."

"Thank you, ma'am." She hauled her suitcase up to the second deck past dozens of chattering young ladies in civilian clothes. The hallway reminded her of her dormitory at Miami University, and so did her new room, except it had two bunk beds instead of two twin beds.

Tess set her suitcase on an empty top bunk and unpinned her hat. Her orders to report for duty had told her to bring enough civilian clothing to last two weeks, since her new uniform had to be tailored. The rest of her belongings had been shipped home to Ohio.

Back downstairs — on the main deck? — Tess followed the sounds of feminine conversation toward the dining hall — the mess hall. She'd heard Navy lingo from Jim and

67

Arch and Dan, but now she'd have to learn it.

"Shiver me timbers," she muttered. "Avast, ye hearties."

In the mess, dozens of women stood in line, and Tess joined the throng. She greeted the young lady ahead of her. "Hi, I'm Tess Beaumont."

"I'm Kate Madison." The gorgeous brunette flashed a dazzling smile and spoke in a Southern drawl. "This is my best friend, Ada Sue Duncan."

"Nice to meet you, Kate, Ada Sue." It was impossible to say Ada Sue without a Southern accent. "Where are you from?"

"Savannah, Georgia." Ada Sue's bright blue eyes beamed, her face framed by sleek, deep golden hair. "And you?"

"Ohio originally. I've lived in Boston this past year, not too far from Northampton."

"It's dreadfully cold here," Kate said. "But it's beautiful."

Tess suppressed a smile. "Wait till the snow comes."

"Next three." A sailor beckoned Kate, Ada Sue, and Tess toward three ladies with tape measures.

Without a greeting, one lady took Tess's name, braced one end of the tape measure on Tess's shoulder, and ran it down to her

68

wrist. "Arm length, twenty-one. Arms up please."

Tess closed her eyes to the indignity of the bust measurement. "I'm glad the Navy chose fashionable uniforms for the WAVES."

"I am too," Kate said.

The single-breasted navy-blue jacket and flared skirt would be so flattering. "They're designed by Mainbocher. I love his work. We sell it at Filene's."

"Filene's? The department store?" An unfamiliar voice.

As the tape measure slipped down to her waist, Tess opened her eyes and sought the voice — a tall woman with frizzy brown hair and a not-too-attractive face. Tess smiled at her. "Yes. Are you from Boston?"

She scrunched up her nose. "I thought you needed a college degree to become an officer. I didn't realize they were taking salesgirls."

What a snob. But Tess maintained her smile as the tape measure transferred to her hips. "I have a business degree. I was training to work in Filene's business offices. But yes, I was an excellent salesgirl."

An eye roll, and the woman looked away.

"What fun to work in a department store," Ada Sue said. "I always thought it would be a glamorous job."

"I don't know about that," Tess said. "But I know our uniforms will be glamorous. I'm so glad we don't have to sacrifice our femininity to serve our country."

The frizzy-haired girl huffed. "I thought the Navy was recruiting leaders, not cheerleaders. And I forgot my pom-poms."

Tess's stomach tightened, but she wouldn't rise to the girl's bait. "Don't worry. I packed an extra pair."

Kate and Ada Sue laughed.

"Well, I agree with Tess," Kate said. "It's important that we look good. The newspapers and magazines will take pictures of us marching in our smart navy-blue uniforms. Then the women of America will flood the recruitment offices."

Tess smiled at her new friend, thankful for her support.

"Done." The lady with the tape measure motioned Tess onward.

In the next line, the ladies received new hats — covers, as the Navy said. Dark blue with a slightly peaked crown, a narrow brim tipped up on each side, and a badge with a silver eagle and shield over golden crossed anchors. This would be the extent of their uniform for the next two weeks.

Tess set hers on top of her curls, glad she'd already had her hair cut above her collar to meet Navy regulations. "How do I look, ladies?"

"Adorable," Ada Sue said. "How about me?"

She looked adorable too. They all did. But Tess put on a mock glare. "This is the Navy, and nothing is cute, much less adorable."

They laughed, then they followed a sailor's directions to go to John M. Greene Hall for orientation at ten hundred.

"Ten o'clock," Tess translated for her friends. "Perhaps we should have chosen the WAAC. At least they speak English."

"But their uniforms aren't as cute." Ada Sue drew out the last word with music only a Southerner could muster.

The ladies ambled down a path toward the auditorium. Ahead of them, a lady walked alone, wearing a dowdy gray suit. She looked familiar. "Nora?" Tess called.

The engineer turned, gave Tess a wave, then hurried on her way.

Tess frowned. Why hadn't Nora waited up for them?

In the auditorium, Tess couldn't find Nora among the nine hundred women in their class. At least she could sit with Kate and Ada Sue.

After half an hour of chatting, they were called to order, and the commanding officer was introduced, Captain Herbert Underwood, who had returned from retirement to run the USS *Northampton,* the Naval Reserve Midshipmen's School at Smith College. He had a grandfatherly look about him with his white hair and kind eyes.

Captain Underwood welcomed them and told them what to expect — physical fitness and drills, lessons in naval etiquette, recognition of rank and ratings, naval history, and more.

The ladies were enlisted as apprentice seamen. If they passed the first three weeks of training, they'd be appointed reserve midshipmen. If they passed the final four weeks, they'd be commissioned as ensigns.

Tess didn't like the "ifs," but she understood. This was the real Navy, as Dan had reminded her. Hard work, discipline, not much time for fun.

He didn't think she could handle it.

How she wanted to prove him wrong.

8

Off Hampton Roads, Virginia
Saturday, October 24, 1942

At sea at last. Dan drank in the brisk morning air and savored the gentle roll of the destroyer USS *Wilkes* as she navigated the waves off the Virginia Capes.

Finally he could learn the destination of this enormous convoy of warships. He entered the bridge superstructure and trotted down the ladder to the wardroom, where many of the destroyer's officers were gathered. Dan nodded at Admiral Howard seated near the head of the table, and then sat near the foot with the other junior officers.

Excitement coursed through every vein. All he knew was they were going into combat, and it would be big.

At the head of the table, Commander Edward Durgin, in command of the destroyer division, greeted the officers and spread out a map.

North Africa.

Dan's pulse skipped a beat, and he scanned the map. The Allies were invading French Morocco and Algeria, both controlled by Vichy France. Just yesterday, British General Bernard Montgomery had launched a major offensive against the Germans at El Alamein in Egypt. By landing additional troops to the west, the Allies could trap the Germans in the middle, securing the Mediterranean and safeguarding Britain's supply of oil from the Middle East.

"Operation Torch," Commander Durgin said, and he outlined the basic plan. The Western Task Force was sailing from Hampton Roads, Virginia, and Casco Bay, Maine, to Morocco, where over one hundred ships would deposit thirty thousand American soldiers.

Meanwhile, the Eastern and Center Task Forces would sail from Britain into the Mediterranean to land seventy thousand British and American troops in Algeria at Oran and Algiers.

Murmurs rose around the table.

Dan let out a quiet whistle. The Western Task Force was steaming 4500 miles across the Atlantic to conduct a surprise night amphibious landing, unsure whether the French would welcome the Americans or shoot them.

Nothing like this had been done before. Ever.

And training had been minimal and hasty.

It could be either a raging success or a historic disaster.

Dan caught Admiral Howard's eye down the length of the table, and his mentor raised a smug smile. Yes, Dan owed him for arranging this.

He'd prefer to serve on the bridge or in the gun director or in the engine room, but serving as an observer and advisor placed a close second.

Commander Durgin briefed them on the composition of the task force and the plan for the two weeks they'd be at sea. Later briefings would cover the specifics of the invasion and the role the *Wilkes* would play.

When the briefing concluded and the officers departed, Admiral Howard motioned Dan to his end of the table and the map.

"Thank you, sir." Dan couldn't contain his smile.

"I knew you'd like this. First major American amphibious landing in the war."

"Other than Guadalcanal."

"This is five times bigger. The Western

Task Force alone is almost double the Guadalcanal force. You and I are here because of the U-boat threat."

Dan traced the course. "Over four thousand miles of submarine-infested ocean."

"Then we'll have to worry about U-boats off Morocco during the landings and while unloading."

"Once they realize what we're doing —"

"They'll come running. The past few weeks, the U-boats have been devastating the North Atlantic convoys off Greenland." Howard shifted his finger to the tip of South Africa. "They've also been wreaking havoc off Cape Town."

"I know." As soon as the Allies plugged one hole, the Germans drilled a new one.

"This is to our advantage." Blue eyes pinned him. "Dönitz has concentrated his forces thousands of miles from our convoy, unaware of the prize slipping through his grasp."

Dan studied the map. "They always patrol off the Straits of Gibraltar to catch British convoys to the Mediterranean."

"Yes, and it won't take them long to reach Morocco. Plus, the Vichy French have fleets at Casablanca and at Dakar, only a few days away."

"So we could have a fight."

"We're prepared. Most of the destroyers are the modern Gleaves and Bristol classes, many equipped with SG centimetric radar."

"And we have auxiliary carriers." Ugly things — merchant ship hulls with flight decks tacked on top — but their potential was more important than their looks.

"The pilots are poorly trained." Howard shook his head. "Most are fresh out of flight school, but they're eager."

Dan would accumulate plenty of data for the civilian scientists to play with.

"That's all for today." The admiral pulled out a small wooden box. "But now is as good a time as any to give this to you."

He'd seen the box many times on Howard's desk. He knew what was inside. "You don't mean —"

"I do." Howard flipped open the lid and slid the box across the table to Dan. "This is the compass my father gave me when I graduated from Annapolis. A Navy man himself. I want you to have it."

Dan fingered the engraved brass casing. "But this is . . . it should stay in the . . ."

"In the family?" He raised an eyebrow. "I have no children. But you — you've become like a son to me. I want you to have it."

Dan lifted the compass and cradled it in his hand. His throat felt tight enough that he didn't trust his voice. He gave a sharp nod to loosen his vocal cords. "Thank you, sir. I'll cherish it always. Someday I'll pass it on . . ."

To whom? He'd chosen not to marry, chosen not to have children.

Why did it feel like a kick to the gut? This wasn't a surprise. He'd made an informed decision for his legacy to be naval rather than familial.

"I'm glad you like it." The admiral's voice sounded husky, and he averted his eyes.

Like a son. Dan's chest filled with emotion and pride. "Thank you, sir. In many ways, you're — well, you're like a father to me."

"Let's not start talking like drippy-faced females." Howard shoved back his chair. "Back to work with you."

"Aye aye, sir." Dan restrained a smile as his mentor grumbled his way back to his cabin.

Like a father.

A father he could actually emulate.

Sure, everyone in Vermilion, Ohio, thought the world of George Avery, a master craftsman and a kind and thoughtful man. The other Avery children adored him.

But when his father had failed in the family's two greatest crises, Dan was the one who had held the household together. Twice. As a child.

Because his father was dreaming and drawing and playing with wood.

Dan snapped the compass case shut. Thank goodness the Lord had given him another man he could look up to.

Northwest of Madeira
Wednesday, November 4, 1942
The seas had picked up. Dan took his morning constitutional on the deck of the *Wilkes* under an iron-gray sky. A chill wind bit at his cheeks, and he dug his hands into the pockets of his mackinaw. A gale was coming, he could feel it.

Adm. Kent Hewitt, commander of the Western Task Force, would have to make a difficult decision.

If the weather reports were right, the landing craft could face twelve-foot waves at the Moroccan beaches. The French wouldn't have to shoot, because the surf would smash the American invaders to bits.

But if they waited offshore for better conditions, they'd lose the element of surprise and allow the enemy to build up defenses.

Dan studied the enormous convoy on the rising seas, over one hundred warships and transports in an area twenty miles by thirty miles. The lives of thirty thousand soldiers and just as many sailors depended on one man. *Lord, help Hewitt make the right choice.*

Someday, Lord willing, Dan might be in a position to make similar decisions. He prayed he'd do so wisely.

Someday, Lord willing, he'd be Admiral Daniel Avery.

Admiral Danny, Tess had called him.

His mouth twitched as he passed a group of sailors chipping flammable paint off the bridge superstructure in preparation for combat. What was it about that woman? She'd be a good month into training by now. Was she thriving, or had she washed out?

She'd taken some hard blows recently, being dumped by her high school boyfriend, finding out her next boyfriend was married, and being treated poorly by her boss at Filene's. She needed a break. *Lord, let her pass.*

Why? So she wouldn't return to Boston? Oh, brother. What a self-centered prayer. Good thing Tess had better people than him praying for her.

"Excuse me, Mr. Avery." An officer approached near the number one gun turret toward the bow of the destroyer. "May I have a word with you?"

"Of course, Dr. Stern."

The medical officer cringed from a blast of wind. "I heard you and Admiral Howard are close."

Dan did enjoy that reputation. He aligned his body to block Dr. Stern from the wind. "He's taken me under his wing."

"Do you have any influence with him? I'm worried about his health."

"His health?" He couldn't keep the alarm from his voice.

"I'm concerned about his heart. His blood pressure is high, he doesn't watch his weight, and he never rests."

"He's a hardworking man."

"Too much so."

"Is that possible?" Dan injected some humor into his voice.

Dr. Stern smiled and pulled his mackinaw up to his prominent chin. "It is. Our bodies are designed to need periods of rest."

A significant design flaw, but Dan nodded.

The doctor narrowed his brown eyes. "Are you a religious man, Mr. Avery? Do you keep the Sabbath?"

Dan drew back a bit. "I do. So does Admiral Howard. We always attend Sunday services."

Dr. Stern shook his head. "Keeping the Sabbath is about more than attending services. The Lord commanded us not to work. Don't you find that odd?"

"I — I never really thought about that."

"I find it fascinating. We think of idleness as a sin, and it is. But in the Ten Commandments, the Lord didn't command us to work. He commanded us to rest. Why, do you think?"

Dan gazed around, as if the clouds held the answer.

The doctor raised one gloved finger. "He knows us. He knows we'll work too hard."

Restlessness tugged at Dan's feet. "We're at war."

"All the more reason to rest when we can, so we're at our best when it's required of us."

Time to end this conversation. "Thank you for the advice, Dr. Stern."

"Will you have a word with Admiral Howard?"

"I will. Good day." Dan continued his constitutional, up to the bow of the destroyer. The sharp prow struck the gray waves, raising plumes of white foam to each side.

Concern squirmed inside. Could the admiral's heart be in danger? And would rest benefit such a driven man — or annoy him?

The doctor's words about rest clashed with everything Dan knew. He repeated his favorite verse, Philippians 3:13–14: "This one thing I do, forgetting those things which are behind, and reaching forth unto those things which are before, I press toward the mark for the prize."

How could a man press toward the mark if he rested too much?

Before Dan talked to the admiral, he had some reading to do.

9

Smith College
Friday, November 6, 1942

"That's it. Smile. Look intelligent and interested."

Tess smiled. She tried to look intelligent and interested. She and Kate and Ada Sue stood on the pier on Paradise Pond, while an exceptionally handsome lieutenant with sleek black hair stood on the deck of a little sailboat and pointed to the rigging.

Flashbulbs popped. "That's it. One more. You, the blonde on my left. Reach over and touch the sail."

Tess fingered the white canvas. This would make a charming recruiting poster or brochure. Three pretty WAVES in their new blue uniforms, learning how to sail. Except they weren't. They were just taking photos.

"That's all, ladies." The photographer and his assistant packed up their equipment.

Kate lunged for her overcoat and burrowed inside. "Oh, this weather. It isn't even fifty degrees."

"I know." Just for fun, Tess draped her coat over her arm. "I can't believe how warm it is."

Ada Sue buttoned her coat up to her chin. "You Yankees have ice in your veins."

"Comes in handy." Tess headed up the walkway toward the Alumnae Gym. "Hurry up, ladies. We're missing first aid, and Mr. Rawlings wants to wash me out."

Kate laughed. "The Navy won't let him. They can't afford to lose their poster girls."

A poster girl — was that why the recruiter had accepted her? A sick feeling congealed in Tess's stomach. Maybe the Navy only wanted her for her looks, not for what she could contribute to the war effort.

"Say, Tess." Kate fluffed her brown curls beneath her officer's cover. "You got two letters this morning. What's the news?"

Tess felt bright inside again. "One's from Mary. She misses me, the sweetheart, but she's doing well. Her boyfriend, Jim, is back in Boston." Mary also said Dan had gone to sea and expected to be away for some time.

Her smile grew. Good. Dan needed to be at sea.

"And the second letter?" Ada Sue asked.

Tess kicked aside some damp brown leaves on the walkway. "It's from Celeste Robillard, the French baker."

"Ooh!" Kate nudged Tess's arm. "Any new clues in the spy case?"

They turned onto the walkway in front of the library, a grand long building like an Italian palazzo. "Nothing really. Madame Robillard says Yvette is acting suspicious. She wonders if Yvette could be the spy."

"Mercy!" Ada Sue said. "How horrible."

Something nasty entwined around Tess's stomach. "It is. I can't believe it. No one loves France more than Yvette."

Kate's eyes glowed. "Maybe she just talks like that to throw off suspicion."

"I refuse to believe it. Besides, I can't do anything here aboard the USS *Northampton*. Now, let's hurry. We're late."

The Alumnae Gym stood before them, a Queen Anne darling with gables and turrets and plenty of ivy. Too bad it was where they were tortured with physical fitness.

The gymnasium buzzed as hundreds of female midshipmen practiced first aid.

Ensign Rawlings approached the three ladies with a frown on his square face. "Late again, I see."

Kate handed him the note from the public

relations officer. "Doing our patriotic duty, sir."

He grumbled. "You're here to become officers, not fashion models."

Ada Sue stood stiff at attention, her face sober. "Sir, mustn't every officer do her duty, no matter how unpleasant?"

He turned on his heel and walked away. "Madison, Duncan, right there. We're on page thirty of your manual. Apply a bandage to the upper left arm, then wrap the right ankle for a sprain. Beaumont, you'll work with Selby."

No doubt, Mr. Rawlings hated her. Greta Selby hadn't concealed her contempt for Tess since their first encounter during the uniform fitting.

Tess worked up a smile. "Hi, Greta. Looks like we're partners."

"Swell." She wouldn't be that unattractive if she didn't always wear a smirk or a sneer. Today she'd chosen the smirk. "You go first. I'll be the patient."

"All right." Tess set down her overcoat and knelt on the wooden floor.

"The supplies are over there. You should have fetched them first."

Or Greta could have told her before Tess sat down. Smile in place, Tess fetched the box and returned to her patient.

"Hurry up. I'm bleeding to death."

If only it were true. Tess pulled out a roll of gauze. "Let's bandage that arm."

"You're supposed to ask me what's wrong first."

"You just said you're bleeding to death."

"But you're supposed to ask. Mr. Rawlings said so in the lecture."

"I missed the lecture. Now, where are you bleeding?"

Greta pointed to a spot on her arm. "Must be nice to be excused from class just because you're pretty."

Tess would rather be in class, but something told her to hold her tongue. She wound the gauze around Greta's upper arm, not too tight, not too loose, and she secured it with a safety pin. "And your ankle?"

"I didn't say one word about my ankle."

Tess raised her sweetest smile. "Where else does it hurt, miss?"

She stuck out her left ankle. "I sprained it."

Mr. Rawlings said to wrap the right ankle. She wouldn't fall for that trap. "You do mean the right ankle, don't you?"

Greta's cheeks colored. "Yes, the right."

Tess gently removed Greta's shoe, then wrapped the ankle crisscross, round-and-about. She might have missed the lecture, but she'd studied the first aid manual.

If only Greta would stop wiggling. The gauze kept popping around her heel.

"How are things going?" Mr. Rawlings stood with his hands clasped behind him.

Greta groaned. "Beaumont is hopeless, sir."

Tess's jaw tightened. "She's wiggling, sir."

"Sir, you said in lecture that patients in pain rarely hold still. I'm trying to be accurate."

"That's correct, Selby. Very good." Mr. Rawlings inspected Tess's ankle bandage, which she hadn't finished yet. "Sloppy work, Beaumont. You have to restrain the patient's movement."

Greta grabbed the bandage around her upper arm and tugged it down to her elbow. "You think that's sloppy, sir. Look at my arm. The bandage slipped off."

Tess gasped, but she refused to call the girl out on her deception.

"Do it again, Beaumont. Get it right this time." Mr. Rawlings shook his head and walked away.

Her hands shaking, Tess unpinned the bandage around Greta's arm. "Why are you doing this to me?"

"Because you don't belong here," she

hissed. "You belong out there, where beautiful girls get everything they want. But here — the WAVES — this is for the rest of us, for those of us who have to rely on brains and hard work. But every time I turn around, they're snapping your picture. They'll make you an ensign, all right, but not because you earned it. Only because of your looks. It isn't fair."

Although her vision blurred, Tess wound the gauze around that stiff upper arm. She'd wanted to do something useful, something that didn't depend on beauty, but everyone was pushing her back in that same old box.

She blinked to clear her vision, and she worked the safety pin through the gauze.

"Ouch!" Greta cried. "You stabbed me."

"What?" She sucked in her breath and inspected Greta's arm. Not one speck of blood. "No, I didn't."

"Mr. Rawlings!" Greta waved her free hand. "Would you please assign Beaumont to someone else before I need actual first aid?"

The ensign's head wagged back and forth. "Honestly, Beaumont."

Tess resisted the urge to skewer Greta with a hateful look. She gathered her belongings and followed Mr. Rawlings.

"What am I going to do with you, Beaumont? Coming in late, missing the lecture, now this. You *can* wash out, you know."

"I know. I'll do better with someone else, sir." Anyone else.

"Work with Thurmond. She and her partner already finished."

Nora. What a blessing. Tess had hoped to make friends with the engineer, but whenever she found time to chat, it seemed Nora had to leave.

"Thurmond," Mr. Rawlings said. "Be a patient for Beaumont. Help her if you can."

"Aye aye, sir." Nora sat on the floor and lowered her brown eyes.

Tess knelt beside her. When they first met, Tess had thought Nora was a good ten years older due to her outdated clothing and hairstyle, but they were the same age. Now with a cute uniform and hairstyle, Nora looked darling. "I'm glad we get to work together. I was hoping to spend time with you. We're always so busy."

"We are. Here are the supplies." She pushed the box closer to Tess.

"Where does it hurt, miss?" Tess asked in her best nurse voice.

"I'm bleeding here, and I think I sprained my ankle."

"Let's take care of your arm first." She wound the gauze around Nora's left arm.

"It does seem silly to teach us first aid, doesn't it?"

"Oh?"

"We'll be working stateside in nice safe offices. The only first aid we'll need is for paper cuts."

"I suppose."

Tess fastened the safety pin. "Let's take care of that ankle."

"Mm-hmm." Not one more word while Tess found a length of gauze for Nora's ankle and removed her shoe.

Time to get the quiet brunette talking while she bandaged her ankle. "What's your favorite class? I love ship and aircraft recognition, but naval history gives me troubles — all those technical details about engines and guns. How about you? What are you enjoying?"

"Please don't do that." Nora's voice came out low and shaky.

Tess jerked her gaze to Nora's face. "I'm sorry. Did I hurt you?"

Nora looked away, her eyes sad. "Please don't pretend to be nice to me."

"Pretend?"

Her eyebrows drew together, and she gazed across the crowded gymnasium. "I've known plenty of girls like you. They were always sweet to me in math and physics, because I'd explain all those technical details. But they'd ignore me in the hallway, and they'd laugh at me behind my back. They thought I didn't know. But I knew."

"I haven't —" Tess's breath quickened, and her eyes stung. "I'd never. I'd never do that to you. To anyone."

Nora turned back to Tess with a gaze born of hurt and strength. "And I don't intend to give you the chance to do so."

Tess's vision blurred again, but she set her jaw and returned to work. It wasn't fair to be accused of something she hadn't done, but it also wasn't fair for those girls to use Nora like that. How could she blame Nora for protecting herself?

She wrapped the ankle and fastened the safety pin. "I'm sorry that happened to you. It isn't right." Her voice wobbled, and she cleared her throat. "Just so you know, I was being nice because you remind me of my friend Mary, my best friend since seventh grade."

"How are things going?" Mr. Rawlings approached.

"I'm done." Tess couldn't look at either her patient or her instructor. Red eyes weren't professional.

"It's passable." He sounded disappointed. "You're dismissed."

Tess sprang to her feet, grabbed her coat, and dashed for the exit, where Kate and Ada Sue waved, happy to see her.

She put on a smile and walked with them back to Capen Hall for lunch. Her friends chattered and laughed, but heaviness descended in Tess's stomach.

Greta was right. Tess didn't belong here.

And Mr. Rawlings was right. She could wash out. And she would if he had any say in the matter. If she didn't fail first aid, then she'd fail naval history.

That would prove she was useless. If the Navy kept her, it would only be for public relations, because she was decorative.

An ache enveloped her chest as she followed Kate and Ada Sue into the mess. After she picked up her tray of fried chicken, green beans, and mashed potatoes, she squeezed between her friends at the long table.

Conversation zinged around her. Tess smiled and nodded, and she must have responded appropriately, because Kate and Ada Sue didn't ask what was wrong.

What was wrong? Quintessa Beaumont was so arrogant she thought she could do something beneficial.

Tess had stolen a spot in the WAVES that belonged to a woman like Nora, or even

Greta, who was brilliant. She was foolish to think she could contribute to the war effort. She should quit. She should deliberately fail a class so they'd have no choice but to wash her out.

Filene's would take her back. It was time to return to Boston.

Why should she stay? They worked constantly and never had time to rest or have fun. This program was too exhausting, too humiliating, too tough.

Tough? Hadn't Dan's going-away card told her, "If things get tough — and they will — stay the course"?

Her eyes slipped shut, and she lowered her chin as if focusing on her meal. Could she stay the course? This was so difficult.

Yet in her heart she knew quitting would be selfish, putting her pride and comfort above the needs of the nation. *Lord, help me. If you want me to stay here, help me be brave and strong. I can't — I can't do this on my own.*

"Tess?" Kate asked.

Her eyes popped open, and she found a smile. "Yes?"

"Nora passed you a note."

Tess stared at a piece of paper and unfolded it, bracing herself for the words inside. The note read, "Dear Tess, I'm sorry.

It wasn't right for me to judge you like that. Can you forgive me? Do you think we could ever be friends? With sincere regret, Nora."

Tess glanced up and found the quiet young woman and her brown eyes filled with that sincere regret. "Yes," she mouthed. Yes, she forgave her. Yes, she wanted to be friends.

Nora gave her a soft smile and returned to her meal.

That night, Tess planned to tuck the note into Dan's card. Both confirmed that Tess was exactly where she needed to be — in a tough place where she'd be humbled. Then she could become a woman who made a difference.

10

Off Fedala, French Morocco
Sunday, November 8, 1942

"The Yanks are coming!" The signal lights flashed Commander Durgin's message to the three other control destroyers four miles off the shores of Fedala in French Morocco.

A cold breeze blew over Dan, scented by earth and charcoal, stirring the adrenaline. Up on the signal deck on top of the pilothouse, he nudged Admiral Howard. "Apparently Commander Durgin didn't get Dr. Stern's message about resting on the Sabbath."

"Dr. Stern will need to have words with General Eisenhower himself." Humor rang in the admiral's tone.

"That he will, sir." On this Sunday, the Allies were invading North Africa. Fedala boasted good landing beaches from which Gen. George Patton could march twelve miles south to capture the vital port of

Casablanca.

The *Wilkes* steamed forward, aiming for Beach Red 2. Dan strode aft and gazed past the destroyer's two funnels. With his binoculars, he could make out phosphorescent wakes behind thirty-one landing craft following the *Wilkes,* each carrying three dozen soldiers. Farther to the east, the destroyers *Swanson, Ludlow,* and *Murphy* shepherded their own flocks.

The Western Task Force had arrived at 2353 on November 7, seven minutes ahead of schedule, undetected by the enemy. However, now the landings had been delayed an hour. It was 0400, with the landings to start at 0500. The soldiers would only have one hour of darkness before morning twilight.

Dan lowered his binoculars. *Lord, let it be enough time.*

God seemed to be smiling on this operation. Only hours before Admiral Hewitt needed to make his decision, his aerologist had contradicted the official weather reports from Washington and London and predicted smooth seas on November 8. Hewitt listened. And the aerologist was correct.

Dan returned to Howard's side. Like Dan, the admiral wore a heavy mackinaw, life vest, and steel helmet. No one knew what the French would do. Would they be moved by the spirit of Lafayette and welcome the Americans? Or would they fight back to appease the Nazis?

As much as Dan longed to experience combat, he wanted to battle the enemy, not America's oldest ally. *Please, Lord. Don't let the French resist.*

"I arranged for us to have the best seats in the house," Howard said.

"I'll say, sir." The *Wilkes* would play three major roles today — as a control destroyer escorting landing craft to the beach, as a fire support destroyer bombarding any hostile gun batteries, and finally screening the force against submarines.

Dan tugged the cuff of his mackinaw sleeve over his glove to cut the cold air. "You realize, sir, that we won't perform antisubmarine duties until late this morning."

"We won't need to."

A question formed about how the admiral knew, but Dan let it pass. Either the admiral had drawn his conclusion based on how quickly Admiral Dönitz could marshal his forces — or the Allies had intelligence unavailable to mere lieutenants.

Dan peered into the moonless night. To the west, Cap Fedala boasted two gun batteries, and to the east the Cherqui headland boasted another. The artillery could enfilade the landing beaches between them.

So far, the guns were silent.

At 0445 the *Wilkes*'s engines stopped, and the clank of anchor chains filled the noise gap. From this line of departure, the landing craft would proceed four thousand yards to the beaches, while the control destroyers would remain to guide later waves of landing craft.

Admiral Howard pointed toward the beaches. "The scout boats must not have received the message about the delayed landings."

Lights blinked in red and blue. "At least they arrived safely and didn't tip off the locals."

Signals passed between the *Wilkes* and her sister ships, and at 0500, the landing craft zipped toward shore and danger and possible death.

"Godspeed." Admiral Howard raised a salute.

Dan followed suit, his heart in his throat.

The landing at Fedala was the most important in Morocco. Smaller forces were landing to the south at the port of Safi and to the north at Mehdia to secure Port Lyautey and Morocco's only airfield with concrete runways. But the soldiers landing at Fedala needed to seize Casablanca and its harbor.

Meanwhile, the US Navy's Covering Group, headed by the new battleship USS *Massachusetts,* patrolled off Casablanca to contain the French fleet should it choose to attack.

Dan's breath puffed before him. It wouldn't be a restful Sunday, but it would be eventful.

He'd rest back in Boston. "Everyone needs to rest now and then," Tess had said, and Dr. Stern had reminded him to "rest when we can, so we're at our best when it's required of us." That conversation had driven Dan to Scripture, to study the command to refrain from work. God must have had a good reason if he'd issued an order.

Thank goodness, Jesus provided an exception when he told the Pharisees, " 'What man shall there be among you, that shall have one sheep, and if it fall into a pit on the sabbath day, will he not lay hold on it, and lift it out? How much then is a man better than a sheep? Wherefore it is lawful to do well on the sabbath days.' "

Well, today the Allies were lifting North Africa out of the Axis pit, and Dan felt good.

A pillar of light shot straight up in the sky from the west, then another to the east.

Dan hauled in a breath. Searchlights at Cap Fedala and at Cherqui. The invasion force had been detected. The search-lights slashed low, sweeping the dark seas, illuminating landing craft and men on the beaches.

"Oh no," Dan said.

The ticking of far-off machine-gun fire crossed the waters.

"We have a fight on our hands. Let's go to the bridge." Admiral Howard headed down the ladder.

Dan followed. The admiral took longer than he used to. Was it just his age and weight, or was his heart affected as the doctor feared? But Admiral Howard had brushed off Dan's concerns as he'd brushed off Dr. Stern's.

Down on the bridge, Cdr. Edward Durgin gave orders, as did Lt. Cdr. John McLean, the commanding officer of the *Wilkes*.

Admiral Howard and Dan went to the cramped radar room behind the pilothouse. The room was lit only by red lightbulbs to preserve night vision. Neon green pulses of light raced across two types of radar scopes.

"How are things going?" the admiral asked the radarman.

"Fine, sir." The young man's face shone red in the eerie light. "We're using the SG radar to fix on the oil tanks at Cap Fedala for navigation."

"Any sign of subs?"

"Not on the radar, sir."

Dan picked up the telephone and contacted the sonar room. They had nothing to report either. The screening destroyers to seaward had the primary role in watching for submarines, but each ship needed to be vigilant.

The admiral beckoned Dan out to the wing of the bridge, where they could observe without hindering operations.

The searchlights had fallen dark, and sporadic gunfire sounded from the shore, but the big gun batteries remained silent. No American ship was to fire unless fired on first. The guns at Cap Fedala were dangerously close to the oil tanks, which the Army hoped to confiscate intact.

At 0600, morning twilight arrived, and shapes of hills and bluffs emerged.

A great boom to the east.

Dan whipped toward the sound. "The guns at Cherqui."

"Batter up!" Commander Durgin cried, the signal to report that the French had chosen to fight.

Lieutenant Commander McLean called out orders to raise the anchor and start the engines and for the gunners to stand ready.

The commands were relayed by talkers and the engine telegraph. Dan craned his neck to see up on the signal deck, where the signalman flashed "Batter up" to the command ship, the cruiser USS *Augusta* with Adm. Kent Hewitt aboard.

The deck rumbled beneath Dan's feet, and anchor chains clanked on the main deck below.

Another boom, to the west this time, from Cap Fedala.

"Fighting back isn't wise," Howard grumbled. "We're taking this port whether they like it or not."

A splash rose in the ocean, some distance from the *Wilkes,* but the French gunners would soon get their range and bearing.

Lieutenant Commander McLean called out a new heading. The *Wilkes* and the *Swanson* steamed west to bombard Cap Fedala, while the *Ludlow* and *Murphy* dealt with Cherqui.

"Sir, Captain Emmet ordered, 'Play ball!' " a talker said.

Then a ball game is what they'd get. "Time for the first pitch," Dan said.

Orders were barked out to the gun director. As the *Wilkes* dashed forward, zigzagging to throw off the coastal artillery, her four 5-inch guns swiveled toward the cape and the barrels rose.

"Commence firing!"

Dan braced himself on the rail. He'd heard naval guns fired in practice but never in battle. Four flashes of orange lit the dim morning, four guns roared, and the deck lurched.

The *Swanson* joined in, and the French fired back. Splashes dotted the ocean around the destroyers.

"The *Murphy* is hit, sir," a talker said. "Light damage. She's retiring. The *Brooklyn* is taking her place."

"Silence those guns," Durgin said.

Another salvo rattled the *Wilkes* and every bone in Dan's body. In a minute, a brilliant yellow fire erupted on land.

"An oil tank," Howard mumbled.

"The Army won't like that." Dan focused his binoculars on the cape, searching for the battery. "But they really won't like it if those guns chew up the troops."

"Cease firing," McLean called.

The guns on the cape had fallen silent. But were they knocked out?

Dan didn't trust them.

Sure enough, within five minutes, they opened fire again. The two destroyers darted about, heaving shells at the cape until the guns fell silent twenty minutes later.

The sun had risen. Dan trained his binoculars to the smoke-shrouded beach. Landing craft sat at odd angles on the sand and lay dashed on rocks.

Yet Dan didn't see bodies, thank goodness. Perhaps the landings were succeeding.

As the morning progressed, the guns at Cap Fedala fired sporadically, silenced over and over by the destroyers and by the cruiser *Augusta,* which joined the ball game. At 0730, they received word that the Army had seized the town of Fedala and the battery at Cherqui, but Cap Fedala's gunfire kept the soldiers at bay.

Farther to the south came great muffled, rumbling booms. Apparently the Covering Group was having a fight with the French fleet at Casablanca.

High above, airplane motors added to the din. Dan gazed up at the F4F Wildcat fighters and SBD Dauntless dive-bombers from the carrier *Ranger* and the auxiliary carrier *Suwannee.*

The British planes at Gibraltar covered the landings in Algeria, leaving no land-based Allied aircraft in range of Morocco. So the Americans brought their air cover with them.

Dan was glad to see the new auxiliary carriers in action. Converted from merchant ship hulls, the "jeep" carriers could be built quickly and held great promise.

"Sir!" a talker called. "A scout plane reports seven French ships steaming from Casablanca toward Fedala at thirty-six knots."

Dan spun to the south. "The Covering Group let them pass?"

"Must be preoccupied with the *Jean Bart.*" The French battleship posed the biggest threat at Casablanca.

"Looks like we'll have a good old-fashioned surface battle." His breath came faster as he counted dots on the horizon. At Fedala, the Americans had two cruisers and ten destroyers, one damaged. Many of the destroyers had to remain to the north and west to screen the transports. At that moment, the *Wilkes* and the *Ludlow* were farthest south, patrolling the new Beach Yellow south of Cap Fedala, separated from the rest of the warships.

Two against seven. Not great odds.

Commanders barked orders, and gunners prepared their weapons.

The shapes on the horizon became more distinct. Five smaller ships, probably destroyers, and two larger ones, probably destroyer leaders.

The French fired first. Geysers sprang up in the water, dyed green and pink and violet to help the French gunners adjust their aim. The *Wilkes* and *Ludlow* fired back, racing and zigzagging.

Plumes of sand shot up from Yellow Beach as shells exploded among the landing craft. Admiral Howard released a mild curse word, and Dan agreed in spirit if not in vocabulary.

American shells zoomed through the air, and a fire broke out on one of the French destroyer leaders.

Commander Durgin ordered the two destroyers to fall back to seaward, to lure the French away from the landing beaches and to gain reinforcement.

The *Ludlow* led the way. A shell burst amidships, and flames rose.

Dan gasped. That could have been the *Wilkes.*

But the *Ludlow* kept underway.

Dan glanced aft. SBDs and TBF Avenger torpedo bombers dived at the French ships. Shells arced through the air toward the *Wilkes* and the *Ludlow,* straddling the ships but falling shorter and shorter.

"They think we're running away," Dan said to the admiral. Now they probably thought they could attack the defenseless transports still teeming with troops. "They're wrong."

"You bet they are."

"Here we go, boys," the commander said from inside the pilothouse. "Admiral Hewitt ordered the *Wilkes, Swanson, Augusta,* and *Brooklyn* to engage."

While the *Ludlow* continued her retreat to bandage her wounds, the *Wilkes* made a tight turn, white foam spraying in her wake, and the *Swanson* drew abreast.

The destroyers surged forward at flank speed, the cruisers right behind. Within minutes, the *Wilkes* and *Swanson* shot salvos of 5-inch shells. The heavy cruiser *Augusta* opened up with the deep roar of her 8-inch guns, and the light cruiser *Brook-lyn* fired her 6-inch guns.

The American ships darted back and forth, dodging French shells and firing their own, carving their signatures on the water, punctuating them with shell geyser exclamation points.

Dan itched to be in command. To be down in the engine room, keeping the engines and boilers running. To be up in the gun director, training fire on the enemy. To be down on the deck as first lieutenant, preparing the damage control parties for any emergency. Or to be on the bridge, co-ordinating all the information, all the departments, all the sailors.

His first battle, and he could only observe.

"They're falling back." Admiral Howard peered through his binoculars.

"Giving up?"

"Or trying to draw us under coastal fire from Casablanca."

Dan winced. If the Americans took chase, they'd abandon the transports at Fedala to any U-boats that might lurk in the area.

"Very well, sir," Commander Durgin said on the Talk Between Ships telephone. He faced McLean. "Admiral Hewitt called in the Covering Group to attack the French ships, and he ordered us back to the transport area."

More orders flew from the bridge, and the *Wilkes* reversed course.

Dan glanced at his watch. The surface battle had lasted only twelve minutes.

But it was magnificent.

11

Smith College
Wednesday, November 11, 1942
"Company left, march!"

As one, Tess's company pivoted and marched across Smith College's athletic fields under a cool autumn sky. Hundreds of black oxfords thudded to the cadence of the drill master.

What fun it was to drill, and in an Armistice Day parade! She wanted to grin at her friends or wave to the girls on the sidelines, the civilian students at Smith College. But she kept a blank expression fixed on the midshipman ahead of her.

The Navy wasn't about being an individual but about working as a unit, about putting others before self, and she was embracing it.

"To the right flank, march!"

She swiveled with her company. A breeze blew a curl against her cheekbone, and it tickled, but she didn't brush it away. Nine hundred women in identical navy-blue uniforms, and for the first time in her life, Tess enjoyed not standing out.

"Company halt!"

Tess stomped to a halt, sharp at attention. They had double reason to celebrate Armistice Day. First, they were commemorating the end of the First World War twenty-four years earlier. Second, they were rejoicing over this morning's news that the French had called a cease-fire in North Africa after three hideous days of friends firing on friends. Meanwhile, the British had soundly defeated the Germans at El Alamein and were chasing Field Marshal Erwin Rommel west across Libya.

"Forward, march."

Tess obeyed.

In the morning paper, she'd read Prime Minister Winston Churchill's moving statement: "This is not the end. It is not even the beginning of the end. But it is, perhaps, the end of the beginning."

"Company halt. Company dismissed."

The ladies marched in formation off the field. North Africa . . . was that where Dan had sailed? There had been a terrific naval battle off Casablanca, and the Americans had sunk half a dozen French warships, maybe more. The papers hadn't reported any American naval losses, but they were often censored, for good reason.

A shudder of fear, but she squelched it. Dan yearned for this, and it was where he belonged. When he returned, Mary or Lillian would tell her what he had done, and that would suffice. Dan certainly wouldn't write her.

The only letter she'd received yesterday was from Yvette, but it was alarming.

The week after Professor Arnaud announced the arrest of his cousin's caretaker, Henri Dubois had named a new informant in the meeting. Henri said this man was the best type of informant because everyone knew him as a Nazi sympathizer. An excellent cover, Henri said.

Now Professor Arnaud had received word that the Gestapo had arrested the informant and tortured him — until they discovered the truth. He really was a Nazi sympathizer.

Henri had lied. He'd named a known fascist to see if the false information would cross the Atlantic. It had. Yvette was certain there was a spy in the group, and she was outraged.

Tess's mouth twisted. Just because Yvette acted outraged didn't rule her out as a suspect.

She drank in fresh autumn air to clear her mind and stop her runaway imagination. Today they were celebrating.

Off the field, the WAVES dispersed and found their friends. Tess gathered Kate, Ada Sue, and Nora. To her relief, Kate and Ada Sue had welcomed Nora. Tess had been ready to put her foot down and say, "If you want to be friends with me, you'll have to be friends with Nora," as she'd done with Mary on the first day of seventh grade.

Tess had never told Mary, but she'd said those words reluctantly. Tess had been the new girl in Vermilion, and coming from Manhattan's glittering art community made her instantly popular in that small Ohio town. Although she'd enjoyed Mary's friendship over the summer, the unpopular girl could have devastated Tess's social life.

Mary assumed Tess had acted out of the goodness of her heart, but she was wrong. Tess had acted out of love of a winter coat in dark gold wool. Her mother threatened not to buy it if Tess abandoned Mary, to make her wear her childish old coat that was too short.

So Tess took her stand. She received her coat. And her friendship with Mary was founded on inauthenticity. Somehow it had grown into a strong, genuine, long-lasting friendship.

With Nora, she'd been prepared to take a stand for higher reasons. But she hadn't needed to.

Tess smiled at the three ladies. "No classes today. Let's explore Northampton."

Kate grabbed Tess's elbow. "Absolutely not. Let's study and enjoy the privilege."

Tess's shoulders sagged. "One little holiday? Please?"

"After we graduate." Nora grabbed the other elbow and tugged Tess toward Capen Hall.

"Forward, march!" Ada Sue led the way.

"You're mean," Tess said. "It isn't good to work all the time."

"We let you haul us around town on Sunday afternoons." Kate pointed forward, her arm ramrod straight. "Forward, march."

"I need new friends."

Ada Sue flashed a smile over her shoulder. "You love us, and you know it."

She did, but she wrinkled her nose at the Southerner.

Back in Capen Hall, the women fetched their textbooks and congregated in the lounge around a table. As much as Tess hated to admit it, final examinations were coming, and she did need to study.

Nora opened her naval history textbook

and explained the Battle of Jutland to Tess. Again. Thank goodness Nora explained things well, because Tess hated this subject with a passion.

Greta Selby strolled by with an armload of manuals. She sniffed. "You're naïve, Nora. They're using you."

Tess gritted her teeth.

But Nora looked up with a beatific smile. "On the contrary. I'm using them. Kate makes naval administration sound almost interesting, Ada Sue keeps me on my feet in field hockey, and Tess draws darling cartoons of ships and aircraft to help with recognition."

Tess raised her own smile, just as beatific, she hoped. "You're welcome to join us. You can use us too."

Greta chose her well-worn sneer. "Are you going to teach me how to sell gloves?"

"Yes. And hats too. Hats are tricky."

With a roll of her tiny eyes, Greta marched to a table in the corner. Alone.

Kate and Ada Sue exchanged a smirk, but Nora gazed at Greta with one corner of her mouth puckered. Tenderhearted Nora felt sorry for mean old Greta.

In a way, so did Tess. Greta was doing well in class and would graduate, but she'd made no friends. And no one deserved to be alone.

She recognized that stirring inside, the unmistakable divine prodding, telling her to put aside her pride and hurt feelings and be kind.

Tess approached Greta's table. This woman had been rejected all her life, and she pushed others away so she wouldn't be hurt. She resented a world that favored beauty over substance, and how could Tess fault her for that?

Greta didn't look up from her naval manual. "Did you want something from me?"

All that acid wouldn't respond to sugar, only to honesty. "I meant it, Greta. We would like for you to join us. We're all good at different things, and we help each other."

She flipped a page and snorted. "You can fool Nora, but you can't fool me."

Tess swallowed her snippy words. Compassion was needed. And sheer honesty. "I understand. You're tired of a world that won't look beneath the surface. You're tired of people judging you on your looks, and you wish they'd judge you on your mind and your work."

Greta glanced up with a flash of connection, quickly muted by suspicion.

Tess crossed her arms and formed a tight-lipped smile. "Guess what? So do I." Her voice wavered, which surprised her.

The sneer returned, sharper and more hateful than ever, but then something sparked in her eyes, and her mouth drifted open.

Yes, they had more in common than either would care to admit. Tess tilted her head to her friends. "My invitation stands. You're more than welcome to join us."

Tess returned to her table. "Do your magic, Nora. Make me feel the thrill of battle."

She ignored the girls' nudges and questioning looks. No gossip. No talking behind Greta's back. The woman had enough of that in her life. "Come on. Finals are around the bend."

Nora turned the textbook to Tess and pointed to a map with lots of loopy lines.

No movement came from Greta's table. No sound.

She wouldn't join them.

But Tess knew she'd done the right thing.

12

Off Fedala, French Morocco
Wednesday, November 11, 1942

The motor whaleboat popped along the waves in the inky darkness. Dan relished the motion and the cold spray of seawater.

The landings on November 8 had gone well, with only light casualties, and the French had surrendered at Fedala that same day. And this morning, Casablanca had surrendered along with all French Morocco and Algeria.

But the Navy's war was far from over. "Is it true, sir? Fourteen U-boats in the area?"

The boat took a hard bump, and Admiral Howard clamped one hand on his cover. "Yes. Admiral Hewitt issued a warning at sunset."

"How much can you tell me about the conference?"

"That's my boy." Howard's smile shone in his voice.

Dan waited for the admiral to condense his thoughts. They were returning to the *Wilkes* from the heavy cruiser USS *Augusta,* where Adm. Kent Hewitt had met with the top commanders. Meanwhile, Dan collected antisubmarine warfare reports that had come to the *Augusta* from the various warships. In the convoy back to Hampton Roads, he'd compile the reports and write a summary.

"Well?" Dan asked.

"Admiral Hewitt voiced concerns," Howard said in measured tones. "All the troops are ashore now, but we still have a substantial quantity of stores to unload."

Vague dark silhouettes hinted at the fifteen transports and cargo ships, the ten destroyers and two cruisers in the harbor of Fedala. "The transports are sitting ducks at anchor."

"Indeed. Hewitt toured Casablanca today. Once again, the French are the very picture of friendly cooperation."

"I'm glad to hear."

"They offered their port facilities to us, but the harbor is littered with wrecks."

"Mm-hmm." Courtesy of fine shooting by the US Navy.

"Casablanca would be safer for the transports, but with so few berths open, unloading would take longer than at Fedala. Also,

120

the first supply convoy is due to arrive on the thirteenth. If the transports went to Casablanca, the convoy would have to wait offshore."

"Where the U-boats could hunt them."

"Precisely. Not everyone is happy with Hewitt's decision, but I concur. Stay in Fedala and unload these ships as quickly as we can."

A loud cry behind them.

Dan whipped around.

The coxswain pointed astern. "I saw something, sir. An explosion."

"One-third speed," the admiral ordered.

As the whaleboat slowed, Dan strained to see through the darkness and to hear over the motor. A pulse of orange light throbbed closer to shore. "Sir? It looks like a fire in the transport area."

"Your eyes are better than mine."

"I see it too, sir," the coxswain said. "What should we do?"

"To the *Wilkes*. Flank speed."

"Aye aye, sir." The engine revved, and the boat sped forward.

What had happened? Was there an accidental fire on one of the ships? Or had a U-boat infiltrated the fleet?

The whaleboat felt small and alone and vulnerable, but that was an illusion. If a submarine were attacking, nowhere was safer. Why would a hungry U-boat pick at such small potatoes when fat juicy transports and rich meaty warships sat on the platter?

Light signals flashed between the whaleboat and the *Wilkes,* and the boat drew alongside and cut her engine. A sailor on the *Wilkes* tossed a line, and a sailor on the whaleboat heaved to. Dan and the admiral stood back as the rope ladder unfurled down into the boat.

Dan followed Admiral Howard up the ladder, not easy in the dress blues they'd worn for the conference, even with overcoats unbuttoned. The admiral puffed and grunted.

A low muffled boom.

Dan sucked in his breath and held tight. A fireball rose from the same area, ugly yellow and white. Was it the same ship or another? Had the fire caused the explosion? Or had a U-boat found another victim?

On the *Wilkes* the alarm sounded general quarters.

"Better hurry, sir," he called up to the admiral.

"Yes . . . indeed. I don't . . . like the sound . . . of that."

Two sailors leaned over and assisted the

admiral onto the deck, then Dan followed.

"What's going on?" Dan asked.

"Don't know, sir." A sailor hauled in the ladder.

The admiral led the way to the bridge. All around, officers and men scurried to battle stations, neatly and in order, orchestrated by training and discipline.

Up in the pilothouse, orders flew.

"What's the word, Captain?" Admiral Howard asked Lt. Cdr. John McLean.

The captain lowered the Talk Between Ships telephone. "Received a call on the TBS. The *Winooski* was hit by a torpedo."

A U-boat. Dan's cheeks filled with air. That explained the fireball. The *Winooski* was the fleet oiler that had refueled the *Wilkes* the day earlier.

"Sir?" The junior officer of the watch looked up from the log. "The *Hambleton* is supposed to be refueling right now."

One of their fellow destroyers in danger from torpedoes and flames.

McLean hung up the TBS. "The *Joseph Hewes* took a fish too."

Dan winced. A transport, laden with vital supplies for the troops ashore.

"Lousy Krauts," Admiral Howard muttered. "Anything on radar? Sonar?"

"No, sir."

A nod from the admiral, and Dan headed to the radar room. "Two ships have been torpedoed, men. Any contacts?"

"The SG radar's down, sir." The radarman pointed to the dark scope. "Blew out a vacuum tube. We're trying to replace it."

A finicky system, but all they had. "Carry on. On the double."

"Aye aye, sir."

Back in the pilothouse, Dan reported the status of the surface radar to the admiral. "Any sound contacts, sir?"

"Nothing. All of these ships, and no one has a contact."

"Are we moving in?"

The admiral shook his head. "We need to keep station in case it's a wolf pack."

Made sense. The cruisers *Augusta* and *Cleveland* and the destroyers *Bristol* and *Murphy* were closer to the *Joseph Hewes* and *Winooski* anyway.

Dan and the admiral stepped onto the wing of the bridge, and Dan grabbed some binoculars. Looked like three distinct fires. Had the *Hambleton* been hit too?

Admiral Howard buttoned his overcoat. "As you can see, we still have work to do in antisubmarine warfare."

A sick feeling slumped in Dan's stomach. Despite a protective minefield and twelve warships with modern equipment, at least two ships had been torpedoed. How many men would die tonight? How much valuable tonnage would settle to the bottom of the Atlantic?

It made him feel helpless, and he hated feeling helpless.

"The *Bristol* has a sound contact," a talker called inside the pilothouse. "She's making a depth-charge attack."

Dan set his jaw. Either another U-boat was trying to penetrate the destroyer screen, or the first U-boat was trying to escape.

This work needed to continue, and for now, Dan was proud to be a part of it. His assignment in ASWU was almost over, and it had been a great opportunity. Participating in Operation Torch had introduced him to some of the top men in the Atlantic Fleet. The ASWU had originally seemed like a diversion from his goal, but it had turned into a blessing. He breathed a prayer of thanks, a moment of refreshment.

Maybe his new commitment to rest would be a similar blessing. What seemed like a distraction from his goals might turn out to be beneficial.

An image flashed through his mind of a golden, sparkling blonde. Would it be the same with a woman?

No. Definitely not.

The exact opposite. Joanie had seemed like a great blessing, but she was a grave distraction. She pulled him away from his work. She disrupted his thoughts when he was on duty. She begged him not to go to sea and leave her. Feminine charms turned to demands.

He refused to make that mistake again.

"Sir, the *Hambleton* reports taking a torpedo, but damage is manageable. And the *Winooski* is staying afloat. But the *Joseph Hewes* . . . has sunk."

Dan closed his eyes against the news.

He had plenty of work to do. He refused to allow anything — or anyone — to interfere.

13

Smith College
Tuesday, November 24, 1942

Ensign Tess Beaumont. She traced the light "reserve blue" stripe above the cuff of her navy-blue jacket. "We're officers. I can't believe it."

Excited feminine voices filled the auditorium of John M. Greene Hall after the graduation ceremony.

"We did it together." Ada Sue squeezed Nora's arm.

Nora's cheeks colored. "Thanks for getting me through field hockey. May we never have to play the foul game again."

"Nothing against you, Nora . . ." Tess raised one hand. "But I solemnly vow to forget everything I learned about naval history."

The ladies laughed together, delightful music never to be played again. Today they'd ship to their new stations.

Ada Sue waved her sealed orders. "If no one's volunteering to go first, I will."

Tess clutched her own envelope. Where would the Navy send her? Sunny California? Bustling Manhattan? Historic Charleston?

Ada Sue squealed. "Florida! I'm assigned to the Naval Air Station in Jacksonville, supervising enlisted WAVES. Good-bye to this wretched cold."

Tess laughed. "It's still autumn. It hasn't even snowed yet."

"There's ice on the sidewalk. That's wretched enough." Kate ripped open her envelope. "Please, somewhere warm. Mare Island Navy Yard in California, working in supply. Hooray! I might meet movie stars."

"Mare Island is closer to San Francisco than Hollywood." Nora eased her finger under the lip of her envelope and pulled out her orders. "Boston Navy Yard. Communications."

"Oh!" Tess gripped Nora's arm. "You can meet my friends."

Ada Sue prodded her. "Come on, Tess. What are you waiting for?"

She stared at her envelope. "I don't know. I want to go somewhere new and adventurous, but I can't bear the thought of leaving you."

Kate lifted her chin with a regal air. "You

are an officer in the United States Navy, Miss Beaumont. Nothing cute about it . . . or sentimental. Open your orders and obey them."

"They should have made you a drill master." Tess opened her envelope and read her orders. Twice. Her face tingled, and her mouth drifted open. "Boston Navy Yard."

"With me?" Nora's smile lit up her face. "That's wonderful. What department?"

The stripe on her sleeve suddenly looked narrower, dwindling away to nothing. "Co-ordinating war bond sales." Because she was pretty and chipper and would sell a lot. So much for becoming a woman of depth and substance.

Nora peered over her shoulder. "There's something more. Supervising WAVE yeomen at the Anti-Submarine Warfare Unit? I've never heard of that."

"I have." Tess groaned. "That's the worst part."

"Well, what is it?" Kate stepped to the side to let another group of WAVES pass.

"We should go back to quarters and grab our gear so we can catch our trains." Tess motioned up the aisle. "I'll explain on the way."

Her friends followed. Greta Selby sat a few rows back, and Tess smiled at her.

"Congratulations, Greta."

"You too." The nicest thing Greta had ever said to her, but at least she'd stopped the mean digs.

A partial success. But her new dilemma . . . she saw no way out.

Tess walked outside into a crisp autumn day. Yesterday's rain had frozen into slick puddles overnight, and the trees were bare.

"Well?" Kate nudged her. "What's this Anti-Submarine Unit?"

"Anti-Submarine Warfare Unit."

"And . . . ?"

"And my friend Lillian's brother is an officer there. That's how I know about it."

"And . . . ?"

Tess glared at Kate. Maybe she wouldn't miss these friends after all. "And I find this brother extraordinarily attractive."

Kate and Ada Sue squealed.

"What's he like?" Ada Sue said.

Tess scrunched up one corner of her mouth. "There's something about him. The strong, silent, no-nonsense type."

"Intriguing." Kate sidestepped an icy patch. "So what's the problem?"

"He doesn't even like me. He thinks I'm silly."

Ada Sue gasped. "He said that?"

"No, but I can tell. He looks right through me."

"Tess?" Nora's brow wrinkled. "He's a naval officer, right? Don't forget —"

"Oh, that stupid rule!" Ada Sue stuffed her hands in the pockets of her overcoat. "WAVES can marry men in the Army, Marines, or Coast Guard — but not the Navy. Who thought of that?"

"Someone who wants us to be seen as professionals," Nora said. "You know what they're saying in some of the papers, that we're a bunch of floozies out to snare men."

"I don't want to date him anyway," Tess said. "I want to forget him, but now I have to work with him. How can I work with a man I'm attracted to?"

Kate shrugged. "Same as you would in any job. Do your duties and maintain a civil distance."

Above her, bare tree limbs formed a tangled web. If only Dan would stay at sea for a very long time. But didn't he always say he was only in Boston until February? November was almost over. Less than three months. She could do this.

Besides, working together might show her an unpleasant side to Daniel Avery, an unsavory habit or annoying quirk. Why, yes. She'd keep an eye out for that.

"Look on the bright side," Kate said. "Now you might be able to catch the French spy."

Yes, she might. A smile inched up. "The game is afoot."

Off Hampton Roads, Virginia
Dan stood at the stern of the light cruiser USS *Philadelphia.*

He was going the wrong way. The day after a U-boat sank the *Joseph Hewes* and damaged the *Hambleton* and *Winooski,* a U-boat sank three more transports off Fedala.

Boom, boom, boom.

Despite the destroyers and minefield and radar and sonar, three more ships were lost.

The following day Dan sailed away. He rapped his fist against his thigh. He had no choice. The reports needed to be delivered and analyzed so the experts could build better weapons and craft better detection systems and formulate better tactics. His work was vital.

Convoy GUF-1 surged over the waves under an overcast sky. An uneventful cruise for the warships and transports returning from Operation Torch. Later today, the convoy would pull in to Hampton Roads, but the *Philadelphia* would proceed north to the Brooklyn Navy Yard.

Tomorrow afternoon in New York, he and Admiral Howard would attend meetings. On Thursday, Dan would eat his Thanksgiving dinner on a train bound for Boston. Then Friday, back to work at ASWU.

He checked his watch. Half an hour until he'd get a turn with a typewriter.

On Sunday, he'd forced himself to take a Sabbath day's rest. Hardest thing he'd done in years. He'd walked the decks, borrowed month-old magazines, and chatted with the crew.

Now he was paying the price. He wanted his reports compiled before the *Philadelphia* came to port, but there were too few typewriters and Dan's reports were lower priority than the ship's orders of the day.

His foot tapped on the deck. Would it be easier to rest in Boston? Jim and Lillian always begged him to join their Sunday afternoon excursions, and now that Tess was away, he could accept more frequently. An excursion appealed to him more than lounging in bachelor officers' quarters. Seemed less idle and indulgent.

"There you are." Admiral Howard's voice rumbled behind him. "Another lazy day for Lieutenant Avery?"

Dan chuckled and faced his mentor.

"Waiting for a typewriter."

"Reports coming along?" His clear blue eyes narrowed.

"Yes, sir. They'll be complete by tomorrow morning." Even if he had to stay up all night.

"Any interesting conclusions?"

"Yes, sir. Two major conclusions. First, what we're doing now still isn't enough."

"Agreed."

"Second, the auxiliary carriers proved themselves. Even with inadequate training, they provided good air cover for the landing forces, and they even sank a sub."

"Also agreed." Howard crossed his arms, resting them on his belly. "Anything else?"

High on the mast, the *Philadelphia*'s antennae etched black hash marks on the clouds. "I've been thinking. We have problems with communication. Radar is up on the bridge, radio's on another deck, and sonar's deep in the hull. We use data from all of them to track enemy vessels and aircraft. It'd be more efficient if they were together. With a plotting table, perhaps."

"That's why you're my protégé."

"Hmm?"

A grin flashed. "Since the battles of Coral Sea and Mid-way, the top commanders in the Pacific have been thinking along those lines. The Combat Information Center, they're dubbing it."

"Yes." The idea picked up momentum. "Put all the equipment together, all the specialists, get them talking to each other —"

"That's why you're going places, young man. You note problems, analyze them, and envision solutions."

"Going places, eh?" Hope and purpose swelled inside. "After a brief sojourn in Boston."

14

Boston

That evening after Tess and Nora dropped off their belongings at their quarters, Tess took her new friend to her old apartment in Charlestown.

"I can't wait to surprise my friends," Tess whispered as she climbed the familiar granite steps. "I know you'll love them."

"I'm sure I will." But Nora's forehead furrowed.

"They'll adore you. How could they not?" Tess winked at her, then rang the doorbell. How strange to ring the bell for the apartment that had been her home for a year.

Mary opened the door and squealed. "Quin—"

"Tess."

"Ah!" Mary dissolved in laughter and pulled Tess into a tight hug. "I'm happy to see you."

Tess squeezed her back, reveling in the

sound of her best friend's voice.

Lillian dashed out of the kitchen. "Tess! What are you doing here?"

"Is that any way to talk to an officer in the US Navy?" She twirled in her navy-blue overcoat and officer's cover.

"You look wonderful." Mary's smile shifted to Nora.

Tess grabbed her arm and dragged her over the threshold. "This is my dear friend, Nora — Ensign Nora Thurmond. She's assigned to the Boston Navy Yard."

Mary shook her hand. "I'm Mary Stirling. Tess has told us wonderful things about you."

"I'm Lillian Avery." Lillian shook her hand too.

Tess shut the door. "Nora, Lillian's the one I was telling you about — the pharmacist. Nora's an engineer."

Lillian grinned. "A fellow stranger in a man's world."

"Mm-hmm. The WAVES has been a bit of a shock. So many women."

"You poor thing."

The ladies laughed as they settled into chairs and the couch. Tess raised her shoulders in glee. She knew Nora would fit in.

"Do I hear my Quintessa's voice?" Yvette stepped out of their old room.

"Nope," Tess called out. "You heard Tess's voice."

"What are you doing here?" Yvette strolled over with a brilliant smile. "I thought you'd left us forever."

Tess stood and hugged her. "I'm assigned to the Boston Navy Yard."

All three of her former roommates squealed as one.

"You are?"

"Oh, that's wonderful!"

"We'll have to go out this weekend to celebrate," Mary said. "You'll join us, Nora, won't you?"

"She will," Tess said. "She has no choice."

"I have no choice." Nora let out a long-suffering sigh.

"How fun." Lillian clasped her hands together in front of her chest. "Arch wanted to go out this weekend since Jim's back in town."

"Arch is Lillian's boyfriend," Mary told Nora. "And Jim is my boyfriend and Lillian's brother."

"Oh." Nora shot Tess a questioning look.

"Too bad Dan is still at sea — my oldest brother," Lillian said. "But we'd have to twist his arm into a double knot to make him go anyway."

Another questioning look, and Tess gave

138

the shortest nod in reply. Yes, *that* brother.

Yvette squeezed onto the couch and tilted her head at Tess. "Since you're back in Boston, perhaps you can come to our meetings. Things have been tense. Everyone suspects everyone else. You have good insight, and you might see things I miss."

"I'd love to go." So many questions bubbled inside.

"And you're just in time for Thanksgiving," Lillian said. "We're making apple-cranberry pie tonight, and you two can help. We saved up sugar from our rations this month."

Nora looked both bewildered and pleased. "That sounds fun."

"It does." Even though Tess had to work with Dan, returning to Boston brought benefits — old friends, new friends, and a mystery to solve.

Wednesday, November 25, 1943
The following evening, Tess opened the door to Robillard's Bakery and drank in the delightful scent of almond.

"Oh! *Ma petite* Quintessa." Behind the counter, Celeste Robillard threw up her hands. "You are here!"

Tess knew better than to correct her elders. "The Navy assigned me to Boston.

I'm so glad to be back."

"It is good. It is very good." She hustled out to Tess and kissed her cheeks. Her deep-set brown eyes glistened. "It hurts to lose one of my American children. My boys in Paris. Oh, it is bad."

Tess gripped the baker's plump hand. Three days after the Allies invaded North Africa, the Germans had taken over Vichy France. Now the Nazis occupied all of France except the city of Toulon, home of the French fleet in the Mediterranean. The French Navy hadn't decided whether to surrender, scuttle the ships, or flee — and risk deadly losses to German attack.

"Any word?" Tess asked softly.

"Non." Madame Robillard dabbed her eyes with a corner of her apron. "They cannot pass letters through Vichy France to Portugal and to me. I do not know if my boys . . ."

Tess put her arm around her shoulder. "I'm sure they are well."

"Hi, Quintessa." Solange Marchand sashayed out of the kitchen with a tray of pastries, dark blonde curls piled high on her head. "It's good to see you."

"Hi, Solange. I just go by Tess now." She smiled at the girl. "When did you start working here?"

"Last month. I was sick of working at the

Navy Yard. I'd rather bake. It's more feminine, don't you think?" She winked at a man seated at a table.

Madame Robillard grabbed Tess's shoulder and pulled her down to whisper in her ear. "Her heart is broken about Henri. She couldn't work with him anymore. She is no good in the kitchen, but . . ." She shrugged.

"How kind of you." Tess gave her a warm look.

"Madame made the almond pastries." Solange transferred the tray to the display case. "Have you tried them, Tess? They're my favorite."

"Henri's favorite," Madame Robillard whispered and rolled her eyes.

Tess approached the counter. "I'm here to buy bread for Thanksgiving." And to seek clues.

"Oh, *non.* You must try." Madame Robillard bustled back behind the counter and sliced up a pastry. "They are *magnifique.*"

Tess took the sample, and her eyes slid shut. "*Magnifique,* indeed."

Solange trotted out to the seating area. "You must try too."

A slender blond man set down his newspaper, stood, and pulled Solange close. "You are the only sweet I crave."

She giggled and fed him the pastry. "For

now, this will have to do."

Tess gaped. That was Jean-Auguste Fournier from the French group. Only months earlier, Solange wouldn't give him the time of day. Had she recovered from her heartbreak? Or was she trying to make Henri jealous?

Solange hugged Jean-Auguste's arm and dragged him to Tess. "Have you met Jean-Auguste?"

"Yes, I have." She shook his hand. "It's good to see you again."

"Welcome back to Boston, mademoiselle."

"We've been dating for a month now." Solange pressed even closer. "He's treating me to a ritzy night on the town on Saturday. We're going to the Cocoanut Grove. Have you been?"

"Not yet." But an idea skipped around in her mind. "It was lovely seeing you again. I'd better buy my bread now."

After Tess picked a nice crusty loaf and said good-bye, she headed into the chilly evening and walked down to the corner to catch her bus.

"I tell you, he is the spy!"

Tess hauled in a breath and peeked around the corner. Under a streetlamp, two men stood close on the sidewalk.

One looked like Professor Arnaud. "Monsieur Guillory, please calm down. We are all Frenchmen. To accuse one another of spying for the *Boche* is unconscionable."

What fun! She could play sleuth. Tess angled her back to the men and stepped closer to the curb, waving her arm as if hailing a cab. They wouldn't recognize her in the dark.

"Uncon—" Pierre Guillory barked out a laugh. "I may work the docks, but I know, I see. You — you are blinded by your big words and fancy titles. We have a spy, and we must act."

"Now, now. It is all coincidence. The caretaker made a sloppy mistake and was caught. The second man — someone in town must have started a rumor out of vengeance. Why would the Nazis care what we say in Boston? Why would they send a spy? It is ridiculous."

"Ridiculous?" The dockworker's voice hardened.

Tess fought the impulse to turn and watch. Headlights approached. *Please, not my bus. Not yet.*

"*Bonsoir,* gentlemen. Are you talking about our spy?" That was Jean-Auguste's voice.

When had he left the bakery? The headlights passed, and Tess eased farther away.

143

"*Bonsoir,* Monsieur Fournier," the professor said. "As I was telling Monsieur Guillory, we do not have a spy."

"I hope not. But there is another possibility. Perhaps our secret was passed overseas by accident."

"Accident?" the professor asked.

"*Oui.* Perhaps someone got drunk at a bar and let information slip. Or perhaps someone was bragging on the job, and a real spy overheard. Someplace like . . . oh, the docks, for example."

A shuffling sound, and Tess glanced over her shoulder.

Arnaud's arm swung up like a gate before Guillory.

The dockworker stared down Jean-Auguste. "Or perhaps . . ." His voice ground out. "Perhaps someone was traveling around, selling bakery supplies —"

Jean-Auguste laughed and pressed a hand to his chest. "Why, that's my job. What a coincidence."

Tess turned away as if that would make her invisible. More headlights approached, brighter and higher from the ground. Now she wanted it to be her bus.

"Perhaps . . ." Arnaud's voice slammed down. "Perhaps we should be as wary of division as we are of potential spies. 'If a house be divided against itself, that house cannot stand.' "

The bus braked before Tess, and she scrambled on board.

Although her heartbeat battered her rib cage, she couldn't help but smile as she took her seat. At last, she had a real mystery.

As an officer in the United States Navy, Tess had taken an oath to protect her country against all enemies. She never dreamed she'd encounter an enemy right here in Boston.

15

Boston Navy Yard
Friday, November 27, 1942

It couldn't be. Dan stopped inside the doorway to his office, and his stomach filled with lead. Of all the people to have to work with.

Stanley Randolph leaned on Dan's desk, arms crossed. On his dress blues, he wore the two broad gold stripes and one narrow stripe of a lieutenant commander, the same rank he'd held when Dan served under him in 1935. He hadn't been promoted. Because of Dan.

He pulled himself together and saluted. "Good morning, Mr. Randolph, Mr. Bentley."

Bill Bentley rose from his desk opposite Dan's and saluted. "Good morning, Mr. Avery."

Dan waited for Mr. Randolph to return his greeting.

Randolph's narrow chin rose. "You're late, Mr. Avery."

Until Randolph returned his salute, Dan was required to hold his. "I had paperwork to deliver to the Rad Lab at MIT."

"Next time report here first." A thin smile barely budged his cheeks. "I'm your new commanding officer."

Nausea twisted his gut. "Commander Lewis — was he —"

"He's in command of the Boston office, but I run daily operations. You report to me."

Tension pulled at his fingers, but he kept his salute as sharp as Randolph's gray-eyed gaze. "Welcome to Boston, sir."

At last Randolph saluted. "I can't tell you how much I'll enjoy serving with you again."

So he could get his revenge. Wonderful. "Thank you, sir."

"You have a lot of work, Mr. Avery. Carry on." Mr. Randolph sauntered out.

Just when he'd reconciled himself to this job. Dan set his portfolio on his desk, pulled off his overcoat, and tossed it on the coatrack.

"What on earth?" Bentley asked in a fierce whisper. "Why does he hate you?"

Dan held up one hand to silence questions, and he plopped into his desk chair.

"If he's changed, I don't want to influence your view of him. If he hasn't changed, you'll find out soon enough why we clashed."

"Staying above the fray? Sounds wise."

"Always."

"Can't wait to hear about your cruise."

No sign of Randolph, but he had to be careful. "I brought home a lot of reports. We'd better get to work."

Bentley's gaze darted to the clock, which indicated 1200. "Aye aye, sir."

"After lunch."

"Thank you, sir. Say, we've had some changes since you left — other than Mr. Randolph." Bentley's light blue eyes glowed. "We have girls."

"Girls?"

"WAVES, and pretty ones. Three yeomen, plus an officer to supervise them."

Dan groaned. Pretty girls in the office would distract the men and slow down work. What was the Navy thinking?

"Ah, don't worry, Mr. Avery. They're pros. They type like the wind. And Commander Lewis reminded us that WAVES aren't allowed to marry Navy men, so he strongly recommends against dating."

"Good man." He pushed himself out of

his chair. "I should meet them before lunch."

"I'll introduce you."

Bentley led him down the hallway and into the workroom. Three young ladies in navy-blue uniforms sat at typewriters with their backs to Dan. On their sleeves they wore red chevrons, the white eagle, and crossed white quills indicating a yeoman rating.

No chatting, no giggling, just speedy typing.

"Attention," Bentley called.

The WAVES sprang to their feet and saluted. "Good morning, sirs."

"Good morning." Dan returned their salute. Was this the first time he'd saluted a woman?

"Mr. Avery, may I introduce Roberta Ingham, Betty Jean Miles, and Edith Sommer. Ladies, may I introduce Lt. Daniel Avery."

"Welcome aboard," Dan said. "I'm sure you three —"

"Four, sir." A feminine voice rose from the corner by the file cabinets, out of his line of sight but reaching into his memory.

It couldn't be.

The ground shifted beneath him like a changing tide. Quintessa. Tess. How was he supposed to address a female officer? "Miss Beaumont?"

"Good morning, sir," she said, her face a blank military mask.

There she stood, saluting him, her blonde curls peeking from under a navy-blue cover. In Boston. In his office. "You — you graduated."

A twitch in the mask. "Yes, sir. I followed your advice and stayed the course."

"Of course you did." But he hadn't returned her salute, as rude an insult as Mr. Randolph had given him. He rectified the situation. "Welcome aboard, Miss Beaumont. We're pleased to have you."

Bentley chuckled. "You know each other?"

Finally he could look at someone else. "Tess — Miss Beaumont and I are both from Vermilion. She roomed with my sister here in Boston."

"Before I joined the WAVES." The gilt buttons of an officer marched up the front of her jacket.

"It's been — two months?"

"Almost. I understand you've been at sea."

"Say," Bentley said. "You two have a lot to catch up on. You should get lunch."

Dan resisted the urge to glare at Bentley and looked at his wristwatch instead — 1203. Asking her would only be polite. She was a family friend, after all. He dipped his chin to her. "Would you do me the honor of accompanying me to the cafeteria?"

The set of her mouth said she didn't want to. Why would a fun-loving girl like Tess want to dine with the most boring man in the world? "Aye aye, sir."

"That — that wasn't an order."

"I know," she said in a breezy tone with a teasing glance. She turned to the yeomen. "I'll see you tomorrow. Carry on."

"Aye aye, ma'am." They sat at their typewriters.

Dan motioned for Tess to lead the way. Tomorrow. She'd be here every day.

Stanley Randolph blocked the doorway. "I'm glad you met the WAVES, Mr. Avery. I put you in charge of them."

In charge? Dan cast a questioning glance to Tess. "I believe that's Miss Beaumont's job."

She nodded. "Yes, sir. It —"

"That's far too important a job to assign to a mere . . ."

If he said *woman,* it would take every ounce of Dan's training and character not to sock the man in the jaw.

"To a mere ensign. I expect a weekly report from you detailing the activities of the WAVES in this unit. In triplicate. And you'll need to type that yourself. We can't risk having the girls falsify information."

Dan's neck muscles felt like iron. To insult the integrity of a rating without cause . . . ? The man hadn't changed one bit. But he still outranked him, and the Navy allowed only one response to a direct order. "Aye aye, sir."

"Carry on." Mr. Randolph returned to his office, his snake pit.

Tess's eyes stretched wide with questions.

He gestured to the door. "Miss Beaumont?"

She blinked and proceeded down the hall.

Dan ducked into his office and grabbed his overcoat, then waited for Tess to put on hers.

Once the door shut behind them, she shuddered. "Ooh. What a horrid man."

"I had the pleasure of serving under his command fresh out of the Naval Academy."

Her heels clicked on the wooden floor. "He doesn't seem to like you."

"No, he does not." Best to direct this conversation away from gossip. He held open the front door. Thank goodness the rain had stopped. "Congratulations on graduating."

"And congratulations to you for going to sea. Are you allowed to say where you went?"

Impressive attention to the need for security. "Yes, now that I've returned. I sailed on a destroyer with the invasion fleet off Casablanca."

"You did?" Her eyes lit up. "Oh my goodness. How exciting for you."

"It was. Our ship did it all — guided landing craft to the beaches, bombarded gun positions, hunted U-boats — even engaged in a surface battle."

She tipped her chin to the soggy sky. "It must have been thrilling. And yet twenty years from now, your battle will be nothing but squiggly lines on a map, boring students of naval history."

"Not your favorite subject?"

"I'm afraid not. If only the instructors could have told stories and made us hear the shells and smell the gunpowder and feel the splash of seawater. That would have been marvelous."

An urge to tell her his new war stories swelled inside, but he squelched it. "What subjects did you enjoy?"

"My favorites were ship and aircraft recognition. I drew cartoons to help my friends. I'll never use it, but it was fun. Oh, and I did well in naval administration. Good common sense, reminded me of my business studies."

A mix of the impractical and the practical.

How interesting. All the more reason not to explore the matter. He led her into the cafeteria, where they picked up trays of meat loaf and mashed potatoes and gray-green peas.

The cafeteria teemed with naval personnel and shipyard workers, quite a few women now, with their hair up in colorful bandannas. The world was changing out of necessity.

Dan found two empty seats at the end of a long crowded table. "Miss Beaumont?"

"Thank you, Mr. Avery."

Military formalities felt strange but right. "So you'll be supervising the WAVES at ASWU."

"Yes. Part of my duties." Her voice sounded stiff.

"Part?" Made sense. Supervising three women wasn't a full-time job. He made dents in his mashed potatoes to allow the gravy to saturate. "What else are you doing?"

"I'm in charge of war bond sales at the Navy Yard. The national First War Loan Drive starts on Monday, so I have my work cut out for me." She stabbed some peas — hard.

"You don't seem happy about that."

Golden-green eyes widened. "I'm an officer in the United States Navy. I have a duty, and I'll perform it to the best of my ability. Besides, bonds are necessary to finance the war."

Dan mixed some peas in the mashed potatoes to mask the flavor. "I also have duties I perform to the best of my ability, duties vital to the war effort. But I don't like my job. I'd rather be at sea, and I don't deny it."

Tess gazed across the busy cafeteria, chewing. She dabbed her mouth with her napkin. "Actually, I think I'll enjoy the work. I'll use my business training to run the sales and track the accounts. And selling bonds will be more fulfilling than selling blouses. I'm just being selfish."

Dan swallowed a bite of peas and potatoes, and followed it with some meat loaf. If Tess liked the work and saw its importance, why was she drawing patterns in her gravy with her fork? "What's the problem?"

Tess mushed up her gravy design. "It's not a problem. I just feel as if the Navy made me their poster girl, patted me on the head, and said, 'Aren't you a pretty little thing?' "

"I thought women liked to be told they're pretty."

Color rose in her cheeks. "They do. Most

do. In fact, many women long to be told they're pretty and never hear it."

Dan sipped his coffee, trying to comprehend the feminine mind. Why would a beautiful woman not want to be told . . . ? "You've heard it all your life. It doesn't mean anything."

She stabbed four peas, one on each tine. "More than that. Most people see me as decorative. That's all. But I don't want to be decorative anymore. I want to do something of worth, to have a purpose, to make a difference."

"And you wanted a worthwhile job in the Navy."

"See? I'm being selfish again."

"But they did give you a worthwhile job. Thirty thousand civilians work at the Navy Yard, and thousands of naval personnel come and go. That's no easy job. It'll require brains, hard work, and business skill. They wouldn't give it to just anyone."

She sat up taller, and something new entered her eyes, the solidness of purpose envisioned. "I suppose you're right."

Of course he was. He took a big bite of meat loaf.

For the rest of the meal, she chatted about ideas for the First War Loan Drive. A rally, competitions between departments, prizes.

What could she offer for prizes? She needed to be careful with her budget since she was just starting. And decorations! What would the commandant allow? Oh, she had so much to do, and she couldn't wait to get started. She had the nicest, smartest girls in her department, and they were going to have so much fun.

Dan didn't have to say much. She was so animated, so enthusiastic. She looked the same, and yet different. Not just the shorter hair and the military uniform, but something more.

She was absolutely dazzling.

Why, why, why, God? For the past decade, he'd successfully avoided feminine distractions off duty. But now he had a feminine distraction smack-dab in the middle of his sanctuary, his duty station.

She continued to chat while they walked back to the office, ideas and joy spilling out. He worked hard to keep his eyes off her, to rein in the smile that threatened to conquer his face.

He opened the door of the ASWU office for her.

"Thank you," she said. "And thanks for everything you said. You helped me."

Dan shrugged. "You just needed to see the truth. You used to get excited about decorating a show window at Filene's. Now you have a gigantic show window."

"I do, don't I?" She giggled. "I'm going to say good-bye to the yeomen, then I'll head to the war bond office."

"I wish you all the best. You'll do well."

Back in his office, Dan hung his overcoat and cover on the coatrack.

"Hi, Mr. Avery." Bill Bentley stepped in right after him, but he leaned out into the hallway, shaking his head and grinning. Then he came inside and hung up his coat. "How come you get to date the WAVES and we don't?"

"Not a date. Remember, lunch was your idea." Dan sat and pulled a stack of reports out of his portfolio. "She's a family friend."

"A family friend, huh?" Bentley leaned against the wall facing the door, too close to Dan's chair. "Wish my family had friends like her."

Dan explained how Tess was Mary Stirling's best friend from way back. When Jim was in high school — when Dan was away at the Academy — Jim's friend Hugh dated Tess. Dan left out the bit about Hugh cheating on Tess, but he was careful to explain he had barely known her until she moved to Boston, thanks to a good five years between them.

He also left out his opinion of high-school Tess as silly and self-centered, because she'd changed and matured.

Bentley's grin didn't diminish. "Here's to friendship becoming something more. You could use someone like that in your life. Soften you up a bit."

Soften him up too much. Dan groaned and sorted the reports. "You know the rules, and so do I. Besides, you know I follow Admiral Howard's advice to avoid women and dating."

"But —"

"It's good advice. I dated a girl just like Miss Beaumont in Annapolis. The beautiful girls, they're used to attention, lots of it, and you can never give them enough. They're never satisfied, always want more of your time and energy. If that isn't bad enough, all you hear is, 'Tell me I'm beautiful. Buy me pretty things.' A girl like that almost cost me my career. Never again."

"Um . . . Mr. Avery . . ." His ensign's face stretched long.

His shoulders tensed. Tess was in the doorway, wasn't she?

Yes, she was, her face white, her eyes chilly. She thumped a pile of papers onto his desk. "The yeomen finished these reports, sir. I'm dropping them off on my way out."

His stomach scrunched into a ball. "Yes . . . thank you . . . thanks."

She strolled to the office door and stopped. "By the way, Mr. Avery, don't ever tell me I'm beautiful. Don't ever buy me pretty things. Tell me I have a purpose. Buy me useful things." She turned on her heel and marched down the hall.

Ah, for heaven's sake. Why'd he always have to be so brusque? Why did he always have to hurt people? Dan lurched out of his chair and followed her. "Tess —"

"Miss Beaumont." She snatched her overcoat from a hook by the door.

"Miss Beaumont. Of course. I apologize. I didn't mean it that way. What you heard."

She worked on her overcoat, her shoulders angled so he couldn't help her. "What did you mean, Mr. Avery?"

Dan rubbed the sore spot on the back of his neck. "I meant — Mr. Bentley was teasing me about our lunch. I wanted to make it clear to him that we aren't dating."

Tess opened the front door and let out a dry laugh. "Dating? Oh, Mr. Avery. You'll never have to worry about that."

Dan grimaced. No, he wouldn't, and that was for the best.

16

Saturday, November 28, 1942
"I can't believe Lt. Daniel Avery lowered himself to a night on the town." Tess sent him a teasing smile across the table at the Cocoanut Grove. The friendlier she was, the more he squirmed. Extremely satisfying.

"Tess, I decided what to call Dan." Lillian leaned forward to see around Bill Bentley. "He's a ship-monk."

Laughter flowed around the table, and Dan was good-natured enough to lift a partial smile. "On the cruise to North Africa, I decided to schedule more rest and recreation. If I require it of my men, I should require it of myself."

Tess laid her napkin on the table next to her empty plate. Dan made rest sound as appealing as swabbing the decks.

She'd hoped to discover an annoying trait, but she'd never dreamed to find so many, so quickly. Yesterday showed her the truth.

He saw her as a vain, demanding, career-destroying vixen.

Well, fine. He was a hard-nosed, rigid, woman-hating killjoy.

And she planned to be excruciatingly pleasant to him.

The busboy cleared the table, pushing his way past a fake palm tree with lightbulbs shielded in coconut shells. The dining room was packed and stuffy. This hadn't been Tess's best idea, but she couldn't resist following Jean-Auguste and Solange and seeking clues.

Tess scanned the room through a haze of cigarette smoke. Where were they?

After the table was cleared, Jim and Arch asked Mary and Lillian to dance. Tess turned to Bill Bentley on her left. The blond ensign was too eager and earnest for her taste, but she could find Jean-Auguste and Solange more easily on the dance floor.

Bill, however, grinned at Nora. "Would you care to dance?"

"Yes. Thank you."

Tess gripped her hands in her lap. How selfish could she be, wishing Nora to be stuck with Dan?

Now she was stuck with him. That was her punishment.

Dan pushed back his chair. "Shall we dance?"

Tess's jaw dangled. When she'd wanted to dance with him, he'd declined. And now that she didn't want to dance with him, he asked. "No, thank you. I'd rather not."

He winced, the same expression he'd worn when she'd told him he'd never have to worry about dating her. Good.

However, she didn't want to look as vindictive as she felt. "Since we'll be working together, it's important to keep our interactions purely professional. Wouldn't you agree?"

His shoulders relaxed, and he scooted his chair back in. "I agree."

Two busboys wrestled another table down onto the edge of the dance floor, crowding out more couples. They'd be better off turning people away at the door than shoehorning them in.

Dan cleared his throat.

Oh no. She wouldn't let him direct this conversation. "Mr. Bentley seems nice. Do you enjoy serving with him?"

"I do." Dan held up his coffee cup for the waiter to fill. "He works hard."

The only trait Mr. Avery valued. "Mr. Randolph on the other hand . . . I don't remember you mentioning problems with

163

your commanding officer."

"First, it isn't proper to gripe about your CO. Second, he's only been my CO for one day. He reported to ASWU while I was at sea."

"But —"

"We have a history." Dan leaned back in his chair and looked out over the dance floor.

He wasn't getting off the hook. Not after making her open her heart, then insulting her. "I don't report to Mr. Randolph, but my WAVES have to work with him. If there's a problem, I should know."

Dan sat forward and cradled the coffee cup in his hands. "Encourage the yeomen to talk freely. Take complaints seriously. Be prepared to intervene."

"Why? What do you know about him?"

"This is only for your ears. I served under him in '35. He was an engineering officer on the USS *Texas,* and I was an assistant engineer. He was . . . harsh with the men. He insulted them, made them work harder and longer than necessary, put them in dangerous situations, neglected their needs. When the junior officers spoke to him, he saddled us with unnecessary paperwork."

"Like weekly reports in triplicate detailing daily activities?"

"Yes." His dark gaze stretched across the table, serious as ever. "So we kept our mouths shut. After a few months, Admiral Howard came on board as the battleship division commander. The admiral and I were well acquainted from Annapolis."

"I've heard you mention him."

"A fine man. I only wanted his advice. I didn't mean to start disciplinary action against Mr. Randolph, but that's what happened. The admiral spoke to the ship's captain, who interviewed the sailors. Mr. Randolph hadn't done anything severe enough to lose his commission, but he was assigned to shore duty. His reputation must have followed him. He hasn't been promoted since."

Tess fiddled with her gilt buttons, resisting the temptation to remove her uniform jacket and cool down. "Mr. Randolph knows you started it?"

"Yes. You can see why he dislikes me."

The WAVES didn't deserve to work with a tyrant. "What should I do if —"

"Talk directly to Commander Lewis, and in private. Don't relate what I just told you, only what the WAVES report to you, what you observe. Mr. Randolph should be judged on the present, not on the past."

"I'll do that." Tess sipped her coffee. Why

165

did he have to be so fair and high-minded, standing up for the defenseless? Just when she was starting to dislike him.

"It's too crowded." Arch Vandenberg returned, his forehead glistening. "Can't dance."

Lillian sat beside him. "It's the strangest thing. I saw Yvette's friend Solange."

"Strange? She's the one who recommended this place." Tess smiled at Jim and Mary as they joined the party.

"That isn't the strange part. I saw Yvette."

"Yvette? I thought she was going to Cape Cod for the weekend." With Henri.

"That's what she said." Mary's brow puckered. "Do you see Solange? Close to the stage by the palm tree."

Finally. There she was, dancing with Jean-Auguste. "Yes."

"Do you see the blonde about five feet behind her in the lavender dress?"

"It's Yvette," Lillian said, eyes huge. "She's wearing a wig, but Mary and I recognized her."

"She won't look us in the eye though," Mary said. "What on earth is she doing?"

Tess stood to get a better look. The blonde had Yvette's build and movements. But her partner was taller and bulkier than Henri. "That man. He isn't Henri."

Who was he? Why would Yvette come in disguise? And why did she lie about going away?

Jean-Auguste and Solange drifted through the crowd, and Yvette and her mystery date shadowed them, keeping Yvette's back to the couple. Was Yvette spying on her friend?

Who was Tess to judge? She'd come to watch Solange too.

Jim groaned. "Please don't tell me you ladies are ferreting out another mystery."

"We don't have to find them, big brother." Lillian grinned. "They find us."

Solange caught Tess's eye and waved.

"Hush, everyone. Solange and Jean-Auguste are coming over." Tess squeezed past the chairs and kissed Solange on both cheeks. Then she introduced everyone.

Solange pulled at the satin bodice of her dress. "It's too hot. Jean-Auguste said we should go to the Melody Lounge in the basement. Why don't you come with us?"

Jean-Auguste's smile thinned. "Please do."

"Is there dancing?" Jim asked.

"No, but it's quieter." Solange clung to Jean-Auguste's arm. "More intimate."

"Oh. We wanted to dance."

"No chance of that." Bill returned to the table with Nora. "Can barely breathe in here."

Someone bumped Tess from behind, and she caught herself on a chair covered with zebra-print upholstery. A rivulet of sweat ran down her breastbone. This was a horrible idea.

At the far end of the table, Dan sneaked a glance at his watch.

"What time is it, Mr. Avery?" she asked.

"Hmm?" He looked up, startled. "The time? It's 2204."

Perfect military precision. "Maybe we should call it a night."

No one disagreed.

While the party pushed in chairs and gathered purses, Solange and Jean-Auguste headed to the foyer. On the opposite side of the dance floor, the blonde in lavender and the big mystery man followed, skirting far from Tess's table.

"Come on. Let's go." Tess led the way, eager to follow the spies as far as possible.

The foyer formed a long broad hallway leading from the revolving door at the main entrance. Ahead of Tess, the two couples strolled under the high-arched ceiling, past walls covered with leather and rattan. The entrance to the Melody Lounge must be at the far end.

At the coat check room near the main door, the men went inside to claim the coats while the ladies waited in the foyer.

Mary pulled on Tess's arm. "Yvette is following Solange. In disguise. Do you know what's going on?"

"No." Tess frowned as the last couple disappeared through the doorway. "Solange was jealous when Yvette and Henri began dating, and now Solange is dating Jean-Auguste."

"Yvette thinks there's a spy in their group." Mary leaned closer. "She must suspect Solange or Jean-Auguste."

"But who's Yvette's date? I've never seen him before." However, another man approaching down the foyer looked very familiar. A middle-aged man, walking quickly with his head down. Alone.

Professor Arnaud ducked past the ladies without noticing Tess, and he handed tickets to the coat check girl. "Two coats, and hurry."

"We're hurrying as fast as we can. It's busy tonight." The girl sifted through coats piled on the floor, of all places.

"Professor Arnaud?" Dan stepped forward from where the men waited, and he held out his hand.

The professor startled.

How did Dan know the professor?

"Lt. Dan Avery from —"

"*Oui, oui.* I remember you." He shook Dan's hand, but he glanced down the foyer, eyebrows tented.

"Here you go, sirs." The coat check girl passed a pile of coats to Tess's friends.

Tess claimed hers, but she didn't plan to put it on until she was outside. It was too warm to breathe.

"And yours, sir."

"Finally." Professor Arnaud grabbed two coats and strode out the revolving door.

Two coats. One man. Where was he going, and what was he hiding?

"Let's go." Tess edged toward the entrance, longing for cool air and answers.

"Just a minute." Lillian pulled on her bottle-green overcoat. "It's below freezing tonight."

Hundreds of people inside, milling around, packed together. So hot. So stuffy. A strange sensation pressed on Tess's lungs. She wanted out, and she wanted out now.

"Are you all right, Miss Beaumont?"

Her vision swam and fixed on Dan's dark eyes filled with concern. She pulled in a breath. "I want to leave now."

"You look pale. Let's get you some fresh air." He took her arm and guided her toward the door. "Come on, everyone. Put on your coats outside. Let's go."

Tess let him lead, her ankles wobbling. She never got claustrophobic. What was wrong with her?

A shout rang from the far end of the foyer. Then a woman's scream.

"Fire!"

"Out. Everyone, out." Dan spoke calmly but firmly, his grip tightening on Tess's arm.

She ached for fresh air. Her vision darkened, and she stumbled.

Dan stopped and caught her about the waist. He motioned the rest of the group toward the door. "Everyone out. Stay calm. One at a time. Don't rush."

"We need to get out." Tess's words sounded disconnected from her body.

"Yes, we do." His voice was deep and soothing, and he pulled her into the confines of the revolving door with him and pushed his way through.

Cold, fresh, sweet air. She drank it in.

"Lillian." Dan pressed Tess's hand into his sister's. "Take her across the street. Sit her down, head between her knees."

"I — I'm fine now." The air's stinging slap had done its work.

"Across the street." Dan ran back to the main entrance, Jim and Arch and Bill on his heels. "One at a time. Don't push."

A lady with bright red hair stood in the

doorway, shivering without a coat. "Louis? Louis!"

"Step aside." Jim urged her away from the doorway.

Louis? That was the professor's first name.

From a cab at the curb, someone waved. The redhead burst into a smile, darted for the cab, and embraced the man inside — the professor.

Tess shuddered. She'd met Mrs. Arnaud, and that wasn't her.

"Sweetie, put on your coat." Mary tugged on the navy-blue overcoat draped over Tess's arm. "Let's cross the street, get out of the way."

She obeyed, her gaze riveted on the entrance. People stumbled out the revolving door, crying, calling for people. Dan and Jim and Arch and Bill directed people away, pulled them out of the doorway, shouted for calm and order.

A bright flash shone through the glass doors, yellow and blue and angry.

Tess gasped.

Flames roared, mixed with screams, horrible screams. Tess joined them. Hundreds of people were inside. "Lord, get them out!"

The men worked faster, grabbed hands, pulled people out, shouted instructions.

"Oh no," Mary said. "The door. Look.

The people — they're pressing up on both sides."

Tess groped for her friends' hands. With people pushing on both sides, the door couldn't revolve. They were trapped. But there were other exits. There had to be other exits. But did they have enough time?

Flames licked out the top of the door, stretching, seeking, hungry, cruel.

"Oh no. Arch," Lillian mumbled. "Please, get away, Arch. It's too late."

Tess strained to see through the crowd on the sidewalk across Piedmont.

A siren sounded. A fire engine.

"Thank you, God!" Tess cried.

Flames poured out the entrance, yellow swords slashing all the way out into the street. Black smoke billowed into the night sky.

In the middle of the street, a woman in lavender huddled with a large man in a gray suit. She glanced Tess's direction, then the two strode down Piedmont.

"Yvette got out," she whispered. "Solange? Oh Lord, please get Solange out. And Jean-Auguste." What a selfish prayer, only for those she knew. "Lord, please. Please protect everyone in there. Get them out."

Several fire engines eased down the crowded street. Firemen fed hoses through the doorway, set up ladders to the roof, and hacked at the walls with axes.

Streams of water hissed on the flames.

Four men in navy-blue overcoats crossed the street toward the ladies. They'd lost their covers. Jim cradled his hand to his chest.

"Jim!" Mary ran to him. "Are you hurt?"

"Just — just a slight burn. I'm fine. Not like . . ."

Tess's stomach twisted. Not like the hundreds of souls trapped in that inferno.

"Arch?" Lillian grabbed his hands and pressed her forehead to his. "Are you all right?"

His hands shook hard. "I'll be fine. I will."

"They're setting up a first aid station over there." Nora pointed to the end of the street. "Tess, we can use our training."

"Yes." She didn't have to stand and watch. She could do something.

Dan stared at his hand. Drops of blood splashed onto the sidewalk.

"Dan! You're hurt." Tess grasped his hand, opened it to see red lines scrawled across his broad palm.

"A woman. She reached out. Down low, under the flames." From behind, the fire lit up the disheveled black waves of his hair. "I thought — I thought I could pull her out. She had — she had red nails."

The streaks blurred in Tess's vision. "You tried. You did your best. At least she knew someone tried to save her, someone was there, someone cared."

He looked up to her, his eyes stark white in a soot-streaked face. "I — I couldn't —"

"No one could have. You did your best. Now, let's get you some first aid." She took his arm. Now it was her turn to guide him.

17

Massachusetts Institute of Technology
Cambridge, Massachusetts
Friday, December 4, 1942

"The Great Dome, MIT's nod to architecture." Dan pointed Tess to the classical structure with its clean white lines. "The school was built for practicality, not beauty."

"Makes sense." Her breath puffed before her.

But Dan frowned at the other, more utilitarian buildings. No school could be more practical than the Naval Academy, yet Annapolis's architecture pleased the eye. And the soul.

"Does it still hurt?" Tess asked. "Your hand?"

His heart wrenched, and his bandaged hand ached. The officer in him wanted to make a stoic statement, but Tess's light green eyes glowed with compassionate strength. She'd reported for duty first thing

Monday morning after the fire, stricken but undaunted.

"Does it?" she asked.

She was a fine sailor, and she deserved honesty. "I don't want it to stop hurting. It should always hurt."

Tess's eyes darkened, and she burrowed deeper into the collar of her overcoat. "Four hundred and ninety people killed. I can't believe it."

Even if he lived through a hundred battles, he'd never forget the screams at the Cocoanut Grove. "I'm thankful we got out in time."

"I never should have suggested the place."

"Don't talk like that. If anything, you saved us. You knew we had to leave. Somehow you knew. If we'd waited for everyone to put on coats . . ."

She glanced away, up at the clear blue sky. "Still —"

"Don't. And be thankful we didn't follow your friends down to the Melody Lounge. That's where the fire started. Did they — your friends . . . ?" This was his first chance to speak to Tess since the fire, other than greetings at the ASWU office.

"Solange and Jean-Auguste. Yes, they were down there when the fire started. They threw themselves to the ground and fol-

177

lowed a waiter out a service exit. They said the fire went straight to the ceiling and raced up the stairs."

That was where a great number of people had perished — at the top of the stairs in front of the emergency exit. Which the nightclub kept locked to prevent theft. His unbandaged hand fisted in his coat pocket. Criminal.

A chilly breeze spun through the space between the buildings, and Tess clamped her hand on her cover. "Yvette and her date must have left just in time, right after Professor Arnaud."

"Speaking of Professor Arnaud, we did come here for a reason."

"Yes, the Rad Lab. My brand-new WAVES reporting for duty."

Dan gestured south toward the Great Dome. "That wing — that's Building 4, where the Radiation Laboratory started in 1940 to study radar. They chose the name to confuse the Axis into thinking they were studying nuclear physics. The next wing over — see that radome on top of Building 6? That's ours."

"Mm-hmm."

Dan turned north. "In '41, we expanded to Building 24, and this May they completed Building 22 for us. That's where we're going today."

"And Professor Arnaud?"

"He's a statistician, helps us analyze our data." Dan led the way into Building 24 and down a hallway.

Tess unbuttoned her overcoat as they walked. "They say a busboy started the fire by accident. He was screwing a lightbulb into one of those fake palm trees, and he lit a match to see what he was doing."

"I saw that in the paper."

Her cheeks, pink from the cold, scrunched up. "I can't help but think — no, I'm being silly."

"What are you thinking? Your French friends?"

"Yes." Something sparked in her eyes. "All of them were down there before the fire. And why was Yvette wearing a disguise? Oh, she denies it. She denies being there, but we recognized her. And Professor Arnaud was sneaking around with a woman who is not his wife."

"Are you sure?"

"I've met his wife." She sighed. "I know. I shouldn't throw around accusations."

He led her down a hallway that crossed to Building 22. "Don't discount your observations. Your suspicions may or may not be warranted, but they shouldn't be ignored."

Her chin edged higher, and her voice edged lower. She rattled off a list of concerns in the group, from leaked secrets to shifting alliances to voiced accusations, all presented with admirable precision of thought and an appropriate amount of shocked fascination.

She tugged at the white silk scarf around her neck. "Nothing concrete, of course. Just a gut feeling that something's wrong and Yvette's in the middle of it."

"So keep your eyes and ears open. But be careful, Tess." He braced himself for a fierce "Miss Beaumont!"

Instead she nodded. "I will."

His shoulders relaxed, and he turned down a hallway inside Building 22. Somehow the ordeal of the fire had eased the tension created by his thoughtless remarks.

"Thank you for coming with me today, Mr. Avery."

Back to military formality. "As I said, I need to discuss the reports from Operation Torch with the scientists."

"Well, I appreciate it. The men will accept me better if you introduce me." Her gaze wavered, and she looked smaller.

And his chest felt bigger. That was one of the great dangers of women. They made a man feel strong and needed, made him want to protect her. He could still feel Tess's warmth as he clutched her to his body and helped her out the revolving door at the Cocoanut Grove.

"Yes. Well, glad to help." His voice sounded gruff, and he shoved open a door.

Inside lay a complex of business offices. Scientists and workers chatted and passed papers. Dan followed the sound of typewriters. "The Rad Lab is a civilian organization under the Office of Scientific Research and Development. Because they work with the Navy, we have yeomen here to type up reports and correspondence. The WAVES are replacing the male yeomen."

"Free a man to fight."

"If only they could free me to fight." Dan introduced Tess around, not relishing the interest he saw in men's faces. Couldn't they see the WAVES were here to work?

In one office, six WAVE yeomen sat at typewriters, as diligent as the WAVES at ASWU. They stood and saluted, and Dan and Tess returned their salutes.

Tess had the WAVES introduce themselves. She had a welcoming way about her, but undergirded with authority. The ladies looked both relieved and impressed with their new commanding officer. What a way she had.

"You're still here, Mr. Avery?" Tess gave him a questioning smile. "I thought —"

"Yes." He snapped to attention. "Wanted to make sure you were situated. I'll return in an hour." He marched out of the business offices, his neck warm.

Two more months. Two more months in Boston, then he'd be gone. Out to sea where he belonged. Away from the lovely Tess Beaumont and the spiteful Stanley Randolph.

He was determined not to complain about Randolph's demeaning orders. All he had to do was keep his head down, work his tail off, keep his temper in check, and trust Commander Lewis to see the truth if Randolph spread poison.

Two long months.

A group of scientists strode down the hall in civilian suits and flapping white lab coats, Professor Louis Arnaud in the center. The professor gave Dan the briefest greeting as they passed, not what one would expect from a fellow survivor of one of the deadliest fires in American history.

But if Tess was right and the professor had been out with a mistress, he wouldn't want to call attention to his presence at the Cocoanut Grove.

Dan climbed the stairs. Tess said the

professor was the leader of the French expatriates, a group allegedly infiltrated by a spy. The professor had access to classified military information. Could he be the spy's target? What if he were the spy himself?

No. All foreign scientists in the Rad Lab had been investigated. They were loyal to the Allied cause and had been trained in security precautions and procedures.

Dan opened the door to a lab filled with oscilloscopes and transceivers and radar dishes. He stepped over wires and squeezed between lab benches crammed with equipment in unholy disarray.

"Mr. Avery." Dr. John Sandler picked his way through the mess a lot faster than Dan did.

"Dr. Sandler." Dan shook his hand. "How's the research going?"

"Excellent." The radar specialist raked his hand through graying blond hair. "But we're concerned about the reports from Torch."

"So are we. When the surface radar worked, it worked well. But we had too many mechanical problems. On many of the ships, the radar broke down when the guns fired."

Brows arched over anxious blue eyes. "It's delicate equipment. You must speak to your men. They need to treat it with care."

This was the continuing problem. Civilian scientists thought in theoretical terms, wanted unlimited time, and required ideal conditions. "I understand. But the purpose of surface radar is to operate on a warship — at sea, in combat. The equipment must be rugged, designed to handle cold and heat, saltwater, and gunfire."

"You don't know what you're asking."

"I do." He worked to keep his voice low and soothing. "I understand this is new technology, experimental. I understand what it must be like watching us destroy your creations."

Dr. Sandler groaned. "You have no idea. We work so hard."

Dan leaned his hip against a lab bench. "I ask you to consider what it's like in battle, when shells are flying, when men are injured and dying. Things happen fast, and you need your equipment to function. Repairs need to be made quickly — not by skilled scientists, but by an eighteen-year-old sailor fresh out of training school."

Dr. Sandler fiddled with an oscilloscope. "It shouldn't be that way."

"But it is. Keep in mind this could win the war."

"I know." But the distance in his voice said he'd forgotten.

"Radar helped win the Battle of Britain, and now radar has the potential to win the Battle of the Atlantic. If we all work together."

"Yes, yes. I'll do my patriotic bit." Humor laced his words. "Let's go over those reports."

For the next hour, he and Dan reviewed the reports, listing specific problems, areas to address in research and testing. It was easier working with military men who thought the same way he did, but if the scientists thought the way Dan did, they wouldn't be as good at research. It took all sorts to win a war.

Even vivacious blondes.

Dan stifled a groan. Another great danger with women was how they invaded his thoughts on duty.

His discussion with Dr. Sandler completed, Dan shook the scientist's hand and headed downstairs to the business offices.

Tess greeted him with her usual sparkle restored. "They're the nicest girls and so smart. They'll do a wonderful job."

"I'm sure they will." Dan retraced their earlier steps through Building 22.

"I'll come here once a week, my CO said. That's not too much extra work, which is good because bond sales keep me hopping.

We had to change all our plans this week. After the fire, no one's in the mood for rallies."

"No, they aren't." The entire city was in a state of stunned grief, slowly changing to outrage over unsafe conditions at the nightclub. So many servicemen had been killed — even a WAVE — that Hitler certainly had to be praising the nightclub owners for furthering his cause.

"So I cancelled the rallies and rewrote my material. Monday was one big blur."

Dan had seen the posters and the article in the *Boston Navy Yard News,* and he'd heard the announcements. She'd struck the right note of sober patriotism and wartime urgency.

"I'll be glad when the drive is over and I can settle into a normal routine, encouraging payroll deductions to buy bonds."

"Over the top by New Year's," Dan quoted the ads and posters.

"Yes." Green eyes gleamed. "You're contributing, aren't you?"

"Yes, ma'am. I know a certain WAVE who'd make me walk the plank if I didn't."

She laughed, a sound he hadn't heard in a week and very welcome. "I would."

Dan turned into Building 24. "When is the drive over?"

"December 23. My CO gave me a week's leave. I'm so excited. I haven't been back to Vermilion for over a year."

A light flipping feeling in his chest. "I'm also going home. Two whole weeks. I'm overdue for leave."

"Do I dare ask how long it's been?"

Dan opened the door to wintery sunshine, and he headed for Kendall Station. He couldn't remember the last time he'd taken even forty-eight hours' liberty. "I haven't been home for — I don't know — three years? Maybe longer."

"Oh my goodness."

Shame plunged into his gut. He couldn't blame the Navy, only himself. "It's time. I need to see my mom and my little brothers and Lucy and her new baby."

Tess shook her head. "No one could ever question your dedication to the Navy."

That dedication meant he neglected those he loved — and reminded him why he couldn't add anyone to the list.

18

"Even a little can help a lot." Tess smiled at the passersby in Boston's North Station and wiggled the poster mounted to cardboard. "Buy your war bonds at our booth on the main concourse."

Men and women of all ages passed, many in uniform, all dressed in their best to travel. But no sign of Yvette.

"Buy your war bonds and help our boys finish the job." Her smile felt forced after three hours. This idea had been brewing since the Cocoanut Grove fire. Did Yvette go away each weekend? With whom and where? Or was she staying in Boston? If so, why lie about it?

Tess's commanding officer heartily approved of setting up a bond booth at the train station on a Friday evening.

From where she stood, Tess could see

anyone coming downtown from Charlestown. She wasn't being sneaky. Selling bonds gave her an excuse to smile at each traveler without looking rude, and Yvette would never question her presence.

If she came.

Tess's heart drifted low. Sure, Yvette could have slipped past, although Tess was also watching the blonde women in case Yvette wore her disguise. She hated to admit it, but it looked like Yvette was lying again.

Then a brunette popped into sight in a red beret and black coat. Yvette! And she was with Henri, arm-in-arm.

"Thank goodness." When the couple drew nearer, she flagged them down. "Hi, Yvette! Hi, Henri! Catching your train?"

"Yes." Yvette smiled and eyed Tess's poster. "We're going to Cape Cod."

"Our favorite hideaway by the sea." Henri gazed at Yvette adoringly.

"On your way, stop by my booth and buy war bonds." Tess gave them an exaggerated wink.

"I gave at the office, remember?" Yvette winked back and sauntered away.

Yes, she had. Yvette and Henri bought more than their share, proving they were loyal to the Allied cause, despite Madame Robillard's suspicions.

And they were telling the truth — at least about going away with each other.

Tess followed them to the main concourse. Yvette and Henri stood in line at a ticket booth, so Tess went to the war bond booth, off to the side so she could watch the lovebirds.

"How is it going?" Tess asked three of the enlisted WAVES from the war bond office.

"No offense, Miss Beaumont." Ruth Feingold arched her dark brows. "But I've had more fun on a Friday night."

Thelma Holt heaved a sigh. "I don't have a date anyway."

"But . . ." Celia Ortega lifted a finger in triumph. "We've sold oodles of bonds."

"Wonderful. Fifteen minutes, and we'll call it a night." Tess ventured a glance. Yvette and Henri were heading to the platforms. "I'll go that way. This time of night there are more arrivals than departures."

She strolled at a distance from the couple, keeping that red beret in sight and selling, selling, selling. "Buy war bonds. Start your weekend right."

Henri held open the door for Yvette. The door outside.

Oh dear. The temperature was below

twenty, and Tess's overcoat was back at the booth.

"For heaven's sake, I'm from Ohio." She gritted her teeth and followed.

Ohio blood or no, the icy air yanked the breath from her lungs. "Buy your bonds. Keep 'em flying."

Puffs of steam blew in the night sky, illuminated by lamps. Far down a crowded platform, Yvette and Henri stood by a sleek locomotive painted in deep green and yellow — the Canadian National Railway?

Tess glanced at the sign. The train was the *New Englander.*

She backed out of sight and found a conductor. "Excuse me, sir. Can you tell me where the *New Englander* goes?"

"Aye, miss." He nodded his white-whiskered chin. "Montréal via Lowell, White River Junction, Montpelier, Burlington, and points in between."

North. Not south to Cape Cod, and Tess shuddered.

"You ought to wear a coat, miss." The conductor gave her a fatherly frown.

"I should. I think I can sell more bonds inside anyway. Thank you for your help." She trudged to the door, her head as low as her heart. Yvette wasn't lying about going away with Henri, but she was lying about her destination. Why?

"Pardon."

Tess glanced up. She'd almost run into a man, a young blond man in a brown over-coat and fedora. "Monsieur Fournier?"

"*Oui.* Mademoiselle Beaumont? You are traveling?"

"Selling bonds." She lifted her poster. "Doing your bit?"

"And then some."

"Going away for the weekend?"

"Alas, for business, not pleasure. I have clients in Burlington. *Bonsoir.*" He tipped his hat and departed.

Tess opened the door to the station and glanced over her shoulder to see Jean-Auguste board the *New Englander* as well. Surely he wasn't joining Yvette and Henri. Wouldn't he be surprised to see them? And wouldn't they be embarrassed to be caught in their lie?

A sigh slipped out as she returned to her booth. Her plan had only been halfway suc-cessful. She still didn't know Yvette's desti-nation, only that it wasn't Cape Cod.

Nevertheless, she hefted up her smile. "Buy war bonds. Even a little can help a lot."

Mama's potato soup warmed Tess's belly, the fire in the parlor warmed her feet, and Papa and Mama's laughter warmed her heart.

Papa's paintings were propped along the walls, waiting to be transferred to studios in Vermilion and New York. A storm on Lake Erie, water and sky in tumult. A sailboat with deflated sails and a lone woman standing pensively at the bow. A lopsided home with two small girls dancing under an elm tree.

Tess traced a brown pigtail on one dancing girl and yellow curls on the other. Not many painters could capture as many moods as Papa did. "I like this one best."

"It's you and Mary."

Tess laughed. "We didn't move here until Mary and I were much older."

"That's who you were in your hearts." Papa settled into his armchair, his short beard gray all the way through now.

Mama set a plate of gingerbread cookies on the coffee table. "We're so glad to have you home. You look so grown up in that uniform."

Faint sounds of singing rose from outside, the tune and lyrics coming into clarity.

"Oh! We have carolers." Mama dashed to the window and lifted the curtains. "It's the Avery family. They do make a complete choir."

Tess's stomach flopped over. She'd enjoyed an entire week in Boston without Dan's silent scrutiny. No matter. She was on leave and it was Christmas, and she wouldn't let the old sourpuss ruin her fun.

Mama flung open the door. The Avery clan, plus Arch Vandenberg, stood on the walkway in a snow flurry, illuminated by the porch light, singing "The First Noel."

Tess hugged herself against the cold and grinned at the familiar faces. Mr. and Mrs. Avery. Dan and Jim. Lillian and Arch. Lillian's twin sister, Lucy, her husband, Martin, and baby Barbara bundled in a carriage. The youngest boys, Ed and Charlie — Ed in a midshipman's uniform from his plebe year at the Naval Academy. They were only missing Rob, between Dan and Jim in age and serving in the Pacific.

They finished the verse, and Lillian reached for Tess's hand. "Come with us. We're picking up Mary next."

What fun! But she shouldn't. "I'm sorry. My train just arrived. It's my first night —"

"Go," Papa said, his face almost stern.

"Yes, go." Mama grabbed Tess's WAVES

overcoat from the rack and tossed it to her.

Tess fumbled for it. "But I —"

Papa set her cover on her head — backward. "Have fun, dolly."

He hadn't called her that in years. She righted her cover and kissed his cheek. "Thank you, Papa. I will."

After she bundled up, she trotted down the stairs to Arch and Lillian. "Let's go get Mary. What are we singing?"

" 'Joy to the World,' " Lillian said. "It's Arch's favorite."

Tess joined in the singing as they crossed the street, a beloved path. The windows of the Stirling home glowed yellow in the night, and curtains shifted.

Mary opened the door, pulling on her overcoat, with her parents behind her.

Tess didn't wait for buttons to be buttoned. She grabbed her best friend's hands, pulled her down to the lawn, and danced in a circle to the carol, tiny snowflakes and laughter spinning around them.

Like Papa's painting.

"You silly girl." Mary tipped her head back in the snow. "You wonderful, silly girl."

"I'm on leave. For the first time since October, I can be silly." When the song ended, Tess halted and buttoned her friend's coat. "But I won't be selfish. You look freezing."

"Not when I'm with you."

Jim bowed to Mary. "May I have the next dance?"

Mary's silvery eyes sparkled in the moonlight. "I thought we were caroling, not dancing."

"Who says you can't do both?" Jim waltzed her down Huron Street.

"Where to next?" Ed called out. "The Andersons'?"

"Yeah." Charlie punched his older brother in the shoulder, then skipped away like a girl. "Peggy hasn't seen him in his new uniform yet."

"Aw, pipe down." Ed chased after his brother.

Tess joined the laughter as the family went next door to the Anderson home. Sensing Dan's presence behind her, she caught up to Arch and Lillian. She didn't want a lecture about conduct unbecoming an officer.

Not only was she on leave, but she was determined to put the gloom of the past month behind her and celebrate the joy of Jesus's birth and the love of family.

Whenever she was in the ASWU office, Dan hovered. Watching. Judging. Disapproving. But she refused to let him faze her. She was doing a fine job, and her commanding officer approved of her work. Part of her wanted to stick out her tongue at the lieutenant. So there.

At the Anderson home, they sang "Silent Night," and on the walk to the Hunters', Tess fell in beside Jim and Mary. But Dan joined them — and Jim and Mary began speaking in intimate, hushed tones.

Grimacing, Tess dropped back to give them privacy, Dan right beside her. "Don't you have work to do, Mr. Avery?"

He smiled. He actually smiled. "Not a lick. By the way, in social situations, officers are allowed to address each other by their given names. Please call me Dan."

Oh bother. "Whatever have you been doing with yourself, Danny?"

"Danny? No one's called me that since I was six." Yet another smile. What was wrong with the man tonight? "For the past week I've read books, watched every movie at the Liberty Theater, seen my old haunts, visited everyone who hasn't forgotten me — and some who have — and I've relaxed."

Tess covered her mouth and made her eyes big. "You know how to relax?"

"With hard work, anything is possible."

"Only Dan Avery could turn rest into hard work."

"True." Snowflakes clung to the dark stubble on his jaw, begging to be brushed away. "I'm conducting an experiment. The Lord commanded us to rest, so I'm obeying his orders. But will two weeks' liberty refresh me and make me more productive? Or will it make me lazy and soft?"

"Are your colleagues at MIT taking measurements?"

He worked one hand under his coat over his heart. "One set of wires here, another there. A transmitter here." He knocked his skull with his fist.

Tess laughed. At least he could make fun of himself.

At the Hunters' two-story clapboard home, Tess stood near Mr. and Mrs. Avery, determined to shake Dan.

But his rough bass sang off-key behind her, mangling the "glorias" in "Angels We Have Heard on High."

In a way, his bad singing was cute. He seemed like the kind of man who did everything well and would refuse to do anything he couldn't master. Yet he sang very badly. But with gusto and a surprising amount of joy.

Her quest to find something annoying

about him was failing. He seemed hard-nosed, but he was fair and kind. He seemed rigid, but she couldn't deny the appeal of his passion and devotion. When she was honest with herself, the only thing she didn't like about him was his low opinion of her.

Standing two blocks from Hugh Mackey's house, she re-called her former boyfriend's starry-eyed adoration. She'd always dated men who fawned over her.

But they weren't men of integrity. Men like Dan Avery.

After the Hunter family waved them good-bye, Tess walked by Mrs. Avery's side. "How have you been? How's the boatyard?"

"We've been drafted." Mr. Avery's dark eyes twinkled. "No sailboats for the duration. We're churning out landing craft."

Mrs. Avery rearranged her red scarf. "We've never been so profitable. We've hired some of the young people in town, even some of the young ladies."

"Good." Dan was there. Again. "I'm proud that Avery Boats is supporting the war effort and the economy as well."

Mr. Avery gazed up through the snowfall. "We all have to make sacrifices, but I do miss my work. It satisfied my soul."

"I understand." Tess couldn't imagine

Papa giving up painting, but his artistic skills weren't needed for the war effort.

"Each sailboat has a unique personality." Mr. Avery cupped his hands as if shaping a wooden hull. "But these landing craft are lifeless, all the same."

"They have a purpose," Dan said. "To safely land men on hostile shores. A sailboat . . ."

"Doesn't have a purpose?" Mr. Avery turned a hard gaze to his oldest son. "Doesn't the joy of sailing serve a purpose? The beauty of a sleek hull dividing the waves? Joy and beauty restore the spirit."

Tess held her breath.

Dan shrugged. "Pleasure is meant to be a counterpoint for work, not the purpose of life."

"Don't forget, son." Mr. Avery's voice stiffened. "Work takes many forms."

"Dan. George," Mrs. Avery said with a warning tone. "We're at the Geigers'."

While they sang "O Little Town of Bethlehem," questions bounced in Tess's head, displacing the lyrics. She'd wanted to chat with Martin and Lucy on the next leg, but curiosity drew her to Dan's side. "What was that?"

He held up one hand and slowed his pace until they lagged behind the group.

"Well? I didn't realize you and your father didn't get along."

His lips mashed together. "Is it obvious?"

"That explains things. At MIT, you mentioned looking forward to seeing your mom and your brothers and sister, but you didn't mention your dad."

"We're different."

He couldn't throw her off the trail so easily, but he did require an indirect approach. "You're more like your mom."

"True. She's a hardworking woman. I respect her."

Didn't he respect his father? Tess studied the couple walking arm-in-arm in the snow. "They balance each other. He's the dreamy visionary, and she takes care of the details."

"Yes. She's good for him."

Tess laughed and whapped Dan lightly in the arm. "Don't you see? He's good for her too. Without his dreams, she wouldn't have supplies to order or ledgers to balance. He provides the beauty. She provides the structure. They're perfect for each other."

Dan used to look right through her, but now his gaze drilled inside. What did he see? Someone who contradicted his values? A flibbertigibbet who danced in the snow? A selfish, vain, career-destroying vixen?

And why did his opinion matter? The only

opinion that mattered was the Lord's.

Dan blinked and turned his attention to the snow-dusted street. "You have a point. I'll have to think about that."

Lt. Daniel Avery considering changing his mind? As long as he did his thinking in private — and for a good long time.

19

Vermilion, Ohio
Friday, December 25, 1942

Nothing had changed. And yet everything had changed.

Dan set his last present beside him on the floor and tightened the belt of his bathrobe.

The Avery offspring sat in their customary spots around the living room while presents were passed around and wrappings were sorted in piles in the middle of the braided rug. But all the children were full grown now, they'd added Martin and Mary and Arch, and baby Barbara sat on her grandmother's lap in a tiny red dress, babbling and chewing on a rattle.

"It's wonderful having Dan home for Christmas again." Mom nestled a kiss in Barbara's fuzzy blonde hair. "If only Rob could be here."

"Probably not for the duration." Jim wore his uniform instead of pajamas, probably because Mary had come over after breakfast. "But soon I may have the opportunity to see Rob."

"What?" Dan's question joined the gasps.

Jim leaned back against the wall beside the tree and tucked Mary's hand under his arm. "I received my orders last week. After my leave, I'll report to San Diego for assignment to a new ship based in the Pacific."

Mary smiled at her boyfriend, brave and serene. Apparently, she already knew.

Dan wrestled back a surge of jealousy and congratulated his brother. The Pacific! That's where the US Navy was making history. The Battle of the Atlantic was a British show, and American contributions were almost a footnote.

More questions flowed, but Jim's answers were short due to security.

Soon he cut them off. "I have one more gift — for Mary." He pulled a small cubical box from his jacket pocket and knelt before her.

Dan held his breath. Was that a ring? But they'd only been — no, they'd been dating over a year. But Jim was too young. No, he was twenty-five. When their father was twenty-five, he was married and had a son.

Jim opened the box. "Mary, will you — will you sail with me? For better or worse?

As long as we both shall live?"

"Oh, darling, yes." Eyes glistening, she held out her hand. "And I'll marry you too."

Jim's grin lit up the room, and he slipped the ring onto Mary's finger. "How does one o'clock sound?"

"Perfect."

More gasps, all around the room.

"One o'clock?" Mom asked. "You don't mean today, do you?"

"We do." Jim sat next to his — his fiancée — beside the Christmas tree.

Mary laughed. "It's all set up. When we came home last week, we got the license and talked to Pastor Reeves and made all the arrangements."

His father leaned forward in his armchair. "But —"

"It'll be a quiet little ceremony," Jim said. "Just our families and closest friends."

"But a reception . . ." Mom clapped a hand to her forehead. "A cake."

"My parents are cooking Christmas dinner," Mary said. "And who needs cake when you have pie?"

Mom waved her hand toward the kitchen, which emitted smells of roasting turkey. "But I have —"

"Bring it all over," Jim said. "We won't go hungry."

"What about your dress?" Lillian asked.

"I bought a lovely new suit at Filene's. I don't need anything special." Mary leaned her head on Jim's shoulder. "I just want to marry Jim before he ships out."

Dan's heart squeezed so hard it hurt. He was almost thirty years old. No one would miss him when he shipped out. No one would be waiting for him when he returned.

But he was alone for a reason, so he could press toward the mark. He'd chosen this course. Now he had to stick to it.

As Pastor Reeves explored the nuances of 1 Corinthians 13, Dan stood at attention and kept his eyes on his little brother and his bride.

The scent of pine boughs filled the church, and candlelight glinted off dark wood. Jim stood straight and still, and Mary looked beautiful in a pale blue suit and a hat with a short veil.

They were good for each other. Mary grounded Jim, and Jim helped Mary to blossom. She didn't hold him back in his career, but Jim's ambitions had never been as lofty as Dan's.

Arch and Lillian were good for each other too. As best man, Arch wore a navy-blue civilian suit, his blond hair neatly styled, his years as a naval officer showing in his upright bearing. Lillian wore a dark green suit and hat, and she kept smiling at Arch. Would they be next at the altar?

Lillian had opened up since she'd met Arch, and Arch seemed less tightly wound. In his career in the family insurance company, a wife would be a benefit rather than a liability.

Dan's gaze slipped to his parents in the front row. Tess's words last night had rocked him. He'd always assumed his mother loved his father in spite of his flaws. But what if she didn't see those traits as flaws? What if she loved those traits? What if only Dan saw them as flaws?

His breath rushed out between tight-pressed lips. Despite everything, his parents had a happy marriage. Sure, they argued sometimes. Sure, they annoyed each other. But they were happy.

Whenever his father drifted away with his dreams, Mom reeled him in to shore. And whenever Mom got mired in details, he pulled her away to watch the sun set.

What about Tess?

Dan faced the bride and groom, but he spied on Tess from the corner of his eye. She wore her Service Dress Uniform, Blue B — same as Jim and Dan did, with the white cover and gloves, appropriate for a formal occasion like a wedding. Little blonde curls fluffed around her face.

What was it about her?

On duty, she was polished and professional. On leave, she danced like a fairy in the snow, the most beautiful thing he'd ever seen.

When she was around, everything felt lighter and airier, and he could see more clearly and breathe more deeply. He craved her light, her air, and he needed to be near her. He couldn't stay away.

But he knew what would happen if he didn't resist. Tess would hold him back as Joanie had.

She was just like Joanie — gorgeous and gregarious.

A grumble rolled too low in his throat to be audible. That's where the similarities ended. Joanie had only thought of herself. Tess thought of others.

Joanie pulled Dan back, demanding more and more. But Tess encouraged him and made no demands.

Of course, that might change if she loved him. But they weren't in love.

That was the way it needed to remain.

Stay the course.

20

Wednesday, January 6, 1943

Tess paused in the doorway to Dan's office. He wrote at his desk with papers spread before him. With his free hand, he kneaded the back of his neck.

Poor thing. Only his third day back, and he was already working too hard.

Tess saluted. "Good morning, Mr. Avery, Mr. Bentley."

In one second, Dan's expression flashed from pleasure to displeasure to professional. "Tess — Miss Beaumont. Good morning."

The men stood and saluted, then Dan glanced at his watch. "Eleven forty-five. You're early. You usually come after lunch."

"I know." An awkward feeling squirmed inside. She didn't want him to think she was chasing him. "I'd like to ask your advice about something. Could we discuss it over lunch?"

His forehead puckered. Could he see the worry on her face? "Very well."

"Thanks." She forced a bright smile. "I'll go check on the yeomen."

"I'll go with you. Mr. Randolph thinks I'm responsible for them." Sarcasm darkened his words.

"Say, Miss Beaumont." Mr. Bentley shuffled papers on his desk. "How's Miss Thurmond? I haven't seen her since the fire. Is she all right?"

"Why, yes. She's doing well."

"Good. If you ever . . . well, pass on my regards."

How sweet. He had a crush on her. "If you'd like to pass on those regards in person, come with Mr. Avery to church. In the afternoon, the whole crowd does something fun."

Mr. Bentley's eyes stretched wide. "Mr. Avery has fun?"

Tess leaned closer and cupped one hand to her mouth. "He only goes so he can look sternly at us."

"Is that so?" Amusement flickered in Dan's eyes.

"He also enjoys grumbling about all the work he isn't doing."

Mr. Bentley grinned. "He does like to grumble."

"He's a grumble-bee."

"All right, all right." Dan motioned to the door. "That's enough fun at my expense. Let's check on the WAVES."

Tess followed him down the hall.

He glanced at her over his shoulder. "Grumble-bee?"

A giggle burst out. "That was clever, wasn't it? And it fits. You're always so serious. I don't think I've ever heard you laugh."

"I reserve my laughter for jokes that are actually funny."

He was teasing her, and she loved it. "I'll work on my material."

"You're beyond hope." But the merriment in his eyes stirred up hope, unrealistic hope.

WAVES weren't supposed to date Navy men. Dan disapproved of her. He thought she'd destroy his career.

If only her heart listened to logic.

In the workroom, Tess chatted with the WAVES about their duties. The yeomen had all worked as secretaries before the war. They were fast and motivated, and they'd learned Navy terminology and procedures.

"Mr. Avery?" she asked. "Are you getting everything you need for your reports? Is there anything else they could do to help you?"

He gave the yeomen a polite nod.

"They've been very helpful. They keep daily tallies, so the reports come together in a snap. Thank you."

"It seems silly though, sir." Betty Jean spoke in a low voice, her brown eyes wide, but then she looked past Dan and sat straighter.

Mr. Randolph strolled into the room. "Another social hour, Mr. Avery?"

Dan stood at attention. "Following your orders, sir. Supervising the WAVES and conferring with Miss Beaumont about their performance, which is exemplary."

His gaze didn't veer from Dan. "I'm glad someone in this office is willing to work."

Tess gripped the back of Betty Jean's chair. How dare he insinuate that Dan, of all people, wasn't willing to work?

"I'd suggest you return to your duties." Mr. Randolph gestured toward Dan's office. "While you enjoyed your holiday, your work piled up."

"Mr. Bentley kept on top of things."

"I just put more assignments on your desk. You'd better see to them, since you're taking another vacation this month."

"It's a special assignment, sir. Not a vacation." Dan clasped his hands behind his back, his fingers bunched up around each other. "Training the crews of the new auxiliary carriers in the latest anti-sub tactics."

Tess clamped her lips shut. It wasn't her place to speak, but ooh — that man!

"With Admiral Howard." Mr. Randolph's eyes narrowed. "You're still his pet, I see."

Dan was in serious danger of snapping his own fingers in half. "He advises me, sir."

"Well, your duties await. Carry on." He glanced at the clock. "I suppose you'll want lunch."

"With your permission, sir."

A touch of sarcasm, and Tess held her breath.

"Very well." Mr. Randolph retreated.

Dan turned to Tess and inclined his head toward the hall.

What a horrible day to ask his advice. She grimaced and shook her head.

He gestured toward the door and departed.

Not a direct order, but not to be denied. Tess said good-bye to the yeomen and followed him, grabbing her coat and scarf by the main office door.

Dan waited in the hall outside.

Tess wound her scarf around her neck. "Are you sure —"

"I won't let him intimidate me. The Navy allows lunch."

She marched down the hall. "The nerve of him. You're the hardest-working person I know. And — oh! Not only did he lie about you, but he criticized you in front of others, in front of ratings."

"It goes against protocol."

"It goes against common decency."

He gave her a warm gaze. "Thanks for the spirited defense, but I'll bear up. Only three weeks left."

"Then off to your little vacation?"

"It'll feel like a vacation without Randolph. That's one reason Admiral Howard gave me this assignment. He's afraid I'll blow a gasket."

She laughed. "I doubt that. You were remarkably composed in there."

"Hard, hard work." Dan held open the door. "What would you like my advice about?"

On to the next item on the agenda. Tess stepped out into the frigid air. "It's about Yvette."

"Is it about the fire? I thought they ruled it an accident. They did press charges against the owner. Blocking the windows, keeping the doors locked — someone needs to go to jail."

"I heard. They ruled out sabotage and arson, and I believe them."

"So what's going on with Yvette?"

Snowdrifts made white hedges around the buildings. "I went to the apartment yesterday evening. Lillian wasn't home yet, and Mary hasn't returned from seeing Jim off in San Diego. Yvette let me in, but she was on her way out. She switched purses, and she was in such a rush that her other purse fell to the floor. After she left, I picked it up. A gun fell out."

"A gun?"

Tess held out one gloved hand. "A tiny thing, no bigger than my hand."

"What did it look like?" He shot her an apologetic glance. "Sorry. That wasn't a good question."

"Yes, it was." Tess opened her purse and handed a piece of paper to Dan. "I drew a picture. Right then, with the gun on the floor. I drew it to scale."

Dan studied the picture. "This is excellent. Very detailed. You even recorded the markings."

"Don't worry. I wore gloves when I looked for them. When I was done, I put it back in Yvette's purse, up on the cabinet. Have you ever seen a gun like that?"

"No." Beneath the bill of his cover, Dan's eyebrows drew together. "I don't like the looks of this. It's designed to be hidden."

"Like a spy would use?" She braced herself for ridicule.

"It's possible. It's also possible Yvette doesn't feel safe with a spy in the group, and she bought this to protect herself."

"What should I do? This is why I — I wanted your advice. You're so levelheaded." She felt like a scatterbrain, but the strength of his gaze built her up inside.

He handed her the picture. "Take this to the FBI."

"The FBI!"

"This isn't a police matter. No crime has been committed. But the FBI wants us to report suspicious behavior."

"Oh dear." The brick walls rose high around her. "I don't think —"

"You have to. First, the FBI will be able to tell if Yvette is a spy or not. Second, if something fishy is going on in that group, they ought to know."

"Oh dear." Tess grasped the knot of her scarf. "Oh goodness."

"I can come with you if you'd like." Such gentleness under that strength.

Part of her wanted to accept, to lean on him, to allow his authoritative presence to carry the day, but she straightened her shoulders. "Thank you, but I'll go by myself. If they brush me off as just a pretty face —"

"They'll have to answer to me." He jabbed his thumb at his chest.

That was better than a hug. "Thank you."

Dan tapped his wristwatch. "We'd better get lunch, or Mr. Randolph will lash me to the main mast and give me forty strokes with the cat-o'-nine-tails."

"He'd enjoy that."

He strode toward the cafeteria. "I have strict orders for lunch conversation. Not one word about fires or spies or Mr. Randolph. I hereby order you to tell me your best jokes. See if you can make me laugh."

"Aye aye, sir. An officer never shirks her duties, no matter how difficult or odious."

Dan chuckled. A little low rumble, but an actual chuckle.

She gasped. "Dan Avery! You did that just to patronize me."

"Guilty as charged. I'll never patronize you again." But the remnants of laughter fanned around the corners of his eyes.

How could she *not* fall in love with this man?

That evening, FBI Agent Paul Sheffield shook Tess's hand. "Miss Beaumont . . . have we met?"

"Yes, sir. I used to live with Mary Stirling from the —"

"Ah yes. She was my little Nancy Drew." He gestured to a large dark-haired man standing to the side of the office. "Do you remember Agent Walter Hayes?"

"Yes, sir." Tess shook Agent Hayes's hand too.

"Please have a seat, Miss Beaumont." Agent Sheffield sat at his desk and picked up a lit cigarette from the ashtray. "My secretary said you had something to report?"

Tess's stomach rolled up like a pill bug. These men hadn't listened to Mary when she suspected sabotage at the shipyard. Why would they listen to silly Quintessa Beaumont? She set the drawing of Yvette's gun on the desk. "I found this in my friend's purse."

Agent Sheffield studied it through his reading glasses. "The picture?"

"The gun. I drew it to scale."

He lifted his sandy head, pale eyes riveted on her. "Tell me more."

Tess told the story of the discovery.

The agent took notes. "Yvette Lafontaine, you said? Rooming with Mary Stirling? She was a person of interest in the sabotage case. Hayes?" He flicked his chin toward the door.

Agent Hayes left the office.

"Actually, it's Mary Avery now, sir." Tess smiled. "She was married on Christmas Day."

"Great." His smile registered little interest. "Anything else with Miss Lafontaine?"

Just the cold hard facts for this man, Mary always said, so Tess cleared her mind of fluff. "After I found the gun, I was curious, so I did a little investigating in Yvette's room."

Agent Sheffield grimaced.

"It's all right," Tess said. "I wore my gloves."

"Don't do that again." He shook his head and made more notes.

"But I found the blonde wig and lavender dress she wore to the Cocoanut Grove on the night of the fire. Yvette wouldn't be caught dead in lavender, and I've never seen that dress before."

"The Cocoanut Grove?" Agent Sheffield took a drag on his cigarette and blew out a stream of smoke. "Does this story have a beginning, and could we start there?"

And she thought Dan was brusque. Tess put on her most professional expression and started at the beginning, with Madame Robillard's suspicions about Yvette's jumpiness. Then she detailed the intrigue in the French group, the arrests of the caretaker and the fascist after they were named in the meetings, Yvette's disguised spying at the nightclub, and how she and Henri took the *New Englander* north when they said they were going to Cape Cod.

Agent Sheffield took plenty of notes. When Agent Hayes returned with a manila folder, Sheffield silenced Tess and reviewed the contents, then he interrogated Tess about every member of the French group.

His urgency filled her with a satisfying sense of validation.

At last he sat back in his chair and smashed his cigarette butt in the ashtray. "Thank you for bringing this to our attention. We'll look into it."

"Is there anything I can do?"

He shot her a glance, and his mouth rounded with the word *no.* Then his lips mushed together. "No more searches. Inadmissible evidence."

She winced. "Sorry, sir."

Then he crossed his arms and scrutinized her. "You're welcome in this group? They speak openly in your presence?"

"Oh yes."

"Would you be willing to bring me a written report after each meeting? Who said what and all that. No opinions or hearsay. Only —"

"The cold hard facts?" She smiled at his surprise and then at her new purpose — Tess Beaumont, official FBI informant. "I'd be honored."

21

Norfolk Navy Yard
Portsmouth, Virginia
Monday, January 25, 1943

She was no beauty, but she was magnificent.

Dan and Admiral Howard strolled along the pier at the Norfolk Navy Yard beside the new auxiliary carrier USS *Bogue*. The shipyard was fitting her out with 5-inch guns and 40-mm Bofors antiaircraft guns.

"When do you think she'll go to sea, sir?" Dan asked.

"Late February, we hope. In time for the spring U-boat offensive."

Dan dug his hands in his overcoat pockets. "If you can't get me to the Pacific, see if you can get me on board one of these babies."

The admiral shook his head. "Ugly baby."

"She certainly is." The Navy had modified a hull for a merchant ship, stacking on a thick hangar deck, topped by a flight deck and an island for the bridge. Semicircular sponson platforms jutted out from the hangar deck to support the guns. Clunky. Unwieldy. Ugly.

But she could carry nine TBF Avenger torpedo bombers and twelve F4F Wildcat fighters anywhere in the ocean, which would allow her to cover merchant convoys.

Nine hundred officers and men were assigned to the *Bogue*. "I wouldn't mind serving on her."

"Patience, son. I'll write your letter of recommendation this week, and I'll mail it February 1. We'll get you a plum assignment."

"One more week."

Admiral Howard shook his head. "If I'd known Randolph had been transferred to ASWU . . ."

"I'm glad you didn't intervene. I survived, and I never complained to Commander Lewis. Had to put in some late nights to finish Mr. Randolph's busywork, but I did it. Lord willing, I'll never see him again."

They headed up the gangway, which jangled underfoot.

Admiral Howard glanced over his shoulder at Dan. "You seem better today."

"Better, sir?"

"Yesterday on the train ride down, you

were distracted. I haven't seen you like that since Annapolis, when you were dating that girl. You're not involved —"

"No, sir. I know better." But he had indeed been distracted by a woman.

His time in Boston was over. His time with Tess. He'd return next week to pack up his things and say good-bye.

"Anything I should know about?" the admiral asked.

"As I said, I've had some late nights. I was just tired."

Admiral Howard paused on the gangway and knifed his hand toward the north. Ironically, toward Annapolis. "The compass needle never deviates."

"Neither do I, sir." That's why he'd prefer to go to the Pacific. Not only did he want to join Rob and Jim in the action, but he'd be a continent and an ocean away from Tess Beaumont.

Being on the Chesapeake served as a good reminder. This week he'd visit Ed at the Naval Academy, and the old sights would reinforce the memory, the message. Joanie always begged him to stop studying and take her out. She begged him not to go to sea. She couldn't bear to be without him. She'd turned him from his goal.

Except Tess encouraged his goals. She was

excited about his opportunity on the *Bogue.* She told him he needed to be at sea. She understood him.

"Mr. Avery?"

Dan snapped to face his mentor — who looked concerned. "Sorry, sir. Another good night of sleep, and I'll be myself."

"Good."

At the top of the gangway, a man in his forties waited for them, wearing the four stripes of a captain.

Salutes were exchanged. Capt. Giles Short commanded the *Bogue.* He had a Midwestern accent, heavy dark brows, thick features, and a contagious grin.

The captain led them onto the hangar deck, filled with a dozen aircraft, their wings folded up over their fuselages for compact storage. Tools clanged as machinists performed maintenance.

Captain Short surveyed the deck. "We'll finish fitting out by the first of the month, then we'll get underway on the bay for more training in flight operations."

"We're looking forward to participating," Admiral Howard said. "Mr. Avery has prepared presentations on the latest in antisubmarine warfare research."

"Excellent." The captain flashed Dan that big grin.

Seemed like a good time to speak. "We learned a lot from the Sangamon-class carriers in Operation Torch, sir. And we're optimistic about what the Bogue-class carriers can accomplish."

"They sank a U-boat, didn't they?"

"A French sub, sir. And they damaged another French sub, which was beached. It'll be in one of my presentations."

"Very well. Let me show you the flight deck." Captain Short led the way. "Still hard to believe we had to fight our oldest allies."

"Yes, sir. I'm glad it only lasted three days." The French were America's friends.

At least most of them were. What was going on with Yvette Lafontaine? Were his sister and new sister-in-law in danger living with her?

Dan climbed the long ladder, Admiral Howard huffing before him.

Thank goodness Tess had gone to the FBI. He was so proud of her. Her face had shone as she'd related her meeting.

Dan hadn't needed to accompany Tess, but he'd savored the look on her face when he offered. She respected him. She trusted him. She made him feel vital.

He climbed up onto the flight deck, and a chilly breeze whipped around him.

That was the danger. Tess didn't distract

him through manipulation as Joanie had, but she distracted him nonetheless.

She invaded his thoughts. He made excuses to be where she was. Since November, he hadn't missed a Sunday afternoon outing. It had less to do with his commitment to rest and more to do with Tess. Her unique light.

Captain Short pointed out the two elevators that lifted planes from the hangar deck to the flight deck. He pointed out the catapult toward the bow to help launch aircraft when the wind wasn't high enough. He pointed out the nine arresting wires to snag landing aircraft as well as the three net barriers to stop them if they missed the wires.

Dan had missed the wires too, daydreaming about Tess. Thank goodness three barriers protected him — the regulations prohibiting Navy men from marrying WAVES, Dan's commitment to not becoming committed, and Tess's lack of interest in him.

On outings, she seemed to try to shake him, but he kept following like a lovesick schoolboy. She called him a grumble-bee, which was fair. She saw him as obsessed with his duties, which was true. And if she fell for him, his serious nature would douse her light. He couldn't allow that.

Dan gazed around the immense flight deck. Although the possibilities of the auxiliary carriers intrigued him, he needed to get away from the Atlantic, from the East Coast.

He faced Admiral Howard. "The Pacific. Please send me to the Pacific, sir."

The action was higher there. And the danger was lower.

22

Boston
Monday, January 25, 1943

The door shut harder than Tess intended.

Nora looked up from the desk they shared in quarters. "Are you all right?"

"Sorry." Tess set her cover in her locker. "I wish I wasn't required to go to ASWU."

"I thought Dan was out of town."

Tess cringed as she hung up her overcoat and scarf. Sometimes she regretted confessing her crush to Nora, but then she needed to confide in somebody. She didn't dare tell Mary or Lillian. "He is. It's that horrid Mr. Randolph."

"What did he do this time?"

Tess plopped on the bed. "First he questioned why I had to come to the office every day. He said there were plenty of men to make sure the girls didn't laze around and gossip."

Nora wrinkled her nose. "Isn't that all we

women do?"

"He thinks so. He says all I do is chitchat with the yeomen. He thinks my job has no purpose." Familiar doubts tugged at her heart. If the WAVES performed their duties well without her supervision, what was her purpose anyway?

"Does Dan agree?" Nora rested her chin on her hand, her brown eyes warm.

"I don't think so. He hasn't said anything." The office felt so empty without his solid presence. If he had his way, he'd only return long enough to clean out his desk. That was what she was praying for. Perhaps her prayers were selfish, to protect her own heart. Yet she knew her prayers were generous, in Dan's best interest and the nation's too.

"Well?"

Tess blinked. "Well what?"

"You are so madly in love with him." Nora's smile conveyed both amusement and compassion.

Tess groaned. "I'm hopeless. I'm glad he'll be transferred somewhere else so I can get over him."

"Mm-hmm. And the question you didn't hear — if Dan disapproved of your work or felt it was useless, wouldn't he say so?"

"Yes." He'd never said anything negative

about her work, had he?

"Then don't let Randolph bother you."

"That man. You know what he called me? A figurehead with a figure."

Nora gasped. "He didn't."

"He did. In front of the yeomen and Mr. Bentley. To his credit, Mr. Bentley protested quite indignantly."

Nora turned and rearranged papers on the desk. "That was . . . nice of him."

Tess smiled. At least she wasn't the only one suffering from infatuation. "He's a perfect gentleman."

"Yes. Well, I'm glad that was the end of it."

"It wasn't. Oh no. He had the nerve to say I only came to the office to see Mr. Avery. He asked if anything was happening between us."

"Oh dear."

Tess's cheeks warmed. "I told him we're only family friends. Then he said if that should change, he'd talk to my commanding officer and have me reprimanded and transferred."

"How dare he!"

Nora's anger, on top of Bill Bentley's, made Tess feel vindicated. "Thank goodness Dan will be transferred soon. That'll silence Mr. Randolph on one front at least."

"But you'll miss him."

"Yes, I will." But how could that be any more painful than her current predicament?

That evening, Tess opened the door to Robillard's Bakery and inhaled the aroma of fresh-baked bread and purpose. Mr. Randolph doubted her, but the FBI thought her useful.

Celeste Robillard bustled behind the counter. "Oh! Quintessa is here. Has everyone arrived?"

Professor Arnaud looked up from some papers on a table. "Yvette and Henri aren't here."

Madame Robillard pulled a tray from inside the display case. "Yvette called. She said Henri was kept late at work. They'll be here around seven thirty."

"I don't see Jean-Auguste."

Solange Marchand wiped the counter. "He's in New York on business. He travels, you know."

"Then we should start."

"That curtain." Madame Robillard dashed to the window and tugged the curtains shut. "It's drafty in here."

"Feels warm to me." Tess tugged off her gloves.

"You are so sweet. Come, come." She carried a tray to a table in the back of the bakery. "Brioche. Everyone must have one. Come, come."

Tess was full from dinner, but who could resist brioche?

The baker beckoned. "We must start, and we must have brioche. Oh dear. I forgot the napkins."

Tess joined the crowd around the table while Madame Robillard hustled behind the counter again.

A crash behind her. Glass shattered.

Tess ducked and clapped her hands to the back of her head. Everyone screamed. What was happening?

Light flashed. A bang!

The force shoved Tess forward. She dropped to the ground and scooted under a table, her breath racing, her ears ringing.

"A bomb!" a man screamed. "Someone threw a bomb through the window!"

"Out! Out the back!" Professor Arnaud yelled.

Everyone staggered to their feet and followed him.

Tess lingered, squinting through the smoky haze. "Is anyone hurt?"

No fire. No cries of pain. Every instinct tugged her to the back door, but she resisted. One table was collapsed close to the shattered window, and she inched closer, covering her mouth and nose.

"Oh no." A parcel lay underneath, smoking. A broken brick lay in a tangle of blackened strings. Thank goodness the explosion hadn't been bigger. Thank goodness the bomb landed in the front of the bakery when all the people were in the back.

But a bomb? In the bakery? Who would do such a thing? She had to call the police.

Tess ran behind the counter, toward the phone in the kitchen.

Madame Robillard huddled with Solange behind the counter next to the window.

Tess hurried to them. "Madame! Solange! Are you all right?"

"*Oui.* I — I was fixing the curtain again, and I saw someone. A woman on a bicycle."

Tess peeked outside. A woman pedaled down the darkened street. "Did you recognize her?"

"I —" Madame Robillard clutched her head. "*Non,* it is impossible."

"What's impossible?" Tess asked.

"I thought it was Yvette."

"Yvette?"

"Oh my goodness," Solange said. "You're right. Her red beret. Her coat. I'd know them anywhere. Oh no."

Tess's stomach soured. Despite her suspicions, to think of her former roommate throwing a bomb into a bakery filled with her friends . . . it couldn't be.

A far-off whine of sirens told her someone in the neighborhood had called the police. "Madame, Solange, go out back with the others. I'll call the FBI."

"The FBI! Oh no." Madame Robillard tugged Tess's arm. "They were here last week asking questions. They must have heard we have a spy in our group. Now look what happened."

Tess's cheeks tingled. She was the reason for the FBI's visit. The spy must have been alerted. And now . . . ?

What had she done?

"Come," Madame Robillard said. "We must go outside, wait for the police."

Tess shook herself. "No, I have to call the FBI. It's my duty as a citizen, as an officer."

Madame Robillard protested, but Solange guided her outside.

Tess opened her purse with shaky fingers and found Agent Sheffield's number in her wallet. Thank goodness he was working late.

In case anyone was listening, she explained the situation in a cool tone, as if she'd never met the agent and had only called the main FBI number. Agent Sheffield promised to come, and Tess joined the others in the back alley.

Despite the freezing weather, the temperature in the crowd was heated.

"It was Yvette," Solange said. "She's trying to kill me so she can have Henri to herself."

Someone laughed. "She already has Henri. And you have Jean-Auguste, remember?"

Solange tossed her head and crossed her arms. Clearly she still had feelings for Henri.

Pierre Guillory wheezed and thumped his chest. The smoke from the explosion must have aggravated his war injuries. "It was Jean-Auguste, I know it."

"He's in New York," Solange cried.

"So he says. The police will check his alibi."

"Non," Madame Robillard said. "It was a woman."

Tess frowned. "We saw a woman on a bicycle, but we don't know if she threw the bomb."

"Jean-Auguste is skinny," Pierre said. "He could wear a skirt and look like a woman."

"That's ridiculous," Solange said. "You only say that because you don't like him."

"He is weak, and he does not stand strong for France."

"Please." Professor Arnaud made patting

motions with his hands. "We mustn't accuse each other. We must wait quietly for
the police."

"How do we know it wasn't you, Pierre?"
a man called out. "You're the firebrand in
this group."

He waved a dismissive hand. "I was in the
bakery, you fool. Not outside."

"Your daughter then."

"My daughter!" He spat on the ground.
"You do not know what you say. She would
not. She could not. Besides, she cares nothing for France. She only cares for the big
bands and the movie stars."

The siren increased in pitch, then stopped.
Thank goodness the police had arrived
before a fight erupted.

"The police are here." Tess tried to open
the door, but it was locked.

"Shoo, shoo." Madame Robillard waved
her off the doormat, pulled a key from
underneath, and unlocked the door. Then
she led everyone through the kitchen and
into the seating area.

The front door burst open, and Yvette and
Henri rushed in. "What happened?"

"You tell us," Solange said. "Where were
you? Where's your red beret?"

"My red . . . ? I was . . ." Yvette wore a
black hat. She gazed around, pale and wide-

eyed. "When I was at work, someone called my apartment claiming to be Henri."

"It wasn't me. I didn't call."

"I know." Yvette pressed a fluttering hand to her chest. "The man told my roommate he'd been kept late at work and asked me to meet him at his apartment at seven fifteen. That's why we're late."

"A convenient alibi," a man muttered.

It was. Tess chewed on her lips. No one could verify an alibi like that. But someone could also fake a call to the apartment and make Yvette late, make her look guilty.

A trio of policemen entered the bakery. For the next hour, they investigated the scene, scooping up the remnants of the bomb, inspecting every corner, and interviewing each person in turn.

Then Agents Paul Sheffield and Walter Hayes arrived. Both men looked right through Tess as if they'd never seen her. They conferred with the policemen, then began their own interviews.

Tess's stomach turned every which way. Her meddling had caused this. Everyone here could have been killed, and it was her fault. She'd wanted to be a sleuth like Mary and Lillian, and look at the trouble she'd caused.

In time, Agent Sheffield pulled Tess aside

to a private table and asked her name and address.

She answered, joining the charade that they'd never met.

The agent wrote in his notebook. "It appears your suspicions were justified."

"I'm afraid so."

He nodded, his face impassive. "Before we start, I want you to know Miss Lafontaine is clean."

"She is? But the gun, the lies —"

"I can't tell you what I know or how I know it, but you and your friends have nothing to fear from Miss Lafontaine."

"But . . ." Tess worked hard to keep her gaze from wandering to Yvette. "But she was late tonight, and her excuse is flimsy, and Madame Robillard and Solange saw —"

"I have all that information. Tell me what you saw and heard, not what anyone else said."

"All right." Tess pulled herself together and gave her most objective report. When she was done, she leaned across the table toward Agent Sheffield. "I stirred up the hornet's nest, didn't I?"

He ground his cigarette in the ashtray and raised half a smile. "A hornet's nest needs to be stirred to be emptied."

That might be true, but how many would be stung in the process?

23

In the ready room of the USS *Bogue,* Dan pointed to his first slide, a photograph of the USS *Suwannee* off the Moroccan coast, and he addressed the pilots of Squadron VC-9.

"During Operation Torch, the US auxiliary carriers proved their worth and showed the great potential of this class of vessel. Without land-based aircraft, the Western Task Force relied solely on the carrier USS *Ranger* and on the ACVs for air support."

In the back of the room, Admiral Howard sat with Captain Giles Short. The captain watched with clear interest, and the admiral sent an encouraging smile.

Dan tapped the pointer in his open palm. "The TBFs, SBDs, and F4Fs filled multiple roles. They established immediate air superiority over the French through air combat and by bombing airfields and destroying aircraft on the ground. They performed ground support by shooting up trucks, tanks, and gun positions. They bombed French surface vessels. But this afternoon I'll focus on their role in antisubmarine warfare."

For the next half hour, Dan described the incidents and the ASWU analysis. In an attack by a single Avenger torpedo bomber on the French sub *Méduse,* the pilot had made a beam attack, a poor angle for an approach. He'd dropped only one depth bomb and from too high an altitude. The sub had received minor damage but had beached herself and was destroyed by other aircraft two days later.

In another attack, four Avengers used clouds to shield their approach, and they came in from a better angle and altitude, dropping four depth bombs each. The fourth TBF pilot held his bombs when the *Sidi-Ferruch* went into her death throes.

In his slides, Dan compared the altitude, angles of approach, and number of bombs dropped, using diagrams to back up the statistics.

Dan clasped the pointer behind his back. "As the *Bogue* joins the Battle of the Atlantic, we at ASWU are looking forward to data from many attacks on U-boats — and plenty of sinkings. Working together, we can refine our tactics and bring the Allies to a speedy victory."

After the applause died, Dan answered questions. His previous talk on surface radar had also gone well, and he was anticipating his future talks, especially the one on upcoming technology.

The captain and admiral stood as Dan approached.

"Excellent job, Mr. Avery," Captain Short said. "Very informative."

"Thank you, sir."

The captain crossed his arms and inclined his head. "Say, the *Bogue* will be the first US auxiliary carrier to escort convoys. We'll be pioneers, but we'll also be guinea pigs. I hope ASWU will put someone aboard."

"Like our Mr. Avery?" Admiral Howard chuckled. "Sorry, Captain. I have plans for this young man."

"Too bad. You'd be welcome."

Dan's chest felt full with the dual compliments. "Thank you, sir. I'm honored."

"Come. I want to show you the catapult today." Captain Short led them out of the ready room, outside, and up a ladder onto the catwalk that ran along the hull. Another ladder led up to the flight deck.

"Go ahead of me. You're young and spry." Admiral Howard gazed up the ladder, his face pale. Sweat glistened on his forehead despite the icy breeze.

"Are you all right, sir?"

"Of course I'm all right. Up you go, young man. Let's go see that catapult."

Dan obeyed. Snow fell, nice and steady, and his feet crunched in the thin layer on the flight deck.

A smile pulled at his mouth. Would he ever be able to look at a snowfall again without picturing Tess Beaumont twirling among the flakes?

Honestly. Would he ever regain control of his emotions? He knew better. He knew to avoid distractions as Admiral Howard always told him.

Where was the admiral?

Dan looked over his shoulder.

The admiral crouched at the top of the ladder with his hands flat on the deck, struggling to pull his knees up under him.

"Sir? Are you —"

"I'm fine," he snapped. "Just have a cramp in my arm."

Helping him wouldn't be wise, but Dan had to grip the lining of his coat pockets to resist.

At last Admiral Howard straightened to

standing. "Wait and see, son. If you live to be my age, you'll have aches and pains as well."

"Yes, sir." Dan gave him a fond smile, then turned to Captain Short. "Tell us about the catapult, sir."

The captain headed toward the bow of the ship. "I know neither of you are aviators. An aircraft needs a certain amount of speed for takeoff, and the *Bogue*'s flight deck isn't long enough. Even if the ship is travelling at a full sixteen knots, we need a boost from the wind. If the air is too still, we can't launch. That's why we need the catapult."

A thump sounded behind Dan.

Admiral Howard lay crumpled on the deck.

"Admiral!" Dan rushed to him and dropped to his knees.

"Perry!" Captain Short yelled. "Call for the medical officer. On the double."

The admiral clutched his arm, panting, his eyes enormous. "I — I —"

He was having a coronary, wasn't he? They never covered that in first aid training. What should he do?

"Help is coming, sir." Dan loosened the admiral's scarf, feeling as helpless as when Lillian had stepped in an animal trap. Dan had released his sister from the trap, but he'd been powerless to save her leg.

Captain Short leaned over the admiral. "Sir? Is there anything we can do?"

"Coat . . . nitro . . ."

Nitroglycerin. It was his heart, just as the doctor on the *Wilkes* had feared.

Lord, help me, help me. Dan plunged his hand into the admiral's coat pocket. There! A tiny glass vial. Fool thing wouldn't open. He yanked off his gloves, unscrewed the little metal lid, and dumped small white tablets into his palm.

But he sensed a void. A stillness.

Admiral Howard's blue eyes stared to the side, to the north. Unseeing.

"No, no, no!" Dan shoved a tablet between the admiral's lips. The medication would work. It had to.

Captain Short stooped and worked his fingers under Admiral Howard's scarf.

Dan waited, praying, his hand freezing.

The captain shook his head.

"No." No, it wasn't too late. It couldn't be.

An officer and two pharmacist's mates jogged down the deck with a medical kit and a stretcher.

"Dr. Mote," Captain Short said. "Admiral Howard collapsed."

Dan scooted aside on his knees. "He has high blood pressure. He looked pale today, sweaty. He said he had a cramp in his arm. Then he collapsed. He asked for his nitro-glycerin, so I gave him a tablet."

Dr. Mote unbuttoned the admiral's over-coat and worked his stethoscope under his service jacket.

Dan clutched Admiral Howard's hand, willing his own heartbeat, his own health to flow to this man he cared for. *Don't take him from me, Lord. Please don't.*

After a minute, the physician pulled the admiral's coat lapels together.

Melted snow soaked through Dan's trouser legs. Why wasn't the doctor doing anything?

Then Dr. Mote rested his hand over Admiral Howard's bright blue eyes and closed his eyelids.

"No . . ." Dan's voice came out in a low, animal groan. He'd never see that blue again, never hear the admiral's gruff voice and wise words.

"I'm sorry," Dr. Mote said. "It was too late. There's nothing anyone could have done."

Captain Short stood. "I'll notify his family."

"He has none."

"None?"

Dan's head shook heavily. "Only child. Never married."

"What a shame," the doctor said.

The admiral's hand felt limp. Dan had never held the man's hand before, never hugged him, never called him anything but "admiral" or "sir." Yet Admiral Howard said Dan was almost a son to him. Dan was the closest thing he had to family.

The pharmacist's mates laid the stretcher on the deck and rolled the admiral onto it.

Dan's compass needle spun. The admiral had died alone. No one to truly mourn him, only his naval colleagues. No one to carry on his name or his legacy, only Dan as his protégé.

The pharmacist's mates covered Rear Admiral Aloysius Howard with a blanket.

Captain Short laid a hand on Dan's shoulder. "Mr. Avery?"

It was time to let go. Dan released his mentor's hand, stood, and raised a sharp salute.

They carried the admiral away, and Dan held the salute in the falling snow. He was the only one who could carry on the man's legacy, and he'd do the best he could. He'd stay the course and have the sterling career the admiral had envisioned for him.

The letter.

How could he be so hard-hearted to think of himself at such a time?

Yet it was still January. Had Admiral Howard written that letter recommending Dan for a transfer to the Pacific Fleet? Even if he had, he'd said he wouldn't mail it until February 1.

The ocean swelled beneath him. The tide that had been carrying him to sea shifted and betrayed him.

24

Boston
Sunday, February 7, 1943

"A bomb?" Dan charged toward Tess and Nora on the sidewalk in front of Park Street Church.

Tess groaned. She hadn't planned to burden him with that, not when he was finally home after two weeks away, not when he had to be reeling from the death of Admiral Howard. She saluted. "Good morning, Mr. Avery. Welcome back to Boston."

"I —" Dan gave his head a little shake, then returned Tess and Nora's salutes. "Good morning, Miss Beaumont, Miss Thurmond. A bomb? Lillian just told me."

At least she wouldn't have to relate the whole story. "Someone threw a bomb through the window of the bakery during a meeting, but no one was hurt. The police and FBI are investigating."

"Agent Sheffield was assigned to the case," Mary said. "He worked on my sabotage case too. Oh! I'd better get to choir."

The group headed up the granite steps to the main door, framed by white pillars against the brick façade.

Dan stuck by Tess's side. "Any arrests?"

"Not yet."

"Suspects?"

In the oval-shaped foyer, twin staircases spiraled up on either side. "Everyone suspects everyone else. Yvette and Henri are the top culprits because they didn't arrive until after the attack, but . . ."

"But what?"

Tess gripped the dark wood curlicue at the base of the banister and waited for the others to climb out of earshot. "After the bombing, Agent Sheffield told me Yvette was clear."

"So the gun —"

"He won't tell me why she's clear, but he says we have nothing to fear."

"Good." Dan took off his cover and smoothed his dark hair. "I've been concerned about Lillian and Mary rooming with her. And about you."

"Thank you." She busied her fingers unbuttoning her overcoat so she wouldn't play with the wayward curl over his forehead. "I didn't tell Mary or Lillian about the gun or about going to the FBI."

"I agree. No need to worry them." He motioned for her to lead the way. "How are you?"

"I'm fine." Tess ascended the stairs. "No one was hurt. The paper said the bomber didn't use much explosive. Either he just wanted to scare us, or he didn't know how to build a bomb."

"But how are *you*?"

She wanted to give a cheery answer, but such a warm and personal question deserved an honest answer. "I feel awful. I started the whole thing."

"You?" A train could run along the tracks across his forehead.

"Mm-hmm. After I went to the FBI, the agents questioned Madame Robillard and the others. The spy must have gotten riled up and —"

"You didn't do anything wrong."

Tess waited for him on the landing. Another pair of stair-cases spiraled up to the gallery where the choir sang. "I went to the FBI for the wrong reasons. I wanted to be a sleuth, to do something important. I wanted attention. I was —"

"Attention?" Dan glared down at her. "I was there when you decided to go. Attention had nothing to do with it. You had information the FBI needed. And don't you see? The bomb proves something is wrong in that group — a spy or a troublemaker. You didn't cause the problem. It was already there. Don't doubt yourself."

She gave him a small smile. "Thank you."

He stepped closer, and the glare dissolved to tenderness. "Will you continue to report to the FBI?"

That look? How could she bear it? She glanced away to all the people who didn't have to worry about spies and bombs and the FBI. "I don't know."

"Tess . . ." His voice rumbled so low and soothing.

She resisted the magnetic pull to his arms, certainly not what he intended, and she made her voice light. "Hmm?"

"Only the Navy can give you a direct order, not the FBI. But I urge you not to let fear win. Be careful, yes, but don't let fear win."

Truth drew her gaze back to his strong face. Here was a man not only willing to face Nazis and bombs and the raging sea — but he longed to do so, drove hard to do so. Her breath caught on the way in. "I did take an oath to protect the nation."

"You did." His mouth twitched into an

approving smile more exhilarating than starry-eyed adoration.

Then he tilted his head toward the sanctuary.

Tess gathered herself, and they filed into a pew beside Lillian, Arch, Nora, and Bill Bentley, a recent Sunday regular.

Dan pulled the hymnal from the pew rack, studied the board at the front of the sanctuary listing the hymn numbers, and located the pages. So like him, planning ahead.

Organ music washed over her, calming her heart, and Tess set her purse under the pew and removed her scarf and gloves.

"Here," Dan said in a low voice. "First hymn, second verse. It's for you."

His hazel eyes were so warm and close, and his message so sweet. She whispered a thank-you.

He held the hymnal open, his palms wide and strong and capable, and he tapped Hymn 236, "All the Way My Savior Leads Me."

She started reading, but then Dr. Harold Ockenga approached the pulpit. After the opening prayer, the organ played the introduction to the hymn. Tess joined in, relishing the choir's sublime singing above and behind her, and Dan's off-key bass beside her.

All the way my Savior leads me — what
    have I to ask beside?
Can I doubt His tender mercy, who thru life
    has been my Guide?
Heav'nly peace, divinest comfort, here by
    faith in Him to dwell!
For I know, whate'er befall me, Jesus doeth
    all things well.

All the way my Savior leads me — cheers
    each winding path I tread,
Gives me grace for ev'ry trial, feeds me
    with the living bread.
Tho' my weary steps may falter and my
    soul athirst may be,
Gushing from the Rock before me, lo! a
    spring of joy I see.

The verse *was* for her. She let the truth
soak in. Her path wound every which way,
her steps faltered, her soul thirsted, but
Jesus led her. She needed to stop doubting
and to relax in his cheer and grace and joy.

All the way my Savior leads me — O the
    fullness of His love!
Perfect rest to me is promised in my
    Father's house above.
When my spirit, clothed immortal, wings its
    flight to realms of day,

This my song thru endless ages: Jesus led me all the way.

Dan's voice warbled on the final verse.

That verse — it was for him. Tess had read in the newspaper about Admiral Howard's death. Was Dan there when his mentor's spirit winged its flight?

Dr. Ockenga preached about comfort in grief, appropriate for a nation at war. Losses continued in unending battles for Tunisia and New Guinea and Guadalcanal, and throughout the world in the air and on the sea.

She could feel Dan's heaviness beside her. She should have asked how he was doing. Instead, she talked on and on about her own problems. If only she could undo that mistake. If only she could take his hand or hug his arm, comfort him in some small way.

After church, Arch suggested a place off Beacon Street that served great clam chowder. A snowy walk through Boston Common would whet the appetite.

The group crossed Park Street and entered the Common, snow covering the slopes, frosty trees stitching lacework in the gray sky.

Mary and Lillian and Arch led the way,

chatting and laughing. Nora and Bill walked together, which made Tess smile.

She lagged behind with Dan, determined to make up for her selfishness earlier. "I'm sorry. I heard about Admiral Howard."

He walked straight, his gaze on the cleared path. "I couldn't do anything."

"You were there?"

"He collapsed on the deck. I gave him his nitroglycerin, but it was too late."

"I'm sorry. I know what he meant to you."

"He was like a father to me. He — he said I was like a son to him." His shoulders hunched up. "He had no family. His funeral — just Navy men."

"How sad."

"It is." His gaze darted to her, then away before she could read his emotions.

They passed a silent fountain with a Victorian bronze sculpture in the center, the classical figures dusted with frost. Up the hill to the right, the Massachusetts State House stood with its dignified Federal architecture, its golden dome painted black as an air raid precaution.

"Wasn't the admiral going to help you get a transfer?"

Dan squeezed his eyes shut. "He was. I — I helped sort his papers that day. No letter. He didn't plan to mail it until February 1, so that means he didn't write it in time."

"Oh dear. But you can request a transfer, can't you?"

"Denied. I returned to Boston yesterday and submitted a transfer request to Commander Lewis. He says he can't spare me. My work's too important. And he — he's heard rumors that I'm behind in my duties." His voice stiffened.

Tess gasped. "Mr. Randolph."

A sharp nod. "I'll have to wait a few months before asking again. In the meantime, Mr. Randolph will be gunning for me. I — I'm trapped."

Tess had never seen him undone like this, and it broke her heart. If only she could hug him, but all she had were words. "I'm sorry, Danny."

He hiked up one eyebrow. "Danny?"

"I know, but when I'm sad and overwhelmed, I feel very little and young. Don't you?"

His gaze stretched far across Boston Common. "I haven't been Danny since I was six."

He'd said that before. "Was it because you started school and wanted to act grown up?"

"No. Because I did grow up. I had to."

"Why? What happened?"

He shot her a hesitant look, unusual for

258

him. "Don't say a word of this to anyone. They all think the world of my father."

"I won't say anything." Her voice hushed with the honor of his confidence.

To the left, the Parkman Bandstand stood empty, waiting for summer's festivities, and they headed right up the slope toward Beacon Street.

Dan cleared his throat. "That was the year the twins were born. Mom had a rough time of it and had to stay in bed. And Lucy was tiny and frail. She almost died a couple times. My father was beside himself worrying about Mom and Lucy, and Mom was trying to take care of the babies. She asked me to watch out for my brothers. Rob was four and Jim was two. So every day I made them breakfast and got them dressed before I went to school."

Tess studied his face, the mix of anger and duty and love and loss. "That was too big of a job for Danny, wasn't it? Dan had to do it."

"And I did. My father wouldn't think to do it. All he could think about was Mom and the babies and his boats."

Three young boys darted across the path, screaming about who was "it" in their game of tag.

Tess paused to let them pass. "So you surrendered some of your childhood."

Dan shook his head slowly, staring at the Frog Pond that stretched to their right. In the summer, children waded and splashed in the shallow waters, but now the pond was frozen and deserted. "I haven't played since I was —"

"Six?"

"Eleven."

He'd said that without hesitation. "Eleven?"

"That was when I stopped playing and became a man." He faced her, his eyes a bit wild. "Do you want the rest of it? All of it?"

She held her breath. Admiral Howard's death had shattered him, and stories were seeping through the cracks. They needed to escape. And she was honored to listen. "What happened?"

"Lillian had her accident." He winced. "Partly my fault. I was being bossy, no surprise, and I refused to let her play with us boys. So she followed us and accidentally stepped in a trap. She was five. Jim tried to free her, but he was too little. I had to be the calm one. I had to get her out and carry her home and fetch the doctor. He amputated her leg. Then Lucy got sick again. Ed was born not long after, and Mom caught a fever and was laid up in bed for weeks."

"Oh my goodness. You had to help again."

"Worse. Almost lost the business." Anger flashed in his eyes, and he marched up the path. "We should catch up."

Tess fell in beside him. "What happened with the business?"

"The summer before the accident, I worked with Mom in the office. She showed me how she did the books and ordering and bills. I liked it. After Ed was born, she asked me to check on things. Good thing I did. She hadn't had time since Lillian's accident. Bills were unpaid, overdue. My father hadn't done a thing. So I pulled it together, kept the business afloat, kept the family from falling apart. He couldn't be a man, so I had to. At eleven."

In all her years knowing the Avery family, this was the first time Tess had heard anything negative about Mr. Avery. "You never complained, did you? Never mentioned what you did. That's why your brothers and sisters think so highly of your dad."

"They need to. Everyone should respect his father." He walked harder, his hands stuffed deep in his pockets.

"And you don't."

His shoulders jumped up to his ears, as if blocking her words. "I know. It's wrong, and I know it."

That explained so much about Dan Avery. It explained his serious nature, why he rarely smiled or laughed. It explained his hardworking spirit, why he put duty above all else. And it explained why he latched on to Admiral Howard as a second father.

Dan let out a short, dry laugh. "And now you don't respect me. For good reason."

"What?" She grasped his arm to stop him. "Oh no. I do. Very much. You did what had to be done. And you did show respect to your dad — you protected him, protected his reputation. That's respectful. You're a good man."

Dan lowered his chin, his face scrunched up.

"You are." She lowered her hand so he wouldn't think she was flirting. "By the way, so is your dad."

His eyes smoldered. "He wasn't when it mattered most, when his family needed him."

Down the pathway, the trees on either side angled together, converging on an imaginary point in the distance. "Perhaps a little perspective would help. What if your father had an accident and were confined to bed? Would your mother build all the boats?"

"Of course not. She doesn't know how to build a . . ." His eyes widened, stricken.

"What would have happened to the business?"

Dan pressed his fingertips to his skull like a cage. He groaned.

"Did your father fail?" she asked softly. "Or did he just lack your mother's business skills?"

He glowered between his fingers. "He should have —"

"Because you hold her skills in higher esteem than his skills." She felt like a heel, but the point needed to be driven home. She felt it.

Silence. Turmoil. Such a strong man, crumbling before her eyes. She didn't want him to stay crumbled but to put his pieces back together in a new and better way.

"It's all right." She reached out and rubbed his upper arm, his muscles bunched up under the layers of wool. "My papa says that without perspective, a painting is flat and dull. Perspective adds depth and life. Now maybe your image of your father will have more perspective, your image of your family . . . of yourself."

His fingers drifted away from his face, and he looked at her with intensity that powered inside her. She didn't resist. Oh, what would it be like if he kissed her with even a fraction of that intensity?

"Color," he muttered.

"Color?"

He blinked, and the intensity washed away. He looked up the path. "We should catch up."

"Yes. We should." She lowered her hand. The moment was over, and he was sealing up his cracks again. If only he'd let her see inside again someday.

25

Boston
Tuesday, February 16, 1943

"Brr!" Tess burst into Dan's office, her cheeks bright pink. "Is Mr. Randolph around?"

Dan eased back in his chair. "He's at the Rad Lab today."

"Thank goodness. May I warm up in here before I see the WAVES?" She unbuttoned her coat.

He'd say yes anyway. "It's cold out there."

"Cold?" Bill Bentley barked out a laugh from the desk behind him. "Record low last night, didn't you hear? Fourteen degrees below zero."

"Yes," Dan said, "but it's supposed to be fourteen above zero this afternoon. Break out the dress whites."

Tess laughed and blew on her hands. "Well, your office is always warm and cozy."

Bill pointed to the wastebasket. "Mr.

Avery and I keep a fire burning there, our hopes and dreams going up in flame."

"Is that so?" Tess cast a sympathetic look to Dan and then to Bill, and she perched on the edge of Dan's desk. "What do you hope for, Mr. Bentley? Going to sea?"

"Not me." His cheeks flushed, and he turned to the papers on his desk. "I like office work."

Dan pushed a piece of scratch paper closer to Tess and sketched a heart. That was Bill's dream, hindered by the Navy.

Tess's eyes twinkled, then she dove into her purse, pulled out a lipstick, and colored the heart red.

He couldn't help but chuckle. She'd done it again — added color.

"What are you two giggling about?" Bill asked.

Dan crumpled the paper. "Nothing."

Tess leaned back against the wall. "So, Mr. Bentley, what is it about office work that you enjoy?" She asked in a friendly way and listened intently as Bill rambled about files and people and aiding the war effort.

Dan slipped the crumpled paper into his jacket pocket and studied the young lady close before him. She did add color, not just her blue uniform and green eyes and yellow hair and pink cheeks and red lips, but her personality and insight and warmth.

Despite all his intentions, he'd fallen hard.

"Now." Tess patted the desk in front of Dan. "We just have to figure out how to get Mr. Avery back to sea."

Dan's heart sank. "It's hopeless. I ought to wait a few months before requesting a transfer again. Meanwhile, Randolph undermines me at every turn."

"I was thinking. Can you get someone else to request you on his ship? How about those carriers in the Chesapeake? Did you meet the COs?"

"They see me as a desk jockey."

"If they could see you in action . . . could you get on board doing ASWU duties, like you did for Torch?"

"I doubt —" A memory flashed through his head. "Wait. Captain Short — the day Admiral Howard died — I forgot —"

"Forgot what?" Tess leaned closer, her eyes lit up.

"Captain Short, on the *Bogue.* He said he hoped ASWU would put someone on board for the maiden cruise. He said I'd be welcome."

She clapped her hands. "Perfect! Do you see? You could fulfill your duties here by gathering data, which would show respect for Commander Lewis. And if the request came from the captain, how could Lewis say no?"

Lewis would be outranked. Randolph would be bypassed. Important work would be done. And no one would be offended. His mind swirled with hope.

"Wow, Miss Beaumont," Bill said. "You're brilliant."

"Nonsense. Dan would have thought of it." She gave Dan a smile. "Just send a tactful letter to Captain Short."

"Tact isn't my strength."

"But it's mine. I could help."

"Right now?" He pulled out a fresh piece of paper.

"Well, sure." She touched the open box for the compass from Admiral Howard. "May I?"

"Please do." He uncapped his pen. Her gifts of tact and encouragement balanced his brusqueness and ambition.

He scrawled down a few sentences, scratched out a too-blunt phrase. How could he concentrate with Tess sitting on the edge of his desk?

Then she stood, tilting the compass up and down. She paced the width of the office, back and forth, then spun in a circle.

Suddenly she stopped, her eyes wide. "Goodness. You must think I'm silly."

"No. No, I don't." She was cute, playful, fun, but never silly. One corner of his mouth edged up. "But what were you doing?"

"Oh, I just find compasses fascinating." She rotated it in her hand. "They always point north no matter what."

"They never deviate."

"Isn't that wonderful? Even if you take side trips or spin around or veer off the path, the compass stays true. You can always find your way."

"Stay the course." Admiral Howard's voice bellowed in his head.

Did Dan have it wrong? Following the admiral's advice, he never deviated from his course. No rest, no fun, no romance.

But that wasn't the purpose of a compass, was it? Or of a goal. Over the past few months, he'd rested. Yet his work hadn't suffered, his goal hadn't changed, and his dedication hadn't diminished.

Could he meet his goal if he added more fun to his life?

Or romance?

Dan stared at the compass in Tess's hand. The right companion could encourage him on the journey, while adding depth and perspective. Color.

"Well." Tess set the compass back on the desk. "That's enough playtime for me. I'll go check on the WAVES."

Dan bent over his paper. "I'll have the rough draft done in fifteen minutes."

"I'll be back."

"Very well." His voice came out gruff.

He wrote hard and fast. Get the important points down, the data, the facts. Tess would soften the wording. He had to focus, focus, focus.

Bill let out a low whistle. "Careful, Mr. Avery."

"Careful?" He didn't turn around.

"You know what Commander Lewis said about the WAVES, about the Navy regulations."

Dan's fingers tensed around the pen. "I would never violate regulations or go against a commander's recommendation. And neither would you."

"Of course not." Bill's voice lowered. "But still, be careful. I told you what Mr. Randolph said to Miss Beaumont. If he suspects anything is happening between you two, he'll speak to her CO and have her reprimanded and transferred."

Dan's shoulders slumped. He could imagine the vile things Randolph would say about Tess. "Nothing is happening between us."

"Mm-hmm." Bill didn't sound convinced.

He grimaced. If Bill had suspicions, so might Randolph. "Don't worry. I'll be careful. I'd never do anything to hurt her."

"I know. I just —"

"And I appreciate it. Now I have a letter to write."

"Yes, sir."

Dan's eyes squeezed shut, and his hand slipped inside his pocket to the wadded-up paper with his penned heart and her red lipstick. He didn't want to end up like Admiral Howard, alone and unloved. Not anymore.

He wanted a companion. He wanted Tess.

But his personal feelings didn't matter. Not only did the Navy have regulations, but Dan needed to guard Tess's reputation and her position. She loved being in the WAVES, and she was doing good work. No matter what, he'd protect her.

Dan shoved the paper into the corner of his pocket and grabbed his pen. The best way to protect Tess was to get away from her, to the sea.

26

Boston
Sunday, March 7, 1943

"Thank you, men. That's perfect." Tess smiled at the four sailors who had set up her war bond booth in North Station. "See you at 1830."

"Aye aye, ma'am." They departed.

Tess gazed around the crowded concourse. Perhaps she should feel guilty. Agent Sheffield assured her Yvette was clean, but Tess couldn't shake her concerns. The *Ambassador* arrived from Montréal at 1830, while trains from Cape Cod arrived throughout the afternoon. Tess could see if Yvette and Henri traveled together, and from which direction.

"Miss Beaumont!" Thelma Holt dashed to her with Celia Ortega and Ruth Feingold in her wake. "Did you hear the good news?"

Her insides tangled up. She knew what the WAVES were talking about.

Celia clasped her hands in front of her chest. "The Navy changed its mind."

"WAVES and Navy men are allowed to marry!" Ruth pointed to her ring finger.

"Which means they'll start asking us out," Thelma said.

"I know exactly who I'm —"

"Not if I get to him fir —"

"And did you see the darling white uniforms they approved for summer?" Celia linked her arm through Ruth's. "Won't we look cute walking out with big handsome sailor men?"

"Ladies!" Tess held up both hands. She never thought she'd see the day when she'd be the voice of calm and reason. "Attention!"

The WAVES looked surprised, but they snapped to attention.

"I understand your excitement. Many of the officers share it." Indeed, only she and Nora seemed to be unsettled by the news.

She stared them down. "But first, as sailors in the United States Navy, you are expected to behave with decorum at all times. Yes, you are allowed to date, but you will not chase after the men."

"Aye aye, ma'am."

"Second, no flirting on duty. How many officers and sailors didn't want women in the Navy because they thought we'd be a distraction? Don't prove them right. That is an order."

"Aye aye, ma'am."

"Third, don't forget what some are saying — that we're nothing better than prostitutes."

Ruth gasped.

Tess fixed a strong look on her. "I know you've heard it, or you've seen it in the papers. Prove them wrong. Be completely professional, dutiful, and ladylike."

"Aye aye, ma'am."

"And remember our purpose. We enlisted to free men to fight, not to snag them. Understood?"

"Yes, ma'am."

"Carry on."

The women turned to their duties, more subdued but still shining with excitement.

"I'll go drum up business." Tess grabbed her poster and headed toward her target platform.

Thank goodness Dan's appeal to Captain Short had succeeded. The captain had called Commander Lewis immediately after he received the letter, and Dan had shipped out on the USS *Bogue* not long after.

He'd been gone two weeks, and she couldn't help but worry. The U-boats had returned to the North Atlantic convoy routes, and many ships had been sunk recently.

But Dan wanted to be in the thick of action. That was where his country needed him.

"Buy your war bonds." Tess smiled at an elderly couple. "Help our boys overseas."

As much as she missed Dan, she was glad he was absent. He'd moved from disdain to grudging acceptance to friendship, but he was adamantly opposed to romance and everyone knew it.

Even if he changed his mind, she'd have to conceal her feelings for him. Mr. Randolph had threatened Tess's position if he suspected anything romantic between her and Dan. What would he do to Dan? She couldn't give him any leverage.

Maybe she should request a transfer. She could go to Mare Island with Kate Madison or to Jacksonville with Ada Sue Duncan. But then she'd miss Mary and Lillian and Nora.

"Do your bit." She waggled her poster. "Buy bonds today."

The Second War Loan Drive was scheduled to begin April 12. This time she had enough notice to prepare. She mentally reviewed her plans for the first drive, set aside after the Cocoanut Grove Fire. Now she could implement them and improve them.

She'd spoken with Rear Adm. Robert Theobald, the new commandant of the Boston Navy Yard, and he'd approved rallies. She'd schedule rousing speeches and entertainment — a band and a singer? A comedy act? Maybe a Hollywood star?

"War bonds," Tess called. "A solid investment for your future — and for victory!"

The Boston Navy Yard had earned the coveted Army-Navy E Pennant in February for meeting production quotas. She could capitalize on pride in that accomplishment to meet bond sale quotas too.

On April 22, Mary was letting her set up a booth at the launching ceremony for two new destroyer escorts. One of the ships was being christened the *Dempsey* after a Lt. Thomas Dempsey, killed in the Battle of Savo Island when the *Vincennes* was sunk. Dan's ship.

Why couldn't she get that man out of her head? She threw on a smile. "War bonds — care enough to give enough."

For the next three hours she patrolled the station. No sign of Yvette and Henri, but it was just now 1830. Tess returned to find the WAVES and the sailors dismantling the booth without a trace of flirting.

Tess joined in the work, keeping the concourse under surveillance. At 1835, Yvette and Henri strolled from the direction of the *Ambassador*'s platform. At least they were consistent.

But where had they gone? Maybe some weekend Tess could take the *New Englander* and see where they disembarked. Wouldn't that be exciting?

Yvette glanced her way, and Tess waved.

"That's the last of it, ma'am," one of the sailors said.

"Thank you. I appreciate it. All right, everyone's dismissed."

Now she could follow Yvette and Henri without looking suspicious. She pulled on her overcoat and picked up her purse.

A man strode down the concourse, a large dark-haired man in a black overcoat. What was it about him? He looked familiar.

Tess gasped. Yvette's date at the Cocoanut Grove!

He glanced around the corner after Yvette and Henri, then swept the concourse with a steely gaze — which landed on Tess for the shortest scariest moment.

Who was he? Did she dare follow?

Why not? She couldn't let fear win.

Tess eased into the crowd. She had every

right to go this direction. She climbed the stairs and stepped outside into the chilly moonless night. The streets glistened, drenched from yesterday's record rainfall.

Yvette and Henri entered a taxi. But where did the mystery man go?

Tess spun around. The station doors opened, and there he was at the bottom of the stairs, leaning against the wall and looking at his watch.

Her breath caught. When did he get behind her? And why?

Yvette's taxi drove away, and Tess hopped into the next one. Everything in her wanted to say, "Follow that cab," but she resisted.

"Where to, miss?"

"Um . . ." She opened her purse and grabbed her notepad. "Let's see. My friend gave me a map, but oh dear, her handwriting. I'll read it to you. Go straight."

"All right, lady." He pulled from the curb.

Tess held up her notepad but kept her eyes on Yvette's cab, which turned toward the bridge. "Let's see. Take the Charlestown Bridge."

She felt very clever and detective-like, but less so when it became clear Yvette was going home. That wasn't exciting or informative.

When Yvette's taxi stopped in front of the

apartment, Tess asked the cabby to stop about a block behind. She peered out the window. "Isn't that lovely? My friend's moving to Boston, and this place is for rent. She wanted me to see if it was nice."

The cabby huffed. "Listen, lady. If you wanted me to follow that cab, you should've just said, 'Follow that cab.' "

"I —" But she'd been caught in a lie, and she couldn't deny it. Her cheeks burned.

"Guarantee that's what the fella behind us said."

"The fellow —"

"Don't look. Big man in a black coat, has a dark look to him, you know what I mean?"

"I do." Tess sank lower in the seat, her face on fire.

"You in trouble, miss? Want me to take you to the cops? Or you want me to shake him?"

"Shake him, yes." She gave him her address. "No, wait. Go slowly at first. I want to see if he was following me or my friend."

"Your friend?" He shook his head and pulled away from the curb. "Listen, lady. I don't know which of those fellas broke your heart or why, but this ain't worth it."

No, it wasn't.

"And he's following us. But don't you worry. I'll shake him so hard, his ears will fall off."

"Thank you." Maybe letting fear win would be wise after all.

27

North Atlantic
Wednesday, March 10, 1943
A frigid mist stung Dan's cheeks, but his heavy mackinaw and gloves kept him comfortable. "Finally got our planes up this morning. Can't wait to hear their report."

"It's about time. I was beginning to wonder why you Yanks were here." The twinkle in Lt. Clive Sinclair's light blue eyes showed he was teasing. Sinclair belonged to the team of Royal Navy observers who were sailing with the *Bogue* on her first cruise to advise on British convoy procedures and communications.

Sinclair had a valid point. The *Bogue* and her escorting destroyers USS *Belknap* and USS *George E. Badger* had sailed from Argentia, Newfoundland, on March 5 to join Convoy HX-228, but high seas and bad weather had limited flight operations to only two days so far. If the carrier didn't provide air cover, she was no use to the convoy.

On the sponson gun platform that jutted out from the port side across from the bridge, Dan stood on tiptoes to see over the flight deck. He felt like a small boy peeking up at the dinner table. "This ship is just here for decoration."

Sinclair laughed. "A rather frightful decoration, if you ask me."

"True." Despite the rough gray seas and the serious threat of U-boats, his mind flew back to Boston, to Tess longing to be seen as useful and not just decorative. *"Don't ever tell me I'm beautiful. Don't ever buy me pretty things. Tell me I have a purpose. Buy me useful things."* She'd said those words in anger, but now he remembered them fondly. She'd more than proven herself.

He could still see her seated at his desk, revising his letter to Captain Short. Her pretty handwriting with its generous loops complemented his angular, utilitarian script. Dan had saved that rough draft.

Love was turning him into a sentimental fool.

Even worse, he didn't half mind it.

Although he couldn't deny his feelings for Tess, he didn't dare admit them, not with both careers at stake. Lord willing, this assignment on the *Bogue* would lead to a transfer.

"The torpedo bombers ought to land soon." Sinclair scanned the sky with his binoculars.

Dan trained his binoculars to the south. The *Bogue* had dropped out of her protected position in the center of the convoy to retrieve her aircraft. "There. I see a TBF."

"I'm sure you chaps hope to sight a sub, but I doubt the merchant marines share that sentiment." Farther east, Convoy SC-121 had been ravaged by a wolf pack of U-boats over the last few days. It wouldn't be long until they turned their periscopes to the next convoy in line.

The Avenger circled the *Bogue,* then came in for the landing approach, wheels down. The landing signal officer stood at the stern, far to port, waving his flags to direct the torpedo bomber. A dangerous job. On the Chesapeake in February, the *Bogue*'s original LSO had been struck by the wheel of a landing aircraft and killed.

Dan didn't envy the pilot his job. Landing a plane seemed tricky enough, but on a short and narrow flight deck, pitching and rolling on the North Atlantic? It required sheer bravado.

The TBF came in lower and lower, right over the stern, and the tail hook snagged one of the nine arresting wires. The flight deck gang rushed to the plane and helped her taxi toward the forward elevator in front of Dan. The pilot, radioman, and gunner hopped out.

The pilot ran toward the bridge, making sharp gestures toward the sea and toward his plane.

"I wonder what happened." Dan climbed the short ladder to the flight deck.

Sinclair followed. "The old boy doesn't look happy."

The two men jogged over to the TBF. The pilot strode back to his plane, followed by Commander Monroe, the air officer.

The pilot squatted under his plane and pointed at the bomb bay. "The bomb rack failed to release."

"Let's go down to the ready room," Commander Monroe said. "We need to clear the deck so the other planes can land. And we need to debrief you, learn everything we can about that U-boat."

"U-boat?" A chilly wind tugged at Dan's mackinaw.

"Mr. Avery, this is Ensign Alexander McAuslan, the first pilot of our squadron to sight a sub."

Dan shook the man's hand, questions brimming in his throat, but he'd wait so he could record every detail.

Down in the ready room, Dan sat around a table with McAuslan's crew, Sinclair, Monroe, and Lt. Cdr. William Drane, the squadron commander.

The senior officers asked questions, and the story poured out. Only ten miles away, McAuslan had sighted a surfaced U-boat. He dove at 180 knots and pressed the bomb release button when he was fifty feet above the sub, a perfect approach. But the depth bombs didn't release. McAuslan yanked back the stick and swung around for another run. By then the U-boat was diving. Once again, the bombs didn't release.

As Dan took down his report, he heard the pilot's frustration. Not only did he want a kill to his credit — who wouldn't? — but that U-boat remained free to summon his friends and attack the convoy.

Protocol demanded radio silence, so McAuslan couldn't call in help. Low on gas, he'd flown to the nearest destroyer and dropped a message to the deck. But valuable time was wasted.

Dan stared at his neatly written report. What a shame. A sighting, a determined pilot, a flawless approach, and a well-executed follow-up run. All foiled by a mechanical glitch.

After he finished his paperwork and ate his lunch, he headed to the open bridge to find out the latest news. An icy wind whipped around the men and equipment.

Sinclair greeted him. "The destroyer didn't find a trace of that U-boat. Neither did the other aircraft."

Dan shook his head and glanced around from his high vantage point, his knees bent to absorb the twenty-degree roll of the ship. "Now we're back in the center of the convoy and can't launch more planes."

Captain Short hung up the telephone-like Talk Between Ships communication system and addressed the senior officers on the bridge. "Our destroyers tried to refuel from the escort tanker again and failed."

Dan winced. The *Belknap* and the *George E. Badger* were old World War I–era destroyers, considered "short-legged." They couldn't make it to Britain without refueling.

The captain glanced at his watch. "We have to turn back."

In the gray mist, sixty cargo ships braved the seas, bearing explosives and oil, grain and sugar, all desperately needed in the United Kingdom. The ships also bore hundreds of merchant marines and passengers.

"We can't turn back now," Dan muttered

to Sinclair.

"You don't have a choice." The British officer leaned his elbows on the railing. "A dreadful shame. The battle is heating up, and we're blind to the enemy's activity again."

Neither Dan nor Sinclair were privy to the classified details, but the Allies had lost a vital source of intelligence. The *Bogue* was needed at sea, but she needed her destroyers for protection. And if her destroyers ran out of fuel . . . "You're right. We don't have a choice."

Sinclair twisted to face Dan. "This wasn't a very fruitful cruise for you, was it?"

"No." Only six days at sea, five days with the convoy, two days with flight operations, and one U-boat sighting and attack — which failed.

Hardly enough to justify Dan's presence. When they returned to Argentia, would Commander Lewis recall him to Boston? If he did, chances were he'd never approve similar duties in the future. Then how could Dan prove himself and obtain a transfer?

The last few days at sea had felt right — the soothing pitch and roll of the ship, the invigorating brace of air, the camaraderie of a crew on duty. Even though Dan was working, he felt more rested than in his office with Randolph's nitpicking and busywork.

The icy air tasted of salt and fuel oil and purpose. Dan closed his eyes. *Lord, help me get this transfer. I need to be here. It — it's like a Sabbath.*

Admiral Howard had taught him much about hard work and strong character and the Navy way, and Dan would always be grateful to him. But in his death, the admiral taught lessons he never intended — the importance of rest and the emptiness of being alone.

Dan leaned on the railing beside Sinclair. He was already applying the first lesson. God had commanded people to rest for their own good, a command born out of mercy and kindness, out of a knowledge of human frailty.

But companionship? The desire wrestled with his ambition. Could he have the career he wanted with a woman at his side? If so, what about Tess?

Dan thumped his hand on the railing. What about her? She thought of him as an annoying big brother. A grumble-bee.

And grumble-bees flew alone.

28

Boston
Tuesday, March 16, 1943

"We missed you last week." Agent Sheffield motioned for Tess to take a seat in front of his desk. "I hope you're feeling better."

"I am, sir. Thank you. Just a touch of bronchitis." The huskiness in her voice proved it. The bronchitis provided a convenient excuse to skip the French meeting the day after she'd been followed. It had taken a week to recover her courage.

"How was last night's meeting?" The agent extended his hand for her written report.

"First, I have to tell you I was followed recently." She related her story.

With each sentence, the agent's jaw jutted out further and further. "Don't do that again."

"Follow Yvette?"

"Follow anyone. You aren't trained, and

this is what happens. I only asked you to attend meetings and bring me reports. Even that is a risk. When you play sleuth, you endanger the entire investigation."

Tess's chin threatened to quiver, but she didn't let it. "And the man who followed me?"

Agent Sheffield pulled a pack of cigarettes from the pocket of his rumpled gray suit. "The description is too vague. Large man in his thirties, dark hair. It could even be Hayes here."

"Oh, it wasn't." She shot Agent Hayes a reassuring smile, but then her cheeks warmed. She sounded silly. "Of course not."

Agent Sheffield busied himself with lighter and cigarette. He probably wished he was working with Mary again instead of babbling Tess.

"Here's my report." She slid it across the desk.

His face brightened, and he read it. "Attendance has fallen."

"The bomb scared a lot of people away."

He nodded and read some more. "So Pierre Guillory wants the group to recruit spies for the Office of Strategic Services? They can handle their own recruitment."

"He made a good point. I'm sure the OSS could use people who speak fluent French and know French ways." Madame Robillard had protested about jumping from airplanes. The thought of the tiny plump baker in a parachute brought up a chuckle, but Tess turned it into a mild cough.

"I see Jean-Auguste Fournier brought up his usual hogwash about Allied spies and the Resistance being bad for France, stirring up trouble and riling up the populace."

"Yes. Madame Robillard agrees because she's worried about Nazi reprisals on civilians. Namely, her sons. Solange parrots everything Madame and Jean-Auguste say."

"No one speaks up for the Resistance anymore except Mr. Guillory?"

"That's right. Everyone writes him off as a hothead, but he's the only one who speaks sense. The Resistance is vital." Each act of sabotage in a factory slowed production of weapons for the Nazis. And when the people were riled up, the Germans diverted troops from the front lines to keep them in check. But the Resistance required outside help — help provided by Allied agents.

Sheffield set down the report and tapped ashes into the ashtray. "And Professor Arnaud?"

Tess sighed. "He used to sound patriotic, but now he wants everyone to stop bickering and discuss food and family and culture."

"Of course he does. Anything else I might be interested in?"

"Not that I can think of."

"All right. We'll see you next week." He stood to shake her hand. "Remember what I said — no searches, no following, no seeking clues. Attend the meetings and bring me reports. Understood?"

"Yes, sir." She raised a polite smile, but it wobbled. How much good did her reports do anyway?

In the reception area, Tess retrieved her raincoat and attached the havelock to the back of her cover. The flap protected her hair and kept rain from trickling down her collar, but it also made her look like a member of the French Foreign Legion.

Tess took the elevator down to ground level and exited the granite-block office building with its Art Deco bronze-and-glass doors. Darkness and rain and the dim-out darkened Post Office Square, and Tess turned right on Congress Street toward the subway station.

She ducked under the eaves at the corner newsstand for a reprieve from the rain.

The evening headlines turned her stomach. Censorship kept most of the details off the front pages, but the message was clear. The Allies were taking a beating on the high seas. The U-boats had sunk dozens of merchant ships in the past few weeks.

How about the escort ships?

How about Lt. Daniel Avery?

No. Tess marched forward through the rain. He needed to be at sea. Would she love him as much if he were the kind of man who chose the safe route over the good route? No, she wouldn't.

Regardless, she missed him. *Oh, Lord, if only he could return my love.*

Tess crossed the street. That seemed like a selfish prayer, and yet it wasn't. In the past, she'd wanted men's affections so they'd give her attention and adoration. But not with Dan.

She wanted to *give* him love. She wanted to walk by his side. She wanted to encourage him, make him smile and laugh, help him play and relax, so he could be an even better officer. She wanted to help him be both the admiral and the little boy.

Tess wiped some raindrops off her face. If she had to love him as a friend rather than as a girlfriend, well then, that's what she'd do.

Turning onto State Street, she twisted her head to shield her face from the rain. The

Old State House rose before her in its solid colonial brick, a regal clock hanging above the balcony where the Declaration of Independence was first read to the people of Boston.

The entrance to the State Street Station lay tucked inside the historic building without a sign to direct newcomers. Thank goodness Mary had warned her the first time she came downtown, or Tess would still be wandering the streets.

She raised her hand to push open the door, but a gentleman jogged up ahead of her and opened it for her.

"Fancy meeting you here, Mademoiselle Beaumont." It was Jean-Auguste.

She smiled, but narrowed her eyes. "Yes, fancy that." Had he been following her? Ridiculous. He came from the west, while she came from the east. The incident at North Station had spooked her.

Jean-Auguste closed his umbrella and followed her into the building. He was handsome in a waifish way that didn't appeal to Tess. "It was good to see you at the meeting yesterday. Yvette said you were sick. I'm glad you're better now."

"Thank you." She headed to the ticket booth.

"I know you and Yvette are friends, but I

am glad you are no longer her roommate. It isn't safe."

Tess paid her fare, her chest tight. "If she hasn't been arrested by now, I doubt she's a suspect."

"I hope you are right. I wasn't in town that night, so I only know what Solange and Madame Robillard saw."

They'd seen a woman in a red beret on a bicycle, but did that woman throw the bomb? And was that woman Yvette? Tess gave Jean-Auguste a good-bye nod.

"You must be busy with your work. I admire you WAVES." He purchased his ticket. "What exactly do you do?"

Apparently she had a travel companion. "I'm in charge of war bond sales at the Navy Yard, plus I supervise enlisted WAVES in other departments."

"Ah, yes. Professor Arnaud mentioned seeing you at MIT. I didn't know the WAVES worked there too." Jean-Auguste motioned for her to lead the way down to the platforms.

Tess frowned and descended the stairs, but that information wasn't classified. "We're everywhere."

"Professor Arnaud's work sounds fascinating, all that research into . . . oh, what's it called again? I'm afraid I was miserable at

295

science."

Time to change the topic. "So was I. That's why I went into business." She strolled onto the platform and found a place to wait for the train.

"Between you and me . . ." Jean-Auguste stepped closer. "Do you ever worry about Professor Arnaud?"

"Worry?"

"He is doing research — military research, am I right?"

Tess didn't like how he was fishing for information. "I'm not familiar with his work."

He shrugged his slight shoulders. "Well, I'm sure he has access to military secrets — new weapons and such. But he also has a history of sneaking letters into Nazi-occupied territory."

"I'm sure a man as intelligent as the professor knows how to keep secrets."

He rubbed his jaw. "I hope so. He could damage the Allied cause. You mustn't forget about the spy in our midst. If the professor made even the tiniest slip . . ."

Tess's stomach felt sour. Even worse — what if the professor were the spy? He worked at the Rad Lab where vital radar research was conducted. Wouldn't the Nazis love to know about Allied technology?

"Well, it was a pleasure as always." Jean-Auguste tipped his hat. "My train is on the other platform. *Bonsoir.*"

"*Bonsoir.*" Tess stepped back as her train pulled up. Tonight she'd write up that conversation for Agent Sheffield.

Maybe her reports helped and maybe they didn't, but she'd do her duty.

29

East of Newfoundland
Tuesday, March 23, 1943

The frustration in the *Bogue*'s wardroom was as thick as the grits in Dan's bowl and as bitter as the coffee.

"I hope we get our planes aloft today." Clive Sinclair took a bite of bacon. "Our second cruise simply must be better than our first."

Dan concealed his smile by taking a mouthful of grits, not the favorite of an Ohio boy, but warm and filling. "You said *our,* not *your.*"

"I'll gladly become a Yankee if it means bacon and . . ." He gestured to his plate.

"Pancakes, griddlecakes, flapjacks, hotcakes — take your pick." Dan scooped out a grapefruit section. "The United States Navy believes in feeding sailors well."

"If only the Royal Navy followed suit."

Dan nodded. "The seas seem smoother

this morning. Perhaps we'll be able to launch." The *Bogue* and her destroyers had left Argentia, Newfoundland, on March 20 to join Convoy SC-123, but foul weather had confined the planes to the hangar deck. Commander Lewis had allowed Dan another cruise, since the first hadn't been a fair test, but Dan doubted he'd be granted a third chance.

Sinclair glanced around the wardroom and sipped his coffee. "These men want to fight."

"So do I. It's time we strike back." The U-boats had inflicted horrific losses in the past few weeks. Convoy HX-228 alone had lost four cargo ships and a destroyer, with the attack starting only hours after the *Bogue* group had detached. At least the escorts had sunk two U-boats in return. But could the losses have been avoided if the *Bogue* group had remained with the convoy? Could they have added to the count of sunken subs?

Dan mopped up the last of his maple syrup with his final bite of pancake. Around the tables in the wardroom, officers were beginning to rise. Dan checked his watch — 0745. "I'd better get going."

"You're meeting with the captain at 0800, are you not? Might I make a suggestion?"

Sinclair held up his bowl of grits with a pathetic expression. "Please, sir? Might I have another bowl of sea duty?"

Dan chuckled. Mimicking Oliver Twist wouldn't impress the CO. "I'll take that into consideration." He went his way up to the captain's office.

Begging for a transfer would backfire, of course. But silence wouldn't advance him to his goal either. *Lord, please give me a natural opportunity to state my case.*

In the captain's office, Dan saluted Capt. Giles Short and sat in a chair at the end of the captain's desk.

"We hope to get some findings for you today." Captain Short flipped through papers. "The aerologist forecasts favorable weather, although not ideal for flight operations."

"The radar plot officer said we had some radar contacts before dawn — icebergs?"

"Icebergs." The captain cracked his wide smile. "We don't expect to sight any U-boats until we reach the 'air gap' between Greenland and Iceland. That's where the wolf packs are."

As Dan had suspected — the Allies had regained their main source of intelligence. "With more B-24s based in Newfoundland, the air gap will shrink, and auxiliary carriers will eliminate it."

Captain Short cocked his head to one side. "In time. The *Bogue* is still the only auxiliary carrier in the northern hemisphere."

"At least we're going in the right direction. I was encouraged by the results of the Atlantic Convoy Conference." The British, Canadians, and Americans had met in Washington in early March and had agreed to more auxiliary carriers and long-range aircraft. They'd also delegated the North Atlantic convoy route to the British and Canadians, with the Americans taking responsibility for convoys across the Central Atlantic. The *Bogue* group remained on loan in the north until the British could send out their escort carriers.

However, Captain Short's time was too valuable to waste on small talk. "Do you have any general observations you'd like me to include in my reports, sir?"

The captain tapped a pen on his desk. "My biggest frustration has been the weather, but we can't do anything about that. If the weather continues to prevent the destroyers from refueling, we'll have to detach from the convoy again."

Dan winced. "I understand, sir. Anything else?"

"In the center of the convoy we don't have the speed and maneuverability we need to launch aircraft, and it takes time to drop out of the convoy for flight operations."

Dan nodded as he wrote. "So we can't launch quickly in an emergency."

"If we had a larger destroyer screen, we could keep station behind the convoy at all times."

"Preferably with longer-legged destroyers — or the new destroyer escorts." Dan posed only a few more questions. Since they hadn't seen action, no observations could be made about weaponry, radar, or air tactics.

"Thank you for your time, sir." Dan stacked his papers and stood. "I'm looking forward to our next meeting."

"So am I." The captain leaned back in his chair. "How's our resident desk jockey holding up at sea?"

Dan's grip tightened on his portfolio. Just the opportunity he'd prayed for. "Actually, sir, I'm in my element. I have salt in my veins."

Heavy eyebrows rose.

"This is my first desk job, sir. And my last, if I have my way. I served on the *Vincennes* for several years, up until February of '42.

302

Engineering, navigation, gunnery — I loved it all."

"The *Vincennes*? I'm sorry."

"Thank you, sir." Dan's voice thickened. Over three hundred of his shipmates had perished in the Battle of Savo Island.

"And you want to return to sea."

"Yes, sir." He tossed up a quick prayer of thanks and another for guidance. "Admiral Howard placed me in ASWU. He thought it would be an excellent step on the way to command."

"Has it been?"

Dan shifted his weight from one leg to the other. "Yes, sir. What I've learned about radar and weapons and tactics is invaluable."

"Admiral Howard said he had plans for you."

"Yes, sir." He'd said that the day he died. "But Commander Lewis doesn't want to spare me."

"The curse of doing a job well." The captain grinned and gave a nod, ending the meeting.

"Thank you, sir. Good day." Dan closed the door behind him, and his mind raced over the conversation. It sounded good. So why did Dan feel depleted?

Later that morning, Dan stood on his usual sponson across from the bridge. Three 20-mm machine gun crews kept him company in the wind and cold.

Ensign Harry Fryatt was coming in for a landing. His was the only Avenger that had launched that morning. The *Bogue* did not make a welcoming runway, pitching and rolling in the rising seas.

The TBF's wings rocked, then leveled, and the plane bumped lower and lower. Just as the tail swung over the flight deck, the *Bogue*'s stern dipped low.

Dan held his breath. The Avenger's tail hook skimmed past the first of the nine arresting wires, then several more. "Come on, Fryatt. Get her down."

The Avenger barreled forward, but the deck plunged away as if the plane were poisoned.

"Come on!" Dan yelled. "Bring her down."

"Lower!" a gunner cried behind him.

Dan clutched the rim of the flight deck, ducking low and peering over the edge. The TBF zipped past the last arresting wires. Only the three net barriers remained.

"Come on, Fryatt!"

The Avenger suddenly dove, aiming for the deck just aft of the barriers. But the *Bogue* pitched upward. The plane's wheels bounced off the deck.

Dan cried out, echoed by crewmen all around him. The TBF soared in an arc before him, up over the barriers, down over the bow. He'd crash into the sea!

The deck gang raced toward the bow, and Dan climbed halfway up the ladder, craning to see.

A tubby gray-and-blue plane lurched into the air. "He made it!"

Cheers erupted, and Dan joined in.

Fryatt's torpedo bomber gained altitude, then circled to port for another landing attempt.

Dan dropped back down to the sponson, his pulse galloping. The gunners grinned and clapped each other on the back. Thank goodness. After all the fruitless patrols, the crew didn't need the tragic loss of a plane and three good men.

The *Bogue* aligned with the wind for Fryatt's next attempt.

Those arresting wires and barriers were meant to save the planes from careening off the deck. Dan had seen the regulation forbidding Navy men from marrying

WAVES as a barrier that protected him from careening into the unknown.

Now the Navy had lowered that barrier. When he'd heard the news after the *Bogue* returned to Argentia after her first cruise, Dan had been stunned, thrilled, terrified.

Elation surged through him once again. He was free — free to soar, free to pursue Tess. Without the Navy's prohibition, Commander Lewis was certain to remove his censure.

Dan had lowered the second barrier on his own. Yes, the wrong woman would hold Dan back, but the right woman would spur him on. Tess Beaumont was the right sort of woman.

Pursuing her seemed like another step toward balancing his life of straight lines and duty.

Dan gripped the ladder rung in his gloved hands. The third barrier remained — Tess. Was he the right man for her? How could someone so full of life fall for a stick-in-the-mud like him?

Would he even know what to do? He hadn't been on a date in a decade, hadn't flirted, hadn't kissed a girl. His natural brusqueness was off-putting enough in everyday dealings with women, but in romance? He was utterly incompetent.

306

Then there was Lt. Cdr. Stanley Randolph. If he knew Dan loved Tess, he could make accusations and have her reprimanded and relieved of duty. Dan knew better than to hand his enemy so lethal a weapon.

He clamped his eyes shut. *Lord, show me what to do.*

Down by the stern, the Avenger came in for another approach. The seas hadn't improved. The *Bogue* continued to pitch. Should Fryatt take the chance?

How could he not? Conditions wouldn't improve, and time was short. If he didn't act, all would be lost.

A chilly breath swirled in Dan's open mouth. Conditions with Tess wouldn't change. Time was short. If he didn't act, all would be lost.

The Avenger dropped lower and lower.

"Come on," Dan muttered. "You can do it, Fryatt."

The wheels inched closer and closer. The stern of the *Bogue* rose to meet the Avenger, as sweet and gentle as a kiss. The tail hook snagged, and the TBF screeched to a halt.

The crew cheered, but Dan laughed out loud, full and hearty. He'd never had a stranger answer to prayer. Or a clearer one.

30

Boston Navy Yard
Saturday, April 10, 1943

At the Boston Navy Yard, Tess held open the door to Building 22 as her friends filed out. "I sure appreciate you ladies giving up your Saturday to help me hang posters."

Lillian eased her way down the steps, then turned and saluted. "Anything to aid the war effort."

"Me too." Mary was especially helpful because she knew which buildings to target. She pointed toward Boston Harbor. "Next down — Building 24 — riggers and the sail loft. Tess, why don't you go there with Nora? Lillian and I will take care of the restaurant in Building 28."

"All right." Tess passed a roll of posters to her friend.

Tess and Nora headed along Dry Dock 1, circling past machinery and workers building two destroyer escorts. Boston Navy Yard was busy with three shifts around the clock, churning out new ships and repairing others.

In Building 24, Tess separated a poster from the roll. "Let's put them here by the entrance."

Nora helped her flatten the first poster on the wall, Norman Rockwell's "Freedom of Worship."

Tess tore off a piece of tape and anchored the top left corner. She was glad the Second War Loan Drive was using Rockwell's "Four Freedoms" paintings. They portrayed exactly what the Allies were fighting for.

Another piece of tape on the top right. People of many faiths, bowed in prayer, free to worship as they chose.

A smile worked at Tess's lips. The poster gave her the perfect opening. "We've missed you at church lately. Will you come with us tomorrow?"

Nora pressed the bottom corner of the poster to the wall. "I'd like to visit another church this week."

Since Nora had praised Dr. Ockenga's preaching, her decision probably had nothing to do with the church itself. "Because of Bill?"

Nora glanced at her, brown eyes wide. "No, of course not. I just . . ."

Tess gave her a skeptical smile.

"All right." Nora heaved a sigh. "Yes, I'm avoiding him. I'm afraid he'll ask me out, but I don't want to hurt him."

"Hurt him? How would you hurt him?"

Nora raised her eyebrows as if shocked by Tess's ignorance. "By saying no."

"I thought you liked him too."

"I do. He seems very nice, but . . ." She shook her head. "But no."

Tess unrolled the next poster, "Freedom from Fear." How appropriate. "Do you remember when we practiced first aid together?"

Nora squinted at the poster of a mother and father tucking their children in to bed. "What does that have to do —"

"I was trying to make friends, and you told me to stop pretending to be nice. You said you wouldn't give me a chance to hurt you."

"I'm sorry. I —"

"Understood and forgiven." Tess smoothed the poster into position. "But I think you're doing the same thing with Bill."

Nora braced the poster in silence, and Tess let her think while she secured the corners.

"I — I don't know what to make of him." Nora's voice wavered. "Men never pay me any attention."

When they'd met, Nora's dowdy clothing and hairstyle made Tess think she was ten years older, but now a cute uniform and haircut made her shine. "Bill's paying attention."

Nora's forehead wrinkled.

Tess nudged her. "And he doesn't need help with his math homework."

A shaky laugh escaped. "I suppose not."

"You're afraid." She patted the poster. "But you can't live that way."

"Oh dear." Nora leaned her forehead against the wall. "You don't understand. I've never been on a date. I wouldn't know how to behave."

Tess swallowed her surprise, then squeezed her friend's shoulder. "Maybe you should tell Bill a bit of what you told me. Be honest and open. It's only fair."

Nora straightened to standing. "I'll think about it. Next poster?"

As she unfurled the poster, Tess had to laugh. "Freedom of Speech." A man stood in a town hall meeting, boldly speaking his mind. "A message from above?"

"Don't read too much into it." But Nora smiled again.

She'd run out of posters, so they went outside, where Mary and Lillian waited for them.

Lillian grinned. "We hung 'Freedom from Want' inside the cafeteria."

Tess laughed. The grandma serving a huge turkey to her family should remind the workers of how America was blessed with food, even with the new rationing of meat, oils, and canned goods.

A worker jostled by the ladies, his hand cupped to his mouth. "Hey, Wally! You oughta see. Big old carrier pulling in to the South Annex. Don't see many of those around here."

Tess's heart flipped. "A carrier?"

"I wonder if it's Dan's." Lillian's face brightened, and she headed down the pier. "Let's get a better look."

"I doubt it. The *Bogue* is operating out of Newfoundland, from what I understand, and her home port is down at Norfolk." But Tess followed her friends to the end of the pier.

She shielded her eyes from the bright afternoon sunshine. The clear sky allowed her to see past downtown to the Navy Yard's South Boston Annex.

"The south jetty is big enough for a carrier," Mary said. "Oh, I wish it were Jim's ship, but he's on the other side of the world."

Lillian pointed. "I see it."

312

Tess did too, a tiny gray silhouette against the dark landscape, long and flat and too high to be a barge. Not many carriers sailed the Atlantic, but the chances of it being the *Bogue* . . .?

"I hope it's Dan's ship," Lillian said.

"Me too." Tess's voice came out ragged with longing.

Mary slapped her hand over her mouth, but a giggle bubbled out. Nora joined in the laughter.

Lillian laughed too. "So it's true? I wondered."

"She hides it well." Mary winked. "Most of the time."

Tess groaned, her cheeks aflame. "Oh no. Please don't say anything. He mustn't know."

Nora planted her hands on her hips. "Weren't you the one telling me to be open and honest?"

"This is different." Since all the posters had been hung, Tess led the way back to the war bond office. "Lillian, you know your brother. You called him a ship-monk. He's vowed never to marry, never to let a woman drag him down. Mary, you've heard him too, I know it."

"I have." But Mary was smiling.

Tess watched her footing as she crossed

the tracks for the giant cranes. "I can't imagine Dan Avery going against his convictions. He's as immovable as the sea he loves."

"Immovable?" Lillian giggled. "The sea? Have you ever heard of the tides?"

"True, and have you noticed?" Mary nudged Lillian. "Dan never leaves her side."

"I did. I've never seen him like this."

Tess stopped and held up her hands like a policeman. "Enough! You're imagining things. We're just friends, colleagues. You need to keep your mouths shut. No winks, no nudges, no teasing glances. Please? It's very important."

Mary inclined her head and studied Tess. "It's not like you to linger in unrequited love."

"I know." She continued on the way, passing the lawn where she'd hold the war bond rally on Monday. The workers had set up a stage, and Tess planned to decorate it tomorrow after church.

"So why —"

"This is where I'm supposed to be," Tess said. "It — it humbles me. Mary, you know what I was like, always looking for adoration."

"I wouldn't say that."

Tess gave her a fond smile. "You're too

good a friend. But it's true. I liked Hugh because he adored me. I liked Clifford, that scoundrel, because he fawned over me. That isn't love. It's selfishness."

"Don't talk that way." Mary's voice was too soothing.

She shook it off. "Dan only wants my friendship. And that's all right. If I love him, I'll want what's best for him. And he believes remaining a bachelor is best. How can I push myself on him? That wouldn't be love. So I need to love him in other ways, by encouraging him and being a friend."

"Oh, sweetie —"

"Don't feel sorry for me." Tess swung a searing gaze at her three friends. "I'm content. This is good for me. Now do you understand why I have to hide my feelings?"

Nora nodded. "I do."

"I suppose," Mary said. "But I still think —"

"No. Not one more word about it." Tess paused outside the war bond office. "Such lovely weather we're having, isn't it?"

Her friends laughed at the change in subject. After all, spring warmth hadn't arrived with the sunshine.

"So what shall we do?" Mary asked. "We have the rest of the afternoon free."

Tess didn't, but she refused to be a killjoy.

Nora shielded her eyes and gazed up Breed's Hill. "Someday I'd like to climb the Bunker Hill Monument."

"I'll warn you — there are 294 steps," Mary said.

"If I can do it, the rest of you can." Lillian inched out her prosthetic foot.

Nora's eyes brightened. "How about right now?"

"Oh yes, please go," Tess said. "I have some more work today with the War Loan Drive starting Monday, but I've already climbed the monument. Here, Mary, I'll take your box back to the apartment. I need a break." She silenced protests with grins and took Mary's box, filled with hammers and nails and rolls of tape.

"You won't need a key," Mary said. "Yvette can let you in."

"Didn't she go away this weekend?"

"No." Mary's mouth puckered. "It was the oddest thing. She said they had the weekend off."

"Off? You take the weekend off from work, not from a romantic getaway."

"I teased her about the same thing, but she said she has problems with English idioms."

"I suppose so." But not like that.

They passed through the gate and climbed

Tremont Street. Monument Square opened before them with its tall granite obelisk that memorialized the men who'd died for freedom.

Tess waved good-bye to her friends and carried the box down Monument Avenue. Idioms or no idioms, if Agent Sheffield said Yvette was clean, she was clean. Tess had to resist the urge to investigate. She'd promised the FBI.

She climbed the steps to her old apartment and raised her fist to knock.

A loud thump. A grunt.

Tess sucked in her breath and reached for the doorknob.

"That is right, my love," Henri said, his voice muffled by the door. "But next time grab the knife first."

Tess clapped her hand over her mouth to stifle her gasp. What on earth?

"All right. Let me try again," Yvette said.

Eavesdropping wasn't the same as following, so Tess edged closer, her ear turned to the door.

"Remember, just as we learned," Henri said. "I grab you around the shoulders, pinning your arms, knife ready to slit your pretty throat, and you —"

A thud, a loud masculine grunt, then laughter. "Yes, that's exactly what you do.

Very good."

Oh goodness. What were they doing? Tess's hand pressed hard over her mouth.

"Your turn, my love," Yvette said. "See if you can do as well as I did."

"I always do."

"Good. This is . . . this is important. We may need to use this."

"We will," Henri said. "And soon."

"June. We're leaving June 1, thank goodness. I can't stand it here any longer. I can't."

"Remember. Don't tell anyone, even Mary and Lillian."

Their voices lowered, and Tess's pulse hammered in her ears, drowning all sound. They'd have to use skills with a knife? And soon? They were leaving town and couldn't tell anyone? Why not?

The possibilities slammed around in her skull, but only one rang true.

They were spies. But for whom? Maybe they were training with the OSS. Maybe that's why they went away every weekend and Yvette always came home exhausted. The so-called trips to Cape Cod were a ruse.

Tess set the box outside the door and padded down the stairs. *Oh, please, Lord. Let it be true.*

Because she couldn't bear the thought
that they were Nazis.

31

Boston
Sunday, April 11, 1943

Dan paced the sidewalk in front of Park Street Church, trying not to stare at the subway station entrance.

"I'm surprised you came today." Bill Bentley leaned against the wrought-iron fence by the church's front steps. "I'd think you'd be at the office. You should see the pile of work Randolph dumped on your desk. He refuses to let me do it. Insists it has to be you."

A muscle tightened in Dan's neck, and he strode the other way. "Of course. Then the work is late, and who looks bad? Me."

"Yet you're here."

"I need to be at church. I need a day off." Even if he hadn't wanted to see Tess so badly, he'd still refuse to work.

The sidewalk was filling with churchgoers, and Bill craned his neck toward the subway entrance.

So Dan wasn't the only one waiting for a lady. "Have you asked Nora out yet?"

Bill spun to him, light blue eyes wide. Then his face clouded over. "Never had a chance. She hasn't returned my calls, and she hasn't come to church since the Navy changed the rules."

Dan winced. "Sorry."

"Don't be. I'm used to it." Bill glanced away, cool and indifferent. Then he stilled, staring across the street. "I guess she decided to reject me in person."

Nora emerged from the subway entrance, wearing her navy-blue overcoat and cover. And so did Tess, a beam of sunshine aimed Dan's way.

His throat clamped shut. Time for the first step in his pursuit — to show her how happy he was to see her and to gauge her reaction.

He pulled in a breath, strode down the sidewalk, and released the muscles that restrained his smile.

Then she saw him. She paused, but he didn't and he let that smile crack his stubborn cheeks.

Tess dashed to him, grinning, curls bouncing. "Dan! You're here!"

"Hello, Tess." For one wonderful moment,

he thought she'd hug him, and he tried to reach for her, but his hands tangled in his pockets.

A flicker of alarm, and she stopped short. Then her grin returned, flooding her face with light. "We thought we saw your ship yesterday. Lillian thought it was yours, but I didn't think it was possible. But it is. And you — you're smiling?"

He hadn't stopped. "I'm glad to be here. It's good to see you."

She studied his face with curiosity and wonder. "Well, I'll be. Time at sea was good for you."

"It was." But not as good as seeing her again.

"I don't understand. Why is the *Bogue* in Boston?"

His mouth returned to normal. "Our catapult's damaged. We were supposed to go to Philadelphia for repairs, but they rerouted us here." A sweet gift from the Lord.

"Wonderful. How long are you here?"

"That's up to Commander Lewis. The repairs will take one week, maybe two, but the commander decides if I'll be aboard."

"Dan!" Lillian hurtled to him and flung her arms around his waist.

"Hi there, Lilliput." He worked his hands

free and hugged her back. He'd rather have Tess in his arms, but at least he'd show he was capable of some affection.

For good measure, he hugged his sister-in-law too. "Hi, Mary."

"Welcome back to shore." Arch shook his hand. "I have to say I'm envious. I've been following the battle at sea in the papers. You must have stories to tell."

"Not as many as I'd like."

"Oh?" Tess asked.

His gaze swung past Bill, Arch, Lillian, Mary, Nora, and straight to Tess. "We escorted two convoys. Both times the weather didn't allow the destroyers to refuel. Both times we had to detach from the convoy prematurely. Both times the convoys were attacked only hours after we detached."

"Oh dear."

"We only sighted one U-boat, but the attack failed."

"Then the auxiliary carriers did what you thought they would." Intelligence sparked in Tess's golden-green eyes. "While you were there, you kept the subs at bay."

Dan dipped his head to one side. "Very likely, but we were just entering their hunting grounds. We don't have enough data to draw that conclusion yet."

"Well, I'm convinced," Arch said. "Whenever an aircraft is overhead, subs dive, and a submerged U-boat is too slow to keep up with a convoy. We need more of those jeep carriers."

"We're building them as fast as we can," Mary said with a smile.

Dan's smile worked its way up again. What fascinating times when men and women could converse together about naval tactics and shipbuilding.

"Since everyone's here . . . I have an announcement." Lillian's eyes glowed in a new way. She glanced at Arch — who shared the same glow — and she pulled off her left glove.

All the women gasped and squealed.

Another engagement? Dan blinked, but diamonds continued to glitter on his sister's ring finger.

"He asked me last night." Lillian leaned closer to her fiancé.

Arch slipped his arm around her waist. "She agreed to be my wife. For richer or poorer."

With the Vandenberg wealth, "poorer" wouldn't be a problem, but the couple's chuckles suggested a private joke.

"I wish Jim could be here." Mary dabbed at her eyes with a handkerchief. "His sister and his best friend. He'll be so happy. What am I saying? *I'm* so happy." She embraced Lillian and then Arch.

Congratulations and hugs and solid handshakes flew around. Dan sent a grin Tess's way, and she responded with a gleeful smile and clap and shoulder lift. Maybe the news would put her in a romantic mood.

First it was time for church.

Dan was careful to stay by Tess's side as they entered the sanctuary, careful to sit beside her, to share a hymnal with her, and to let his shoulder rest against hers from time to time.

She didn't pull away.

In fact, for the closing hymn, she leaned into him, pointed to the title, and covered a chuckle with her fingertips.

The hymn, "Jesus, Savior, Pilot Me," had a nautical theme appropriate for the sailors, merchant marines, and Navy families in the pews. Dan joined in heartily.

Jesus, Savior, pilot me over life's
    tempestuous sea:
Unknown waves before me roll, hiding
    rocks and treach'rous shoal;
Chart and compass come from Thee —
    Jesus, Savior, pilot me!

As a mother stills her child, Thou canst
hush the ocean wild;
Boist'rous waves obey Thy will when Thou
say'st to them, "Be still!"
Wondrous Sov'reign of the sea, Jesus,
Savior, pilot me!

Unknown waves did indeed roll before
him. *Yes, Lord, pilot me. Show me the bearing. Tell me when to speed up and when to stop my engines. Be my only compass.*

After the benediction, the group filed out
of the pews, down the stairs, and onto the
sidewalk. Dan swept his arm in a grand
gesture. "The city awaits. What fun excursion shall we have today?"

Lillian laughed. "I never thought I'd hear
you talk like that."

"It's tradition, isn't it?"

"It's also tradition for you to sneak away
to your office."

"Not anymore. It's a day of rest, and I
refuse to work. So what's the plan?"

Everyone turned to Tess.

Her eyes danced between mischief and
guilt. "I'm setting up the stage for tomorrow's War Loan Drive rally at the Navy
Yard."

Dan gave her a teasing look. "Sounds like
work to me."

"You don't have to come, but I intend to make it a party. We'll have sandwiches and potato salad at Mary and Lillian's place first."

"Very well." Dan directed his admiral's gaze around the group. "Who's on board?"

"I am."

"I don't have a choice."

Bill sent a challenging look to Nora. They hadn't spoken to each other yet. "I'm in."

Nora gazed at her shoes. "Me too."

Dan snapped his best salute to Tess. "Your crew reports for duty, Captain."

"Captain? Ooh, I like that."

"I thought I was the ambitious one in this crowd." He motioned for her to take the lead, and he fell in by her side.

"Mr. Bentley?" Nora's voice cracked. "Bill? May I have a word with you?"

A pause, and Dan resisted the urge to look behind him. "Yes," Bill said.

Tess wore a small, secretive smile. Maybe Bill wouldn't have his heart broken today. Even if he did, at least Nora had the guts to speak her mind.

They trotted down the stairs to the subway, and Dan paid the fare for the group. Down more stairs and tunnels, and they boarded the train bound for North Station.

Dan swung in to the seat beside Tess. She

327

gave him an unusually nervous smile for her, and Dan had to remind himself to smile back. It would be hard to break this habit.

As the train pulled away from the platform, Tess's gaze roamed his face. "I've never seen you smile so much."

"Time at sea makes you think, helps you see clearly."

"What did you think about, Dan Avery?"

She didn't want to know. Not yet. Probably not ever. But she did want to know why he was smiling. "When I was a boy, helping my family, I needed to be taken seriously. So I acted serious. Playing, laughing, smiling — those were for boys. And I was a man."

"And now?"

"Now I actually am a man. People take me seriously. I decided I can smile a little." He put on a mock stern face. "Not a lot, mind you. And never on duty."

"Of course not." She looked at him from under the bill of her cover. "No merriness on duty, Mr. Avery."

"No danger of that when Mr. Randolph's around. But —" He raised one finger. "It's the Sabbath, and there will be no talk of ASWU."

"What shall we talk about then?"

Dan liked how the train's motion jostled

her shoulder against his. "How was your birthday?"

"My birthday?" Her eyes widened.

"Mary mentioned it in a letter. I'm sorry I missed it. I brought you something." He wrestled a small package out of his coat pocket.

"You didn't have to —"

"You'll understand. Open it."

"All right." Tess unwrapped the brown paper and opened the polished mahogany case. "Oh my. It's a compass."

"I bought it in Annapolis when I was at the Academy."

Her jaw dropped open. "It's yours? I couldn't —"

"Admiral Howard gave me his compass. I want you to have this. I know you'll enjoy it."

She stroked the brass casing. "I will. Thank you. It's beautiful."

He couldn't have asked for a better connection. "I'd prefer to say it's useful. Practical. Has a purpose."

Tess looked him full in the face, her eyes shimmering. "You remember."

How could he forget? Dan tapped the compass. "But you're right. It's also pleasing to the eye. Proof that something can be both beautiful and useful."

He held his gaze firm, praying she'd hear the full meaning of his words, see a hint of how much he admired her and loved her.

Tess returned her attention to the gift, her cheeks pink. "It is."

Dan's bearing was true. He'd continue his pursuit.

32

Tess set her hands on her hips and scrutinized the rough stage. "Let's put bunting along the base on all three sides. We'll hang the banner across the top, with streamers draped in an arc below. The sides — oh, they're ugly — let's cover them with posters. We'll decorate the podium too."

"We have plenty of bunting and streamers." Mary patted one of the boxes. "And I brought hammers and nails and tape."

"Wonderful. Thanks for letting me use your supplies for ship launchings."

Bill Bentley picked up a hammer. "I did roofing work to put myself through college. I don't mind climbing the ladder to hang the banner and streamers. Nora, would you like to help me?"

"Sure."

Tess stifled her smile. After making her friends vow not to tease her, how could she tease them?

"I'll take care of the podium," Mary said. "Arch and Lillian, why don't you work on that side of the stage, and Dan and Tess can do the other."

So innocent, that Mary Avery. And so conniving.

"Let's get to work." Dan grabbed a box and flashed Tess a grin.

Her knees buckled. Thank goodness he walked away so he didn't see her catch her balance on the stage.

It wasn't fair. She'd always considered him arresting, fascinating, and insanely attractive — but when he unleashed that grin? It snatched the breath from her lungs and the sense from her head. How was she supposed to conceal her feelings for him?

At the back left corner of the stage, Dan opened a box of nails. "Why don't you get out the bunting?"

"All right." Her voice squeaked. She'd have to be careful not to make him laugh. She'd probably swoon like some silly B-movie heroine.

A sober conversational topic would help, and she had several to choose from. Tess pulled out a pile of bunting and laid it flat on top of the stage. "Did you hear the verdict in the Cocoanut Grove case? It came in yesterday."

"Mm-hmm. They found the owner guilty, but not the inspector or the contractor."

"Involuntary manslaughter. They think he'll get twelve to fifteen years." Tess held the end in place while Dan tapped a nail through a grommet in the canvas tape. "It doesn't seem like enough. They kept the exits bolted and the windows blocked."

"Four hundred and ninety people died. They're tossing the public a morsel."

Tess blocked the memory of hands groping through the flames, the smell of the smoke and the feel of the heat, and she stretched out the first loop of bunting for Dan.

He set the nail in place and waited for Tess to move her fingers out of the way. "Say, did you ever figure out who that man was —Yvette's date at the Cocoanut Grove?"

Tess smoothed the next section. "No, but I saw him last month. He followed me."

"What?"

She turned him back to his work. As they decorated the stage, Tess told him everything that had happened while he was at sea. Following Yvette and being followed by the mystery man. Agent Sheffield's warning. Yvette and Henri practicing hand-to-hand combat, and their secret plan to leave town in June.

Dan drove a nail into the front corner of the stage. "So, what do you think?"

"You don't want to know."

"I do, or I wouldn't have asked." He pointed the hammer at her. "Since you're being reticent, you must be back to the theory that Yvette is a Nazi spy."

Tess pulled the next batch of bunting from the box. "I prefer to think she's training with the OSS, but that sounds just as outlandish."

"May I add a third theory?"

"Oh, please. I hate the others."

Dan anchored the end of a new string of bunting. "Yvette sounds terrified. She's the one who first suspected a spy in the group, and she was right. Everyone thinks she threw that bomb. Maybe she thinks the spy is out to get her. Maybe she bought the gun to protect herself. Maybe she and Henri are learning to defend themselves — those are defensive moves you described, not offensive. Maybe they're leaving Boston to escape."

Tess smoothed a swag of red, white, and blue. "That makes sense. But we still don't know who the spy is, the bomber. Either Yvette and Henri are guilty — or someone is working very hard to make them look guilty."

Dan slid the box of nails along the stage and selected one. "Who dislikes Yvette?"

Tess lifted a wry smile. "Solange, but only because she's jealous of Yvette. She doesn't have what it takes to be a spy or a bomber."

"All right. But if she hates Yvette, she might be willing to work with the real spy. Who is she closest to?"

"Madame Robillard, but she couldn't be guilty. She's the sweetest woman in the world. She was heartbroken when the contact was arrested and she couldn't get letters to her sons. And she'd never let someone smash the window of her bakery."

"Good point."

Tess held the canvas tape flat. "Then there's Jean-Auguste, Solange's boyfriend. He . . . he fished for information about my work, about Professor Arnaud's work. I didn't tell him a thing, of course."

Dan clutched a nail, and his eyes darkened. "Tell me about him."

"He's a salesman for a bakery equipment company. That's how he met Madame Robillard and got involved with the group." Tess untwisted a wayward swag. "He's been preaching about the dangers of an Allied invasion, how innocent civilians would be killed. He says the Resistance and the SOE and OSS bring danger to France."

"Danger?" Dan straightened, his mouth grim. "Talk like that is the real danger."

"It makes my skin crawl. Someone like that might want to betray a Resistance member."

Dan gazed around, his eyebrows low. "And the bombing. Wouldn't he love to break up a group that helps the Resistance? There's your man."

Black-and-white Dan, with his straight lines and precise corners. How she loved him. "He was in New York the night of the bombing. They checked his alibi."

He jerked his head to one side. "Very well. Who else? Who doesn't like Yvette?"

Tess stretched out another section of bunting. "Pierre Guillory. He's no Nazi, that's for sure. Fiercest patriot in the bunch. He's angry at Yvette and Henri because they don't speak up as much as they used to. He says they switched sides."

"If he's a patriot, he wouldn't betray a contact."

"No, but he's a loudmouth, and he could have accidentally spilled the information. Loose lips sink ships, you know."

"Believe me, I know." The next nail went in with two strong strokes. "If he thinks Yvette and Henri are traitors to the cause, he might want to frame them for the bomb-ing."

"He was inside the bakery, but he could have accomplices."

"We have some excellent suspects. Anyone else?"

Tess prepared the next section. "You won't like this one — Professor Arnaud."

"From the Rad Lab? I thought he was the leader."

"He is. When I started attending, no one spoke more poetically about aiding the Resistance and fighting for France. But then he refused to admit there was a spy, even when Henri proved it. Lately, he just begs everyone not to argue."

Dan's jaw jutted out, and the hammer rang on the nail head. "You're right. I don't like that theory at all."

"Bear with me. Let my imagination play for a moment. Can you do that?"

He gave her an adorable sidelong glance with a touch of amusement. "Only because it's my day off."

"Good boy. Now let me spin my tale. Let's imagine a dastardly Nazi spy infiltrated a classified organization so he could steal Al-lied secrets. Let's say he started a group of French expatriates and talked like de Gaulle himself to earn their trust. Let's say he helped the members pass letters, tucking in his classified papers."

"And the bomb, oh tale-spinner?"

Tess pressed down the next bit of tape. "This odious spy wants to shatter Allied morale. So he terrorizes his own group with a bombing and silences the most loyal voices. Voila! A toothless wine-and-cheese club."

Dan's hammer strokes were slow and methodical, as if he were processing her words.

"Should I sell it to Hollywood?" She put extra perkiness into her voice.

He gave her his old not-quite-a-smile. "Your imagination is . . . colorful."

"Thank you. I think. If it makes you feel better, I didn't tell that one to the FBI. Only the cold, hard facts for Agent Sheffield." They'd reached the front right corner, where Lillian and Arch had stopped in order to hang posters. "I don't know what good I do for the FBI. I just report what people say and keep my mouth shut."

"Good." Dan drove in the final nail. "That's your job, not to investigate, and not to solve the case."

She fluffed out a red, white, and blue arc. "I know, but I wish I could have some thrilling insight that breaks the case."

"Tess . . ." His voice rolled in a gentle but firm way that made her heart vibrate. "Be careful. You're doing the right thing, but there are some shady characters in that group. Please be careful."

"I will." Her voice caught.

That intense gaze of his delved inside. Not so long ago, he'd looked right through her. Then he'd looked inside and seen and judged. But now there was a softness in the corners of his eyes, as if he were looking inside and appreciating her, all of her, mind and character and personality.

Appreciation was far better than adoration, a heady feeling.

"Are you done with that box?"

Tess startled and spun around.

Bill pointed at an empty box. "Are you done?"

"Yes. Yes, we are."

"I'll take it back to storage." He slid it off the stage and headed toward the storeroom with Nora.

"Well," Dan said. "It looks like Bill and Nora called a truce."

Tess smiled as they walked away. "Oh, it's more than that."

"I don't know. They're barely speaking."

"Trust me. Women know these things. See how he looks at her? It's darling."

"Is that so?" The humor in his voice turned her to face him.

His smile. Not the full knee-buckling grin, but a warm and personal smile she'd never seen before and prayed she'd see again. Completely and utterly darling.

"Well?" he asked, that smile deepening.

She pulled herself together and tried to remember his question. "Yes, it's so."

Dan leaned closer, one eyebrow raised. "But is she looking at him the same way?"

Was he talking about Nora . . . or Tess? How could she think straight with his hazel eyes so close, the smell of his aftershave making her wonderfully woozy? She tilted her head in a playful way and returned his smile. "She is."

"As you said, women know these things." He glanced over her shoulder toward Bill and Nora.

Tess only hoped she was right.

33

Boston
Monday, April 12, 1943

A spasm buckled the back of Dan's neck, and he gripped it with both hands. Randolph had his revenge. Dan was ruined.

"I'm sorry, Mr. Avery," Bill said. "I couldn't disobey orders."

Dan stood in front of his desk, piles looming before him. "I know. It's not your fault."

"I did as much as I could." Bill laid his hand on one stack. "This stack hasn't been started, but I did the preliminary work and organized it by project. The stack in the middle contains reports ready to be written up, with the facts and figures in each folder. The stack on the right — complete and ready to be typed."

"He insists I type them myself, even though we have yeomen."

"Yes, sir. He said he'd be able to tell if you typed them yourself."

Dan slapped the edge of his desk. "Yeah, by all the typographical errors. Doesn't he care that sloppy reports reflect poorly on the whole unit?"

"Apparently not."

His hands were tied. He had to obey orders. Going over his commanding officer's head with petty complaints violated Navy protocol and was beneath him as an officer.

With delegation of duties and some grueling late nights, he could plow through this paperwork in a week or so. But without delegation? Impossible.

So much for balancing work and rest. So much for spending time with Tess. Other than this morning's trip to the Rad Lab, he'd only see her in passing for the foreseeable future.

He slapped the desk again. "I need to get started, but first I have to report to Commander Lewis."

"I'll come with you." Bill opened the office door. "I'll take whatever blame I can."

"No." Dan grabbed his portfolio and headed down the hall. "I won't let you do that. You've done everything you possibly could."

"I'm coming anyway."

At the end of the hall, Mr. Randolph's office faced Commander Lewis's. Mr. Randolph looked up from his desk with a mean little smile that begged to be knocked to kingdom come.

Instead, Dan greeted Mr. Randolph properly, then turned on his heel and entered his commander's office. After salutes, Dan and Bill sat in front of Commander Lewis's desk.

Over the next fifteen minutes, Dan relayed the salient points from his two cruises. Mr. Randolph sneaked into the back of the office, but Dan ignored him.

"Excellent work," Commander Lewis said in his rich Louisiana accent as he flipped to the last page of Dan's report. "Thorough but concise."

Mr. Randolph huffed. "I wish he'd be as conscientious with his work here."

Dan swallowed a dozen retorts and kept his gaze on Commander Lewis. "I give my all to my work, sir. I always have."

His eyes narrowed. "You do have a large number of outstanding reports."

"After my visit to the Rad Lab this morning, I'll get to work. I'll get it done."

"You have a week."

Dan's chest seized. "A week?"

"The *Bogue* is scheduled to ship out on Saturday. Captain Short requested your presence aboard. At first I refused, but then he told me his crew will spend two weeks at the British antisubmarine training facility in Belfast. I want you there. That would be an excellent opportunity to swap notes with the British."

"Yes, sir." He could barely speak over his dry tongue. "It would."

"Sir?" Mr. Randolph said. "Perhaps you should send another officer, someone who's caught up in his work."

"No, it should be Mr. Avery. He knows the ship, the crew, and their work, and Captain Short speaks highly of him."

"But, sir." Annoyance tinged Randolph's voice green. "You haven't seen how much work he has. It's reprehensible. Negligent."

Dan's mouth hardened. The only reprehensible and negligent man in the room was Mr. Randolph himself.

Commander Lewis leveled a glare at Dan. "You have until Saturday at 0800. If you aren't finished, I'll send Mr. Randolph in your place."

Dan's chest caved in from the pressure. Mr. Randolph might as well pack his sea bag, because Dan could never meet that deadline with current orders in place. "Aye aye, sir."

Commander Lewis looked above Dan's

shoulder and smiled. "Good morning, Miss Beaumont. May I help you?"

Tess stood right outside the doorway, as bright and colorful as light through a prism. "I didn't mean to interrupt, sir. I just wanted to catch Mr. Avery's eye and let him know I'm ready to go to the Rad Lab whenever he is."

She'd caught his eye, all right.

Then she gave him an affectionate smile, and his gut lurched. If Mr. Randolph saw her look at him that way, he'd destroy her as surely as he'd destroyed Dan.

An idea flashed in his mind, perfect in its brilliance, solving all his problems at once. If only Bill would play along.

Dan flicked his ensign hard in the forearm. When Bill startled, Dan shot him a significant look, then addressed the commander. "Sir, may I have a quick word with Miss Beaumont?"

"Very well."

Dan put on his sternest expression and approached Tess. Her smile drifted south into confusion. He motioned her farther into the hallway to give the illusion of privacy while ensuring Commander Lewis could hear every syllable.

He glowered at her. He hated doing so, but what better way to conceal his love, to protect her from Randolph? "Miss Beaumont, would you care to tell me why I have a stack of papers ten inches tall waiting to be typed?"

"I . . ." She blinked sleepily, as if clearing her vision. "I don't understand."

Dan knifed his hand in the direction of his office. "On my desk. Some of the reports are weeks overdue. Why haven't your yeomen typed them up?"

Tess's mouth drew up tight. "They've typed every report they've received. They work hard, and it isn't fair —"

"Mr. Avery!" Bill leaped to his feet. "It isn't the yeomen's fault. I never gave them those reports."

He wheeled to Bill and caught a flicker of a smile. Hallelujah! Message received.

Dan worked up some restrained steam. "They're ready to be typed, the yeomen were waiting for them, and you didn't pass them along?"

Bill feigned bewilderment well. "But — but, sir. They can only be typed by you."

"By me? I'm not a yeoman."

Commander Lewis pushed his chair back. "A strange idea, Mr. Bentley."

Bill gazed between the two men with innocent blue eyes. "But those were Mr. Randolph's orders, sir."

"That's ridiculous," Mr. Randolph spluttered. "Why would I give an order like that? You — you must have misunderstood me."

Bill lowered his head and dropped Dan a surreptitious wink. "Yes, sir. I must have."

Victory surged in Dan's chest. He marched to Commander Lewis's desk. "Sir, do I have your permission to delegate tasks in an appropriate manner as I see fit?"

"Of course." The commander frowned. "That's your duty as an officer."

"Thank you, sir." He wanted to throw Randolph's smug smile back in his face, but ignoring him was the higher ground. "Mr. Bentley, let's get to work."

Now he had a fighting chance. What a perfect, flawless plan.

Tess stood in the hallway, her face pale and cold.

Uh-oh. The only flaw, but it was a whopper. His mouth opened, but no words came.

"Good day, Mr. Avery. I'll go to the Rad Lab by myself. I don't need an escort." She strode away, tall and proud.

"Miss Beau—"

"No, thank you." She tossed a wave over her shoulder. "I'd rather not wait for you."

Dan mashed his lips together and returned to his office. He'd work till midnight Monday through Friday, turn in his work Saturday morning, and sail away. He'd never get another minute alone with Tess, and he deserved no better.

Bill shut the office door behind them. "I guess you didn't show her the script."

"No time. At least you figured it out." He laid a hand on his friend's shoulder. "I'll never forget this. I owe you."

"You'd do the same for me." He jerked his head toward the door. "The Rad Lab?"

"I'll give her a head start so she can avoid me." Dan picked up the right-hand stack of papers. "Let's get this ball rolling. Take this to the WAVES. They'll shriek when they see it."

"Aye aye, sir."

While Bill ran his errand, Dan thumbed through the middle stack and plucked out the highest-priority reports for Bill to work on in his absence. When the ensign returned, Dan handed him the papers. "This should keep you busy. I won't be gone long." No lingering with Tess, that was for sure.

"Finally have something to do. I've been twiddling my thumbs."

"Unconscionable." Dan yanked on his overcoat. "Listen, if I ship out on Saturday and you see Tess on Sunday, could you —"

"Tell her you're sorry you were a jerk? Aye

aye, sir."

"Thanks." Dan trudged out of the building toward City Square Station.

He passed the stage for the rallies that would take place today at 1200 and 1800. Just yesterday, he and Tess had hung that bunting, hands close, conversation closer. By the end of the day, he'd convinced himself she might be falling for him.

If it were true yesterday, it wasn't today. He'd blown it. He meant to protect her, but he'd only hurt her. Why did he think he could pursue a woman like Tess? He was nothing but a bulldozer.

The platform at City Square Station was more crowded than usual, and people checked the clock and their watches. The train must have been delayed.

Dan scanned the crowd. Tess stood not too far away, and she hadn't noticed him. He'd enter a different car to give her space.

Guilt and longing mingled in his chest. Or he could follow her and give her an apology.

Dan eased over, careful to stay out of her sight. In a minute, a train pulled up. Tess slipped into a seat by the window, and Dan plopped next to her.

She gasped, hiked up her chin, and faced the window. "I don't wish to speak to you,

349

Mr. Avery."

He didn't blame her. She held a handkerchief in her lap, and she balled it up in her fist. Oh swell, he'd made her cry.

The train pulled out of the station, and Dan leaned closer. "Tess —"

"Miss Beaumont!"

More than anything, he wanted to fold her in his arms and murmur apologies in her hair until she melted and forgave him. But he didn't have that right.

"Tess . . ." He drew out her name until it was almost an apology in itself. "I'm sorry. I shouldn't have spoken to you like that."

"I'll say. You accused me and my girls of dereliction of duty, which isn't true and you know it."

"I do, and I apologize. I wish I could have let you know what I was doing, but —"

"Oh, I figured it out." Golden fire blazed in her eyes. "Mr. Randolph ordered you not to delegate, which is wrong — it is — but what you did was wrong too. You made us take a fall for you, all to protect your precious reputation. You put your career over your friends. Fine, enjoy your career — alone."

That was untrue and unfair, but he'd hurt her feelings and he couldn't get defensive. "May I explain?" he asked softly.

"If you can."

He pulled in a slow breath. "With those orders, Mr. Randolph would have destroyed me. I have piles of work and a Saturday morning deadline. If I can delegate and I work sixteen hours a day, I might finish on time. Might. But if I couldn't delegate, I was sunk."

"I'm so glad you're still floating." Those prickles could sink any lifeboat.

Dan gripped his hands together. "I'm sorry I turned on you, but I knew you and the WAVES would never get in trouble. They can't be held responsible for work they never received."

She thrust up her chin. "What about Bill? He's such a good friend, and you made him —"

"I didn't make him. I —" Then he groaned, and his eyes slipped shut. "You're right. I put him in a tight spot. He didn't have much of a choice."

"I'll say." A Boston winter held nothing to the chill in her voice.

"I'll apologize to him too. But just so you know, he isn't in trouble. It's in his best interest that the work is completed. It's in the nation's best interest. Mr. Randolph . . ." He shook his head hard. "Well, the Nazis don't need spies with him in their camp.

How dare he impede important work?"

The train rattled its way over the Charlestown Bridge, and Tess twisted the hankie in her lap.

Maybe he was getting through to her. "I really am sorry."

"You didn't have to be mean to me." Her voice quivered.

Why did he have to be such a heel? "I was also protecting you."

"Protecting me? By chewing me out?"

Dan nodded. "Bill told me Mr. Randolph threatened to have you reprimanded and transferred if he suspected anything was happening between you and me."

The red in her eyes made the green stand out starker. "There's certainly no danger of that."

No, there wasn't. Dan gritted his teeth. "That isn't the point. If he knew how much . . . how much I care about you, he'd destroy you to hurt me."

Tess's face collapsed and darkened, shadowed as the train descended into a subway tunnel. "Oh. I see."

"Mm-hmm. But the way I chewed you out? That'll throw him off the trail."

She tucked in her lips. "It will."

"When he's around, we need to be polite but distant. That's vital."

"And off duty?"

"Depends." One corner of his mouth puckered. "Can you forgive me?"

"Oh, all right, you big oaf." She nudged him with her shoulder. "But don't you ever talk to me like that again."

"Never."

By the time they reached MIT, he had her smiling again. His hopes for romance had been smashed to smithereens, but at least he'd salvaged their friendship.

Inside Building 22, they headed to the office where the WAVE yeomen worked. Professor Louis Arnaud strode down the hallway, his nose in a book, muttering to himself.

He almost bumped into Dan, but then he made an abrupt turn into an office — his own office. The professor stopped inside the doorway and dropped the book. "I told you never to come here."

Dan pulled Tess toward the wall right outside the office and put a finger to his lips.

She nodded and pressed her ear to the wall.

"You can't keep me away, Louis. We have an agreement." A woman's voice, thickened by a central European accent.

Arnaud slammed the door, but it bounced

off the latch and floated back open. "You promised not to come here."

"You promised a lot of things too. Things you never delivered."

Delivered? Dan's hand tightened around Tess's arm, and she covered her mouth with her hand, her eyes enormous.

"I can't, Helga. It is not as easy as you think."

"It is as easy as you want it to be. I am beginning to question your loyalty."

Instinctively, Dan drew Tess closer, and she didn't resist.

"My loyalty?" The professor let out a harsh laugh. "If I were loyal, I wouldn't be in this mess."

"A mess? Is that what you call it? You wanted this as much as I did."

"I did. I do. Oh, darling, you must never doubt me again."

"Then do what you promised. You have one week."

"One week? Please, Helga. I need more time. It is very complicated. Please give me until June."

A chair scraped along the floor. "You have until June 1. If you break your promise, I will tear you into little pieces. It would not be difficult to convince a jury that you offered to sell me military secrets."

"You wouldn't!"

Fear sparked in the giant green pools of Tess's eyes.

"Oh, my Louis, my treasure. You've seen what I'm capable of. Do not test me."

High heels thumped toward the door.

Dan froze. They had to cover and fast.

He flung his arm up on the wall, arching over Tess's head, and he leaned close with his best impersonation of a roguish grin. "I'm flirting with you," he said in a light, low tone. "Can you see? I'm flirting with you and you'd better flirt back."

Tess batted her eyelashes. "Flirt all you want, sailor boy. I'm not giving you the time of day."

The door slammed, and a slim redhead stomped down the hall, shooting Dan and Tess a dismissive look.

After she passed, Tess sagged against the wall and her hand fluttered to her mouth. "Oh no."

Dan guided her down the hall and into the stairwell. When the door shut, he turned her to face him. "Keep your voice low. You know her?"

"No, but I've seen her. She was at the Cocoanut Grove. Do you remember? Professor Arnaud left alone, but he fetched two coats. She came out later and joined him in the cab. She's his mistress."

"I figured that much."

"It gets worse." Tess clutched the lapel of Dan's coat. "She's wearing a red beret."

How could he think with her so close, touching him? "A red beret?"

"The bombing. The woman on the bike wore a red beret. I know, thousands of women in Boston own a red beret, including Yvette, but . . ."

"But this looks bad. This looks like the professor has a German mistress who's coaxing him to give her military secrets."

"It could be. Or it could be he has a mistress with a German name, and she wants him to divorce his wife as he promised. That also fits everything they said."

"Regardless, we can't take any chances. We're going straight to the FBI."

"Now? I — I can't." She pressed her hand to her forehead. "The rally. It's at noon. I'm in charge. I have to be there."

His cheeks puffed out with air. "Very well. Immediately after the rally we'll go —"

"We? You can't go. You have all that work."

"I'm a witness too. As for my work, if God wants me to finish, he'll make it happen."

Her eyes rounded. "I can't let you do that for me."

Dan rubbed her upper arm and offered

half a smile. "This time, let me choose friends over career, okay?"

"Okay." But her face reddened and crumpled, and she swayed closer. "Oh, Dan."

She was asking him to hold her? How could he refuse?

"Come here." He gathered her close and caressed her back.

She felt so right in his arms, even with the heavy layers of wool between them and her cover preventing him from nuzzling in her curls.

If only she could stay there, but this would be his only chance to hold her.

"Goodness." She let out a nervous chuckle and backed away. "If Mr. Randolph saw us, it'd all be over, wouldn't it?"

"Yes, it would." It was all over anyway.

34

Wednesday, April 14, 1943
Tess glanced at her watch — 1900. She motioned for Nora and the WAVES from the war bond office to tiptoe closer, then she lightly rapped on the outer door of the ASWU office.

Bill Bentley stepped into the hall and shut the door behind him. "He doesn't suspect a thing," he whispered.

"Everyone's gone?"

"Just me and the WAVES. He's trying to shoo us out, but we won't budge."

"Good. Ready?"

"Yes, ma'am." He grinned at the women, flung open the door, and burst into the birthday song.

The ladies joined in the song, carrying their burdens inside. The ASWU yeomen came singing down the hall from the other direction.

Dan poked his head out of his office, and

his jaw dropped. Then he raised his arm and leaned it against the doorjamb. He'd taken off his jacket and loosened his tie, and his hair stuck up on one side. He'd never looked more befuddled, more rumpled, or more delicious.

When the song ended, Dan stared at his guests. "What's going on?"

Tess stepped forward. "Lillian told me your birthday is on Friday. You're turning thirty."

He raked his hand through his hair on the sticking-up side. "I — I don't need a party."

"Yes, you do. Mr. Bentley told me you'd stayed up till midnight both Monday and Tuesday but sent him home at six."

Dan rolled an annoyed look at his ensign.

Bill spread his palms wide. "Would you rather I lied?" Tess set down her heavy basket and stretched her fingers.

"We know you don't have time for a fun party, so we're throwing you a work party."

"A work —"

"We're all working late tonight. Everyone volunteered, so don't fuss. We want to help you. The yeomen here said they have a huge logjam of typing, so three of the yeomen from the bond office came — with typewriters."

"Where should we go?" Celia Ortega lifted

her typewriter case.

"This way." Betty Jean Miles motioned her toward the workroom. "Thanks for coming. Mr. Avery's so good to us, always treats us right. We're all glad to help."

Nora raised her slide rule. "I'm here to do calculations. Mr. Bentley said you have lots, and I'm speedy with numbers."

"Thank you, Miss Thurmond." Bill beckoned. "Mr. Santini said we could use his office this evening and give Mr. Avery peace and quiet."

That left Tess alone with Dan. "I don't know how useful I'll be, but I'll be your Girl Friday. Anything I can help you with, let me know. Oh, and I brought dinner for everyone."

Dan's gaze was liquid and unbelieving. "You didn't have to do this."

"I wanted to. It's my birthday gift to you — from all of us, really."

"It was your idea though." His lips curved up. "You put it together."

"It was fun. Anything to get you on the *Bogue* when she sails." He couldn't say when, only that it would be soon.

"Trying to get rid of me, eh?"

"You see right through me." She winked. "I'll set up dinner on that big table in the workroom. Come get one of Madame Robillard's gorgeous sandwiches. Oh, and an almond pastry. Wait until you taste them."

She turned to leave, but he grasped her arm. "Thank you. This is — this is the best present ever."

The emotions in his expression — gratitude and guilt, affection and disbelief — all she wanted was to pull him down for a kiss that lasted until his actual birthday.

But that would put her selfish pleasure above his needs. Dan believed romance would hinder his goals, and Tess loved him too much to stand in his way.

She managed a smile. "Give me five minutes to set up, then come get dinner. You can't work on an empty stomach."

In the workroom, Tess opened her basket and set the wrapped sandwiches on napkins. Roberta Ingham showed her how to use the coffeemaker, a task Tess could adopt for the evening so the yeomen could type.

For the next few hours, she kept coffee percolating and cups filled. She ran papers from Dan to Bill and from Bill to Dan and from Dan to the yeomen. She ran data to Nora and completed calculations back to Dan. She sorted reports, stapled them, and inserted them in folders.

It was nothing but busywork, but it kept everyone else working hard.

At ten o'clock, Dan handed her a tall stack of signed reports and his empty coffee cup. "Please put these on Mr. Randolph's desk — they only need his signature. And may I have a refill?"

"Aye aye, sir." What a lovely sight, all those reports tucked neatly in their folders. Wouldn't Mr. Randolph be shocked at the quantity?

Tess's steps slowed. What if he ignored them . . . pretended to lose them? Oh no. She wouldn't give the man that power.

In the workroom, she wrote a note and paper-clipped it to the top folder. Then she set the stack of folders on Commander Lewis's desk and smiled at her note: "To Cdr. Thomas Lewis: Completed reports from Lt. Daniel Avery. Sincerely, Ens. Quintessa Beaumont."

The commander could ask Randolph for his signature and write off the confusion to a loopy dame. Most importantly, he'd see Dan had completed the work.

Then she refilled Dan's coffee, no cream, no sugar, and took it to his office. He sat hunched over his desk, writing hard, kneading the back of his neck.

"More coffee?"

He looked up, his eyes bleary. "Thanks. Please. Yes."

The poor man had worn himself ragged. She set down the cup, picked up the paper he was working on, and set it to the side.

"What are you —"

"You're taking a break."

"I don't have time for a break."

"You can't work like this." She grabbed a blank sheet of paper and set it before him. "Draw something."

"Draw?" He ran his hand along the thick dark stubble on his jaw.

"It's what you do when you need to relax. I've seen you." She tapped the paper. "Draw something — a sailboat, a flower, a lady-bug."

"A ladybug?" A black eyebrow arched.

"Anything you want. You have fifteen minutes." She studied the clock. "Until 2225."

Dan groaned, but he leaned back in his chair and started sketching. "Why are you doing this to me?"

Tess giggled. Because she loved him. "Because I don't want you to die young of a heart attack."

He jerked up his head, his eyes stricken and sad.

"I'm sorry." She perched on the edge of his desk. "I didn't mean to hurt you."

"No, you're right." He shaded the top of

the paper with long strokes. "Admiral Howard died of overwork and underrest. I've learned the lesson, but this week . . ."

"Some weeks are like that, but you still have to trust God enough to rest."

"Trust God?"

Tess smoothed her navy-blue skirt over her knees. "The other day, I didn't want you to come to the FBI office with me, but you insisted. You said if God wanted you to finish your work, he'd make it happen."

She remembered his voice when he said it, so close she felt his breath, his hand caressing her arm, infusing her with courage. And she remembered how he sat at her side in Agent Sheffield's office, his presence lending her story weight. Because of Dan, the agent took her even more seriously.

Dan sighed. "I did say that, didn't I?"

She gathered her thoughts, willing the warmth in her cheeks to be invisible. "I think the Sabbath is kind of like tithing."

"Interesting. Explain."

She leaned back against the wall. "Think about it. God gives us a paycheck and says, 'Keep 90 percent, give me 10 percent, and trust me to meet your needs out of that 90 percent.' Tithing is an exercise in trusting the Lord."

"True." Dan sketched an arced line.

"It's the same with time. God gives us a week and says, 'Work hard on six days, give me one day for worship and rest, and trust me to meet your needs out of those six days.' Choosing to rest is an exercise in trust."

"I didn't work on Sunday, remember?" He winced and tucked up one shoulder.

Tess slid off the desk. "Yes, but you also need daily rest. You're working too hard this week, and your body's fighting back."

"I don't have a choice, and I'm fine." His voice turned gruff.

"You're not fine." She stood behind Dan's chair and set her hands on his shoulders.

He sucked in a breath and sat forward. "What are you —"

"Your neck hurts. I'll work out the knots while you draw." She pulled on his shoulders.

He sagged back in the chair. "Don't forget I outrank you."

"On Sunday you called me captain." She pressed the heel of her hand into the triangle of muscles at the base of his neck, stiff and lumpy under his white shirt.

"I — regret it." His voice edged higher.

"Poor thing. You have knots the size of Bunker Hill. Loosen that tie and undo one more button."

"Tess . . ." His voice darkened with warning.

"Relax. I'm not getting fresh, but your collar's in the way."

He grumbled, but he obeyed.

She worked her fingers down under his collar, trying to ignore how warm and supple his skin felt. Had they truly touched before, skin to skin? She'd touched his coat sleeve. He'd touched hers. But this?

Thank goodness he faced away from her and couldn't see her tingling cheeks.

Dan grunted and gripped the edge of his desk.

"You're not drawing," she said.

"How can I when you're torturing me?" His voice squeaked.

"Stop it, you big baby." She glanced at the clock. "Only nine more minutes. Draw."

More grumbling, but he picked up his pen. Soon his posture relaxed, his muscles softened and warmed, and he stretched his head to the right to allow her to massage.

"What are you drawing?" She peeked over his shoulder.

"A sailboat." His tone was low and dreamy. "I don't have my father's gift. I can't create beautiful things that call to the soul. That's what Dad does, you know."

"I know." It was good to hear him say that,

good to hear him say "Dad." He always said "my father," respectful but impersonal.

"All these years I've disdained his work, but he's right. There are different kinds of work, and they're all good. Mom does the books, Dad crafts the boats, you encourage —"

"Me?" Her hands stilled.

"Don't stop. A little lower, to the right." He tipped his head to the left.

"Encouraging isn't work." Tess followed his instructions and found a new knot.

He jerked and grunted. "Sure, it is. The yeomen sing your praises. You ran a stirring bond rally. And you organized this work party. With your gifts, you help the yeomen work better, you sell heaps of bonds, and now you're helping me get my work done and putting this cranky toddler down for a much-needed nap."

She chewed her bottom lip. "It doesn't feel like much."

"It is. You're generous and cheerful, and you make people feel better about themselves. I can't think of anything more . . . more useful."

Useful. No one made her feel better about herself than he did. Her pinky finger strayed into the hair at the nape of his neck, thick and soft. "Thank you."

"No, thank you. Thanks to you and your friends, I'll meet my deadline. I might even — I might finish early Friday."

"Friday?" She gasped in delight. "Your birthday. You could go out and celebrate."

"That's my new goal, and I'm determined to meet it."

She fought the urge to hug him and plant a kiss on that stubbly cheek. "Oh, Danny, that's wonderful."

"Now, my fifteen minutes is over, my neck feels like warm jelly, and my reports await." He held up his drawing. "My best yet."

Tess snatched it out of his hand and sat on his desk. The lines were looser but no less firm, somehow gaining confidence in their relaxation. "Oh, it *is* good. Very good."

"Color it for me?" He had never looked more appealing, his tie hanging loose, his shirt collar open and inviting, his smile even more open and inviting. Yet he was still the same rock-steady, no-nonsense Dan.

She hugged the paper. "I will."

35

In the ballroom of the Bradford Hotel, while Frankie Masters and his orchestra played a swing tune, Dan set a birthday card on the table and smiled at his friends. "Thanks, everyone."

"You're not done yet." Tess pulled a flat box from under her chair.

"I said no presents."

"Hush. I only put it in a box so it wouldn't get crumpled. Besides, you asked for this."

He gave her a skeptical look and opened the box. He had indeed asked for this. She'd colored his sailboat bright blue and drawn a little man lounging along the bow, wearing an officer's cover and red swim trunks. He read the caption out loud, "Danny at play."

Lillian laughed. "He has never been a Danny."

He was now, but only with Tess.

"I wish I had that other sailboat drawing," Tess said. "Do you remember?"

Remember? He had it in his wallet at that moment. "I do."

"I'd call it 'Dan at work.' The first boat was solid and practical, and you were in uniform. The second is fluid and playful."

"Six days, one day." With her at his side, he could achieve that balance. Which reminded him it was time to get underway. He tucked the drawing and the cards in the stationery box Tess had used. "Thanks again, everyone. It's not every year a man gets two parties."

Bill scooted his chair back. "It's not every year a man turns eighty."

"Thirty."

"Oops. Sorry. You only *act* eighty." Bill winked, stood, and offered his arm to Nora. "Would you like to dance?"

Arch asked Lillian. Each of the men had promised to give Mary a whirl around the dance floor, but she glanced away from Dan, kindly freeing him to ask Tess.

He stood and approached Tess's chair. "The drawing reminds me of a grave wrong I committed against you."

She looked up at him with amusement. "Which one?"

He bowed his head. Fair enough. "The

night I drew that first sailboat, you told me it would be polite if I asked you to dance, and I refused. I was wrong." He held out his hand. "Would you do me the honor?"

She hesitated one painful second, then settled her hand in his.

He led her to the dance floor. He could have offered his arm, but holding hands felt more personal, more proprietary.

" 'In My Sweet Little Alice Blue Gown,' " Tess said.

Strange thing to say. "Hmm?"

She laughed, her hand small in his. "The name of the song. I heard Frankie Masters perform it when I was in Chicago. Only then I was wearing an actual gown, not a uniform."

She couldn't have looked any sweeter. He pulled her into his arms and immediately forgot how to dance.

Tess stood so close, her face tipped toward his, a flush on her cheeks, her eyes round, her mouth curved. "Has it been that long?"

Since he'd danced? Or since he'd kissed a woman? Too long for both. "It has, but I'll make do."

He forced his feet in the old patterns, but his mind was more interested in the position of his hands — one on the curve of Tess's waist, the other holding her hand.

Such a pretty hand, yet capable of inflicting the sweetest agony.

The sweetness of those fingers caressing his neck and shoulders and hair and reducing his brain to mush. The agony of not being able to pull her down to his lap for a passionate kiss.

Dan turned his attention to the couples dancing and the swing band on stage. A kiss was months away, but tonight he'd set his plan in motion and give his speech to Tess.

Once he managed to get her in private, he'd cut to the chase and tell her he wanted to ask her out after he received his transfer. Commander Lewis had been impressed with how Dan met his deadline, and he'd praised Dan's humility in giving credit to Bill, Tess, and the WAVES. With a good recommendation from Captain Short, Dan was sure to succeed.

As soon as he was out from under Randolph's thumb, he'd be free to pursue Tess openly.

Next he'd explain why he'd rejected Admiral Howard's instructions to avoid romance and how Tess had helped change his mind. It was too early to tell her he loved her, but he'd list everything he admired about her and why he wanted her in his life. That could take a while.

Then he'd order her not to answer until he returned from his cruise on the *Bogue*. He'd be gone at least a month, which would give her plenty of time to pray about it. He only asked for the courtesy of considering his offer.

It was a fine speech.

"You're quiet."

Dan blinked.

Tess's eyes were mesmerizing this close, the gold and green in rays of brightness and life. "Thinking about the steps?"

He was indeed, but not the dance steps. "You could say that."

"Well, aren't you mysterious?" Then the music changed, and her eyes faded.

"What's the matter?"

She gave her head a small shake. "Nothing. I just don't like this song."

"I don't recognize it."

"You're hopeless. It's called 'Scatterbrain' — a Top Ten hit a few years back. It's Frankie Masters's theme song."

"And you heard him in Chicago."

Her mouth pursed. "My date said it should be my theme song too."

Dan tuned in to the gentleman singing about his darling scatterbrain with her delightful smile and insane chatter. He frowned. "That wasn't kind, and it definitely isn't true."

"I didn't allow him a second date."

"See? Proof you're no scatterbrain." Part of his speech threatened to tumble out prematurely, but he restrained himself. The other day she'd massaged words right out of his skull. If the neck rub had lasted another fifteen minutes, he would have proposed marriage.

When the song finished, Tess relaxed. But then the band switched to a peppy Latin beat, and Dan released her. "Sorry. I can't keep up with this."

Tess spun to face the crowd. "Look! They're starting a conga line. What fun! Let's join in."

"Not me." He backed toward the edge of the room. "Bunch of nonsense."

She bounded to him and grabbed both his hands. "Even you can do the conga. Three steps forward, little kick to the side. Follow me." She congaed backward. "One and two and three — kick! One and two and three — kick!"

He followed, enchanted. She was right. Even a no-nonsense man could have a little nonsense in his life, a little rest, a little romance.

Dan let a grin rise. "Lead on, Carmen Miranda."

She cheered, whirled around, and planted his hands on her waist. Then she congaed her way to the snaking line with the drummer at the head. The line opened and swallowed them.

Dan had a strange woman's hands on his waist, and Tess had her hands on a strange man's waist, but Dan didn't mind. He held Tess's small, nimble waist. Her hips bounced and swayed to the beat, and she kept glancing back at Dan, laughing for joy. And his laughter welled up from an old and neglected vault in his soul.

All too soon, the song ended and the crowd clapped and whistled.

Tess's face glowed. "Wasn't that fun?"

"It was." He ran his hand over his hair, the waves gone wild.

She looked past him. "Mary's trying to get my attention."

The rest of their party was at the table, and Mary beckoned. Dan guided Tess back through the crowd.

"I'm sorry." Lillian patted her knee. "I don't want to spoil the party, but I'm getting sore."

"I'll take her home," Arch said. "And Mary too."

"And I'm not feeling well." Nora rested a hand on her stomach. "I hate to —"

"I'd be glad to take you home," Bill said.

Dan's gut tightened. It was only nine. He'd hoped for another hour.

"Oh dear. I'm sorry you're not feeling well." Tess's voice was softened by compassion but also held a tinge of disappointment.

Dan turned to her. "I'd rather not call it a night yet. Would you like to keep dancing?"

She brightened. "Oh yes. It's too early to go home, and you have so much to celebrate."

"I do." He directed a deliberate look at Arch. "Which is why I won't see you at church on Sunday."

The former naval officer nodded. "I see. Congratulations."

Dan hugged Lillian and Mary, shook hands with Arch, saluted Bill and Nora, and sent them on their way.

"Tomorrow?" Tess asked by his side.

He leaned closer to her ear. "I report to the ship at midnight tonight."

"Or you turn into a pumpkin?"

"Yes, ma'am."

"When should we leave?"

"At 2200. That'll give me time to take you home, get my sea bag, and return to the ship."

Tess's eyes glistened, but then cleared. "I'll miss you, but I'm so happy for you."

His chest ached with a good pain he'd never felt before, as if his heart were stuffed full to the top. How he wanted this woman in his life, a woman who would miss him when he was at sea and welcome him back to shore, supporting him wherever he was.

"So!" She grabbed his hand. "You have one more hour. Use it well."

He did. For the next hour, he danced with her and talked with her, breathing in her air and basking in her light. His speech muddled in his mind. He rearranged it, adding bits. Then he chided himself for editing such a fine speech.

The hands on his watch spun to ten o'clock. Time to give that speech. Time to say good-bye.

He checked out their coats and his cover, and they headed outside. A taxi sat at the curb, and Dan hailed it and opened the back door for Tess. A cab ride would be a good place for his speech, private enough to declare his intentions.

But Tess stared up at the sky. "Too bad I live so far away. It'd be a lovely night to walk."

The temperature hovered around forty degrees, but a three-quarters moon lit the starry sky. Dan leaned into the cab. "Excuse me. Could you please meet us about three blocks from here?"

"Sorry, pal. I've got guaranteed fares if I sit here."

Dan slipped out his wallet. "I'm hiring you for at least an hour and a half. I'll pay you in advance and then some." He handed the man three dollars.

The cabby whistled and pointed over his shoulder with his thumb. "I'll meet you at the corner of Tremont and Stuart. Take your time."

Tess clasped her hands before her chest. "Thank you. I didn't want the evening to end yet."

Neither did he. Something even older slipped out of that hidden vault, a bit of mischief. "You said something about going for a polka?"

"A polka?"

"That's what I heard." He yanked her into his arms and careened down the sidewalk. They left a river of laughter behind them, her laugh the water and bubbles, his the banks and rocks.

He interrupted the polka long enough to guide her safely across the street, then resumed it. But at the next intersection, he could see the taxi waiting at the far end of the block. Time to slow down. Time for his speech. Time to catch his breath.

Tess remained in his arms, laughing, and she rested her forehead on his shoulder. "Oh, Danny. You dance as badly as you sing."

His face screwed up. "Why don't you give me another neck rub and add injury to insult?"

She giggled and gazed up at him. "But I love how you sing. You may sing badly, but you sing with joy. And when you dance, you laugh. Oh, your laugh. You need to laugh more often. It's wonderful."

He had a speech to give, didn't he? He had so much to say, but the speech dissolved and flowed out of his mind, every word lost.

Only one thought remained — Tess.

Tess warm in his arms, smiling and breathless and light and air and everything he wanted. He bent nearer, unable to stop himself, and her laughter stilled and her eyes widened and her lips, oh, her lips, they parted, and she didn't push away.

His lips touched hers, and a blaze of color and warmth flooded his being. He hovered, barely touching her, every sense awakening from dark sleep, tingling from the pain of it, the exquisite pain.

Then she lifted closer, her breath escaping over his lips. She cared for him too. She did, and he pulled her close and kissed her with everything in him, the fullness of the kiss jolting him awake, to life.

What good was a speech anyway? This was better, communicating the depth of his love, his esteem, his every thought of her, how he wanted her in his life now and forever.

Tess pulled away, and he dragged his gaze from her mouth to her eyes. Why did she look . . . worried?

"I — I don't understand." She pressed one hand to his chest, right over his thumping heart. "You said — you always say you don't want a woman in your life, that — that a woman would ruin your career. Why now? Why — why me?"

Wasn't that obvious? Hadn't he just told her?

Not in words, he hadn't. And the words, the speech, it was gone. He fished around in the recesses of his brain, but every thought lingered on the kiss, not the reasons behind it.

Why her? Because he loved her, every bit of her, heart and mind and soul. Everything about her was . . . was . . . "You're so beautiful."

She drew farther away, too far, her gaze sweeping his face, and she blinked faster and faster, two creases forming between her eyebrows. "Beautiful?"

Why did she look even more worried? Hadn't he made himself clear? "You are. You're so beautiful."

Her mouth contorted, and she broke free of his embrace and clapped one hand over her mouth. "How could you? How could you say that?"

The general quarters alarm clanged in his head, but what was the source? Torpedo? Air attack? Fire? Collision? He couldn't identify the danger, didn't see where he'd gone wrong. "That — that's a compliment."

She let out a strange sound, not a whimper, not a sob, and she hunched over as if he'd kicked her in the stomach. "How could you? Beautiful? I thought you knew me better than that. I thought you saw inside. I thought you liked me for who I am."

The loudspeaker blared the error in his ear. Of all the words to pick, why had he chosen that one? His mouth drifted open, groping for that speech, that fine speech, but nothing remained.

Tess groaned. "All this time, all this time, and I'm nothing to you, nothing but a pretty face."

Until the words came back, he needed to hold her, console her, and he reached out.

"Don't you dare!" She flung down her

arms, striking his hands away, and she pulled herself tall, her arms shaking by her sides, her eyes deep and dark. "I don't want your compliments. I don't want your kisses. And I never want to see you again."

His hands hung suspended in the air, empty. His mind reeled, emptier still. What could he say? How could he fix this? "Tess, I'm —"

"No! Not one more word. No stupid apologies. No stupid explanations. I never want to hear your voice again." She took off running toward the taxi.

He unglued his feet from the sidewalk and chased after her. "Tess! Wait up!"

"No!" She yanked open the cab door and glared at him, her cheeks glistening wet in the moonlight. "I'm locking the doors. Good night, Mr. Avery, and good-bye."

The door slammed.

The cab pulled away.

Dan threw himself back against the brick wall of the building and thumped the heels of his hands against his forehead. "Why? Why? Why?"

Beautiful? Beautiful? She'd told him not to call her that. Calling her beautiful was an insult, not a compliment, and he knew it. But in the moment he'd lost his mind and his memory and his fine, fine speech.

And now he'd lost Tess.

At 2300, Dan lugged his sea bag down the south jetty to the *Bogue.* For the first time ever, he didn't want to go to sea. If only he had one more day, maybe two. Tess needed time to cool down, but then maybe she'd hear him out. He'd never win her over, but at least she'd know she was more than a pretty face to him. She deserved to know that much.

An officer strolled down the jetty toward him, away from the ship. "Mr. Avery."

Dan stopped cold. "Mr. Randolph?"

"Is that any way to address your commanding officer?"

His insides twisted, but he saluted. "Good evening, Mr. Randolph."

The salute wasn't returned. "I came to say good-bye. You won't be serving in ASWU any longer."

He sincerely hoped not, but for the second time that evening, an alarm sounded. "Did Commander Lewis say something about a transfer, sir?"

"Not yet, but you'll get one. You're going to Washington, to the most obscure desk job I can find."

Dan's salute stiffened.

Mr. Randolph's smile gleamed in the

darkness. "You thought you were so high-and-mighty when you destroyed me. A puny little ensign. Well, you're no better than I am. One man took me down, and one man can take you down."

"There's a difference, sir." His words ground out. "I haven't done anything wrong."

"But you have." He inspected Dan's upraised arm with that hateful smile. "You were away for six weeks and failed to instruct your ensign to handle your work in your absence."

Dan's left hand tightened to a fist around his sea bag. "You know very well why, and Mr. Bentley can vouch —"

"Mr. Bentley? My word against his, and whose makes sense? You heard Commander Lewis. It'd be ridiculous to order an officer to not delegate his work. The commander wonders whether Bentley was making excuses for his laziness — or yours."

Dan glared at the man. "Attack me all you want, but leave Mr. Bentley out of it."

"I do intend to attack you." Mr. Randolph strode in a circle around Dan, a wolf surveying his prey. "You might have temporarily blinded the commander when you finished those reports, but I reminded him that most are long overdue. Your dereliction of duty impeded the war effort."

Only years of discipline as an officer restrained his tongue and his fist. Randolph probably wanted Dan to strike him. Then he'd have legitimate grounds for a court-martial.

"Wait until the commander hears how you were able to finish those reports so quickly."

"I already told him, sir."

"You told him the WAVES helped you. But did you tell him you shoveled piles of work on them and forced them to work till midnight?"

"Forced?" Dan's voice came out too loud. "They volunteered."

"Volunteered?" His condescending tone scraped Dan's frayed nerves. "That's not what it'll look like when I'm done. No, I see you using your influence with Miss Beaumont — a family friend, you say? Or more?"

After tonight, neither. The pain and weight of it slammed into Dan's chest, but he kept his face neutral.

Mr. Randolph shrugged. "I'll find out. Girls gossip. They can't help it. And how could those WAVES resist Miss Beaumont's pleading? Can an officer ask a rating for a favor? Doesn't it automatically sound like an order? You tell me."

Dan's salute shook from anger and pain.

He'd be away at sea, unable to defend himself. Randolph had omitted the truth, twisted Dan's motives, and condemned him.

"Such a shame about that Mr. Avery." Mr. Randolph crossed his arms and clucked his tongue. "Such a promising officer. Such potential. And he threw it all away."

Dan's breath came hard and fast. If he didn't leave now, he'd flatten Randolph to the jetty and lose his commission along with everything else. "May I please be dismissed, sir?"

Mr. Randolph drew in a long breath. "I suppose. Very well. Enjoy your last cruise ever. I must say it's been a pleasure serving with you again. A great pleasure."

Dan stomped to the gangplank, silent. Tonight his words could only do harm.

36

Boston
Saturday, April 17, 1943

Tess's eyes opened, dry and swollen. Dull sunlight illuminated Nora's alarm clock — six o'clock. It wasn't like her to sleep past sunrise, but after last night . . .

Her face crumpled, and she covered her mouth and rolled over in bed to face the wall. She hadn't cried so hard since Hugh betrayed her and got Alice Pendleton pregnant, since she found out Clifford was married and had deceived her from the start.

Dan's betrayal shouldn't sting more, but it did. Hugh and Clifford never looked below the surface, but Dan? She thought he'd looked below and seen and appreciated, and after that kiss she'd allowed herself to believe for one blissful moment that he loved her for who she was.

A fresh wave of grief, and she pulled her knees to her chest.

Oh, that kiss, that glorious kiss. First, the gentle hesitation, both of them caught up in the wonder of it all, and then the passion, the fervency, everything she'd ever hoped for.

Thank goodness she'd asked him why he kissed her, or she'd still be fooling herself.

She didn't want Dan to adore her for her looks. Adoration allowed her to be as self-centered as she pleased.

She wanted him to love her. Love delved deep and inspired her to give, to help, to change and improve. That's what she longed for.

But she'd never receive it. She'd never be more than a pretty bauble.

The alarm clock clattered, and Tess startled. Then she burrowed in the covers. How could she speak to Nora or anyone else today? But she didn't have a choice. With the War Loan Drive in full swing, she had to report for duty at 0800.

Nora silenced the clock, her covers shifted, and soft footsteps crossed the narrow room. "Tess?" She rocked Tess's shoulder. "You overslept. It's 0615."

"I'm awake." She ripped her attention from her own dilemma to Nora's, but she didn't roll over. "How's your stomach?"

Nora chuckled, and her bedsprings

creaked. "I have a confession to make. I lied. We all went back to Mary and Lillian's place. That's why I came home after you were already asleep."

"What?" Tess stared at the blank white wall.

"Lillian was telling the truth about her leg, but she wanted to stay and let Arch dance with Mary. Then we all decided you and Dan needed privacy since he ships out today. Oh, his face when you dragged him into the conga line — simply darling. He's head over heels —"

"Stop!"

Nora gasped.

Tess flopped over and shoved curls out of her eyes.

"Oh my goodness." Nora sat on her bed in pajamas and curlers, her eyes wide. "Have you been crying?"

Tess kicked off her covers and sat up. "All night."

"You poor thing. Because he's leaving?"

Hardly. She stumbled to the mirror on her locker. Her hair was a tangled mess, her face splotchy. Dan wouldn't call her beautiful today. Then he wouldn't kiss her either. Her chin quivered. "I cried because he kissed me and called me beautiful."

Nora sat in silence for a long moment.

"And then?"

"Then what?"

"What happened to make you cry?"

Tess spun to her. "Don't you see? He only kissed me because I'm beautiful. He said so. You know — I've told you — I want to be more than a pretty face. I want a man to love me for who I am inside. But Dan — of all the words in the English language, he picked *beautiful.*"

Nora's face clouded. "Don't take this the wrong way, but he doesn't strike me as the kind of man to make flowery speeches."

"No, but he also doesn't strike me as the kind of man to focus on this." Tess motioned in a frenzied circle around her face. "That's one of the reasons I liked him so much."

Nora stood and opened her locker. "What did you do?"

Tess unbuttoned her pajama top. Like it or not, she had to report for duty. "I was upset, of course. He knew I didn't want to hear that, but he kept repeating himself, hammering it in. I thought — I thought he cared for me, but he doesn't. I — I'm just a trinket to him. So I left, told him I never wanted to see him again. And I don't."

Nora was silent as they finished dressing. While she often took time to think things through, this was longer than usual.

Tess peeked over. Nora wore her white blouse and navy-blue skirt and black tie, and she yanked out curlers, brown curls springing free. In the mirror, Nora's face reflected red.

"Nora? Are you all right?"

"Of course, I'm all right." Her voice wavered. "I have no reason to be upset. No one had the gall to call *me* beautiful last night."

Tess's mouth dropped open.

Nora swiped her brush through her hair. "Some of us have never been kissed. Some of us have never been called beautiful."

Tess's heart went out to her. "I didn't mean it that way."

"I know what you meant. How long have you and Dan worked together? Hasn't he shown you through his actions what he thinks of you? Isn't it obvious he respects you? And you — oh! How selfish can you be? You shooed him out of your royal presence because he chose the wrong adjective."

"Nora!"

"I can't talk to you right now." She slapped her cover on her head and grabbed her jacket and purse. "I just can't. Later. But not now."

Tess stared as Nora fled the room, and she vacillated between shock and outrage

391

and sorrow. She'd never seen Nora angry before. If only Tess had more time to explain. If she'd heard everything Dan said, she'd understand.

With shaking hands, she finished dressing and applied an extra layer of face powder. However, nothing could conceal the condition of her eyes.

Her cover and purse — why weren't they in her locker? There — in her misery last night, she'd tossed them on the desk.

She picked up her cover and saw the compass Dan had given her.

Pain hollowed out her chest, but then fire filled the empty space. The mahogany box felt cold in her hand. When he'd given it to her on the train, she'd called it beautiful, but he said it was useful and had a purpose.

Her grip tightened and shook. Her own words, parroted back to her. He knew! He knew what it meant to her. He had no excuse.

Tess's arm coiled up, ready to pitch the stupid compass against the wall and watch it shatter.

"Proof that something can be both beautiful and useful." His words raced through her head and captured her breath.

When he'd said that, he'd looked at her with such warmth, as if he meant it about her as well as the compass. Why couldn't he have said something like *that* last night? Why couldn't he have said nice things like he had . . .

All the breath drained from her lungs, and she grasped the desk for balance.

Like the nice things he'd said when she was massaging his shoulders? What had he said? He'd praised her for how she encouraged people and helped them and made them feel better about themselves. He'd called her generous and cheerful and . . . and . . .

Useful.

A groan erupted from deep in her belly, and she set down the compass before she could drop it. "Oh no, oh no. Lord, what have I done?"

Dan had indeed said it. Just not at the exact moment she wanted.

She doubled over, moaning. Nora was right. Dan had shown her respect through his actions each and every day. Even when he chewed her out, he did it to protect her.

That day at the office when he'd offended her, she'd stormed off. Last night, she'd done the same. Only last night, Dan couldn't catch up to her. He couldn't apologize. He couldn't explain. She hadn't let him.

Tess stood up straight. Maybe she could catch him. Maybe the *Bogue* hadn't sailed yet.

She snatched up her purse, then halted. No, she couldn't. She had to report for duty. A romantic emergency didn't qualify as an excuse in the US Navy.

Woozy, Tess sank into her chair and let her forehead thud onto the desk. Her pain was more acute than it had been last night, because now it was directed inward.

All this time, Tess wanted Dan to take her seriously, but then she threw a silly fit. She wanted him to see her as selfless, but then she'd treated him selfishly.

She pressed her hand over her stomach. She thought she'd changed and grown, but she hadn't.

She was still Quintessa. Not Tess.

37

Argentia, Placentia Bay, Newfoundland
Friday, April 23, 1943

Dan shook hands around the wardroom of the USS *Bogue* after the briefing. Morale was high for the auxiliary carrier's third cruise, and Dan had labored to prevent his bad mood from infecting the crew.

After he excused himself, Dan made his way down a crowded passageway. Later this afternoon, the *Bogue* would get underway from Argentia. In two days, she'd join Convoy HX-235 bound for the United Kingdom. The convoy had been routed farther south to avoid known concentrations of U-boats. The lower latitude would also present better weather conditions for flight operations and refueling.

Dan turned down another passageway. With plenty of U-boat prey, frequent flights, and an experienced crew, the *Bogue* had an excellent chance of success. In Belfast, the crew would receive training and the carrier would be fitted with the latest technology, High-Frequency Direction-Finding equipment, which homed in on U-boat radio chatter. Combining "Huff-Duff" with radar and sonar, plus vigilant eyes in aircraft — how could the U-boats win?

As Dan strode to his cabin, optimism pushed toward the surface. He'd obtain plenty of data on this cruise, learn from the British, and assist the crew. An extraordinary opportunity.

If it weren't for the career guillotine poised over his neck.

Dan shut the cabin door behind him. At his desk he organized his notes from the briefing, and he placed the folder in the desk drawer.

On top of the stationery box from Tess.

Darkness swamped him, but he pulled out the box, glutton for punishment that he was.

A week ago. It felt like only hours ago. And a lifetime ago.

He spread out his mementoes of Tess — the rough draft of his letter to Captain Short, the lipstick-stained heart, and the two sailboat drawings. All showed his structure and her color.

Without her, his life seemed rigid and lifeless and unbalanced.

He traced his finger over "Dan at work" then "Danny at play," and grief wrenched through him. In both drawings he was alone. A few months ago he'd preferred to be alone, but now that he'd tasted companionship, his solitary life felt like punishment.

Punishment he'd earned.

Dan rested his forehead on his fist. She'd actually cared for him. The kiss proved it. She had ample time to push him away, but she didn't. She kissed him back. Even the forcefulness of her anger showed she cared.

Dan rapped his other fist on the desk. "I ruined it."

Not only had he destroyed any chance for romance, but he'd undermined her confidence in her abilities, the last thing he wanted to do.

"Why?" Why had he let himself get carried away with that kiss? If only he'd followed his plan and given his speech. From what he knew now, she would have listened joyfully.

Dan leaned back and let his head sag. She'd have the speech soon. It had taken him the entire week to recall it, write it, refine it, and mail it. But no letter could make amends. She'd probably rip it to shreds without reading it anyway.

"I never want to hear your voice again."

Dan winced and grabbed his neck. Why did she always do that? Why did she always run away? She didn't even give him the chance to explain himself. It wasn't fair. She knew he was brusque. She knew he was no good with words. How many times had he offended her in the last few months? And every single time, she ran away.

His mouth and fist and heart hardened. It wouldn't have worked anyway. What kind of marriage would they have had? She couldn't run away every time he misspoke. That wasn't right. How many times was he supposed to chase her down and beg her forgiveness? Honestly, a man needed to retain some pride.

Dan gathered the papers, slapped the lid back in place, and shoved the box deep in the drawer. It was better for him to remain alone. He should have stayed with Admiral Howard's counsel after all.

He ran his hand through his hair. This was what love did to him — upended him into turmoil and grief.

He couldn't even take comfort in his career.

The cabin door opened, and Lt. Clive Sinclair entered. "Ahoy, Dan old man."

"Ahoy."

Sinclair opened the locker. "I'd say I was

surprised you're not watching the preparations to get underway, but considering your dark mood since I came on board yesterday . . ."

"You do have that effect on me." Dan stood and recovered his mackinaw from the open locker.

Sinclair slapped him on the back. "Still have that stirring sense of humor, my boy."

At least he had that. "I'm going topside."

"Without me? I say not." He slipped on his own mackinaw. "Perhaps you can tell me what plunged you into darkness."

Dan grunted and held open the cabin door for his friend.

Blue eyes studied him as he passed. "Did you talk to your commander about your transfer?"

"I will be transferred — to Washington, DC."

Sinclair looked back with alarm. "Washington, DC? Please tell me that's the name of the Yankees' newest cruiser."

"It isn't." He held up one hand to request silence in public. "Let's go to the catwalk just below the bridge. We'll have a good view but be out of the way."

They climbed the ladder to the hangar deck and stepped outside onto the starboard catwalk. After they passed the winch for the motor whaleboat and two 20-mm machine guns, they found positions along the rail.

The *Bogue* was moored to a buoy in Placentia Bay along with dozens of other ships. Under a clear sky, the waters stretched serene and blue. Low hills dotted with hardy pines surrounded the picturesque town of Placentia with its red-roofed clapboard buildings.

Dan gazed to the bridge above him, his lifelong goal. Denied. At the age of thirty.

"Washington?" Sinclair asked.

A glance behind him revealed unmanned guns and a long stretch of privacy. Sinclair would be leaving the *Bogue* in Belfast, and he'd earned Dan's trust. "I received an unsatisfactory evaluation from my immediate commanding officer. He's recommending the transfer."

"Unsatisfactory? That surprises me. I sized you up as an exemplary officer."

"Exemplary." His sigh rolled into the cool air. "Eight years of exemplary service. No matter how well I do my job, how thorough my reports, how sage my advice, how astute my observations, how solid my character — none of it matters anymore. All undone by one man."

"I find that hard to —"

"He accused me of neglecting my duties,

failing to delegate, and abusing command."

Sinclair frowned at the whaleboat, which was motoring to the buoy. "Is it true?"

"No, but he manipulated the situation, and I have no recourse."

"Why would he . . . ?"

"There's bad blood between us."

"Like the Hatfields and McCoys? I'll never grasp American culture."

Dan almost smiled. "Nothing like that. Eight years ago, I served under him. He was harsh with the men, and I asked an admiral friend for advice. The admiral saw to it that he was disciplined. His career was destroyed. But now he's had his revenge."

A sailor hopped out of the whaleboat onto the buoy, where a doubled chain had moored the *Bogue* for the past three days.

"What about your next in command?" Sinclair asked. "Have you told him about this vendetta?"

"No." Dan's jaw clenched. "I wanted to be noble and high-minded, and I wanted Commander Lewis to judge the man on the present not the past. Look where that got me. If I tell him now, it'll look like sour grapes. Besides, it'll be too late by the time I return."

Down below, the sailor climbed back into the whaleboat. Calls and signals passed between the forecastle deck and the whale-boat, and sailors passed the chain back through the ring on the buoy, using a line bent to the end of the chain.

"Chin up, old man," Sinclair said. "We may be attacked by a wolf pack, and you can perform some valiant deed to save the ship. Heroism erases unsatisfactory evaluations."

No chance of valiant deeds in his data-collecting role. "I'll write the most heroic reports Commander Lewis has ever read."

"That's the spirit."

But Dan's nerves rattled like the chain being drawn to the deck. He hated feeling weak and defenseless.

Since his first day at the Academy, he'd been marked for that exemplary career. His mind, character, and drive impressed every officer. Especially Admiral Howard.

Grief mingled with his frustration. Dan missed his mentor, his friend, his champion. If the admiral had lived, he'd have written that letter and Dan would have left Boston in February.

Pain flamed through his neck. Why hadn't Admiral Howard written that letter? Dan wouldn't have gotten in this mess with Randolph to begin with. He wouldn't have gotten in this mess with Tess either.

At last the *Bogue* was unmoored. The whaleboat was hoisted aboard. And the carrier got underway, both boilers steaming.

Dan's last time on a warship, slicing through the waves, wind on his cheeks, salt in his lungs.

And there was nothing he could do.

38

Boston
Monday, May 3, 1943

Tess poked at the baked beans on her plate. The supper chatter in the Navy Yard cafeteria mocked her solitude, but it seemed best to keep to herself.

Even her acts of selflessness hurt people.

She swallowed a bite, but the beans' sweetness tasted cloying and heavy. Cdr. Thomas Lewis had just interrogated her about the work party she'd held for Dan. She'd meant to help, but she'd done his career more harm than good.

She'd asked the WAVES to volunteer, woman to woman, but they weren't her friends, Commander Lewis reminded her. She was their commanding officer. Now he thought Dan had coerced her into drafting the ladies.

Tess took a bite of pot roast, but it tasted dry and flavorless. Hadn't she hurt Dan enough? What was she thinking? Was she even capable of selfless giving?

Not at all. In her arrogance, she thought she could actually help. In her selfishness, she said she did it for him, but hadn't she cherished the appreciative look he'd given her?

Her eyes felt hot, and she closed them. *Oh Lord, I thought I'd improved, but I haven't. Why did I join the WAVES anyway? To serve my country? Or just so I could feel worthwhile? Lord, please forgive me.*

Tess stared down at her supper. She couldn't keep another bite down, so she stood to bus her tray. It was time to go to the meeting at Robillard's Bakery anyway.

Maybe she should go home. Why was she mixed up in this? Was she playing sleuth to get attention? So everyone would praise her for being clever and helpful?

Her stomach turned, and she marched out of the cafeteria, past the poster her friends had hung only weeks earlier — "Freedom from Want."

Buy war bonds. Keep 'em flying. All together now.

Regardless of her motive for reporting to the FBI, she had to keep her promise.

Half an hour later, Tess entered the bakery.

The usual delectable smells pulled her in, but the usual warmth was lacking.

"*Bonsoir,* Quintessa." Madame Robillard stood by the table closest to the door. "I do not have enough sugar this week, but please take a sandwich."

Tess's heart turned inside out at the pretty sandwiches, just like she'd brought to her work party for Dan. Although she couldn't eat, she took a plate to be polite.

Madame Robillard fiddled with the tie to her apron, gazing around the bakery with moist eyes.

"Madame, are you all right?"

"*Oui.* Everything will be all right." Her face buckled, and she darted behind the counter. "More sandwiches. We need more sandwiches."

Tess joined Yvette and Henri at a table. "Do you know what's wrong with Madame Robillard? She seems upset."

"No, I don't." Lately Yvette's features had changed from sleek and svelte to lean and defined. She shot Henri a glance, and a twitch of his eyebrows said he didn't know either.

About a dozen people sat at the tables, less than half the attendance before the bomb.

Professor Louis Arnaud stood in the back

of the room, his gaze flitting between his wife and the door. Was he afraid his mistress would burst in and make a scene? Or was he watching for the FBI to arrest him for selling secrets? The man wiped his mouth and nose with a handkerchief. "Shall we begin? Who would like to start?"

"May I, Professor?" Jean-Auguste Fournier stood and smoothed his gray suit. "Has anyone been to Rousseau's recently? Mademoiselle Marchand and I dined there this weekend. The meat was overcooked, and the béchamel sauce lacked all subtlety. We were disappointed to say the least."

Solange bobbed her head in agreement.

"The owner is a friend of mine," Henri said, his hand entwined with Yvette's. "His chef was drafted, and he hasn't found a replacement."

"Yet another wartime sacrifice we —"

"Food?" Pierre Guillory bellowed, his chair tumbling to the floor behind him.

Tess jumped and edged back.

Pierre gestured wildly, his wide face red. "Our homeland is occupied by Nazi swine. They send our young men to Germany as slave labor. They round up our Jewish neighbors and send them who knows where. They turn Frenchmen against Frenchmen. Collaborators spy on patriots. The Milice arrest the Maquis. Everyone lives in fear of the Gestapo. No one has enough to eat. And you — you whine about the béchamel sauce?"

Jean-Auguste lowered his chin. "I apologize, monsieur, for choosing a topic you know nothing about."

"Why, you —" Pierre charged forward.

"Don't." Henri stepped in front of the dockworker, his dark eyes hard as onyx.

Tess held her breath, but she couldn't hold her opinion. Monsieur Guillory was correct.

"You . . ." Pierre shook his finger in Henri's face. "I used to call you friend. You used to stand for France. And now you stand in my way."

"I always stand for France."

"You say nothing. You do nothing."

Yvette rose to her feet. "You do not know what you say, monsieur. There is more than one way to aid France."

Tess gazed up. The strength and conviction reminded her of the old Yvette.

"More than one way?" Pierre snorted and jabbed his finger in Henri's chest. "I would be happy if you picked one."

Professor Arnaud's forehead wrinkled. "What would you recommend? We lost our sources in France, and we can't send letters anymore."

Pierre's gaze hadn't budged from Henri. "Name one way you help."

"I do what I can." Henri's voice lowered to a growl.

"You do nothing. You are a traitor!"

Tess joined in the gasps.

"Please, Monsieur Guillory. You mustn't say such things." The professor waved his hand as if cleaning his blackboard.

The dockworker glanced around the room and took half a step back, chagrined.

"You must see how it is," the professor said. "We can only aid the war effort from here in America. Do your job, buy bonds, save scrap. Someday we shall invade and drive out the Nazis."

Jean-Auguste sank into his chair. "If France survives the invasion, that is."

Another roar from Pierre. "That is how traitors talk! There is only one punishment for traitors." He marched forward.

Henri held up one hand. "Don't do anything you'll regret."

"You! You're the worst traitor of all!" Pierre swung at him.

In one swift move, Henri blocked the punch, swept the man's feet out from under him, and threw him to the floor, one hand poised like a blade at the man's jugular.

Tess cried out, and others did too. Then silence forced its way to the top.

Pierre moaned and stared up at Henri.

But Henri was looking at Yvette with alarm, as if he'd done something wrong.

Tess's heart pounded, and her grip tightened on her purse.

Suddenly, Henri offered a hand to Pierre. "I apologize, monsieur."

Pierre swatted away the offer and scrambled to his feet. "I do not want the help of a traitor. You — all of you — you're all traitors. You all deserve to die!" He stormed out of the bakery.

"Oh my goodness," Tess whispered, and she faced Yvette, expecting to see disdain.

Instead, something unfamiliar flickered in Yvette's golden-brown eyes, and then it was gone.

Fear.

Tess still felt shaky as she returned to quarters. The meeting had fallen apart after Pierre left. Was that an actual threat? Or a hothead letting off steam? Either way, she'd report every word to the FBI tomorrow.

And every move. Tess knew nothing about fighting, but Henri had used no ordinary moves to take Pierre down. He'd had training, and the alarm on his face said the training was meant to remain secret.

Tess opened the door. Her new roommate, Lorena Gibbons, brushed past her. "Hiya, Tess. I'm going to Mabel and Anne's room — Mabel's mama sent fudge. Want to come?"

"No, thanks." That threesome did too much giggling and gossiping.

"Suit yourself." The pretty brunette strolled down the hall. "By the way, some letters came for you. I put them on your bed."

"Thanks." Tess shut the door, her heart aching for her former friendship with Nora. The day after the disaster with Dan, Tess had apologized and told Nora she was right and Tess had been horribly wrong, but Nora hadn't trusted Tess's sincerity. Only a few days later, the Navy sent Nora back to Smith College for specialized communications school. After she graduated, she'd probably be assigned somewhere other than Boston. They'd never have the chance to make up.

Tess stashed her purse and overcoat and cover, and she picked up the letters. From Ada Sue, Papa, and —

Pain crushed her lungs. "Dan."

Solitude intensified the pain. She wanted a friend. Mary would let her cry, gently reprimand her, and then comfort her. But she couldn't tell Mary how she'd hurt Dan. Mary and Lillian and Dan were family, and that complicated matters. She had to be discreet.

By the time he returned, Tess would figure out a statement that was both honest and kind. In the meantime, she'd told her friends she didn't want to talk about him. Mary and Lillian assumed she was sad because he was away at sea.

At least the sadness was honest.

Tess stared at the envelope, at Dan's strong handwriting. How could she bear to read it? Maybe she should throw it away. What could he say that she hadn't already said to herself? Nothing was to be gained from the letter but more heartache.

Yet her fingers clenched the envelope. That night, she'd fled before he could respond. This was his response. If she loved him, she'd listen to every painful word.

Tess changed into pajamas and gathered handkerchiefs. If she was going to cry herself to sleep, she might as well be prepared.

She sat on her bed and pulled the covers over her lap. Then she bent her head over the letter. *Lord, please use Dan's words to humble me. Show me how to be selfless.*

With a long ratcheting breath, she pulled out two sheets of stationery, covered front and back. Oh dear. For a man of few words, he'd certainly found his fair share.

Dear Tess,

I owe you many apologies, but let me start with my major regret. I'd planned a speech to explain my change in heart. I hadn't planned the kiss. If I'd followed my plan, I wouldn't have hurt you and I apologize for that. On the other hand, someday both of us will be grateful for that mistake. The kiss revealed why our romance never would have worked. Better we found out now than later.

Second, I apologize for calling you beautiful. While true, it was unkind. I know exactly what the word means to you, and I'm grieved that my careless words undermined what you've worked for these past months.

Since I was unable to explain myself that night, now I'll relate the speech. I'd planned to say I wanted to ask you out after I received a transfer and was no longer under Mr. Randolph's thumb.

I anticipated the confusion you voiced. For a decade, I avoided romance. At the Academy, I dated a girl named Joanie.

She resembled you in a superficial way — attractive, gregarious, and full of life. That's where your similarities end. Joanie whined when I chose to study rather than see her. She manipulated me. She cried when I mentioned going to sea, saying if I loved her I'd never leave her.

Admiral Howard saw how my work suffered, and he gave me a stern lecture. He was right. Joanie distracted me from my goal, so I ended the relationship.

However, the admiral was also wrong. A dedicated bachelor himself, he saw all women as a distraction to the serious officer.

For ten years, I followed his advice. Then you came along. Although I found you attractive, I set you in the same category as Joanie and ignored you.

However, working with you changed my opinion of you and of Admiral Howard's teaching. You encouraged me in my career, helped me toward my goal, and cheered when I went to sea. I began to wonder if the right type of woman would be more help than hindrance.

When Admiral Howard died with no family to grieve him, I was shaken. I was no longer content to be alone. I wanted someone in my life. And I wanted that someone to be you.

Over the last few months, I wrestled with my final reservations. And when the Navy reversed policy last month, I decided to pursue you.

The speech was part of my plan. The kiss wasn't. I had guarded my feelings while I fell in love with you, and I knew it wouldn't be fair to lower that guard all at once. Now we see how right I was.

When you asked me why I kissed you, my brain was addled by the kiss. The long list of reasons I loved you boiled down to one concept — you are beautiful inside and out. That's the single word that fell out of my mouth.

Here's what I should have said. I love how you want to be useful. I love how you've challenged yourself in the WAVES and have dedicated yourself to something important. You bring energy, intelligence, creativity, and generosity to your very worthwhile work. You have my respect.

I also love how you care about your friends and family, and how you've encouraged me. Your kindness, pushing, and teasing have helped me become more balanced as a man. You have my affection.

But there's also something about you that I struggle to describe. You add color to my black-and-white life. When you're around, I feel lighter and see clearer and have deeper perspective. Tess, you have my love.

I didn't plan to tell you I loved you that night. I knew it would be too much. But since this is the last time I'll speak freely to you, I want you to know the truth. You doubted — with good reason — that I cared for the real woman inside. Only by revealing my love can I hope to erase those doubts.

Before you get the notion that this grumbling, bumbling oaf is trying to win your heart, rest assured that I have called off the pursuit.

Part of me wants to apologize for ruining our chance at love. The fact that you accepted my kiss shows you had some romantic interest in me.

However, it was only a matter of time. I am brusque. My words have often offended you. No matter how hard I tried to change, I would have continued to offend you, even inadvertently. You need a man who will shower you with sweet words, softly spoken. I am not that man, and I never will be.

The second half of the problem is the way you walk away and refuse to listen when you're offended. I need a woman who will listen to my explanations and allow me to apologize. All men — all people — deserve the opportunity to apologize when they've hurt someone. No one should have to resort to writing a letter that will probably be ripped to shreds without being read.

May I offer one piece of advice? I urge you not to condemn the next man who calls you beautiful. Like it or not, the word applies to you. To expect a man to sift through a dictionary while he's holding the woman he loves in his arms is too much to ask. Don't do it again.

The last matter to address is how we shall act when I return. I intend to act as an officer and a gentleman, with polite military distance, and I will not pursue you again. I only ask for a measure of courtesy in return.

Sincerely, Dan

Tess let the tears dribble down her chin. What could he say that she hadn't already said to herself? Only that he'd fallen in love with her.

She doubled over from the pain of it. He'd fallen in love with her? He loved her?

When he kissed her, he hadn't been carried away at the sight of a pretty face. No, he'd kissed her because he loved her, all of her.

She brushed her eyes against her sleeve and gazed at the blurry words. "This — this is what I could have had." If she hadn't pitched a childish fit.

But she had. His righteous anger seeped out at the end of the letter, and she was glad he didn't hide it. Otherwise, she could have deluded herself into believing she could change his mind.

She couldn't. She'd gained his love, only to lose it forever.

Londonderry, Northern Ireland
Wednesday, May 12, 1943

The dive-bomber plunged, engines whining, guns chattering, and the *Bogue*'s machine gunner ducked out of the way, breaking his fire.

A dozen other gunners burst into laughter, but Dan shook his head.

"Nice shootin' there, Ray! What do you call that? *Duck* hunting?"

"Aw, pipe down," Ray said. "It looks real."

"Precisely." The Royal Navy gunnery instructor flipped on the lights inside the dome teacher.

Dan blinked as the film being projected inside the huge concrete dome faded to pale gray.

A Women's Royal Naval Service technician carried a film can to the projector, and she changed reels.

The instructor strode forward, hands

clasped behind his back. "The dome teacher is designed to look and sound real in order to train you for combat. The natural instinct is to duck, but the consequences in battle would be dire."

"I'm sorry, sir," Ray said.

"You will learn to curb your natural impulse, and next time you will do better. Next?"

"Beecher, that's you. Kill that duck."

Beecher grinned at his buddy and took his place behind the dummy gun.

The instructor showed him how to operate the device. "When you press the trigger, you will project an image of a gunsight on the dome. Don't forget to aim off. I believe you Americans call it 'leading,' but 'aiming off' is a more accurate term."

To Dan's left, two of the *Bogue*'s gunnery officers nudged each other. Since the carrier had docked at Belfast on May 2, the men had engaged in spirited discussions with their Royal Navy brethren, comparing British and American terminology, tactics, training, and technology.

The Wren fed the last bit of film through the projector and turned it on. Out went the lights.

The film played on the inside of the dome as in a planetarium. The footage had been shot on a ship in convoy, complete with sounds of battle.

An enemy aircraft appeared low on the horizon, and Beecher lined the gun up with the target and kept the projected gunsight well in front of the plane's nose, aiming for the spot where the plane would be when the bullets arrived.

The bomber zoomed overhead, and Dan sucked in his breath on instinct. But he didn't duck, and neither did Beecher. Then a dive-bomber came into view, and Beecher swung his gun up to meet it.

For the rest of the afternoon, the gunners took turns, improving with each pass.

Dan's mind hummed with possibilities. Although antiaircraft gunnery had nothing to do with antisubmarine warfare, Commander Lewis had asked Dan to observe training in the dome teacher. The concept was excellent — simulating combat conditions while minimizing danger and damage.

In the faint light, Dan sketched an idea on the notepad in his portfolio. Perhaps the technology could be adapted to train aircrew to attack submarines. A scaffold with a dummy gun, perhaps a dummy depth bomb release. Film could be projected on the floor.

The past ten days in Belfast and Londonderry had been productive. He'd even spent two entire days with the Huff-Duff experts as they trained the officers and men.

He couldn't wait to share his reports with his commander.

Dan's gut contracted. But then it would all be over. The *Bogue* was scheduled to sail in three days, and in two weeks she'd arrive in Argentia. Orders would be waiting for him — orders to return to Boston only long enough to turn in his reports and clean out his desk. Then he'd catch a train to Washington, DC.

After the gunners and officers grabbed supper in the base cafeteria, they boarded a train back to Belfast. Dan sat in a compartment with the *Bogue*'s gunnery officers, Lieutenants Chandler, Moody, and Lorenz.

Dan shared their eagerness to return to sea. While escorting Convoy HX-235, they'd conducted flight operations on all but one day, and a TBF had attacked a surfaced submarine. Ricocheting depth bombs foiled the attack and inspired discussion about how to prevent ricochets in the future.

Now the crew had experience and even more training. Now the carrier boasted Huff-Duff as well as radar and sonar. And now the tide of the Battle of the Atlantic was turning, the power swinging at last to the Allies, Dan could feel it. After horrific losses of merchant ships in March, May brought change as fresh as spring. U-boats were going down by the handful, sunk by surface ships and aircraft, often working together.

Perhaps it wasn't the turning point yet, but it had a momentous quality to it, bearing the weight of Allied production and ingenuity and strength. With the last bit of North Africa expected to fall into Allied hands any day now, defeating Nazi Germany seemed more than possible. It was inevitable.

Soon his fellow officers leaned back for naps, but Dan couldn't sleep, his mind churning with both purpose and frustration. Irish green hills rolled by, lit by the gold of the sunset.

Tess's eyes.

Dan grunted and opened his portfolio. At such a time in the war, America needed good officers at sea, not filed in Washington because they'd made enemies with the wrong man. Plenty of officers preferred desk jobs. More and more WAVES were reporting for duty, perfectly capable of performing those jobs. How could the Navy disarm an officer who longed to fight?

Dan's ambition and indignation wrestled

with his helplessness and resignation. It wasn't like him to surrender. It never had been.

Bad enough he couldn't fight for Tess. She'd made her wishes clear. He wouldn't humiliate himself by crawling to her. Nor would he break the promise he'd made not to pursue her. Why would he pursue her anyway? Why would he want to walk on eggshells for the rest of his life?

Dan tapped his pen on the notepad in his portfolio. But his career . . . there had to be a way to fight for it.

If only Admiral Howard had lived. If only he'd written that letter.

The top piece of paper felt thin in Dan's fingers, yet a single sheet of paper held the power to make a career or shatter one.

What would Admiral Howard have written? Dan could hear his mentor's voice in his head, gruff but warm.

With his life in shambles, Dan needed to hear those words, so he scratched them on the notepad: *The finest midshipman in your class. Not just smart. You have drive and character and presence. The other mids know — you're the one to watch. . . . Daniel Avery is known for his integrity. Even as an ensign, he exhibits a noble sort of compassion, bearing grievances with a stoicism befitting the greatest admiral. . . . You're going places. You note problems, analyze them, and envision solutions. . . . I have plans for this young man.*

Then Dan scribbled down his accomplishments as Admiral Howard would have described them, focusing on the breadth of experience and depth of knowledge, including the year at ASWU learning technology that would make him an ideal officer in the modern Navy.

What if Admiral Howard had added a warning about Randolph in his letter, a subtle statement to nullify any possible negative evaluations?

Dan stared at the page in the fading light.

This was the letter the admiral would have written, should have written. Indeed, he'd meant to write it and would be grieved to know what had happened to his protégé.

Perhaps Dan could write it for him.

Nonsense. He yanked down the blackout shade and turned on the lamp. That would be forgery, a crime and grounds for losing his commission.

He closed the portfolio, but his breath came deeper and slower and harder.

Death had stolen the letter from him. Admiral Howard would be furious to see Dan languishing in Washington, his talents wasted.

Randolph was stealing his career from him. All because Dan insisted on being high-minded. Dan should have told Lewis every sordid detail of their time on the *Texas* and every petty offense at ASWU.

Dan might not be able to salvage his own career, but he could ruin Randolph's — and for good this time. The man didn't deserve his commission.

A naval officer needed to be aggressive and fight for what was right.

And this was right.

40

Boston
Saturday, May 22, 1943

"What matinee shall we see?" Mary spread the newspaper on the coffee table in her apartment.

"No men with us this afternoon, so we can pick something romantic," Lillian said.

With the War Loan Drive over, Tess had her Saturdays free again, but she couldn't stomach anything romantic.

"How about *They Came to Blow Up America*?" Mary tapped the paper. "It's about those German spies who landed in New York and Florida by U-boat."

Tess made a face. She also couldn't stomach a spy movie. "Anything else?"

"There's a new Humphrey Bogart movie," Lillian said. "*Action in the North Atlantic*. Oh, probably not."

Two sets of concerned eyes turned to Tess.

"You poor thing," Mary said. "I hate to

see you so sad and quiet. But cheer up. He'll be back soon."

Time to tell her friends the truth, or as much of it as she could. She drew a deep breath. "I'm not sad because he's at sea. I'm sad because it won't work between us."

"What?" Lillian's hazel eyes widened. "I thought . . . but on his birthday . . ."

Tess tugged at the sleeves of her navy-blue jacket, longing for her new dress whites, for a fresh start. "That night I did something selfish, and we realized it would never work."

"What happened?" Lillian said.

"I can't tell you. You're his sister — and Mary, you're his sister-in-law. We need to be discreet."

"Oh, sweetie." Mary leaned her shoulder against Tess's. "You've been keeping this to yourself for over a month? But you need to talk to people. And Nora's gone now. Were you able to talk to her?"

"I told her everything." Tess's voice came out strained. "She was still angry with me when she left, and I don't blame her."

"That bad, huh?" Lillian's voice sank low in understanding.

"That bad." The squirming sensation in her belly — when would it go away? She was writing Dan a letter, but it wouldn't reach him until he returned. It was so difficult — how could she communicate the depth of her regret without sounding as if she were trying to change his mind?

Tess scooted forward and studied the movie listings. "How about a western? There's a new one with Dana Andrews and Henry Fonda, *The Ox-Bow Incident*."

The apartment door opened, and Yvette entered.

"You're home early," Mary said. "I thought you and Henri went away for the weekend."

Yvette paused with her back to them, her hat perched over the coatrack. "I — we changed plans. I'm moving to New York today."

"Moving!" Lillian cried. "To New York?"

"Today?" Tess peered over the back of the couch and clamped her lips so she wouldn't mention the conversation she'd overheard. It wasn't June yet. What had changed?

Mary stood, concern etched on her face. "But . . . but what about your jobs at the Navy Yard?"

Yvette braced one hand on the wall, fingers wide, and then she pushed back and slipped out of her coat. "I'll call from New York and quit."

Her voice sounded odd, and Tess exchanged glances with Mary and Lillian.

Lillian stood. "Why today? What's the rush?"

"I — I —" Yvette strode to her room. "I have to leave."

What was wrong? Tess and her friends followed Yvette.

She pulled a suitcase from the closet and flung it onto the bed. Where was the one she'd used for the weekend? Why hadn't she brought it home?

"What's wrong?" Mary asked.

"Nothing." Yvette grabbed an armload of dresses and stuffed them in the suitcase, her movements frantic and jerky. "I need to . . . too many dresses. I need slips, stockings."

Tess held her breath. Something was horribly wrong.

"Shoes, a hairbrush —" Yvette's voice cracked. She gripped the dresser, clothing tumbled from her hands, and a low moan spilled out. "Henri . . . he's dead."

"What?" Tess gasped. "Henri?"

"Oh no, oh no." Yvette turned wild eyes to Tess. "I'm not supposed to tell. You can't — you can't tell anyone. Do you hear?"

"What do you mean?" Mary's voice quivered. "Henri's dead? How —"

"I was supposed to die too. That's why I need to leave now." She clutched the edge of the dresser, but her knees buckled and she slipped to the floor. "Oh, Henri. Henri."

Tess fell to her knees in front of her. "What happened?"

"Start from the beginning." Mary sat beside her friend and put her arm around her shoulder.

"We — we went to our usual hideaway." Yvette's voice trembled, and she pressed her hand to her forehead. "When I went to his room this morning, he — he opened the door, but he was down on his knees. He was bright red — like a cherry — and he was breathing hard. He said the pastries were poisoned, and — and he was glad he was greedy and hadn't waited for me. He went into convulsions, and he — he died. It happened so fast."

"The almond pastries that were delivered yesterday?" Lillian knelt, arms wrapped around her middle, her face pale. "Almond? Cherry-red skin? It was cyanide."

Yvette's gaze homed in on Lillian. "You took the delivery from Robillard's. Tell me everything. Every detail."

"Oh goodness. Oh goodness."

Tess felt a bit sick. "From Robillard's? Madame Robillard? Solange?"

"No," Yvette said. "Definitely not. Please, Lillian. Every detail."

Lillian stared at the ceiling, working her lips between her teeth. "The girl was in her twenties or thirties, taller than I, and slim — it wasn't Solange. She had very red hair, and she wore a red beret. They clashed, and I wondered why she wore it."

Tess's fingertips dug into her forearms. Like Professor Arnaud's mistress, Helga.

"Anything else?" Yvette leaned closer. "Eyes, facial features?"

"I didn't notice."

"That's why she wore the red wig, the red beret, to draw your eye away. Tell me exactly what she said. Yesterday you told me Pierre Guillory sent the pastries as a gift."

"Pierre Guillory!" Tess cried.

Yvette didn't look away from Lillian. "Every word."

Lillian drew a deep breath. "She said she had a delivery from Robillard's. The pastries were a gift from Pierre Guillory to apologize for his behavior. He hoped Henri could forgive him and you could still be friends."

"His behavior?" Mary asked.

Yvette gathered the clothing on the floor. "He called Henri a traitor and said he deserved to die, said all of us deserved to die. He carried out his threat. He bought almond pastries, because he knows they're Henri's favorite and he wants to make

Madame Robillard look guilty. He poisoned them, then had his daughter deliver them wearing a red wig."

Tess's mind swam. "I know he's a loud-mouth, but a murderer?"

Yvette stumbled to her feet with an arm-load of clothing. "He's the bomber too. A girl in a red beret."

Tess frowned. Or it could have been Professor Arnaud and Helga, and they were taking advantage of Pierre's death threat.

Clothing overflowed the suitcase. "That Pierre. He thinks we're complacent, but he has no idea — no idea what he's done."

"What about the police?" Mary asked softly.

"They came. I called them. Of course, I called them. I'm not a suspect, so they let me go."

"To New York?" Lillian's forehead crinkled.

"They want me to go for my own safety."

Tess picked up the straggling items of clothing. As Henri's girlfriend and the only witness, Yvette would top the suspect list. Why would they let her leave the state?

She needed to call the FBI. Yvette was certainly innocent, but the FBI needed to know about the murder before she fled town. But she couldn't call from the apart-

433

ment with Yvette listening. She had to leave, to find a pay phone. What excuse could she give?

Yvette snatched toiletries from the dresser top. "That's why I have to leave now. If Pierre finds out I survived, he'll come after me. That's why the — why the police don't want me to tell anyone about Henri yet. They won't go to arrest Pierre until I'm safe, in case he has accomplices or he escapes. You must promise to be quiet."

"We will," Mary said.

Tess had no intention of keeping quiet. She rose to her feet. *Lord, give me a reason to leave.*

"Oh no." Yvette bowed her head over the suitcase. "Madame Robillard. She's in danger. Pierre used her pastries. He hates her too. I — I have to warn her. She's like a mother to me."

"Call her," Lillian said.

"No!" Yvette whirled around. "The phone might be bugged — ours, Madame Robillard's. I have to go in person. But I — I can't be seen. And I have to leave town."

What a quick answer to prayer. "I'll go."

"Would you?" Yvette turned grateful, red-rimmed eyes to her. "Tell her in private. Tell her not to tell a soul. Solange mustn't know. She can't keep a secret. Tell Madame Robil-

434

lard to leave town for a few days. I couldn't bear it if anything happened to her."

"I'll tell her all that."

"Thank you." She closed her eyes and pressed her fingertips to her eyelids. "Would you mind? I need some privacy."

"Of course." Tess led her friends out of the bedroom and shut the door behind her. "I think you two should leave the apartment for a while."

"That sounds like an excellent idea," Lillian said. "And the choice of movie . . ."

"It doesn't matter anymore, does it?" Mary's eyes glistened. "Poor Henri. Poor Yvette."

Tess squeezed her friends' hands. "Be careful. I'll see you later."

She grabbed her raincoat and cover from the coatrack and jogged down the stairs to Monument Avenue. *Lord, guide me every step of the way.*

41

South of Greenland
Saturday, May 22, 1943

The Avenger streaked past Dan's position on the machine gun sponson, and propwash blustered in his face.

A perfect landing. Two of the four TBFs from the morning patrol had returned. The third would supply plenty of material for Dan's reports.

The U-boats had discovered Convoy ON-184.

The *Bogue* had been informed that twenty-three U-boats were converging on the convoy as well as on Convoy HX-239, which was steaming nearby in the other direction.

Before sunset the previous evening, Lt. Cdr. William Drane, the squadron commander, had spotted a surfaced U-boat. To avoid ricocheting depth bombs, he'd slowed down by lowering his landing gear. The bombs straddled the U-boat and damaged the conning tower, but the U-boat dove and escaped.

This morning, the American destroyers *George E. Badger* and *Greene* had each attacked U-boats, Lt. Roger Kuhn's Avenger had attacked a sub to the southeast, and Lt. Richard Rogers's Wildcat had spotted another to the southwest.

Twenty-three U-boats. Thirty-nine Allied merchant ships. The six warships of Canadian Escort Group C-1. And the *Bogue* and her five destroyers.

Dan drew a deep breath of cool air. It was going to be a long, tense, and exciting day. He was ready.

Kuhn's TBF approached with flaps and landing gear down. Dan frowned. The torpedo bomber seemed a bit high. Sure enough, it glanced over the arresting wires and slammed into the net barrier.

Dan's groan was echoed by the machine gunners behind him. Although the *Bogue* had increased her complement of Avengers from nine to twelve, she couldn't afford to lose any to damage.

The deck gang rushed to the TBF, and the crew climbed out unharmed.

Dan scrambled down the ladder to the aviators' ready room. Before long, Kuhn's three-man crew arrived, and the air officers debriefed them while Dan filled out his reports and asked clarifying questions.

Kuhn had spotted the U-boat fifty-five miles away from the convoy. Taking advantage of the clouds, he sneaked up on the Germans, then dove. To his shock, the U-boat's gunners shot back — something the squadron hadn't encountered yet.

After Kuhn let loose his four depth bombs, the U-boat settled by the stern and trailed oil.

Following the latest protocol, the pilot radioed his attack to the *Bogue.* However, he sent incorrect coordinates, and the other aircraft and escort ships couldn't locate him. For an hour, he circled the damaged sub, out of depth bombs.

When the U-boat submerged, Kuhn sent another radio report, allowing the *Bogue* to fix his position. But the sub escaped.

Dan rubbed his neck as he filled in the last of the data. So many U-boats, so many attacks, but nothing to show for it.

Since no more planes were due to land for a while, he'd visit the Combat Information Center and check the latest transmissions.

Dan headed down the passageway that crossed to starboard. An officer in khakis was coming toward him, and Dan's stomach clenched.

The chaplain.

"Good morning, sir," Dan said.

"Good morning, Mr. Avery." The chaplain gave him a serene smile. "We missed you in services last week. Will we see you tomorrow?"

"If the battle situation allows." Dan gave him a polite nod and continued on his way. For once, he hoped the battle would keep him busy.

Dan climbed the ladder to the outside catwalk. He worked his way forward, passing guns and gunners, cool briny air filling his lungs.

He didn't want to hear God nag him. After he gave his letter to Commander Lewis and exposed Mr. Randolph's deeds, then he'd listen. But not yet.

If he couldn't have the woman he loved, he'd better have the career he loved. And if he couldn't have that, at least Randolph was going down with him.

When Dan reached the bridge tower, he descended the ladder into the cluster of compartments at the base. He passed the aerology office and entered the Combat Information Center.

It took a minute for his eyes to adjust to

the dimly lit compartment and for his ears to adjust to the cacophony of radar pips, sonar pings, crackling radio "squawk boxes," and the two dozen crewmen calling to each other and speaking into phones.

In Dan's opinion, the CIC ranked high among the Navy's best ideas of the war. All combat information flowed into and out of this compartment. Radio, radar, sonar, Huff-Duff, and intelligence were received and marked on the plotting table. The officers evaluated the information and sent filtered reports to the bridge, gunnery, other ships, or the aircraft.

A radio operator took off his headphones and turned to the CIC watch officer. "Sir, a transmission from Doty. One hearse, two-six-zero, eighteen."

Dan charged to the plotting table. A surfaced U-boat, bearing 260 degrees, eighteen miles from the *Bogue* — to the west. Since the *Bogue* was now permanently stationed behind the convoy, the U-boat was in an ideal location to attack the merchant ships. Doty had better sink that sub or keep him occupied.

The officer repeated the transmission to the talker to send to the bridge, while a sailor marked the U-boat's position on the plotting table.

"Sir!" The Huff-Duff recorder looked up with bright eyes. "I'm receiving something."

Dan strode over, heart beating fast. "Dits and dahs" of Morse code filled the air. A U-boat was sending a message. While Dan would have loved to have been able to decode the message, the content didn't matter — only the location of the sub. On the round oscilloscope screen, a neon green figure eight flashed, tipped at an angle. A contact.

The operator tuned the oscilloscope until one of the lobes of the figure eight grew larger than the other, pointing to bearing two-six-zero. It worked! Apparently the U-boat was signaling the wolf pack about Doty's Avenger.

The talker informed the captain that Huff-Duff confirmed Doty's sighting and reported back that another TBF was preparing to launch.

Dan marched to the plotting table. Dozens of little circles indicated the Allied warships and merchant ships, and *X*'s indicated U-boat sightings. Far too many.

And getting far too close.

Boston

Tess held open the door of Robillard's for a lady who was leaving with a baby in one arm and a pastry box in the other.

No other customers remained. And where was Madame Robillard?

A grunting sound came from toward the kitchen. Oh no! What happened?

Tess dashed to the half-door that led behind the counter. Madame Robillard was down on hands and knees scrubbing with a rag. "Madame? What happened?"

"Oh, Quintessa." Madame Robillard sat back on her heels and smiled at her, but then she made a face. "That Solange. She spilled a full gallon tin of cooking oil. It is hard to get oil now, and she is careless."

"Oh dear."

"I am so angry, I sent her home early. It is a quiet time of day anyway." Madame Robillard flung oily rags into a wicker basket. "What would you like? Bread? Croissants?"

Tess gripped the top of the half-door. "I'm afraid I came with bad news."

"Bad news?"

The poor woman would be devastated. Tess held open the door. "Let's have a seat."

"Oh no." The baker pulled herself up and darted to the nearest table. "Is it Yvette?"

Tess nodded and sat in a chair with her knees facing Madame Robillard's. "She came home early from her weekend away.

Henri — I'm afraid Henri is dead."

"Henri?" Her hands flew to her mouth. "My Henri? He cannot be dead."

"I'm so sorry, but it's true." An ache spread throughout her chest.

"And Yvette? She is fine? That is good. But — but how?"

"Someone poisoned him. And — and I'm afraid they used your pastries."

"My . . . ?" Fire flashed in her brown eyes. "Pierre Guillory. *Oui.* He bought two pastries on Friday. The almond, Henri's favorite. He threatened to kill Henri and Yvette. You heard him."

"I — I did. But we don't know who it was. A redheaded woman delivered them to Yvette's apartment, but —"

"Pierre's daughter in a red wig. I know it. A red beret too?"

Tess nodded, but her mouth went dry. Why would she ask about a beret?

"Like the bomber. I knew Pierre did it." Madame Robillard slapped her knees. "He used my pastries? He knew almond would hide the taste of cyanide. How dare he?"

She'd put that together even faster than Lillian.

The front door opened, and an elderly couple entered the bakery.

"Oh, I cannot!" Madame Robillard cried.

443

"I must close. Bad news. Very bad. Please forgive me."

The couple nodded, concern on their faces, and they left.

Madame Robillard stood, twisting her apron. "I must close. Oh! I am so sad. So angry."

"How can I help?"

The baker bustled behind the counter. "Turn over the sign on the door, then draw the shades. I'll close down back here. Oh, poor Henri. And Yvette — she did not eat?"

Tess flipped the sign from open to closed. "He warned her in time, thank goodness."

"*Oui,* thank goodness."

"She is very upset of course, and she's scared. She thinks she's still in danger." Tess found the cord for the blinds and released them to cover the door. "She thinks you're in danger too. The murderer used your pastries."

"Me? In danger? *Non.*" By the cash register, Madame Robillard flapped her hand. "Pierre would never hurt me. We are old friends."

Tess pulled down a shade in the seating area. "We don't know for sure it's Pierre."

"Yes, we do."

Tess frowned. For an old friend, she was quick to accuse. "Still, Yvette wants you to

444

leave town for a few days, just to be safe."

"Oh, but my bakery!" The cash register drawer slammed shut.

"You're closed today anyway, and tomorrow is Sunday. You should leave town. The police won't make any moves until they know Yvette is safe."

"Safe? What do you mean?"

Tess pulled down the next shade. "The police want her to leave town immediately."

"Leave town? No, she cannot."

Why wouldn't she want Yvette to flee? Tess studied the older woman's face. "She must. For her own safety."

"She — she would leave? Without saying good-bye to me?"

Tess's breath came more easily, and she headed for the next window. "She sent me to say good-bye for her. She doesn't dare come out in public. She can't take the chance of the murderer seeing her."

"Oh dear. Oh dear. I have to tell —"

"Tell? No! You can't tell anyone, not even Solange. She only wanted you to know so you could leave, to protect you. But you can't tell anyone until the murderers are behind bars."

Madame Robillard lowered the window shade at the end of the counter. "Oh dear. All right. I — I would like to be alone now.

My poor Henri."

Tess drew down the last shade. On such an overcast day, she hated to snuff out the little bit of light. "Are you sure you don't want me to help you close up?"

"No, you go. I have so little to do. I need to be alone."

Just as well. Tess had postponed calling the FBI to warn Madame Robillard, but she shouldn't wait any longer. "Promise me you'll leave town."

"I — I promise." She disappeared into the kitchen. "Good-bye, Quintessa."

Tess opened the front door, making the bells jingle, but she paused. Maybe she was too hasty. Should she leave Madame Robillard alone in her grief?

From back in the kitchen came the clicking of a phone dial.

Tess sucked in her breath. She'd told Madame not to tell anyone. Whom was she calling? And why?

"Jean-Auguste? Oh, it is bad. Henri is dead."

Jean-Auguste? Why would she call Jean-Auguste? Tess's heart hiccupped. She squatted below the level of the counter in case the baker peeked out, and she held the door open a crack.

"No, no. Yvette — she survived. *Oui, oui.* I

446

know. She is leaving town today."

Tess strained to hear through the silence.

"I do not like that. You know I do not. Oh dear. I know, but she will not come. She does not want to be seen."

Tess's thoughts tumbled, and she squeezed her eyes shut against the dizziness. Madame Robillard? Jean-Auguste? What was going on?

"All right. Yes, I see. I'll do that. *Au revoir.*"

Oh no! Tess had to leave, and she eased the door open, careful not to set the bells to jingling.

But the phone dial clicked again, and Tess stopped.

"Oh, Yvette! Quintessa told me about Henri. You poor thing. But you cannot leave town without saying good-bye."

Tess braced her free hand on the wooden floor. She'd told Madame exactly why Yvette couldn't come.

"I cannot leave the bakery. Solange is home sick, and it is so busy. So many customers. You understand."

Tess understood one thing — Madame Robillard was a barefaced liar.

"*Oui,* I understand. But maybe . . . could you wear a disguise? Please? You are like my own daughter." She sobbed. "You cannot . . . you cannot . . ."

Not just a liar, but a manipulator.

"Oh, *merci. Merci, ma petite.* You have made an old woman happy. Please come soon."

Her heart thudding, Tess backed out the open door. Then she eased the door shut and stood. A mother with two young children stared at her.

She must have looked very strange indeed. Tess gave them a shaky smile and strode down the street, scanning for the nearest pay phone.

Madame Robillard was lying, and Yvette was falling into a trap.

Tess had to warn Yvette and call the FBI.

She couldn't wait another minute.

42

South of Greenland

"I got him! He was straight up and down." Ensign Stewart Doty ran his hand through his blond hair, enthusiasm shining on his too-young face.

Dan nodded, but he and the other officers had to pry under the enthusiasm for the facts. And the facts didn't confirm a sinking yet. Doty had flown through a curtain of the U-boat's antiaircraft fire to drop four depth bombs from sixty feet. Three missed, but one exploded under the sub and tipped her on her side. Leaking oil, she tilted up with her bow in the air. But then she regained control and dove.

The destroyer USS *Osmond Ingram* and two more Avengers were searching the area, but no reports had come in.

Dan asked questions until his form was complete. At least the U-boat had been damaged, which might keep her out of the battle.

After Doty's crew departed, Dan tidied his report and Lt. Cdr. William Drane briefed two Avenger crews, preparing them to launch when needed.

Dan tucked his forms in his portfolio — impressive in its thickness, but not in success. If only he could bring home one confirmed sinking to catch Commander Lewis's eye and validate his work in ASWU.

The phone buzzed, and a sailor answered. "Mr. Drane, it's the CIC. Mr. Stearns attacked a sub, bearing three-four-zero, distance twenty-five."

Dan darted to the chart on the wall. That position was close to where Doty had attacked.

"Very well. Inform conn and CIC that two TBFs are preparing to launch." Mr. Drane showed the crews the new position on the chart.

The six men pulled on the rest of their flight gear and jogged to the ladder that went down to the hangar deck.

"I'm heading to the bridge," Mr. Drane said in his Virginia accent.

Dan grabbed his portfolio. "I'll go with you."

"Have you had lunch yet, Mr. Avery?"

Dan motioned with his thumb to the table of sandwiches and coffee in the back of the ready room. "Sandwich."

"And breakfast?"

"Doughnut."

"Have you been on duty since we sounded flight quarters?"

"Yes, sir." At 0350, bright and early.

"Take a break."

"But sir, we're in the middle —"

"I took a break this morning. My pilots take breaks. One hour. That's an order."

The lieutenant commander wasn't Dan's CO, but he did outrank him. And Stearns wouldn't land for at least an hour. "Aye aye, sir."

Dan checked his watch so he wouldn't stay off-duty one minute longer than ordered, then he descended the long ladder to the hangar deck.

What was he supposed to do for an hour? A hot meal and a fresh cup of coffee sounded good but wouldn't occupy him for fifty-eight more minutes.

The hangar deck bustled with activity. Aviation machinists repaired damage, performed maintenance, and fueled aircraft. Sailors pushed two TBFs to the forward elevator by the catapult.

Everyone had something important to do

but Dan.

Reports and more reports.

His gut simmered, and he stepped into the hatch, scrambled down to the main deck, and strode to the wardroom.

Conversation drifted into the passageway. "I hope we ditch that bureaucrat in Argentia."

Dan stopped outside the door. Bureaucrat? There weren't any bureaucrats on board.

"No kidding," said another man. "I'm sick of his reports. He wants even more information than Drane does. Waste of our time."

They were talking about Dan, and his jaw clenched.

"Come on, be fair," a third officer said. "He's doing his duty. All that data will help the Navy work out better tactics."

"Fine," the first pilot said. "You help him fill out his stupid forms and keep him out of my way so I can fly."

Dan's stomach hardened around the flimsy sandwich. He turned on his heel, marched to his cabin, and slammed the door.

A bureaucrat with forms. That's all he was now. If Randolph had his way, that's all he'd ever be.

Enough. Dan slammed his portfolio on

his desk and stood there, his fists opening and closing. He was meant to be at sea, created to command. And he was going to make it happen.

He sat at his desk, yanked open the drawer, and pulled out his letter to Commander Lewis.

An excellent letter, thorough and strong. He started with a diplomatic touch, stating that although he and Randolph had a bad history, Dan granted him mercy by allowing him to be judged on the present not the past. However, since Randolph insisted on enacting revenge, Dan insisted on revealing the truth.

Then he listed Randolph's offenses on the *Texas,* which could be confirmed in Randolph's personnel records. Dan detailed the man's mistreatment of the sailors and how he silenced his junior officers by burying them with busywork.

On the next page, Dan listed all the snake's offenses at ASWU, stating that Mr. Bentley and the other personnel would back him up.

Dan closed the letter with a bang. At best, Randolph was guilty of deliberate dereliction of duty, forcing his men not to perform their duties — work necessary for the war effort — all to satisfy his desire for revenge.

At worst, he was a saboteur, a traitor, impeding the work of the United States Navy in time of war. Dan respectfully requested that Commander Lewis have Randolph court-martialed.

The letter was more than excellent. It was perfect. Dan would deliver it to Commander Lewis in person, and he couldn't wait.

A sense of rightness burned inside, dark around the edges.

Dan opened the stationery box to return the letter. His notes from the train from Londonderry to Belfast sat on top, listing kind words Admiral Howard had spoken.

How he missed that man. Heaviness settled in his chest, and he picked up the sheet of paper.

A jolt of color bruised his eyes. A sailboat picture lay underneath, the one he'd drawn in his last period of forced rest. "Danny at play," lounging on a yacht, Tess's whimsy polluting the simplicity of his sketch.

"Fine!" he said to the laughing blonde in his head. "You want me to draw? I'll draw."

He grabbed a blank sheet of paper and took his pen to it, slashing out a sailboat, all points and sharp edges, and he scribbled over the hull and made it as black as his life would be if he didn't present that letter.

"A desk job in Washington?" His pen ripped a hole. Not only would Dan hate that kind of work, but he'd be bad at it. He endured the paperwork at ASWU because he saw the connection to combat.

But in supply or personnel? He'd be as useless as his father.

The pen stilled. That wasn't true. Tess had helped him see. Sure, Dad was lousy at bookkeeping, but he was a first-rate craftsman, creating beautiful designs and bringing them to life with his hands and tools.

Now Dad had dedicated his workshop to the war. He didn't want to build landing craft. He wanted to build sailboats. It was what he was created to do. But he built landing craft anyway.

George Avery was a good man, doing good work with integrity.

Integrity? Horror thudded in Dan's gut. He snatched up his list of Admiral Howard's compliments. "Daniel Avery is known for his integrity. Even as an ensign, he exhibits a noble sort of compassion, bearing grievances with a stoicism befitting the greatest admiral."

Bearing grievances? When had that stopped?

When the grievances threatened his greatest goal.

Dan's breath came shallow. Admiral Howard had written those words in a letter of recommendation in 1935, after the first incident with Randolph.

"A noble sort of compassion?" Dan's words grated on his throat, and he sifted through the desk drawer to find his Bible. Where was that passage? The one he'd forced himself to read every week in the Academy at his mother's urging. She and Dan were so alike, and she knew Dan needed more than talent and brains and fortitude. He needed balance.

Colossians 3:12–13. When was the last time he'd read it? "Put on therefore, as the elect of God, holy and beloved, bowels of mercies, kindness, humbleness of mind, meekness, longsuffering; Forbearing one another, and forgiving one another, if any man have a quarrel against any: even as Christ forgave you, so also do ye."

Dan rested his forehead on his fists and screwed his eyes shut. Every word in his letter to Commander Lewis was true. But where was the humility? Longsuffering? Forgiveness? Where was that noble compassion he'd cultivated and Admiral Howard had praised?

More importantly, where was the image of the merciful Savior he claimed to love?

His fingernails dug into his palms. "Lord, help me get back on course. Not my career, but my character."

A new sense of rightness filled him, tinged with light and sadness. His father built landing craft with integrity. Dan would rather be a desk jockey with integrity than an admiral with vengeance in his heart.

If he handed that letter to Commander Lewis, he'd be no better than Randolph.

Dan picked it up, gritted his teeth, and shredded his last hope of command into bits.

Boston

Tess hurried to the pay phone on the corner, flung open her purse, and inserted a nickel.

Dead silence.

"No, no, no." She clicked the switch in the phone cradle, but no dial tone. Broken.

She stepped out of the phone booth and gazed around. There! At the end of the next block.

Tess crossed the street, dodged a taxi, and strode down the sidewalk.

Madame Robillard was involved in Henri's murder. Sweet, motherly Celeste Robillard. No matter how hard Tess tried to deny it, she couldn't. The baker had put the story together too quickly, as if she already knew

457

the details — the red beret, the cyanide, even the fact that Tess's bad news concerned Yvette.

Raindrops struck her nose, and she pulled up the collar of her raincoat.

Madame Robillard had lied to Yvette about the bakery being busy. Why? To entice Yvette to the bakery. It was a trap.

And Jean-Auguste was behind it. Why would Madame Robillard call him first when she heard about Henri's death? Why not Solange as Yvette and Henri's old friend? Why not Professor Arnaud as the leader of the group?

Jean-Auguste was the murderer, and somehow he'd drawn the baker into his plot. Was he the spy too? The bomber?

But he was out of town the day of the bombing, and Madame Robillard was inside the bakery.

Pierre had accused Jean-Auguste of disguising himself as a woman. He did have the right build. Could he have been the pastry delivery girl? The bomber? If so, how had he fooled the FBI with his alibi?

A middle-aged man occupied the next phone booth. When he saw Tess, he turned his back to her.

She groaned. She didn't have time to wait. Yvette's life was at stake.

Tess shielded her eyes from the rain and located another phone booth.

Dan thought Jean-Auguste was the spy. Tess's chest caved in. He was right. He was right about so many things.

If Jean-Auguste was a spy, he'd want to extract information. He'd done that. He'd had contacts in France arrested by the Gestapo.

A spy would want to crush groups that supported the French Resistance. Jean-Auguste had eviscerated the group in Boston with the bomb and his collaborationist rhetoric.

Tess's steps slowed and her mouth hung open. The bomber had tried to frame Yvette and Henri. For months, Madame Robillard and Jean-Auguste raised suspicions about Yvette and Henri.

They were the targets from the start.

"Lord, protect her." Tess picked up the pace toward the phone booth.

What if Henri and Yvette had been training with the OSS? Wouldn't a Nazi spy want to eliminate them before they landed on French soil?

Henri and Yvette had been planning to leave Boston in June. Had they finished training? Were they preparing to head overseas? If so, Jean-Auguste had run out of time.

So had Henri.

Tess shoved open the phone booth door, poked a nickel into the slot, praised the Lord for a dial tone, and dialed the apartment.

It rang. And rang. And rang.

"I'm too late." Tess would have to intercept Yvette before she reached the bakery.

She put in another nickel and dialed Agent Sheffield's office. Thank goodness he was there.

Tess told him everything as quickly as possible — Henri's death, Yvette's plan to leave town, Madame Robillard's call to Jean-Auguste, and their plot to lure Yvette to the bakery.

Jean-Auguste had intended to kill both Henri and Yvette. Except Yvette had survived. He wouldn't let her survive this time.

After she spilled the story in one long sentence, Agent Sheffield put her on hold for an hour-long minute. When he returned, he asked more questions, listening with maddening calmness. He kept slowing her down to ask for unimportant details or to make Tess repeat what she'd already made plain. Couldn't he see this was an emergency and they couldn't waste a precious second?

And he wouldn't confirm or deny any of Tess's theories. None. He revealed absolutely nothing, and Tess wanted to scream in frustration.

"All right, Miss Beaumont. Thank you for calling. The FBI will take care of everything. You need to go home, stay out of the way, and let us do our job."

"You'll stop Yvette?"

The pause. That was not a comforting pause. "We have everything under control. Now please leave the area and go home."

"I — I will. Thank you." Tess hung up. He hadn't promised to stop Yvette. What if the FBI didn't arrive in time? Tess would indeed go home, but not until she'd warned her friend.

She jogged down the street, rain stinging her cheeks and tears prickling her eyes. How could she have suspected her friend of being a spy? Of betraying both her native country and her adopted one? Why had she let Madame Robillard fill her ears with words as poisonous as those pastries?

Tess had failed Yvette this past year, but she wouldn't fail her now.

She rounded the corner. The bakery was in sight a block and a half away. A man stood by the door, his head bent over a newspaper. Why would he read outside on a day like this, even with an awning overhead?

Tess broke into a run. A blonde woman approached the bakery from the other direction. She paused by the door and tilted her head at the "closed" sign. Was that Yvette? Wearing the disguise she'd worn to the Cocoanut Grove?

"Yvette!" Tess's voice was drowned by the shush of taxi tires on the rain-soaked street. "Yvette! Stop!"

The man with the newspaper rapped his fist on the window behind him. The bakery door flew open, and Madame Robillard hugged the blonde woman, drawing her into her venomous web.

"Yvette! Stop! It's a trap!" Tess stepped off the curb to cross the street.

A horn blared, and a bus barreled toward Tess.

She screeched and jumped back onto the curb.

When the bus finally passed, Tess glimpsed the man lowering his newspaper and ducking into the bakery.

Jean-Auguste.

Tess was too late.

43

South of Greenland

"We came out of the clouds at the coordinates at 1200 feet, and there she was, five miles away." Lt. Robert Stearns rubbed his mustache. "We immediately attacked."

"She put up a lot of flak," his gunner said, "but that didn't stop us."

Dan made his notes. This was the same sub Doty had attacked earlier. U-boats always dove under aerial attack. Had Admiral Dönitz changed tactics to encourage shooting back?

Stearns described his attack — four depth bombs dropped from 125 feet, which exploded close to the sub. Then the U-boat submerged. Due to damage? Or to evade Stearns's guns?

Dan studied his diagram. The U-boat was farther north now, farther from the convoy, indicating she'd been damaged. At least this sub wouldn't attack the merchantmen.

Captain Short had attended the debriefing, and afterward he talked to Mr. Drane and the air officer, Commander Monroe.

When Dan completed his report, he clasped his hands behind his head to stretch his shoulders.

They didn't ache. He'd lost his dream, surrendered his goal, resigned himself to his fate, and a curious sad peace filled his mind.

Randolph would get away with everything, but it was God's job to deal with Randolph, not Dan's. If the Lord chose not to punish Randolph, he had his reasons and had no obligation to explain himself.

Captain Short sat next to Dan. "The afternoon watch is almost over, and the first dog watch is about to begin."

"Yes, sir." It wasn't like him to state the obvious.

"This isn't an order, but I'd like to offer you a chance to serve as junior officer of the watch."

On the bridge. Dan's mouth dried out at the memory of his conversation with Clive Sinclair. If Dan could perform some valiant deed in battle, that could override Randolph's evaluation. If not, at least he'd have four hours of pure fun.

"You've done an excellent job, and you deserve a reward."

"Thank you, sir. There's nothing I'd like more." This wasn't a reward for the job he'd performed, but for the decision he'd made a few hours earlier, choosing mercy over vengeance.

"I'd like to see you in action, see what you can do."

So would Dan. "You think we'll see more action?"

He shrugged. "Twenty-three U-boats in the area. We've probably damaged three. So, you'll take my offer?"

The words "yes, sir" poised on his tongue, ready to leap into the captain's ear, but something niggled. He needed a minute of Sabbath rest. "May I have a moment to consider it?"

Thick brows shot high, but he nodded. "Very well."

While the captain stood and inspected the chart, Dan inspected that niggling sensation. *Lord, what's going on? What do you want me to do?*

At the chart, the senior officers discussed the convoy's upcoming change in course.

Stay the course.

Dan frowned. He'd just surrendered his goal of making admiral. Did God want him to stay that original course and take his turn on the bridge?

That niggling poked him in the gut. Or did God want him to stay the course Commander Lewis had assigned? The commander hadn't sent him on this cruise to play on the bridge.

Dan swallowed hard, swallowing his ambitions and desires and the knowledge that he'd serve well on the bridge. When it all digested into nothingness, he approached the senior officers.

The captain faced him. "Yes, Mr. Avery?"

"Thank you for your offer, Captain. I'm honored, and I'd love to accept. However, if I'm on the bridge, I can't debrief pilots or advise the CIC. Commander Lewis's orders were for me to observe, advise, and gather data. As much as it pains me, I have to decline."

"Very well." The captain returned his attention to the chart, to the action Dan wouldn't participate in.

For the second time today, Dan had chosen integrity. For the second time, he'd surrendered. For the second time, he'd shot himself down.

Dan headed to the CIC.

To a new destination.

Boston

Yvette had fallen into a trap, and Tess was

too late to stop her.

She stood on the corner and searched for FBI agents. But everyone scurried by in the rain, hunkered under umbrellas or hunched low in their raincoats. No one lingered. No one observed.

A young woman strolled up to the bakery and leaned by the door, just as Jean-Auguste had done. She wore a raincoat and sunglasses, and she pulled a magazine from her coat pocket.

Sunglasses? In the rain?

It was Solange, serving as lookout for her boyfriend.

Tess's chest burned. Solange had once been Yvette's friend.

Down the side street, Tess glimpsed motion. A small heavy-set woman darted out of the alley and down the street away from Tess. Madame Robillard.

That left Yvette alone with Jean-Auguste.

A strange sense of hope chased away the burning feeling. Tess had seen Henri's fighting skills. Yvette had received the same training. Given a chance, Yvette could land that scrawny Jean-Auguste flat on his back.

All Yvette needed was a diversion. *Lord, what can I do? What should I do?*

Tess wouldn't be able to get in the front door without raising the alarm, but what about the back door? Did Madame Robillard still keep the key under the mat?

Desperation pinged around in her chest but slowly transformed into resolution. No matter what happened, she couldn't abandon Yvette to certain death. She had to act now.

Tess lowered her head and strode across the intersection and down the side street. She peeked down the alley. An empty car sat by the bakery door, but no one stood guard.

She took even breaths as she approached, willing her heart rate to slow down. A closer inspection revealed the car was truly empty.

Please, Lord. Let it be there. Tess lifted the rubber doormat. A key smiled up at her.

As she stood, her raincoat rustled. That wouldn't do. She shed the coat, her cover, her shoes, and her jacket.

Then she slid the key into the lock, rotated it slowly and quietly, and turned the doorknob with just as much care. *Lord, this is the bravest and craziest thing I've ever done. Please don't let it be the stupidest. Please help me save Yvette.*

Tess eased the door open. Angry voices sounded from the seating area. The kitchen was empty. She slipped through the door and wedged her jacket in the gap so it wouldn't click shut. If the FBI came, they could sneak in the same way.

"You're a fool. You might have gotten away with one murder, but not two." That was Yvette's voice, strong and determined.

"Oh, I have a plan." Jean-Auguste chuckled. "By the way, I had an alternative plan in case you died and Henri survived."

Tess's stomach tightened. So he'd confessed to the murder, the pig. She tiptoed across the kitchen, testing each wooden board for creaks.

"It's an excellent plan, my sweet," Jean-Auguste cooed. "Solange wants you dead. I told her you heard a rumor that she and Henri had a tryst. She'll tell the police you flew into a jealous rage and poisoned your lover. Madame Robillard sold you the pastries and —"

"That's a lie."

"What does it matter? Madame Robillard will say you came to the bakery today, distraught. You confessed the murder and were determined to commit suicide. She talked you out of it. Then she respected your request for solitude and left — to fetch the police to arrest you. But when they arrive an hour from now, they'll find you hanged yourself. A tragic end."

Tess gripped the counter by the phone,

and the blood tingled its way out of her face. He planned to hang Yvette. Not if Tess had any say in the matter.

She lowered herself to hands and knees and crawled behind the half-door that led to the seating area.

"Even if I knew anything, I wouldn't talk," Yvette said, low and dark. "And if you torture me, you'll leave marks. They'll know it wasn't suicide."

"That's why you're in a straitjacket, my pet. But if you're a good girl, I'll give you cyanide and you'll die a quick and honorable death, rather than the lingering death you deserve."

A straitjacket? How did Jean-Auguste and tiny flustered Madame Robillard get Yvette into a straitjacket?

Tess crawled past the basket of rags and along the back of the display cabinet.

"See the cyanide capsule? Isn't it pretty? Just give me the names of the other OSS agents."

OSS? It was true. Yvette was indeed a spy . . . for the Allies!

"I am not —"

"We know you are. We knew when they recruited you and Henri last July. We followed you to the training camp you attended every weekend. We knew you were about to leave for France."

We? Wasn't Jean-Auguste alone? Tess lifted her head just enough to see through the glass.

Yvette sat in a chair, bound in a white straitjacket. Jean-Auguste strolled in front of her with a gun. And a man and a woman stood by the chair. The woman held a gun to Yvette's head.

Tess sank to sitting. Oh no. Three people with guns. Yvette needed more than a diversion — she needed a miracle.

"Death by hanging," Jean-Auguste said. "Fitting for a traitor."

"You are the traitor, Nazi swine." The sound of spitting.

"Such passion, sadly misplaced. The Nazis are good for France. I know. I am from Strasbourg, on the border. My father was French and my mother German. My father died in the trenches for France, but do you know how his countrymen rewarded his sacrifice? They raped my mother in front of me and killed my older brother for trying to stop them."

Tess clapped her hand over her mouth so she wouldn't gasp.

"The French . . ." Jean-Auguste's voice ground to new lows. "I went to Germany when Hitler came to power. I saw what he did, the order and prosperity he brought. And I cheered when he conquered France. He is bringing the same order to France."

"He brings no order," Yvette said. "He brings terror and disorder, and so do you. You tore this group apart, turned us against each other, betrayed our sources."

Tess's head spun. Jean-Auguste had been sent by the Nazis to do all those things — and he'd succeeded.

"Betraying a traitor is honorable. Your Henri made a deadly mistake when he gave me a false lead. They were quite angry with me in Germany. Now I've redeemed myself."

"The bomb. You tried to frame us, but you failed."

"True, you didn't get arrested as I'd hoped, but it turned the FBI off my trail, since I made sure I was seen in New York. Liese here threw the bomb on Madame Robillard's signal."

Tess pressed a hand to her head. Fixing the curtains? That was the signal?

"How could you involve Madame Robillard in this mess?" Yvette asked, her voice hard. "She's been like a mother to you, to me, to all of us."

"She is so simple. She has only one care — her boys in Paris. Anything that threatens them must be eliminated. I convinced her France must submit to German rule, and that Resistance attacks and Allied invasions will destroy the country. That includes OSS spies stirring up trouble. She will not stand for that."

Queasiness turned in Tess's stomach. How could the kindly baker allow Jean-Auguste to turn her against two friends? How could she become an accomplice to murder?

"And Solange?" Yvette said. "You hoped she'd spill information on Henri and me. I followed you at the Cocoanut Grove in disguise. You got her drunk and tried to make her talk. But there was nothing to spill."

"She certainly doesn't know anything. But she was a pleasant diversion."

"What will you do to them?"

Breath froze in Tess's mouth.

Jean-Auguste's chuckle — she hated the sound. "One evening this summer there will be a tragic fire when they're closing the bakery. I'm afraid no one will survive. But that is your last question. Now you will answer mine. Who else is in the OSS?"

"If I knew, I wouldn't tell you. But I don't understand . . . whatever made you think we were in the OSS?"

"No more stalling. Your FBI friends will

not storm in. They don't know you're here. And if they came, we'd shoot you with your own little spy gun and we'd shoot them too. So the choice is yours — cyanide or hanging?"

"I will never talk."

"All right. Klaus, Liese, get the gag back on her. The noose is tied to the ceiling fan. It'll hold — I tested it. Get her up on the table."

Tess squeezed her eyes shut and covered her ears against the sounds of struggling. Whatever made her think she could help? One unarmed, untrained woman against three armed spies? And Yvette bound and gagged?

She buried her face in her knees. If they found her, they'd kill her too. If she left and called in help, she'd be too late. Again.

I'm so sorry, Yvette. I failed you.

Tess couldn't save Yvette. She could only save herself.

44

South of Greenland

The flight deck rumbled above Dan's head, and the men in the CIC braced delicate equipment.

Two TBFs had landed without sighting U-boats. However, the convoy remained unmolested. Either the Allies' defenses were keeping the Germans at bay, or the submarines were gearing up for a coordinated attack.

Dan cruised the cramped compartment in the dim light. The SG microwave radar scope and the SK long-wave radar scope sent out plaintive unanswered pips, bright green light sweeping circles around the fluorescent screens.

Speakers on the bulkhead broadcasted sonar pings and radio chatter, none revealing enemy activity.

Dan leaned over the plotting table as if it would yield new insight. Convoy ON-184 had cut a curving path through the seas south of Greenland, now bearing to the southwest. Dark crosses for enemy ships lay strewn in the convoy's wake, but how many lay ahead?

The last Avenger had landed from the afternoon patrols, and the *Bogue* was scheduled to secure from flight quarters. But something restless stirred inside Dan.

"Sir?" the Huff-Duff operator called to the CIC watch officer. "I might have something."

Dan charged over. A green light pulsed feebly in the center of the oscilloscope, and occasional tapping sounds came from the speaker. "Tune it some more."

As the operator fiddled with the switch, the light and sound only grew fainter.

The watch officer coached him, but nothing helped.

Dan's foot jiggled. A U-boat was sending a message nearby, but without bearing and range, the *Bogue* couldn't vector aircraft. They needed that information before the transmission ended.

His fingers itched to get to work. "Sir, may I have a try?"

The watch officer and operator stared at him.

He gave them a slight smile. "I was trained too."

The operator turned a pleading look to his officer. "Please, sir?"

"Be my guest," the watch officer said to Dan.

"Thank you, sir." Dan tossed his cover onto the desk, sat down, and pulled on the earphones. *Please, Lord. Show me.*

"Now hear this," blared over the loud-speaker. "All hands, secure from flight quarters."

Dan and the watch officer exchanged a look of alarm. The *Bogue* needed to launch aircraft, but first they needed coordinates.

Holding his breath, Dan focused his eyes and ears on the Huff-Duff. He massaged the switches under his finger, listening for taps and watching for the green blob to elongate in any direction.

Dits and dahs tickled his eardrums, and he homed in on them. The blob stretched longer, east to west, turning more and more into a figure eight.

Either east or west — but which?

The watch officer grabbed the closest intercom phone and flipped the switch for the bridge.

Dan swiped moisture from his upper lip and resumed his assault. *Come on. Come on. Where are you?*

The figure eight flickered, then pushed its way slightly northeast — 067 degrees, off the *Bogue*'s port quarter.

The watch officer thumped Dan on the back and spoke into the intercom.

Dan tugged off the headphones and handed them to their rightful owner. "Thanks for letting me play with your toy."

"Yes, sir. Any day, sir." The sailor plopped into his seat.

Men sprang into action. After the watch officer informed the bridge, he contacted the other Allied ships with Huff-Duff. One more reading was required for distance, but at least the pilots had a bearing to chase down.

The alarm sounded flight quarters only six minutes after the *Bogue* had been secured. But it had been a false security.

Dan stared at the plotting board. Another black *X* on the blue sea.

Another wolf ravenous for blood.

Boston

Tess crawled toward the kitchen, tears hot in her eyes. She thought she'd changed, but she was as arrogant as ever, thinking she could help Yvette.

Thumps and grunts rose from the seating

area. "Ow! Why you —"

"Don't hit her. We must not leave marks."

On hands and knees, Tess passed the half-door. In front of her in the kitchen, a bank of ovens ran along the wall, the knobs all pointing true north.

Memories of Dan dug sharp claws into every corner of her heart.

She could picture him in his office, watching her with a cute little smile as she played with his compass. What had she told him? *"Even if you take side trips or spin around or veer off the path, the compass stays true. You can always find your way."*

Not today. How had she veered so far off the path? She'd prayed with every step.

Except about her decision to escape.

Tess paused, her hands splayed on the oily floor. *Why did you let me come here, Lord? I can't save Yvette. Only you can.*

Something crashed, wood on wood, and the men cussed.

"Don't let her kick over the table again," Jean-Auguste said.

Tess's jaw tightened. Good for Yvette. She wouldn't die without a fight, a good member of the OSS to the end.

And what was Tess? An officer in the United States Navy, sworn to protect her country against all enemies.

479

Three enemies stood in this building, and they didn't know Tess had overheard their confession. She could report to the FBI and have them all arrested.

That was why she'd come. Tess crawled past the basket of rags. Dampness seeped through her stockings at her knees. Madame Robillard hadn't finished cleaning up the spill.

A fire hazard. Tess could envision flames licking up from the rags, from the oil on the wooden floor. Jean-Auguste had planned such a fire. But if Tess reported to the FBI, there would be no fire and Madame Robillard and Solange would survive to face a jury for their crimes.

No flames clawing for the ceiling. No black smoke rolling through the building. No one stampeding for the exits, the locked exits. No hands stretching through the door, begging for rescue. No screams ripping the night air.

No spies fleeing the flames into a rainy afternoon.

Tess stifled a gasp. A diversion.

"Don't let her sag. Get her upright. She needs to be standing for the noose to reach."

More thuds and grumbles and swearing.

Starting a fire? It was a crazy idea, a stupid idea, and she latched onto it. If she could drive away the spies, she might be able to save Yvette. If not, at least Tess wouldn't die a coward and Yvette wouldn't die alone.

The basket sat behind the half-door. A fire there would block the spies' exit through the back and force them out the front — away from the getaway car and away from Tess.

She crawled to the oven and grabbed a matchbox from on top. Then she snatched the phone book for kindling.

Back to the basket. She trailed rags along the wall to the half-door. Anything to spread the flames.

The spies and Yvette made enough noise to cover her rustlings and the occasional squeak of a floorboard. But she had to act fast.

Hunched beside the wicker basket, she struck a match. She grimaced at the noise, but the sounds in the seating area didn't change.

Tess held the match to the phone book. When orange flames raced along the cover, she set the book among the rags and arranged a drenched rag in the fiery path.

Now to hide. But where? The cabinets under the display case would be full, and she had to remain close to Yvette.

Her breath came faster and faster. She

spotted a dark space — a kneehole under the cash register down by the window. Tess slipped in and pulled her knees to her chest, her heart pummeling her thighs. *Oh Lord, please, please, please.*

A faint crackling, a whiff of burning oil. Thank goodness the fire had taken.

"There! I got the noose on."

Three sets of feet thumped to the ground.

"The next few minutes must be perfect," Jean-Auguste said. "As soon as I kick the table out from under her, Klaus will grab her legs and I'll stand on a chair to remove her gag. Then we'll let her hang. After a minute, we'll remove the straitjacket. She must have claw marks on her neck as she regrets taking her life. Then we'll pack the guns and bindings in my briefcase. Leave nothing behind. When we're sure she's dead, we'll escape."

Couldn't they hear the fire crackling? Tess pulled a hankie from the breast pocket of her blouse and pressed it over her nose and mouth.

"Do you smell smoke?" Liese said.

"Fire! Put it out!" The half-door banged against the wall.

Tess tucked in even tighter. What if the fire was small enough for them to extinguish? Then they'd come looking for the source. For her.

They cried out and cussed. "Put it out!"

"Smother it. Use your jackets."

But the crackles only increased.

"It's too late!"

A crashing sound in the seating area, and a muffled feminine grunt.

Oh no. They'd knocked the table out from under Yvette.

"Grab her legs," Jean-Auguste said. "Take off the gag and straitjacket. We can't wait."

Smoke scratched at Tess's eyes and throat and lungs, and the urge to cough swelled inside. She stifled the cough against her knees.

"We can't get out the back," Jean-Auguste said. "We'll have to go out the front and soon, before someone calls the fire department."

"Let's go!"

"Not yet!" Jean-Auguste said. "Get that gun. No, not hers. Leave hers."

"That's the last of it. We must leave now."

"Oh, Yvette, my sweet," Jean-Auguste said. "I must bid you adieu."

The door opened, footsteps led outside, and the door slammed.

Tess waited a second to make sure they'd left. Then she unfolded herself from her hiding spot.

Yellow and orange flames coiled up the wall and snaked toward Papa's painting of the Pont Neuf. Thick black smoke roiled along the ceiling toward —

Yvette! Hanging from the ceiling fan, still wearing the blonde wig, her eyes bulging, feet flailing, hands grasping the rope around her neck.

"I'm coming!" Tess coughed.

With the half-door engulfed in flames, Tess would have to climb over the display cabinet. She pressed her hands on top of the glass, hoisted herself up, and swung her legs around to the other side. Stupid skirt slowed her down.

She jumped to the floor and slid a table under Yvette. "Set your feet down."

Yvette did, but her knees buckled. She was too weak.

"Hold on. I'll help you." Tess hiked her skirt to her hips and climbed onto the table. It creaked and swayed, but Tess hugged her friend and lifted her to relieve the pressure. "Can you? Can you get the noose off?"

Yvette gasped and fumbled with the rope, her movements slow and jerky.

"Hurry, sweetie. I don't know how long I can hold you." Smoke stung her eyes and brought up another cough, and Tess stumbled under Yvette's weight.

Then Yvette collapsed into Tess, and both ladies tumbled to the ground. Pain shot through Tess's hip and arm, and she cried out. But Yvette was free!

"Let's get out of here!" Tess pulled Yvette to her feet and struggled to the door. Yvette leaned hard on her, gagging and coughing and rubbing at her throat.

Tess shoved the door open, dragged her friend outside, sucked down clean air.

From either side, two men dashed to her, guns high.

Tess screamed.

"Miss Beaumont?" Agent Sheffield lowered his gun. "What are you . . . ?"

"Never mind me." Hugging Yvette to her side, Tess jerked her head toward the street. "Jean-Auguste! Two others! Don't let them —"

"Already arrested. Mrs. Robillard and Miss Marchand as well." The agent holstered his gun and wrapped his arm around Yvette's waist from the other side. "We were waiting outside."

Agent Walter Hayes took Tess's place, and the men guided Yvette to the other side of the street, where a black sedan sat in the rain.

Tess followed, her breath burning from the fire and from indignation. "You were waiting outside? Why didn't you barge in? Why did you let —"

"No!" Yvette barked, glaring over her shoulder at Tess.

"No?" Tess stopped in the middle of the street, the wet asphalt cold and sharp on her stocking feet. Rain pelted her face and shoulders.

"You'll have to come with us, Miss Beaumont." Agent Hayes motioned to the car. "Quickly, before the fire draws spectators. And reporters."

Small groups clustered on the sidewalk, and a siren howled a few streets away.

"Now, Miss Beaumont." Agent Sheffield shot her a hard look. "We'll answer your questions in the car."

Tess slid into the backseat with Agent Sheffield and Yvette. Agent Hayes took the wheel, and a third man sat in the passenger seat — a large, dark-haired man.

Yvette's date at the Cocoanut Grove! The man who followed her.

So many questions crowded Tess's mouth that none could burst free.

Agent Hayes drove down the street. Darkened car windows obscured Tess's view.

Finally, a question tumbled out. "Why didn't you save her? They tried to kill her."

Yvette rubbed her rope-burnt neck. "I —

didn't — want —"

"Rest your throat, Miss Lafontaine," the mystery man said.

"She didn't want us to save her," Agent Sheffield said.

"Yvette . . ." Tess clutched her friend's arm. Even though she mourned Henri, she shouldn't have wished her own life away.

Agent Sheffield took off his damp fedora and smoothed his sandy hair. "After we learned of Mr. Dubois's murder this morning, we stationed an agent near the bakery. When you called in your tip, I put you on hold to notify him by radio. He intercepted Miss Lafontaine and briefed her. At that point we didn't have enough to convict Mr. Fournier — it was all circumstantial evidence and conjecture. We needed a confession."

"I knew — I could —"

"Please, Miss Lafontaine." Agent Sheffield glanced around Yvette at Tess. "She wanted that confession too, and she knew she could get it. She went in willingly, knowing she would die."

Tess's chest simmered. "Why couldn't you storm in and save her?"

"If we'd stormed in, they would have shot her, and we would have shot them. We wanted to catch them alive, put them on trial, and send a message to the Nazis."

"We got that confession," Agent Hayes said.

Tess sat up straighter. "I can testify too. I heard every word."

"That won't be necessary. We listened in from next door and recorded the conversation. Mr. Fournier will be convicted of espionage and murder."

He'd go to the electric chair. "Oh my goodness."

"Miss Lafontaine is a true heroine."

She was, and Tess gazed at her former roommate with admiration and regret.

"Where . . ." Yvette coughed and frowned at Tess. "Where did you . . . ?"

"Where did I come from? After I called the FBI, I tried to stop you, but I was too late. I couldn't abandon you, so I sneaked in the back door. I thought I could cause a diversion."

"You started the fire," Agent Sheffield said.

"You saved my . . . life." Tears welled in Yvette's golden-brown eyes.

She had, hadn't she? But only Yvette deserved accolades. She was willing to sacrifice her life for the cause. "Is it true? What Jean-Auguste said about you?"

Yvette pressed a finger to her lips. "Tell

no one. Not Mary. Not Lillian."

"We'll construct a story for you, Miss Beaumont," Agent Sheffield said. "First we need to take Miss Lafontaine away."

"Are you able to travel?" the mystery man asked, concern on his broad face.

"Oui." Yvette's chin rose, exposing the red mark around her neck. "And I'm ready."

Tess's throat tightened. "I won't see you again, will I?"

Yvette clasped Tess's shoulder and kissed both her cheeks. "Maybe someday."

In the confined space of the backseat, Tess saluted her friend and her heroine. *"Au revoir, ma amie."*

45

South of Greenland

How much longer? Dan stared at the VHF radio receiver, willing Lt. William Chamberlain to send word of a sighting. His Avenger had been in the air thirteen minutes. The pilot should have arrived at the coordinates predicted by Huff-Duff.

Dan resisted the urge to pace in the jampacked CIC. He needed to stay out of the way and let the crew work. But his foot tapped on the deck, sending a Morse code message.

The radio receiver crackled, and Chamberlain announced his call sign. "One hearse, zero-eight-seven, twenty-three. Dropped four depth bombs in straddle. Hearse dove."

One sailor whooped, but everyone else stayed on their tasks.

Elation drove Dan to the plotting table. Bearing 087 degrees, twenty-three miles away. The sub was farther south than on Huff-Duff, reasonable for half an hour's travel.

Chamberlain had forced the U-boat to submerge, possibly damaged, but he was out of depth bombs. He needed reinforcement.

Within minutes, the flight deck rumbled as Lt. Howard Roberts took to the air in another Avenger.

Then they waited. And monitored.

Dan cruised by the stations. The Huff-Duff worked. It allowed Chamberlain to attack a sub that hadn't been detected by radar or sonar or aerial search.

Twenty minutes. Still nothing from the radio, and Dan buried his hands in the pockets of his khaki trousers so he wouldn't fiddle with the dial. The pilots would notify the *Bogue* in due time.

Thirty minutes. So the Germans were staying submerged, a wise choice if they wanted to live.

From a defensive point of view, the day's actions were a success. The two escort groups had prevented attacks on the cargo ships. But to win the war, the Allies needed to sink enough U-boats to make the battle unbearably costly to the Germans.

The radio crackled, and Dan dashed over

as Roberts identified himself. His report flew in, clipped and professional, but no less exultant.

Roberts and Chamberlain had attacked the U-boat, and a white flag flew from the periscope.

Dan whooped this time. All around the CIC, sailors and officers cheered and clapped each other on the back. The *Bogue* had her first victory.

The celebration didn't last, however. Duties needed to be performed.

Two more Avengers were ordered to launch in case the Germans were being tricky. Roberts was vectoring the Canadian destroyer *St. Laurent* to his coordinates to pick up survivors. And Chamberlain was returning to the *Bogue*.

Dan headed to the ready room to debrief Chamberlain. All along the catwalk, crewmen grinned and cheered in the late-afternoon sun. The training and trials had turned to success.

An Avenger whizzed down the deck and lifted into the blue sky, and a minute later a second joined it, off to help Roberts.

A white flag of surrender. Wouldn't it be something if they could capture an intact U-boat with code books and everything? That would be a greater victory than a hundred sinkings.

In the ready room, Dan pulled out fresh forms. For the first time, he felt eager to fill them out.

The flight deck rattled overhead, and the men in the ready room stared up in expectation.

In minutes, Chamberlain's crew assembled around the table. The pilot's smile stretched from one of his prominent ears to the other.

Chamberlain had surprised the sub on the surface, his attack coming so quickly the Germans didn't have time to shoot back. Four depth bombs in a perfect straddle and down she went. Chamberlain circled until Roberts arrived.

The U-boat surfaced directly under Roberts, but the Avenger's depth bombs drove the sub under again. A minute later the U-boat popped to the surface, bow high. Then the two Avengers strafed the dying sub to keep the sailors away from the deck guns and to prevent them from scuttling the ship.

The U-boat bobbed down and up one more time, then in a flurry of American machine-gun bullets, the Germans strung a white sheet to the periscope.

Dan and the senior officers sifted through

the jubilation for the data. Now more than ever, they needed complete reports.

"Sir?" The talker held the intercom phone to his chest. "The *St. Laurent* arrived at the coordinates. The U-boat is scuttled, confirmed sunk. The *St. Laurent* is picking up survivors."

Capturing an intact U-boat was an extreme longshot anyway. But they had a confirmed sinking, and Dan wanted to put exclamation points all over his report.

The *Bogue* was the first American auxiliary carrier to sink a submarine, and the first of the Allied auxiliary and escort carriers to sink a sub without assistance by surface ships.

They'd made history.

A few minutes later, Howard Roberts landed and added more details to Dan's report, details the ASWU would love of excellent attacks, communication, and coordination.

Dan had missed dinner, but he grabbed a sandwich and took it up to the catwalk. He leaned on the railing and munched on his drying sandwich, savoring the cold sea air and the majesty of the ocean. The sun rested low before him, scattering gold light over the gray waves. This was his last time at sea on a warship, but he'd gone out well. No heroics, no valiant deeds, but he'd done his part. More importantly, he'd obeyed God.

Back in Boston, he could face Commander Lewis and his censure. He could face Stanley Randolph and his smug retribution. He could even face Tess in her pain and anger.

Tess. Dan picked off a chunk of bread and rolled it into a pea-sized ball in his fingers. He'd promised her polite military distance, but that sounded less and less appealing.

Was it even fair? That niggling returned, but this time it poked at his heart.

After the kiss, Tess had fled with a handful of hurt words and accusations. But five weeks had passed. She'd had time to think and pray and talk to her girlfriends — that last thought made him flinch. She might even have read his letter.

Tess had a kind and generous heart. She wasn't stubborn and unbending like Dan. What if she had explanations and apologies? Would it be right to shut her down with cool indifference?

Dan chewed on his ham sandwich and his dilemma. Hadn't he told Tess that he had a right to be heard? How could he deny her the same right? And if she only offered more hurt words, couldn't he take it like a man?

The sun sank lower, the golds deepening

to reds and purples.

He missed her. He missed her humor and her insight and her compassion.

Should he give their relationship another chance? He'd told her their differences were insurmountable, but that wasn't true. That was his wounded pride.

One problem. He'd promised her he wouldn't pursue her, and he always kept his promises.

Dan jammed the last bite into his mouth. Perhaps he'd have to break a promise for the first time he could remember.

What was it about that woman that turned the tides of his will as surely as the moon?

Boston
Sunday, May 23, 1943
The sermon was wonderful, Tess was sure of it, but she could only think of the previous day. Everything in her ached for Yvette's loss. No doubt remained that Yvette loved Henri. No doubt remained that Yvette was the bravest woman Tess had ever met.

And no one could know just how brave.

For Yvette to remain with the OSS, her presence at the bakery and her role in the arrest of the spies had to be kept secret, so Tess was coached in a story.

The Sunday morning papers trumpeted

how the FBI had arrested three Nazi agents. A courageous draftsman named Henri Dubois had learned they were spies, so Mr. Fournier murdered him. But that murder provided the clues the FBI needed to arrest the little gang.

In a separate story, the papers reported how Celeste Robillard had set her bakery on fire with the help of her employee, Solange Marchand, in order to collect insurance money. With decreased business due to shortages of sugar and butter, Mrs. Robillard resorted to crime to pay her bills.

The fire had almost cost the life of Miss Marchand. An officer in the WAVES, who wished to remain anonymous, had visited the bakery but found it closed. Hearing screams, the officer let herself in the back door to find the bakery on fire. Mrs. Robillard escaped, but Miss Marchand was trapped. Beating back the flames with her raincoat, the officer led Miss Marchand to safety out the front door.

Tess gripped the black leather cover of her Bible. That was the story she had been ordered to tell for national security.

When Madame Robillard and Solange learned they would be charged for aiding enemy agents and serving as accomplices to murder and attempted murder, they agreed to testify against the spies and to plead guilty to false charges of arson.

An officer in the WAVES had indeed been seen leading a blonde woman out of the bakery, but only Tess knew it wasn't Solange, but Yvette in a blonde wig. And only Mary and Lillian knew Tess had been that officer.

Last night, Tess had told Mary and Lillian the false story. They were astonished, but no more than if Tess had told the truth. As for Yvette, her friends would think she had fled to New York, despondent over Henri.

When the church service ended, Bill Bentley leaned forward in the pew and smiled at Tess, oblivious to her ordeal. "Here's hoping we have another pleasant week at ASWU."

Tess blinked and returned his smile. Mr. Randolph had been away on special assignment, and the office was relaxed, cheerful, and productive. "I hope so too."

"Maybe Dan will come back. It's about time."

Tess's heart lurched. Bill had no idea what had happened between her and Dan, nor should he. Dan deserved discretion and courtesy.

Bill stood. "Of course, he won't be in town long. You heard he's being transferred?"

Another lurch with a painful jab at the end. "No, I hadn't. Where . . . ?"

"Commander Lewis won't tell us until Dan receives his orders. But I didn't like Mr. Randolph's barbs about Dan being better suited for a desk job in DC. I hope Commander Lewis sees through him."

"Me too." Her voice choked.

On Tess's other side, Lillian stood and smiled. "Well, look who's here."

Dan? Tess whipped around. No sign of the man she loved. However, a WAVE officer sat in the back pew with sad brown eyes. "Nora!"

Tess squeezed past her friends, barreled down the aisle, and slid into the pew beside Nora. "Please forgive me. I'm the most selfish, thoughtless —"

"Hush. No, you're not."

"But I am."

Nora's mouth bent with a hint of teasing. "Well, maybe that one night."

Tess's eyelids drooped shut. "Not maybe. Definitely."

"Nonsense." Nora's warm hands gripped Tess's. "Anyone who recognizes she made a mistake as quickly as you did could never be called thoughtless. And anyone who humbles herself like this could never —

well, don't you dare call yourself selfish again."

"Only if you forgive me." She offered a slight smile.

"Already done. But can you forgive me? I wrote letters, but they sounded awful and I ripped them up."

Tess hugged her. "Please let's be friends again. And please, please, please tell me you're stationed in Boston again."

"I am. Now please let me breathe."

They laughed together, a shaky kind of laugh. In the aisle, Mary and Lillian and Arch waited to welcome Nora, but Bill stood back, his face dark and determined.

Oh no. What happened? Everything had been going so well before Nora left for training school.

Tess followed Mary, Lillian, and Arch into the second-floor lobby.

"Welcome back, Nora," Bill said from behind Tess. "Would you like to have lunch with me, just the two of us?"

"No, thank you."

Tess had to use every ounce of will not to stare back at them.

"For the same reasons you didn't answer my letters this month?" Bill's tone sharpened.

"I — I was busy in training school."

"I thought we were friends."

"We are." Disappointment lowered Nora's voice. "We're friends. So let's have lunch with the rest of our friends."

Tess gripped the banister, her mind spiraling down with the staircase. Did Nora think Bill was only interested in her friendship, her mind? No one had ever told her she was beautiful. No one had ever kissed her.

And poor Bill had no idea why she was pushing him away.

Tess shouldn't get involved, yet a strange sense of urgency led her to hang back at the doorway while Nora marched past her and down to the sidewalk.

The darkness in Bill's blue eyes — she couldn't bear it. Tess grabbed his arm and pulled him out of sight inside the front door. "Tell her she's beautiful."

"What?" His lip curled in confusion.

"Have you ever told her?"

"No, but —"

"Tell her right now." Her fingers dug into his arm.

His face cleared, and his jaw edged forward. Then he stepped onto the front stoop, and Tess followed. Nora waited on the sidewalk with the others, her back to the door.

"Nora Thurmond!" Bill yelled, standing

501

at perfect military attention. "I think you're beautiful!"

She whirled around, her eyes large with shock, with hope. Then her gaze flicked to Tess, and she set her mouth in a thin line and stomped up the dozen steps, straight to Tess.

Oh dear. She'd lose Nora's friendship for good this time.

Nora glared at her. "I don't want to hear it like that. Not under duress."

Bill stepped closer. "It wasn't under —"

"I don't want to hear it." Nora held up one hand to silence Bill, and her gaze drilled into Tess. "How could you?"

"Oh, for heaven's sake," Tess whispered. "You're punishing Bill for not calling you beautiful. How's that any different from what I did to Dan?"

Nora gasped and clapped her hand over her mouth.

"It isn't fair to expect a man to say what you need to hear if you don't tell him." Tess's voice warbled. "For heaven's sake, it isn't fair to expect him to say it even if you *do* tell him."

Tears glimmered in Nora's brown eyes. "I . . . I . . ."

"May I have a say in this?" Bill pushed closer. "Since you're talking about me."

Nora swung to Bill, her hand tight over her mouth, then she ducked her chin.

Tess needed to fade away, but she was trapped with a brick wall behind her, a wrought-iron railing in front of her, a white column on one side, and Bill on the other. She pressed back against the wall.

Bill took the hint and slid into her spot. "Nora, I didn't think you'd want flowery talk like that. You're so practical and down-to-earth."

Nora shook her head, her gaze on Bill's black shoes. "I don't want to hear it if —"

"If I don't mean it?" His voice softened. "But I do. Look at me."

Tess squished past him and padded down the stairs with a few other curious church-goers, and she watched her friends out of the corner of her eye.

Bill set one finger under Nora's chin and tipped her face up. "I mean it. You're so beautiful. Your eyes — I just want to fall in. And when you're thinking hard — that cute little thing you do with your lips. And your fingers — even your fingers — they're so pretty."

As Tess descended the steps, her smile rose higher and higher.

"What's going on?" Mary asked.

Bill murmured sweet somethings, and

Nora's hand lowered from her mouth and fluttered for Bill's shoulder.

Tess's fiasco with Dan had produced unexpected fruit, and the sweetness of that fruit satisfied her soul. "They won't be joining us for lunch."

46

Argentia, Placentia Bay, Newfoundland
Wednesday, May 26, 1943

"Welcome back to Newfoundland."

In the wardroom of the USS *Bogue,* the officers applauded Captain Short. Dan might not be a member of the crew, but he shared their emotion.

"I just received a note from Adm. Royal Ingersoll, Commander in Chief of the US Atlantic Fleet."

"Never heard of him," an officer wise-cracked, and everyone laughed.

Captain Short wore his customary grin. "The admiral offers high praise. Not one merchant ship in Convoy ON-184 was at-tacked by a U-boat, despite overwhelming presence of the enemy. The *Bogue* and the *Archer* have sent a message to Admiral Dönitz."

"The *Archer*? We were first!"

More applause, a few catcalls. The British

escort carrier HMS *Archer* had sunk a U-boat attacking Convoy HX-239 on May 23, but yes, the *Bogue* had been first.

"Now." The captain lowered his eyebrows in an expression reminding his men that high spirits were never an excuse for interrupting a commanding officer. "I have our new orders from Cinclant. We'll sail from Argentia on May 31 for the Central Atlantic convoy routes — but Admiral Ingersoll isn't tying us to a convoy. He's giving us free rein to chase down fixes from Huff-Duff and intelligence, and to cover convoys when needed. We're no longer on the defensive. We're going on the offensive."

Dan wholeheartedly joined the cheering. Although he wouldn't be along for the ride, a soft sadness had replaced his harsh bitterness. And he'd be sailing with the *Bogue* in spirit. Over the past few days, he'd worked with the senior officers as they developed tactics to deal with antiaircraft fire. Now the Avenger torpedo bombers and Wildcat fighters would fly in pairs. When a U-boat was sighted, the Wildcat would strafe the deck to chase the Germans from the guns, then the Avenger would swoop in from another angle with her depth bombs.

Captain Short concluded his address, and Dan chatted with the officers at his table.

His supper of Salisbury steak, potatoes au gratin, and buttered beets nestled warm in his belly.

The ship's mailman entered the wardroom and distributed mail brought from shore to the carrier at her mooring buoy.

Dan received a thick stack.

The officer to his right let out a whistle. "She must be crazy about you."

No, she wasn't, but Dan would survive. He held up months-old letters from Rob and Jim, both somewhere in the Pacific. "Big family."

Dan flipped through — several letters from his parents and from each of his brothers and sisters, but none from Tess, not that he expected any.

Two letters stopped the blood in his veins. The first from Cinclant — his new orders. The second from Commander Lewis — his censure.

It was one thing to know it was coming and another to see it in brutal black-and-white.

The wardroom began to empty as the men prepared for the second dog watch, when the other half of the officers would dine and hear from Captain Short.

But Dan sat holding his letters. Washington, DC, wouldn't be so bad. He could visit historical sites and the Smithsonian. He had friends from the Academy in town. When he had leave, Ohio was a reasonable distance away.

And his work would have worth. Personnel manned the ships, and supply met their needs. Both were essential. Dan would put his all into his duties.

With a deep breath, he worked his finger under the rim and pulled out his orders.

Lt. Daniel Avery is ordered to proceed to Norfolk Naval Operating Base on 15 June 1943 to report for duty aboard the auxiliary carrier USS *Bogue* as assistant communications officer.

Dan couldn't breathe. The *Bogue*? At sea? A line officer?

His gaze whipped to Captain Short chatting by the door with the chief engineer. Dan bolted to his feet, to the door.

After the engineer left the wardroom, Captain Short faced Dan.

He couldn't speak. He could only lift his orders.

The captain gave them a glance. "Good. I got my way."

"You —"

"When we were in Boston in April, I

talked with Commander Lewis. We agreed you needed to finish your current projects at ASWU, so I'm afraid you won't join us on our next cruise."

"That — that's fine, sir."

"Looking forward to having you on board in June."

"Thank you, sir. Thank you." Dan meandered back to the table, staring at his orders. He went the wrong way and had to try again.

Captain Short had arranged for his transfer in April. Before Randolph's campaign to ruin Dan. Before Dan's vicious plan to ruin Randolph. Without Admiral Howard's help.

He stood by his chair, his breath in disorganized clumps. God had answered his prayers, but in his timing, not Dan's. God waited until Dan surrendered his goal and stopped fighting in his own feeble strength. Even if the Lord had sent him to Washington, he would have been fine. But the Lord hadn't done that. He'd sent him back to sea.

Dan laughed out loud, grabbed his mail, and retreated to his cabin. At his desk, he ripped open Commander Lewis's letter to answer the remaining mysteries.

The Monday after the Bogue sailed, Lt.

Cdr. Stanley Randolph presented charges against you and demanded you be transferred and court-martialed.

His demands seemed extreme, but I promised to investigate.

His first charge was that you had failed to delegate while away and were therefore guilty of dereliction of duty. This hadn't happened in your previous absences, so I summoned Ensign William Bentley. He reiterated his claim that Mr. Randolph had ordered him not to complete the work and that you were to perform all duties yourself, including typing. He was aware that Mr. Randolph denied giving such orders.

I stated that I had noticed tension between you and Mr. Randolph. Mr. Bentley claimed not to know the source, but said it was longstanding and personal.

The second charge involved the "work party" arranged by Ensign Quintessa Beaumont. She assured me it was entirely her doing and that she had surprised you, which was confirmed by Mr. Bentley and the WAVES. Miss Beaumont was mortified that her actions might have caused you trouble.

I also asked her about the tension. She said you had told her the source but had asked her not to say anything for Mr. Randolph's sake. Then she offered a hint — I should look at the personnel records from 1935.

That was all I needed. I found the record of Mr. Randolph's transgressions on the USS Texas and your role in bringing them to light.

His current transgressions bear a strong resemblance to those in the past, but this time he interfered with the duties of this unit and tried to destroy the career of a fellow officer.

Mr. Randolph is currently under suspension. Upon receipt of your written statement, I will transmit a request for a general court-martial to the Secretary of the Navy.

The rest of the letter faded to a blur. Dan hadn't spoken one word against Randolph, but the man had still been brought to justice.

"Thank you, Lord. Thank you." He rested his head in his hands until the spinning stopped, praising God for his mercy and praying for Randolph to turn to the Lord and change his ways.

When he opened his eyes, the paragraphs about Tess came into focus. She'd defended him and shown concern for his welfare, while still respecting his wishes — for the most part. He ran one finger along his favorite sentence. She defied him enough to drop one hint — an impulsive little Tess-twist.

Kind and merciful and generous, she'd chosen to help him. He wanted her in his life forever. If only she'd give him a second chance.

Dan opened the desk drawer and retrieved the two sailboat drawings.

Something was missing.

He grabbed a pen and got to work. "Lord, help me bring this sketch to life."

47

Boston
Sunday, May 30, 1943

Tess had never known such a meaningful Memorial Day. In Boston Common, she and the WAVES from the war bond office untied the bunting from the wrought-iron railing that ran around the stage of the Parkman Bandstand.

The WAVES looked fresh and bright in their new dress whites, cut in the same flattering pattern as the dress blues.

"Here, Miss Beaumont." Thelma Holt handed Tess a pile of folded bunting.

"Thank you." She trotted down the curving stairs to the brick pavement. She hugged the bunting and sniffed for a hint of Dan's scent.

None, of course.

Tess nestled the bunting in its box. Dan would return to Boston any day now, but he wouldn't stay long. On Friday, the

ASWU office was buzzing over Dan's transfer and Mr. Randolph's court-martial.

Seeing Dan would hurt, but she could hand him her letter, give him a proper apology, and end the matter. Then they could have a fresh start. Apart.

Tess returned to the stage and untied another string of bunting. She'd joined the WAVES for a fresh start, and she'd found her purpose — not by developing new skills but by recognizing the worth of her natural skills. She encouraged people, built up morale — and yes, she sold a lot of bonds.

Especially today. The early afternoon Memorial Day service had been touching. Everyone remembered those who'd died freeing North Africa, Guadalcanal, and Papua New Guinea from Axis control, as well as those who'd died on the sea and in the air and in countless unsung ways. Like Henri Dubois.

Tess drew a shaky breath and gazed at the site on the pavement where sailors dismantled her booth. The WAVES had sold hundreds of bonds.

"That's the last of it, Miss Beaumont." Celia Ortega pointed to the boxes at the bottom of the stairs.

"Thank you, ladies." Tess smiled at them. "You did a wonderful job. The sailors will load the van and unload it at the Navy Yard. You can get a ride in the van if you'd like, but you're free to enjoy the rest of your Sunday afternoon. I'll take the subway."

"Thank you, ma'am." The WAVES headed toward the van and its handsome crew.

Tess leaned her elbows on the wrought-iron railing, relishing the sunshine. Nora was on a romantic picnic with Bill, so Tess would go to Mary and Lillian's apartment to relax before the special evening service.

To the east, Park Street Church's white steeple soared into the blue sky above the trees in the Common.

Tonight at 2100, Park Street was holding a Singspiration and Dr. Ockenga was giving an evangelistic message that would be broadcast on Boston Common, reaching hundreds of servicemen and civilians. After the service, the congregation planned to mingle on the Common. What an unusual and exciting idea, and Tess couldn't wait to see what happened.

She smiled down at the people milling around the park. Children capered, and ladies and gentlemen strolled, their steps lighter without heavy winter coats. Dozens of sailors wore dashing white for the first time that year.

A sea breeze tossed curls against Tess's

cheek, and she brushed them away and faced into the breeze.

One figure in white caught her eye — a naval officer with a familiar determined gait.

Tess's breath leaked from pain-stabbed lungs. "Dan?"

Although his stride didn't waver, he gazed from side to side like a lost child at Filene's, frowning and squinting.

Oh goodness. Now was her chance. Not some hideously strained meeting at the office in public, but just the two of them. He could ignore her or rant or pout or whatever he wanted to do.

Tess scanned the bandstand, frantic. Where was her purse with the letter? "Oh no. That's right." After church, she'd put subway change in her pocket and sent her purse with Mary so she wouldn't have to fuss with it.

But Dan — he deserved that letter.

He came closer and closer. Then his gaze swept up the bandstand. He spotted Tess, and the frown and squint disappeared. His face stretched, raw with regret and longing.

"Oh, Dan." That wasn't polite military distance, and this was no time for letters, no time to hesitate, no time to hold back.

Tess scrambled down the stairs and ran to him, dodging startled passersby. "Dan! Dan!

Danny!"

His face darted in and out of view, shifting to surprise, to hope.

Oh goodness, he'd forgiven her! He'd forgiven her, and she hadn't even apologized yet. "Danny! I'm sorry. I'm so sorry. I love you, I love you, I love you!"

He stepped off the path onto the grass, the hope broadening to joy.

She launched herself at him, flung her arms around his neck, and kissed him full on the lips. He grunted but kissed her back, one arm tight around her waist.

She had too much to say, so she pulled back an inch. "I'm sorry. I really am. I was selfish and horrible, and I shouldn't have run away, and I'll never run away again. Never. I promise. If only you'll give me another chance . . . Oh, you already have, haven't you?"

His eyes, his incredible dark eyes, swam with so many emotions. "You — you love me?"

"Very much." She caressed the back of his neck, his hair springy from a fresh haircut. "You've forgiven me?"

"Of course, and it seems you've forgiven me too." He lifted something in his free hand. "Guess I didn't need to bring you this bouquet."

Tess twisted in his embrace to see a brown paper grocery bag with the top rolled in his grip. "A bouquet? Darling, you don't need to apologize to me, but you will need to apologize to those poor flowers."

He laughed. Oh, it really was the loveliest sound in the world. "Flowers? I wouldn't dare give you flowers."

She gave him a quizzical look, but the sight of his firm mouth open in laughter almost dissolved her leg muscles.

"Come on," he said. "Let's go somewhere else. We've given these folks enough of a show."

Oh dear. Tess glanced at the amused faces of a dozen park-goers. "Oh no. The Navy has rules."

"Yes, we do." Dan took her hand and led her over a knoll and up a side path. "As for the bouquet, you once told me never to buy you pretty things. Flowers are pretty. That wouldn't do. So I bought you a useful bouquet."

"A useful bouquet?"

"I bought out the store on the *Bogue* and in Argentia." Dan traipsed up the slope to a bench shielded behind an elm tree. He set the bag on the bench, looked inside, mumbled something about kisses making a mess of things, and tinkered inside the bag.

"What are you grumbling about, Dan Avery?"

"Here you go." He handed her a drinking glass stuffed with pencils and a toothbrush and a comb and a ruler and a spoon and a fork, tied with two black shoestrings in a sloppy bow. "Every item is completely practical."

"Oh, Dan." She fingered the two shoestrings — one wouldn't be practical, would it? — and everything inside her felt soft and warm. "It's the most . . . the most *beautiful* gift ever." A giggle popped up.

Dan's face split in a smile. "You like it then."

"I love it."

"And I love you."

That was the first time she'd heard the words from his mouth, seen them in his eyes. He looked all the way inside her, knowing her and loving her.

Without breaking his gaze, he nudged aside her hand that held the bouquet, and he lowered his mouth to hers, one hand on her waist and the other stroking her cheek, her jaw, her hair.

His lips said things to her, more than any words could. His was a love that appreciated her as she was but would also challenge her and steady her and cause her to grow.

Dan murmured and pressed his forehead to hers. "A kiss like that makes a man want to go to sea just so he can come home."

Tess trailed her fingers over the roughness of his jaw. "I heard about your new assignment. I'm so excited for you. When do you report?"

"June 15. I thought I'd have the longest, most brutal two weeks of my life."

"Two weeks. Now it seems too short."

"Plenty of time." He rearranged his arms around her waist and studied the leaves of the elm tree. "Let's see. Today's Sunday. Are you free on Saturday?"

"Well, yes." She frowned at his chin. She didn't want to wait until Saturday to see him.

"Good. That should be enough time to get a license. We'll get married on Saturday."

"What?" She gaped at him. "Married?"

"Why not? I love you, you're the right woman for me, and I want to marry you."

The man certainly knew his mind. But he was choosing a wife, not a blouse for his mother. "Six days? It's so soon. I mean, we just now . . ."

"Oh." He released her and sank down onto the bench. "I suppose I've had longer to think about this than you have. I've been in love with you for months, but you . . . ?"

"You're not the only one who guarded your feelings." She raised a mysterious smile. "I had a crush on you before I joined the WAVES, and I've been falling in love with you ever since."

His mouth crept up on one side. "You have?"

"I'm madly in love with you." She rested her hand on his shoulder and kissed the tip of his nose. "But I never let myself think about marriage. Goodness, at first I thought you didn't even like me. I never let myself dream about love, much less a life with you."

"So you need time."

"I do. Let me get used to this. Let me dream. And let's just enjoy ourselves."

"Speaking of enjoying ourselves." He plucked the bouquet from her hand and stashed it in the bag. "There's something fun I've always wanted to do here."

"Fun? Shouldn't you be at the office?"

He arched one eyebrow, handed her some papers from the bag, grabbed her hand, and marched her up the slope.

Tess glanced at the papers, but she had to watch her step on the uneven ground. "Your sailboats."

"Our sailboats. That's why I want to

marry you. I'm the straight lines, the black-and-white, the structure."

"That's why I love you."

A surprised little smile, then he nodded at the paper, never slowing his pace. "You provide the color, the perspective, the life. That's why I love you. But something was missing from the drawings."

"What?" She glanced at the papers but stumbled on a root.

Dan stopped and faced her, his face solemn. "I was alone. In both pictures, at work and at play, I was alone. I don't want to be alone anymore."

She heard the hurt of a little boy who'd forced himself to become a man too young, of a man who'd deprived himself of love for too long. "Oh, Danny."

He tapped the papers. "I fixed them. You'll have to do your part with paint or crayon or whatever you use."

"All right." In the first picture, "Dan at work," he'd drawn a little woman in a WAVES uniform standing beside him at the helm. "That's darling."

In the second picture, "Danny at play," he lounged on his sailboat. The woman knelt behind him in a modest bathing suit. And her hands . . . Tess frowned. "Why am I strangling you?"

"You're giving me a neck rub." The eagerness in his expression . . .

She laughed. "I thought you hated it. You grumbled the whole time."

His eyes turned smoky. "You don't know how much I wanted to pull you onto my lap and kiss you."

Her cheeks warmed. "I wish you had."

"Maybe I should have." He huffed out a breath and marched up the slope. "But there's a time for work and a time for play. And now is a time for play."

"Where are we going?" She peered ahead. "The Frog Pond?"

"This winter we all walked up this way. I told you I hadn't played since I was eleven."

She squeezed his hand. "I remember."

"We were standing over there." He pointed west. "I was looking at the Frog Pond, thinking of the kids wading in the summer. That's what I want to do."

"Today?" It wasn't even seventy degrees.

"Today." Dan sat on a bench beside the bean-shaped concrete pond, and he plucked off his shoes and socks.

Only two children splashed in the far end of the pond, and they were shooed out by their scolding mother. "It's still too cold."

"Not for a sailor." He rolled up his white trousers to reveal calves Tess had never seen . . . so masculine. He stood and tossed his cover onto the bench. "Come on."

"Me? I can't. My stockings. I — there's no place to take them off. And we don't have a towel."

He shook his head and marched straight into the shallow pond. "That's the problem with you, Miss Beaumont. You're too practical."

She laughed and sat on the bench. "And you, Mr. Avery. You're too silly."

"I'll try to be more serious." He put on a stern expression and marched, knees high.

Tess watched in wonder and amusement. It might not be "conduct unbecoming an officer," but he was pushing the limits, probably for the first time in his career, and it was adorable.

Dan marched past again and snapped her a salute, water splashing around his bare ankles.

One day he would indeed make admiral, and Admiral Avery would be the finest sort of leader, firm and fair, brilliant and compassionate. She would be honored to be his wife.

He flashed a smile and flicked water in her direction, nowhere near enough to splash her, but she squealed to make him happy.

How she'd love making him happy all his life, letting him be Danny with her.

Affection for him welled inside, bolstered by certainty. "Yes!" she yelled.

He turned to her. "Yes what?"

"Yes, I'll marry you. But not next week."

He didn't smile. Not one bit. He walked to her, hands and feet dripping. Leaning over, he braced his hands on the back of the bench behind her.

His hair was mussed up in irresistible black waves. The wildness of it.

He was going to kiss her with all the passion she'd seen when he talked of ships and the sea, and she raised her face to accept it.

She wasn't disappointed.

48

How could this be real? She was walking down the aisle of Park Street Church — to him.

Dan hadn't seen her in anything but her WAVES uniform for almost a year, and she didn't look like his Tess with all those layers of white swishing around her feet, her face veiled.

She looked like a bride. His bride. It couldn't be real.

Yet the air in his lungs felt real, the sweat on his palms, the weight of his dress whites on his shoulders. So did the presence of dozens of family and friends in the wooden pews and the wedding party beside him — Arch and Jim and Bill and Lillian and Mary and Nora.

Arch and Lillian had planned an autumn wedding, but when Jim's ship came to Mare

Island in California for refitting and he received a month's leave, Arch and Lillian moved up their wedding date so Jim could attend. The *Bogue* had docked in Norfolk on August 23, and Dan had spent the first two days convincing Tess to make it a double wedding.

Now he wanted to run. Not because he doubted his love for Tess. He never would.

Not because of Admiral Howard's advice. He had a hunch his mentor would grudgingly approve of Tess's influence on him.

But at that moment, Dan needed more time. He couldn't believe this lovely creature was about to join herself to him. Forever.

And she was smiling about it.

Dr. Ockenga asked Mr. Beaumont who was giving this woman to this man, and Mr. Beaumont said he was, and he lifted his daughter's veil to reveal all her light and color.

Something kicked the back of his foot. Dan glanced to his side, and Jim jerked his head toward Tess.

Time to get underway. Dan lifted anchor, started his engines, and heaved to alongside his bride.

She slipped her warm hand in his, and love glistened in her golden-green eyes. Yes, he wanted to run — but to her, with her, all the days of his life.

Dan wandered around the reception room on the first floor of the church, accepting congratulations. So many naval personnel in dress whites — men from ASWU and the *Bogue*. Crew from Arch's former ships, the *Atwood* and the *Ettinger*. And WAVES. Lots of WAVES.

Plenty of civilians too — Lillian's coworkers from the drugstore, Arch's from his insurance company, and the Avery, Beaumont, and Vandenberg families.

Jim and Mary approached, and Jim gave Dan a broad grin. "Never thought I'd see my big brother take a wife."

Dan chuckled. "Never thought I'd worry about my little brother outranking me."

Jim wore two stripes for a full lieutenant and a bunch of medals on his chest. He pointed to Dan's shoulder boards, which now bore a third thin stripe. "You always stay one step ahead of me, Lieutenant Commander."

Dan nudged his sister-in-law. "That pipsqueak of a husband of yours is making a name for himself, I've heard."

"I know." She looked up at Jim adoringly. "But I'll keep him in line."

"Tess will have a harder job keeping this

man in line." Jim jutted his chin at Dan. "The *Bogue* is singlehandedly responsible for ending the Battle of the Atlantic."

Dan broke out laughing. "Not true at all, and you know it." But the *Bogue* had sunk five U-boats and damaged many more. "You know full well there are many factors."

Jim nodded. Convoys, technology, air cover, intelligence, and massive production — combined with the courage of Allied sailors and merchant marines.

Dan sobered. "And you know full well the battle isn't over."

"But the tide has turned. The Allies finally have the upper hand."

"We do." Dan was thrilled to be playing a role.

Arch and Lillian Vandenberg strolled over, hand in hand. Lillian wore her twin sister Lucy's wedding dress, much frillier than Lillian's usual style, but she looked radiant.

Dan kissed his sister on the cheek, then shook Arch's hand with a solemn face. "My deepest sympathies."

"Daniel!" Lillian gasped.

Mary laughed. "I'm glad I don't have brothers."

"Now you do. Tons of them." Dan tugged a lock of Mary's hair.

"And I have brothers and sisters for the

first time ever." Wonder shone on Arch's face. He'd done well for himself since his medical discharge from the Navy. His Boston branch of the family insurance company was flourishing. More importantly, Arch was flourishing as he hired former servicemen who had been injured and maimed in the line of duty.

Dan clapped his new brother-in-law on the shoulder. "In all seriousness, we're glad to have you in the family, and we know you'll take good care of our Lilliput."

"Thanks, Dan." Lillian smiled and leaned her head on Arch's shoulder. His sister had never looked so happy, open, and confident. "And what about you? You aren't our ship-monk anymore."

"No, I'm not." But where was the responsible party? Dan gazed around the room.

There were Bill and Nora, talking to each other as if no one else existed. They'd get married soon, no doubt.

And there were his parents, looking happily dazed at the increase in the Avery Aviary. Wait until the newlyweds added more grandchildren to the flock. For Dan and Tess, babies would have to wait until after the war so Tess could continue to serve in the WAVES. But Dan didn't want to wait one minute longer than necessary.

Dad caught his eye and nodded.

Warmth filled Dan's chest, and he raised a smile. With Tess's encouragement, Dan had written a long letter to his father, asking forgiveness for judging him and withholding respect. Thanks to Tess, Dan had seen the truth — George Avery was the best sort of man, and Dan was honored to be his son.

Where was Tess? His . . . his wife?

Her laughter floated from the corner, where she stood with a dozen WAVES.

He couldn't be prouder of her. She did excellent work at the Navy Yard, and she knew how to keep secrets vital to national security. When he'd asked about Yvette and the spy case, she'd merely shown him two newspaper articles and stated which elements were true. Tess had been involved in something bigger than rescuing one woman from a fire, but Dan knew better than to ask questions.

Right now, he needed her in his arms. Dan excused himself and weaved through the crowd, eyes on his goal.

Tess met his gaze, and her color rose. She stepped away from her friends. "My, you look like a man on a mission."

"I am." He wrapped his arms around her waist.

Her cheeks turned bright pink, and she pressed her forehead to his shoulder. "I've always loved your determination, how you know your mind."

He sighed. "Yet you're the one who changed my mind."

"Aren't you glad?"

Dan pressed a kiss to the top of her head, to the blonde curls that fit perfectly around his fingers. "You know I am. I have the most useful bride in the world."

"You sweet-talker, you." She raised her face to him, so close, so lovely.

"And you're beautiful. So, so beautiful."

Her smile deepened and softened. She understood he loved her inside and out.

The kisses he longed to give her would have to wait for a more private moment, but they had a whole lifetime ahead of them. They'd work together, rest together, play together, loving and encouraging and supporting each other.

He squeezed her waist. "Ready to chart our new course together, Mrs. Avery?"

"Aye aye, Captain." She pressed a sweet, tantalizing, too-short kiss to his lips. "Anchors aweigh, my love."

Dear Reader,

Thank you so much for traveling with Dan and Tess. I hope you enjoyed reading their story as much as I enjoyed telling it. It was great fun writing about the WAVES (Women Accepted for Voluntary Emergency Service), which was established on July 30, 1942. Although the Navy was initially reluctant to take women, the WAVES quickly proved their worth. By the end of the war, 86,000 women served at 900 various stations in dozens of positions.

Sadly, the Cocoanut Grove Fire was a real event, taking the lives of 492 men and women in one of the deadliest fires in American history. In the story, I used the initial figure of 490 deaths that was reported at the time. The theory that a busboy accidentally started the fire with a match while changing a lightbulb is still held as the most likely cause, and the nightclub's policy of keeping emergency exits locked or blocked to prevent theft led to hundreds of tragic deaths. However, as with many disasters, this led to major reforms in fire safety.

In Dan's story, the Anti-Submarine Warfare Unit and the ships USS *Cleveland,* USS *Wilkes,* and USS *Bogue* were all real. The war diaries of the latter two ships helped me describe their accomplishments. The auxiliary carriers (renamed escort carriers — CVEs — on July 15, 1943) played important roles in Operation Torch and in the Battle of the Atlantic, eventually forming the nucleus of the hunter-killer groups that would turn the U-boats from hunters to prey. Please visit the book page on my website (www.sarahsundin.com/books/when-tides-turn) for pictures of *U-505,* captured by the hunter-killer group led by escort carrier USS *Guadalcanal* on June 4, 1944, and currently on display at the Chicago Museum of Science and Industry.

The Battle of the Atlantic peaked in March 1943, when the U-boats sank 95 ships. The German Navy began using a new Enigma code on March 10, temporarily blinding the Allies to U-boat activities during this crucial and deadly time period. May 1943 represents the turning point in the Battle of the Atlantic, when U-boats sank 41 ships, but 44 Axis subs were lost. The improvements in air cover, convoy escorts, radar, High-Frequency Direction-Finding equipment, and intelligence all contributed to these successes. On May 24, 1943, Adm. Karl Dönitz withdrew his U-boats from the North Atlantic, officially ending the battle. Although the U-boats remained active until V-E Day in May 1945, they never again posed as serious a threat. Victory in this battle allowed American and Canadian troops to safely cross to Britain to prepare for D-Day in June 1944.

Since I used real ships and units in this novel, many real-life naval personnel appear as well. In the ASWU, all characters are fictional except Cdr. Thomas Lewis. On the USS *Cleveland,* USS *Wilkes,* and USS *Bogue,* all personnel are real except Dr. Stern, Lt. Clive Sinclair, and gunners Ray and Beecher. Dan's mentor, Rear Adm. Aloysius Howard, is fictional. Other real-life people mentioned in the book include Dr. Harold Ockenga of Park Street Church, Capt. Herbert Underwood of the Naval Reserve Midshipmen's School at Smith College, Rear Adm. Robert Theobald at the Boston Navy Yard, and bandleaders Jack Edwards and Frankie Masters. It always feels odd to put fictional words in the mouths of real people, and I did my best to show respect to these men who are my heroes.

If you're on Pinterest, please visit my board for *When Tides Turn* (www.pinterest .com/sarahsundin) to see pictures of Boston, WAVES, auxiliary carriers, and other inspiration for the story.

Please join me in spring 2018 for my new World War II series. As D-Day approaches, three estranged brothers battle the Nazis on the sea, in the air, and on the ground. Will the women they love and the dangers they face lead them to redemption . . . or destruction?

ACKNOWLEDGMENTS

Finishing a series always feels bittersweet, and I'm thankful for the people who accompanied me on this journey, especially my husband and children.

I am grateful to some wonderful professionals who aided my research. The staff at the Ritter Public Library in Vermilion, Ohio, downloaded photos of microfiche copies of the *Vermilion News*. Likewise, Margaret Dyson at the Boston Parks Department provided me a link to the original City of Boston Fire Commissioner's report on the Cocoanut Grove Fire, which was extremely useful.

Many thanks to reader Steffani Webb, who suggested the title *When Tides Turn* in a title brainstorm game on my blog!

I deeply appreciate my brainstorming and critique buddies, who help me build my stories and polish them. Cathleen Armstrong, Judy Gann, Sherry Kyle, Bonnie

Leon, Ann Shorey, and Marcy Weydemuller — you're the best!

I'm continually thankful for all the people who make these books come to pass — my agent, Rachel Kent at Books & Such, my editors Vicki Crumpton and Kristin Kornoelje at Revell, Cheryl Van Andel's cover team, and Michele Misiak and Karen Steele in marketing. What an incredible joy to work with such talented and fascinating people!

And I adore my readers! Thank you for your emails, Facebook messages, prayers, and encouragement. Without you, there would be no books at all! Please visit me at www.sarah sundin.com to leave a message, sign up for my quarterly newsletter, read about the history behind the story, and see pictures from my research trip to Boston — and my trip to Vermilion! I hope to hear from you.

DISCUSSION QUESTIONS

1. In this story, Dan Avery experiences Operation Torch, the climax of the Battle of the Atlantic in March 1943, and the turning point of the battle in May 1943. Have you heard of these events before? What did you find interesting?

2. The WAVES (Women Accepted for Voluntary Emergency Service) was established on July 30, 1942. Do you know any women who served in the military in World War II or since? Would you have served?

3. Dan longs to go back to sea and he is driven to make admiral. In what ways is his ambition good? In what ways is it bad? How does he change? What do you think of his decisions at the climax of the story?

4. At the beginning of the story, Quintessa Beaumont sees herself as useless and selfish. She hopes that changing her name to Tess and joining the WAVES will help her

become useful and unselfish. How does she change throughout the story? Have you ever tried to transform yourself as Tess did?

5. At the beginning of the book, Dan Avery is "already married — to the United States Navy." How do Admiral Howard and Tess influence his views on romance? How does he grow? Have you ever had to change your views about love and romance? If so, how?

6. In the past, Tess was always "drawn to men who showered her with starry-eyed adoration," but she's come to long for a deeper sort of love. Why does she long for this? How does this influence her character development — and setbacks?

7. Both Nora Thurmond and Greta Selby are accustomed to being rejected. How do they differ? How do they change?

8. "Stay the course" is Dan Avery's motto. How does the compass represent his motto? How do his views shift and mature?

9. A hardworking man, Dan struggles with the concept of rest. What does he learn and how does it change him? Do you tend toward overwork or "under-work"? How can you achieve better balance in your life?

10. Adm. Aloysius Howard has served as

Dan's mentor and hero. How is this relationship good for Dan? How is it bad? Have you ever had a mentor or role model? What have you learned from this person?

11. What did you think of the various members of the French group? Whom did you suspect of being the spy? What do you think of Tess's role?

12. Dan has a strained relationship with his father. How does Tess help him see his father in a new light? Do you expect these men to have an improved relationship in the future?

13. Before joining the WAVES, both Tess and Nora struggled to be taken seriously in their careers. How have things changed for women since World War II? How do you think women like the WAVES aided in those improvements?

14. The sailboat drawings form a connection between Dan and Tess. How do they represent their romance?

15. If you read *Through Waters Deep* and *Anchor in the Storm,* did you enjoy the updates on Jim and Mary and Arch and Lillian? What do you imagine in the future for the Avery family?

ABOUT THE AUTHOR

Sarah Sundin is the author of the Waves of Freedom series, as well as the Wings of the Nightingale and the Wings of Glory series. Her novel *Through Waters Deep* was a finalist for the 2016 Carol Award, won the INSPY Award, and was named to Booklist's "101 Best Romance Novels of the Last 10 Years." In 2011, Sarah received the Writer of the Year Award at the Mount Hermon Christian Writers Conference.

A graduate of UC San Francisco School of Pharmacy, she works on-call as a hospital pharmacist. During WWII, her grandfather served as a pharmacist's mate (medic) in the Navy, and her great-uncle flew with the US Eighth Air Force in England. Sarah and her husband have three adult children — including a sailor in the US Navy! Sarah lives in northern California, and she enjoys speaking for church, community, and writers' groups.